AN
ECHO
THROUGH
THE
SNOW

AN
ECHO
THROUGH
THE
SNOW

ANDREA THALASINOS

FORGE®

A TOM DOHERTY ASSOCIATES BOOK
NEW YORK

AN ECHO THROUGH THE SNOW

Copyright © 2012 by Andrea Thalasinos

A Forge Book
Published by Tom Doherty Associates, LLC
175 Fifth Avenue
New York, NY 10010

www.tor-forge.com

Forge® is a registered trademark of Tom Doherty Associates, LLC.

The Library of Congress has cataloged the hardcover edition as follows:

Thalasinos, Andrea.
    An echo through the snow / Andrea Thalasinos. — 1st ed.
        p. cm.
    "A Tom Doherty Associates book."
    ISBN 978-0-7653-3036-9 (hardcover)
    ISBN 978-1-4299-6842-3 (e-book)
  1. Sled dog racing—Fiction.   2. Women mushers—Fiction.   I. Title.
    PS3620.H344E28 2012
    813'.6—dc23

                                                                2012017241

    ISBN 978-0-7653-3253-0 (trade paperback)

First Edition: August 2012
First Trade Paperback Edition: February 2013

Printed in the United States of America

0 9 8 7 6 5 4 3 2 1

FOR LOIS LEONARD AND THE REST OF US
WHO COULDN'T SAY NO

AN
ECHO
THROUGH
THE
SNOW

CHAPTER 1

Sometimes a story has to be told if for no other reason than to unburden the heart.

–Anonymous

OCTOBER 1929–UELEN, CHUKOTKA, NORTHEASTERN SIBERIA

He strained to catch a glimpse of them through the morning mist. Tariem wiped his runny nose on his sleeve. A truck engine rumbled from the outskirts of the village; the soldiers must have discovered that he'd escaped. Earlier he pried off a few loose boards from the temporary stockade and slipped out.

It was snowing lightly, the clouds low hanging and billowy. Snowflakes gathered in lacy patterns along the folds of his sealskin sleeves, like the mountain ridges where he'd soon be headed. It might have been a peaceful morning if not for the smoke from burning houses, the Red Army's truck or that his wife was gone. Today all remaining Chukchi along the Bering seacoast were to be evicted. Evacuation orders had been tacked up in Russian on family *yarangas* for weeks, though no one could read.

Tariem fumbled as he attached the gangline to the remaining sled. The engine sounds stabbed his stomach like spoiled whale meat.

The remaining team of dogs watched in silence as he readied the loaded sled. It was his wife Jeaantaa's team. The dogs looked wary, especially Kinin. The lead dog's blue stare pierced the mist. From a puppy he'd been Jeaantaa's leader, and leaders often ran for no one else.

Tariem lashed the frozen salmon tighter onto the heavy sled.

The gut line dug deeply into his palm as he leveraged his weight, securing it to the sled's driftwood stanchion. He prayed it wouldn't snap. Losing food on the tundra was death.

He looked to Kinin. The Guardian had bear-thick fur, as blue-black as the Siberian night. Above each crystalline eye a white fur circle grew. These markings proffered guidance from the Old Ones, whose spirits swirled in colorful trails across the sky. Tariem hoped for Kinin to get him out of the village, to the Cave of Many Points, and from there find the twelve-hundred-mile trail to their reindeer-breeding cousins.

The dogs' whiskers were frosted into snow beards. Though they ordinarily would be yelping with excitement as a sled was being readied, the events of the past few days made them hushed and suspicious. Gaps in the yard stood like missing teeth—only twenty dogs left where there had been eighty.

"Kinin," he called. The dog lowered his head and didn't move. Tariem slowly approached, trying to be calm, though the army truck was getting louder. Harness in one hand and a piece of seal meat as an offering to Kinin in the other. Just like Jeaantaa questioned his judgment, Kinin also had doubts.

"They're coming, Kinin," he explained. Palms up, he laid the meat down. Dogs couldn't be forced to run. They'd just lie down. You could beat them, cut off their tails in anger; they still wouldn't get up.

Tariem glanced at the family *yaranga* out of habit. "Ku, ku"— he'd not had time to burn their birch and walrus-skin house to free the House Spirit. Now the Spirit would follow, even harm them.

Tariem and the dog turned in the direction of the truck. Kinin's eyes softened. His one ear twitched; then his body relaxed. "Thank you," Tariem whispered. Kinin slipped his head and front legs into the harness and then surged, dragging Tariem to the front of the gangline as he toggled him in lead. Kinin pulled the line taut and then watched as the remaining nineteen dogs were quickly attached.

Tariem stepped onto the sled runners and pulled the wooden stake.

"Ke!"

Kinin charged. The Guardians lunged in unison. Tariem fell back from the momentum, grabbing on to the handle to steady himself.

The truck rounded the bend, barreling down the shoreline coming closer to the *yaranga*. Two soldiers stood in the rear. They pointed, yelling in broken Chukchi for him to stop.

"Ke, ke, ke, Kinin," Tariem urged, but the smell of fear was enough. Kinin raced to beat the truck, to get past the last *yaranga* and out to the snowpack. If they didn't start shooting he'd have the advantage. The sled runners would glide, leaving the truck's wheels to break through, spinning and whining like a frustrated reindeer scratching off spring's growth of itchy antler velvet.

Tariem spotted a child's empty *kliak* molded in the shape of a foot. Dread spread through his lungs. Blood dotted the snow.

"Ke, ke," he repeated.

Kinin's paws flicked snow as he jettisoned the team forward. All twenty spines undulated with speed, their breath syncopated with pounding feet.

Charred Chukchi *yarangas* blared by, burning in fragrant streams, their smoldering birch poles like red eyes. Tariem braced his knees against the stanchions for balance anticipating the first steep mogul. The runners hit and the sled was airborne. He used his weight to counterbalance, but the sled flipped on its side. Dogs darted back looks as it dragged.

"Ke, ke-e-e-e," he hollered. The truck gained. Tariem grasped the sled handle, worn smooth from Jeaantaa's touch.

Soldiers jeered from behind as he struggled to right the sled.

"Ke, ke, Kinin," he shouted. A gut lash snapped. Bundles of frozen salmon rolled out along with the heavy anorak that Jeaantaa had made for him. The team accelerated on the brief downslope. As he yanked the handle, the sled flipped upright.

Spires of the Siberian tree line were immediately visible to the west, close enough to make out individual branches. If only his will could catapult them. A painful spasm gathered in his throat. He lowered his chin to his sleeve, crouching to make a smaller target, his fingers numb and stinging with cold. Mittens would have to wait until deep within the forest. The gangly-limbed Russians must be cold. He was shorter, more compact.

"Ready." A command came from behind.

He glanced back. A young soldier unslung his rifle. Tariem turned forward, watching only Kinin and the trail before them. He held his breath, as if doing so could block bullets.

"Fire!"

A shot chipped and sprang one of two strands of walrus-gut ganglines. The team surged, startled. "Forest Keeper," Tariem cried out to Jeaantaa's guardian spirit. He eyed the straining gangline. "Breathe your life here."

With a crack, truck wheels broke through the ice behind him. Curses echoed off the surrounding hills, in first broken Chukchi, then Russian. Soon nothing but the rhythmic breath of the dogs as Kinin entered the stillness of the trees.

Tynga was limping.

"Whoa." Tariem kicked in the wooden stake. His legs were rubbery; he staggered like a drunken man over to the dog. Her back paw was up. Tariem bent over, and when he touched her leg Tynga yelped and pulled away. Her blood warmed his fingers as he touched them to his lips. She looked up adoringly. Her eyes crinkled as her ears lay flat, tail wagging and thumping against his thigh. In the dim forest light he checked her shoulders, abdomen and back. "Easy," he said. They'd run two of twelve hundred miles. He could leave her here, or sacrifice her.

Tears burned his eyes. Why Tynga? She was the only one to single him out. From a puppy she claimed him, following him everywhere. It was as annoying as it was touching, but he'd gradually come to accept this love. Crouching down, he looked at Tynga. She bunched her shoulders and licked his face. This was Bakki's daughter, the color of early orange sunlight, with lichen-colored eyes.

Pride had deafened him to Jeaantaa's warnings. A day earlier he struck her and then stared dumbfounded as blood dotted her nostrils. Though he was furious at how she'd broken the laws of the Lygoravetlat, or the original ones, he ached for her. She'd never been freely his and now even less so. He hated that he was so powerless to despise her. "A man should never love more than a woman," years ago the elders warned. "She's bewitched you."

The day before, Jeaantaa left with a man named Ramsay who'd come with an Inuit guide from Alaska. Tears cramped Tariem's throat as he thought of his sons. He imagined them waiting for her at the Cave, not wanting to leave for the longer journey inland in case she'd show.

He dreaded the two-day journey. The burden of not-knowing would drag beside him, like the anxious soul of a dead relative. He'd trudge long past the Valley of Flowers, down the frozen River of the Dead, hoping all the way to the Cave that he was wrong. Praying to Aquarvanguit for the moment when the boys would reach the Cave with Cheyuga and spot their mother's beautiful face. There she'd be with a fire already started, a bubbling pot of marrow and seal stew. And from there, together they'd begin the monthlong journey inland to their reindeer cousins.

But even if she changed her mind and left for the Cave, Bakki, her fourteen-year-old dog, couldn't run that far. She had him in lead and not Kinin when she left. And while Bakki wouldn't make it to the Cave, the dog *could* make it across the frozen Bering Sea to Rochlit.

Tynga licked mucus from his nose as he squatted. Tariem lifted the dog, stumbling as he carried her back to the sled, her tail thumping. He laid her down onto the sled and raised his knife, arching his back to gain force for a quick kill. Tynga lay quiet and trusting, lifting her leg to expose her belly as she did for only him.

A convulsive sob stopped him. "No more blood," Jeaantaa had pleaded yesterday. The knife dropped, he buried his face in Tynga's fur, gasping in spastic heaves. The dog's musky warmth was a momentary comfort. He picked up the knife and began sawing off a length from the bottom of his anorak. He scooped a handful of snow, packed Tynga's flesh wound and tightened the bandage around her leg.

"Lay still," he scolded. "We have a long way." The dog's tail thumped against the load as she settled in on top of the sled, her eyes fixed on him.

CHAPTER 2

Despite heavenly intentions, sometimes the wrong soul makes its way into a human body.

—Anonymous

NOVEMBER 1992–BAYFIELD, WISCONSIN, THE SOUTH SHORE OF LAKE SUPERIOR

Locals say that winter in the snowy north is a land of extremes. Some days are so dreary that the bluntness of low-hanging gunmetal clouds is enough to steal your soul. On others the sun is so bright you can hardly see. Everything that's gloomy becomes brighter, and everything that's bright becomes blinding.

Her stomach squeezed as Mrs. Cleo plopped down at her station. Rosalie MacKenzie hated how the old woman clutched her purse like the body of a stillborn child. One of the stylists had cropped the woman's hair too short—like a botched grooming job on a white poodle—and her raw pink scalp made Rosalie shudder.

As the eighteen-year-old lifted a comb to set Mrs. Cleo's hair, the old woman's blue marble eyes fixed on her. The kind of stare you sometimes see in the truly mad. Rosalie's cheeks flushed under the scrutiny, beads of sweat formed on her upper lip. Except for an occasional "oww" from a bent bobby pin, everyone understood the woman to have "lost the power of speech" from a stroke. At least Mrs. Cleo didn't require an audience.

Maybe it was more out of shyness, but while speaking Rosalie would restlessly avert her eyes, as if searching about for help or fishing for things to say.

She fumbled the comb. It clanked loudly on the black-and-white floor. Rosalie sneaked a glance as Marge peeked over to check, her latex gloves red with hair dye. Rosalie nodded in apology and reached for a clean comb. Being a disappointment is exhausting. When shop gossip would target an absentee local, Rosalie would smile slyly as the lynch mob formed, never chiming in, just relieved it wasn't her that time. She'd get a perverse sense of superiority at someone else's being an "incompetent piece of you-know-what."

She smoothed a swatch of Mrs. Cleo's hair and checked the clock. Marge caught her. She'd already been warned; clients complained that her "clock-watching" made them feel like she couldn't wait to shoo them out.

Tuesday evenings were "Old Lady Day" at the Frosty Tip Salon. After the last paying customer left for the day, a van pulled up from Ashland's assisted-living complex, nine miles east on the shore of Lake Superior. All those who were still mobile enough to navigate frozen sidewalks were delivered for a wash and set. A weekly treat designed to lift even the lowest of winter-worn spirits.

Rosalie caught herself about to sigh and stopped—last week's "talking-to."

"You're a spy," Mrs. Cleo blurted.

Rosalie looked up. Their eyes met in the mirror. "She speaks," a few remarked. "Why, I've never heard her . . ." Clients in the adjacent stations chuckled. Stylists paused beside spiderweb tangles of bouffant hairdos. A lone hair dryer droned.

Mrs. Cleo's voice was low and deep. It sounded as if coming from a long way off, yet it got right under Rosalie's skin. She tried to break eye contact but couldn't. Marge stepped up with red-stained gloves. "No one's a spy, Mrs. Cleo. That's Rosalie, my right-hand girl."

To listen to Marge you'd think it was true. But Rosalie was

scrutinized more closely than the other trainee. Just last week Marge exploded on the shop floor right in front of stylists and customers alike. "Do something with that hair for cripe sakes, Rosalie. Put some makeup on." The woman's hands tapped her cheekbones for emphasis. "Take off those boots; get some smart shoes on those tootsies—look like a stylist and not like you're shoveling shit."

Her chest had collapsed into her fingertips, her wounded spirit hovering just beneath her ribs. No one rushed to her defense. She glanced around for the soft eye-rolling smile of an ally, but she hadn't a friend in the place and knew it. Even the few to whom she listened endlessly as they chattered on about their "man problems." Others fired off looks of moral rectitude, as if "glad someone finally had the nerve to say it." The next day Rosalie made the good-faith effort to don her "woman face" with blue shadowed and lined eyes only to end up running late.

"Rosalie washes and sets you every week, Mrs. Cleo," Marge continued. "Remember?"

Rosalie folded her arms and peeked at the clock. Her dark brown, shoulder-length hair was pulled tightly back into a ponytail. Tall and willowy with the high Ojibwa cheekbones of her mother fused with her father's nose and Irish green eyes. Her sheared-off bangs fluttered like fringe with every turn of her head.

Mrs. Cleo's eyes fixed on her. She wasn't buying it. Her spotted bony finger repeated the accusation.

"Oh my, you're such a card." Marge dismissed it with a playful wave. She turned to her audience of patrons, crossed her eyes and made a face. Everyone but Rosalie laughed. Instead she stood motionless in her pink clown suit, bangs fluttering, arms crossed, fingertips tucked into the soft folds of her elbows. She looked at the floor.

Mrs. Cleo agitated in the chair. "Let me up," the old woman growled. She spoke with an air of authority. Razor sharp one instant, mad as a hatter the next. Clutching her purse with one arm, she pushed against the chair arm with the other. "False prophets stand among us—" She began to yank out the top few curlers. Clips clinked as they hit the floor, threads of white hair in each.

"Stop it, Mrs. Cleo." Marge took command. She peeled off her latex gloves and chucked the latest issue of *Midwest Living* onto the old woman's lap. Mrs. Cleo collapsed as if all the air had been let out of her body. The woman felt for the certainty of her purse, lowering her head to whisper secrets into its handle.

Marge nudged Rosalie aside. "I'll finish, hon. You can go on home now."

Rosalie grabbed her blue parka from the coat tree by the front door and wrestled into the sleeves. Too embarrassed to turn around and wave or think of something funny to say, which she never could anyway, Rosalie pulled open the door.

The icy fresh air felt good on her hot eyes. She inhaled deeply, trying to rid her nostrils of the stench of perm chemicals. Though relieved to be out, she hoped Marge wouldn't dock her the last two hours. It would be just her luck that Jerry would notice the difference in her check.

The sky was ink and the moon unnaturally bright and high as she walked home. It felt like someone was watching from inside the chain-link fence across the street. The Bayfield junkyard. She slowed down and scanned the street. She had an odd feeling, more like being studied than watched. Her steamy breath etched itself into the frigid Wisconsin night air. The silence rippled with expectancy.

"Who's there?" She whirled around. The streetlight shone on the outlines of car fenders and stacks of bumpers through the chain link. Maybe she was imagining things. Often she thought people said things when they hadn't. The doctor at the clinic advised her that feeling edgy was common.

Just beyond the street lay the vast expanse of Lake Superior, spinning the chemical properties of water into ever-thickening crystalline sheets of ice. Lake thunder crackled in striations of menacing laughter beneath the freezing surface before booming in release. Pressure ridges groaned with the evening's plummeting temperature. Soon the ferry would stop running for the season and the ice road to Madeline Island would open.

Something rustled and she gave a startled cry. Like the noise of an animal having a bad dream, her voice embarrassed her. Holding her breath, she tipped an ear to listen. She grasped an aluminum hair clip in her pocket with the iron grip of a newborn. The sign *Warning: Patrolled by Guard Dog* still dangled from a rusty piece of baling wire. Her blue parka, the green plaid scarf hastily roped around her neck, slid farther down her shoulders.

No more trouble. She had enough of it from Jerry, her husband of four months. He hadn't even bought her a wedding ring, though Arlan, her father, lent her money to buy his. For the ceremony they borrowed one from the Judge's secretary to use as a prop. Everyone was embarrassed, except for Jerry. Seconds after the kiss, he popped his ring off, tucking it into his pocket. "It makes my finger sweaty," he explained. And when Jerry was drinking, a malicious twinkle would pucker his eyes, as he laughed at her, wearing his flannel shirt. "Rosalie, Rosalie," he'd say, shaking his head like she was the biggest inside joke in the world. With that she'd lose all sense of herself, silenced with humiliation that transmuted into rage.

A hubcap fell and startled her. She listened as it pinged, riveting manically on its axis until it finally stopped. Holding her breath, she guessed it was that new guard dog, Smokey, getting used to his nighttime digs.

"Smokey?" she asked tentatively, and stepped towards the curb. The town of two hundred knew that Kurt, the junkyard guy, wasted no time in getting a replacement after the legendary Raggs had died. For over a decade Raggs hurled himself at unsuspecting passersby until a bulge formed in the chain link.

Locals crossed the street out of habit. The dog could be heard going off from the dock in summertime, even with the ferry engines running. For years Raggs was the most popular write-in candidate for city mayor.

She peered across the street trying to get a good look into the yard. It was probably those idiotic Shannon brothers from over in Cornucopia looking to rip off a radiator from Kurt's yard. They'd already stolen a tourist's car just last week and driven it out onto the not-quite-frozen Chequamegon Bay just to watch it sink. Though the same age, her eighteenth birthday just the week before, she considered herself grown-up. She was married after all. And what were the little jerk-wads planning? To jump her? She snorted to herself. She hadn't enough pocket change to buy gum.

"You think it's funny?" She put her whole heart into the holler and it felt good. "I know you're there, you little fuckers."

She rushed across the street, her boots clopping through November's first sloppy snowfall. She mentally rehearsed a choke hold she learned in a self-defense class Lorraine, her best friend, dragged her to.

A hand between her shoulder blades seemed to guide her closer to the bulge in the fence. The hair on her body prickled. Maybe it *was* hormones. Maybe the miscarriage wasn't just the lame excuse she'd been peddling at the Frosty Tip. It hadn't been two months.

Not one breeze blew off Superior. The air felt cold, colder than she knew it to be. Pulling up the scarf over her nose like a bandit, she absentmindedly chewed on the wool. Maybe Jerry was right. There was nothing to choke hold except her moronic self.

A misty form darted from behind a car fender. A stack of hub-caps tipped over and crashed. Her heart heaved against her chest as she dashed towards the bus station. What a relief to see Jerry's burly profile through the sliding ticket window, stamping people's bus tickets and then scolding them for walking towards the wrong gate. She catapulted up the back steps of the bus station two at a time, to their second-floor apartment, and slammed the rickety door shut.

Leaning against the kitchen counter, she touched her chest and tried to catch her breath. Another four hours before Jerry got off work. Better not mention it. Why did these freaky things happen? Jerry wondered the same thing. He already called her Wacko.

She wrestled the Frosty Tip uniform off her damp back. Absentmindedly fiddling with the TV antenna, she searched for reruns of *Happy Days* from the Duluth station, then gave up and turned it off.

She stepped into the bedroom and reached underneath the bed for the satin sewing box that had been her mother's. Aunt Edie had given her a special *rush order* project. Her mother and Edie had been founding members of the Northern Workers Beading Guild. The Guild was an association of Indian Beaders on the Red Cliff Reservation who used traditional techniques to create designs for exclusive bridal and couture salons. Better, according to Aunt Edie, than cranking out beaded key chains, bracelets and bookmarks for tourists. This dress was a test for entry into the next level of the Guild. Once Rosalie passed, more complex and involved projects would be assigned, which meant more income.

She sat down cross-legged on the bed, lining up a white satin pincushion on the night table. Needles sprang from the satin like porcupine quills. Tiny boxes of seed pearls, silver beads and sparkling sequins glistened together like a winter garden under the bedside lamp.

The darting figure nagged at her. It was as quiet as fog—like a ghost trapped in the junkyard. She popped a thimble on her middle finger and picked up a threaded needle. She twisted the silk thread against her finger on calluses that had formed over years. Aiming the needle, she missed a row of tiny seed pearls. Her hands were still shaky. The completed fern design on the front bodice was due at Aunt Edie's by seven for the first Federal Express shipment to a Minneapolis bridal salon. Being let off two hours early was a blessing. Rosalie was under the gun, though Edie had given her plenty of time. If she missed this deadline she was out. They'd train someone more dependable.

She missed the row again, pricking herself instead. Jumping up, she sucked the finger. *Great, bloodstains on the wedding dress bodice.*

Last night she'd striven to make headway, even after Jerry came home drunk and insisted on lights off. She sat on top of the closed toilet seat in the bathroom to the tune of his snoring, working on the bodice until 3 a.m. Freehand beadwork couldn't be rushed. And when you hadn't put in enough time up front, you couldn't rush it on the back end. The graceful flowing flowers, fronds and leaves flowed only through a relaxed hand. The aesthetic had evolved for centuries. Though she beaded alone, most never did. Edie and the others would sit together in a circle, bitching about their husbands, chatting about their children and remarking on how quickly Superior had frozen over that year. Machines couldn't do it. The skills of the Northern Workers Beading Guild were in high demand by those who could afford their work, work spun from the hands of people from some of the poorest census tracts in America.

Rosalie sighed. She stabbed the needle into the pincushion. The junkyard sprint had worn her out. Her cheek touched the pillow's edge. Exhaustion replaced adrenaline in equal measure. Her eyes fluttered. Her lips rested on the edge of the white satin bodice near the tiny cluster of five bloodroot blossoms she'd created as her trademark signature. Drool seeped, instantly absorbing into the silk.

The dream came on suddenly. It was more real than the mattress on which she slept. The east wall dissolved into low gray storm clouds, and she stood out on the surface of sea ice. It was not Lake Superior but somewhere else. Black jagged cliffs like shards of glass jutted up from the sea into the sky. They formed a curvilinear wall that surrounded her like a curtain. Rosalie stumbled over pressure ridges as clear as glass. Beneath the ice a fish swam between her feet.

An Indian-looking woman appeared as if in the middle of a conversation. There was dried blood on one of her nostrils. Long scatters of hair blew around her, black like the darkest of nights. Rosalie was crying, though it was unclear whose memory or sadness she felt. The woman told of loved ones who were taken.

Winds exploded into gales like an assault from every direction. It was colder than anything Rosalie'd ever felt, yet the lady of the ice stood in a loose skin dress and boots. She gestured to come closer. The woman peered into her; those pooling eyes passed a burden so heavy Rosalie's legs felt they would buckle. But as the woman spoke, the wind screamed back, scattering her words to all the directions before Rosalie could catch them.

Rosalie cupped her ears, but the winds were in her mind. Tracks of fresh blood dotted the snow, almost black against its whiteness, tramped down like an animal's footprint.

"Watch out, there's blood," Rosalie yelled a warning, only the woman no longer was listening. "Someone's bleeding."

She bolted up gasping. Batting away what felt like chilly spiderwebs brushing against her face. Frantic as she tried to calm down, she forced herself to focus on the here and now. Rosalie acknowledged the bedroom dresser with the missing top drawer. Turning to the kitchen area, she saw the same old table with three mismatched chairs, the cracked plastic TV casing with the crooked antenna. Her heart slowed, her breathing approaching normal. But her fingers were stinging. She lifted her hands to look. Each fingertip was white like frostbite.

"What the hell?" She touched them to her cheek. It felt like they'd been in the freezer all night. Reaching into her armpits, she yelped. Getting up, she stepped over to the kitchen sink and leaned against the counter. Nudging the leaky hot-water faucet with her palm, she rested her elbows on the edge and held her fingers under a quiet stream of warm water. She then dipped them into the accumulating pool in a standing pot. Mottled patches of pink spread like blots of diffusing red ink.

The smell of ozone filled the room.

"Leave me alone."

She leaned her forehead on her arm.

CHAPTER 3

Jeaantaa loved dancing on the sea ice. Especially in the Season-of-the-Fresh-Air-Going-Out. She dashed out just as the Cove was freezing. Her waist-length ink hair tied back, bangs quivering like butterflies, wearing her best beaded and embroidered reindeer-skin anorak and boots. Just in case Uptek showed up to watch. Hiding behind a whale skull perched on the shore, she always knew when he was there.

Uptek had been like her brother. They'd grown up playing together as children, until a few weeks earlier when Jeaantaa turned fourteen. She was sitting on the shore mending nets with the gossipy older women when sixteen-year-old Uptek and his older brother Tariem returned from a hunt, dragging their umiaks onto shore. Uptek hauled a dead seal up the pebbly shoreline. She watched his back muscles work, the arc of his chest as he bent over to pour a cup of water into the seal's mouth. Uptek closed his eyes, asked forgiveness and gave thanks for the creature. She could almost breathe the smell of Uptek's skin. And though Tariem had noticed her first in that way, it was Uptek's sea gray eyes that claimed her breath.

Days later, using the skin of that very seal, she began to prepare betrothal clothes as an offering to him. If accepted, it would announce him as her husband.

Warm breezes blew through the *yaranga* that evening, gifts from the Forest Keeper in the brief arctic summer. She brushed her bangs aside and leaned with all her weight onto the smooth gray stones she used to tan the hide. She rhythmically worked its underside, a stone in each palm as she thought of him, imagined the children they'd have. So far no one else had claimed him. And even if one of the girls offered, he'd decline. He already suspected she was preparing his clothes—she could tell by the looks that passed between them.

She tested the hide against her cheek. Smelling it, she envisioned the shirt brushing across his brown shoulders.

Bakki lay on his side beside her, his back legs laced together with her bare feet. The dog's blue eyes supervised lazily and a long canine tooth peeped below his lip on one side. Though still young, he'd already proven to be the best lead dog.

The stones clunked together in her lap as she paused to inspect the hide. The dog rolled over onto his back and pawed the air, drowsy in the warm *yaranga*.

"Look—Bakki approves," Gyrongav, her aunt, joked. Her name meant "springtime." Lighting a moss wick afloat in seal fat, Gyrongav positioned a stone lamp close to her niece. Though it was never fully dark in the white nights of the arctic summer, the light grew weak.

Jeaantaa used her knife to flick off the last bits of dried flesh. It was almost pliant enough to slip through her fingers and as smooth as a newborn's head. Tomorrow the anorak would be finished. And after Uptek was presented with the clothes he'd come to her.

The completed boots stood propped against a pile of skins. They seemed eager to receive his feet. She couldn't stop admiring them; they turned out far better than she'd hoped. The boots would reach his knees. Edged with contrasting triangles of white fox and darker sable and embroidered with aqua-colored glass trade beads, the color of Bakki's eyes. "Such tiny, tiny gut stitches," Gyrongav had remarked while examining them. "Invisible." The tiniest she had ever seen. The woman shook her head and made clicking noises with her tongue, not believing it was she who taught Jeaantaa how to sew. Such work was evidence that Jeaantaa would make a good wife.

Moisture made gut stitches swell, rendering garments watertight. For the anorak shirt, decorative appliqué fur figures of seals and dogs would line the edges of the hood, cuffs and bottom hem.

Tomorrow the clothes would be passed off to Tariem, to be walked to his brother after Cheyuga's blessing to Aquarvanguit. She was too embarrassed to deliver them, though most girls weren't. But Tariem would do it; he'd do anything for her.

"A guest!" her uncle, Cheyuga, called from outside to give fair warning.

Jeaantaa looked up. The two front walrus-skin walls had been rolled up and tied so they could enjoy the breeze. The untied back walls swayed gently.

It was Tariem, looking as eager as usual, she thought with irritation. He always seemed to show up uninvited at the worst possible times. He followed Cheyuga with an unsure expression, his arms loaded with fresh red seal flesh. Darting a quick look, he searched out Jeaantaa as he entered. She rolled her eyes and looked away, contorting into an awkward position to block his view. It was bad luck for Tariem to see Uptek's betrothal clothes before they were finished.

"Tariem brought gifts." Cheyuga lifted a slab of seal meat, showing off both sides as he admired it himself. It was forbidden for village shamans to hunt, so others supplied their meat. Uptek and Tariem were the bravest hunters and harpooners. Launching their walrus-skin umiaks from the Cove during open-water months, they hunted walrus, seals, even bowhead whales. Though young and cocky, they had a well-earned reputation for generosity, known for giving away far more meat than they kept. It was generosity that sprang from goodness, not out of fear of Aquarvanguit's punishment for greed. Year-round they kept Cheyuga's *yaranga* well stocked with meat.

Gyrongav positioned a bark basket under the seal meat.

Tariem's eyes settled on Jeaantaa. She'd nicknamed him the Watcher behind his back, an insulting Chukchi word for which Cheyuga had scolded her. Even while Tariem was deep in discussion with her uncle, his eyes would wander off in search of hers. His face permanently fixed as if on the verge of asking her a question. "That one sits with thorns in his pants," Gyrongav would joke after he'd leave.

Gyrongav set a kettle to boil, preparing the meat as a meal of thanks for Tariem. A sudden gust of wind rustled the skin walls. The back ones burst up like bird wings, startling them all. An evening storm was blowing in from the Cove.

"Jeaantaa." Gyrongav motioned for her to come and help roll down the *yaranga* walls to secure them before the storm hit.

With any luck Tariem wouldn't stay, but so often he did. Sometimes he'd chat with Cheyuga by the inside cook fire until dawn, going on about the hunt, spirits, the *Lygoraveltlat*. With the aid of strong Russian tea, she'd make every effort to be polite and stay attentive. Yet over the course of an evening she'd creep inch by inch towards the *yorongue*, the inner sleeping chamber, hoping Tariem wouldn't notice her disappearance.

Jeaantaa's parents had died early in a coughing sickness epidemic. She had lived with Cheyuga and Gyrongav since she was eight years old. Though they were good to her, her closest family were the dogs. At night the girl would sneak out of the *yaranga* and climb into the kennels with the old dogs, even during the coldest nights. Sucking her thumb, she'd lie twisting a strand of her hair and inhaling the comforting scent of their fur as she thought of her mother. Every morning she woke covered with reindeer blankets that Gyrongav must have thrown over her.

Two years before they died, her parents drove their dog teams to the edge of the forest to gather the spring's first cloudberries and nagoonberries. They eyed the spongy forest floor, careful not to trample what might be a good meal. Twigs snapped underfoot like sparks as they ducked under the lower branches of fir trees still laden with heavy, wet snow.

Something made them glance at their daughter. The little girl reached to touch the face of a caribou that was busy munching fat buds from low-growing cranberry bushes. She took the caribou's face in her chubby hands as she giggled. Its tail fluttered and head cocked as it looked at her inquisitively. She talked, stroking its nose and face until it relaxed. For her parents it was confirmation. Their daughter was to be the Keeper of the Guardians. And while honored, they were equally as saddened. For Keepers, their first responsibility and loyalty was always to their Keep, far and above anyone or anything else, including their own well-being. It was a designation not taken lightly.

After her parents' deaths, even though she was young, Jeaantaa was given full charge of the old dogs. She knew them well enough to notice changes in their faces and eyes when death neared. A quiet curiosity filled their eyes in the hours before each passed, their pupils opening wide for the exit of their souls into the next world. How she missed saying their names when they were gone. The sound of each became trapped inside her chest.

By age nine she'd startle awake at the slightest howl, knowing which dog's voice of the seventy-five was signaling.

No one remembered moving to the village. Neither were there stories of living elsewhere, which is why they called themselves the Lygoravetlat, or the original ones. Cousins and relatives lived only footsteps away. The fenced kennel area was located within a crescent stand of trees, growing in the hills overlooking the Bering Sea. The Guardians, as they were called, had been at the center of Chukchi life since woolly mammoths had lumbered alongside them.

Pups were whelped every spring and by fall were integrated into teams with older, more experienced dogs. During these months pups tumbled around, biting the scruffs of older dogs, who didn't hesitate to flip them onto their backs and hold them down until they stopped struggling. Manners and hierarchy were instilled through a mix of harsh discipline and play.

During the brief spring and summer, two of the seven seasons of Chukotka, all dogs ran free. They foraged for quick kills— mice, hares, moles, not to mention an occasional theft from a family cook fire. Every fall mass feedings of whale blubber, salmon roe and seal porridge were set out in troughs of hollowed-out tree trunks, designed to lure them back.

At the first sign of gathering snow clouds the adult dogs were tied, ganglines checked for cracks in the gut, worn lashing on sled joints replaced. The first seasonal snows would set the dogs off into squeals and howls of anticipation. Smaller teams of five or six dogs would travel out onto the sea ice to hunt. Experienced lead dogs would sniff out the breathing holes of seals and walrus. The larger teams, sometimes over twenty dogs long, would run a trans-Siberian trail, traversing thousands of miles. Sleds loaded with seal meat and dried salmon were hauled to distant inland villages for trade or to help cousins on the brink of starvation.

As the storm began, Jeaantaa crept into the *yorongue* to finish Uptek's anorak. Outside the bustle of clothing and clank of kettles near the front doorway signaled a meal.

"Oh, Jeaantaa-a, come eat with us," Cheyuga started to tease. She didn't answer.

"Jeaantaa," her aunt teased. "Don't be rude; come eat with us."

"Tell Tariem what you're working on so eagerly," Cheyuga kept up the kidding. As the walls of the *yaranga* boomed in unison from the drop in air pressure, Jeaantaa sighed. She tucked the anorak under her arm and got up, climbing out of the *yorongue*.

"Tonight you'd better stay with us," she heard Cheyuga say.

With that she stepped outside, Bakki following on her heels.

She tied the door flaps shut behind her before running to the crescent stand of trees.

"Where are you going?" she heard Gyrongav calling after her. "It's going to storm."

Climbing into the reindeer-skin shed, she cuddled up with the old dogs and the warm, nutty smell of their fur. They looked up only briefly, sniffing her hair as they lay panting in the thick, stormy air. Bakki settled in quickly to find his spot beside her.

She heard Tariem call out from the *yaranga*, "It's going to be a bad storm."

She ignored him and pulled out Uptek's anorak in the dim light, twisting the gut thread with her fingers to thread the needle.

CHAPTER 4

"Somethin' wrong with yer fingers, Rosalie?" the senior stylist called out loud enough to make every head turn. The ordinarily preoccupied wash and rinse assistant seemed more distracted than usual.

Rosalie paused to look at her fingers, touching them to her cheek, forgetting what she'd been in the middle of doing. Used towels were placed back in with the clean. She had mistakenly soaked combs in the vinegar solution used for cleaning mirrors instead of the beauty supply disinfectant. Mrs. Shockenthaler called the instant she got home. "I smell like Eyetalian dressing," she shouted into the phone.

"For God sakes, Rosalie—" Marge hung up the phone. Her smile fixed in an unnatural way. "You're not a stupid girl."

She wasn't sure how to take it.

"Breathe and focus," Marge ordered, placing her hands up on Rosalie's bony shoulders. "Follow me—breathe. Now slow down— you rush like you gotta train to catch for cripe sakes."

But the dream chased her like a ratty little dog. Sadness pulsed in waves—like a broken radio that picks up faraway stations clearer than local ones. She kept tearing up. Blinking madly, her eyes would well again. "We're running low on developer. . . ." She chirped off a phony excuse just to walk back to the storeroom and gain some composure. There in the quiet darkness of the storeroom she bent over, elbows resting on her knees, to clear her head. Something had changed or something was wrong, or both. One thing was certain: she had a *really* bad feeling.

. . .

Earlier, she glanced into the junkyard. Winter was pushing out the last bit of fall's warmth. No sign of a dog, though—only muddy boot prints on patches of melting snow, rusty water drippings. Spying on Kurt, she slowed to a crawl. He gesticulated wildly and then gently cupped the receiver as if sweet-talking his way out of something he just said. Despite the chill, he stood outside in a T-shirt and jeans, cord twisted and pulled taut as far as it would stretch. Inside his office was cluttered with collapsing piles of spark plug boxes, fan belts and catalogues of engine parts. And while admittedly an odd place for a junkyard—densely packed into a city lot on the main thoroughfare, despite the efforts of newcomer-cum-developer types stricken with condo fever—the family business had been grandfathered into perpetuity.

Thank God it was closing time. She mopped the entire floor, flipped off the overhead lights and reveled in the silence—funny how nobody heard the buzzing all day. She slipped into her coat and out of new stylish flats into her boots. Tiptoeing outside, she held on to the mop. Reaching in, she swabbed the front entrance to give Marge the illusion she'd floated out. Anything to absolve the day's mistakes so that tomorrow Marge might comment: "Hon, that floor was the best thing that happened to me all day."

Jiggling the shop key, she locked up. *Come In—We're Open*! Shit—*the sign. Ah, just leave it.* But then why add another way to show Marge she didn't care? Sighing deeply, she slipped out of her boots, unlocked, tiptoed back in, flipped the sign and polished her footmarks out with her socks.

The cool boots felt good on her hot, tired feet. First time she relaxed all day, all week. Even so, it felt like someone was waiting to yank another rug out from under her. It often felt that way. Ever since that snowy morning when, at seven years old, she awoke to discover her mother had been killed on the highway. Anna Marie had worked third shift because of the higher wage, trying to squirrel away extra money for Rosalie's college fund. Ever since it seemed no one was safe.

Rosalie stood on the snowy, moonlit banks of Superior. Steam from people's houses was thick and lethargic, rising like ruched fabric in the chilly air. Lights from the bus station were immediately visible across the Bay. It was a straight shot across frozen Chequamegon Bay to avoid the junkyard, but two hunters on ATVs broke through yesterday as they tried the shortcut to the Ice Caves. No ice fishermen out yet. Once you saw them out on their buckets, sitting in formation like an army of toileted men, it was safe to cross.

Instead she trudged towards her and Jerry's apartment, slowing as she neared the junkyard. Snowy patches glowed with an unnatural blue fluorescence from the moon. She approached the chain link, now more curious than scared.

"Hh-h-h-h . . ." She drew breath in and gasped. Blinking several times, she peered into what appeared to be the curious blue eyes of a wolf.

"So *you're* Smokey."

His ears perked at his name.

He studied her with the patience of one who's waited all day for the sound of familiar footsteps. Mucus ran from his black nose. The odor of old feces, urine and grime surrounded him. His eyes were weepy and crusted in the corners. His pale gray winter coat was thick, albeit soiled a grimy brownish-yellow color around his face and shoulders where he brushed against the salvage. There were large bald spots along his back where he scratched down to his skin.

She crouched down, sitting on her heels and holding on to the chain link. She wanted so badly to touch him. Reaching her fingers through the little diamond squares, she wiggled them as if to entice him over. He didn't move.

"Hi, Smokey." His ears perked again. "Come here, come on." She wiggled her fingers again as she studied him. "Don't be scared." Fur tufts dotted his shoulders and haunches. The coat along his spine separated like quilt batting, not having the benefit of stiff forest branches to help shed it. His eyes looked remarkably human.

"Come on—don't be a chicken." But he turned and trotted off as if weightless, his long legs and huge paws light-footed as if he floated. Quickly, he retreated back into a space between stacks of car fenders. He seemed to vanish then reappear beside objects as he cocked his head and searched her face. He seemed terrified by the radiators he was supposed to be guarding. As he sniffed tentatively, puffs of steam circled his head. His face half peeked out at her, one blue eye watching from behind a washing machine.

She stood and walked over to the gate. Slipping out of her coat sleeve, she squeezed her arm through two fence posts, chuckling at the prospect of getting stuck. She reached towards him. "Smokey."

But he gingerly backed away, keeping a fixed eye studying her. He was asking for help; she was certain. And just when it seemed clear that she understood, he vanished like mist on Superior after the sun burns through.

————

"Sorry, Rosalie—legally he's Kurt's property," Franklin reported when she stopped by the police station on her way to work. "I hear rumors."

"What kind of rumors?"

"Rumors that tell me Kurt's up to his old tricks."

"He's gonna shoot him, isn't he." Her stomach jumped as she said it.

"Need more than rumors. Hell, if that was the case I'd have

half the goddamned town locked up. Now"—he paused, looking at her in that coy way that meant "off-the-record"—"if someone were to go and *take* the dog . . ." He stared long and hard. She left for work with a heavy heart, her throat aching with the dilemma.

Late that afternoon she flitted about the salon, mumbling.

"How can a living thing be property?" she muttered, snipping way too much from Mrs. Burhaulter's bangs.

"Excuse me?" the woman asked with a belligerence that made Rosalie snap out of it. Marge craned her neck from the register to look.

"Oh, sorry, not you. I-I-I was just thinking out loud."

Mrs. Burkhaulter glared in the mirror. Mumbling was another bad habit. Rosalie had muttered as an only child, growing up on a remote part of the Red Cliff Reservation, often with only herself as company. Even now it took conscious restraint not to embarrass herself in public.

"Who ya talking to, Rosalie?" Jerry'd snicker. "You know, you do that a lot." He'd laugh and look around at the empty chairs in their apartment as if cuing from an audience just waiting to agree.

"Yeah, so—"

"So-o-o—," he'd mimic. "Only crazy people talk to themselves, Wacko."

Later that evening, sweeping snips of hair in staccato bursts, she paused contemplatively to bite her nails. She could take the dog, but then what? Jerry would rat her out. He and Kurt were tight. She rested the broom in her armpit, chomping on what was left of a hangnail. Maybe it was time to call Lorraine.

"Rosalie," Marge interceded, looking at her watch. "Time to finish up the mirrors, hon." Marge handed over a bottle of glass cleaner and a roll of paper towels. "Scat; go on."

She couldn't stop thinking about Smokey. His sad, quiet face and the way his two white canine teeth poked out from below his lip. She couldn't help it. Always remembering the names of dogs but not their owners, as a kid crying more for the "poor horsey" in TV western gunfights. God bless Arlan, who piped up as interpreter in ever patient tones, "Yep, she's her ma all over again, God rest her soul—bawling whenever the mousetrap went off."

From the mirrors, Rosalie saw Mrs. Burhaulter complain to Marge at the register. Her job was doomed. She knew the instant she burned through the final quota of grace; Marge gave her the "dead look," the precursor to getting fired. It was a disengaged, chilly stare—the last look the condemned see before they're snuffed out. Disfavor has a distinct odor and if you're sharp enough you get to walk before you're fired. People don't find flakiness endearing, as they might a family puppy who keeps knocking over the water bowl.

Lorraine remained her only true friend. There were a few others who found humor in stupid things, befriended the outcast. All of them turned up pregnant—disappearing into the initiation of way-too-early motherhood. So far only Lorraine had skillfully avoided it. And while Lorraine bore the status of a tramp and a juvey, Rosalie had no status at all. She was so invisible that nobody picked on her. There was nothing to be gained by either tribal or town girls. Even when she tried to be noticed, they'd issue a dismissive and rather annoyed, "Shu-ut u-u-up, idiot." Marrying Jerry might have been one way to jockey for status, had he not been a bullet so many of them were smart enough to dodge.

"Rosalie? Mirrors?" Marge called, and snapped her fingers. "Focus. Remember? We had that talk the other day?"

Yes, yes, clean the mirrors, Jesus H. Christ. Rosalie climbed up onto an empty workstation. She knelt on the counter, sprayed vinegar solution over the glass surface and with vigor began polishing her own reflection. How could she save Smokey when she couldn't even save herself? Her thoughts drifted to her dream and the sadness of the lady on the ice.

The console began to wobble. She paused, waited for it to stop, but it had come to life. The workstation jumped in incremental jolts like a beating heart. Bins of curlers flew off, scattering like mice. Customers shrieked. Rosalie scurried on all fours to gather clips and bobby pins until Marge hauled her up by the back of her smock, like a lifeguard pulls a drowning person from a tidal pool.

"Go home, Rosalie." She held out her hand for the shop keys. Rosalie fished them from her pocket and, shoulders drooping, dropped them onto Marge's outstretched hand. Marge linked arms and escorted her to the chrome coatrack, picking up Rosalie's parka. She set the coat on Rosalie's shoulders like the end of a sentence.

"Good luck, Rosalie," Marge said in that way older women do when they see trouble ahead. Rosalie wanted to stand in the doorway to absorb the gravity of the moment, but Marge pulled open the door for her. She shoved her hands into her pockets and left. Walking down a few doors, she ducked and sat in the doorway of an art gallery that was closed for winter.

"Bitches." Head in hands, she couldn't even cry. It wasn't a relief to be out of there. Nothing was a relief. Restlessness crawled in her skin. She rocked, leaning on her knees, trying to find comfort where there was none. Neither would there be any for Smokey. A surge of responsibility turned her cranky. No way could she take on a dog and tempt the wrath of Kurt, who was known to be even crazier than Jerry. And damn that idiotic dream—who was that stupid woman anyway?

She glanced up; a metal newspaper box was at eye-level. With two quarters she could get a paper—maybe even another job before Jerry found out. Just yesterday a Walmart had opened in Ashland. If she was home, Lorraine would give her a ride. But the thought of another job made her want to hitch to Arlan's, crawl back into her childhood bed and go to sleep.

.   .   .

Rosalie met Jerry on the Fourth of July after her junior year of high school. She went to the Pow-wow at Red Cliff to watch Lorraine's younger sister, wearing the beaded flower shawl Rosalie had made, in grand entrance. It had traditional flower patterns of the Anishinabe meandering along the borders with a porcupine beaded in the center. She also beaded a buckskin vest for Franklin, her uncle and the town sheriff. As a veteran, Franklin marched with the color guard procession. Images of eagles were beaded into his vest also using porcupine quills. She could tell Franklin was proud of it. He darted looks at her as he carried the Flag—a small, embarrassed smile turning his lips. She loved how her mark of the five bloodroot blossoms gleamed in the firelight along the hem of each garment.

After, during the parade in Bayfield, she saw Jerry standing outside a bar on Rittenhouse Avenue. Fireworks were going off. A parade of police cars, search and rescue and ambulances were flashing their lights and whooping their sirens to the cheering crowd. She'd been walking back on Highway 13 to Red Cliff with Lorraine and a few other friends when Jerry cruised by. He pulled alongside and rolled down the window of his vintage Camaro.

"You want a ride?" he asked, looking at only her.

"Sure," the four of them sounded off. They hopped onto the hood of his car, giggling, three-quarters drunk as he slowly drove towards Red Cliff. Glancing back, Rosalie saw his gaze, illuminated through the windshield, fixed on her. She counted that as their first official date, though in Jerry's words he knew she was jailbait. Still, it hadn't stopped him.

"Who needs high school anyway," she explained to Arlan after she found herself pregnant. She and Jerry went together to find Arlan and break the good news. He was working that summer on the Bayfield City Dock as a subcontractor, repairing the jetties—since Arlan seemed to be the only one who knew how. After the dock, he'd drive to his regular job at Consolidated Paper in Two Harbors, where he worked third shift.

The strangest look crossed her father's face as the couple

approached. As if he were seeing people he thought had died in
Vietnam. He looked sadder and older than his fifty-three years
as she stood eyeball-to-eyeball with him, as tall and willowy as
her mother had been. Her straight dark hair glistened like glass
in the summer sun. Wearing cutoffs, a tank top and a flannel
shirt longer than her shorts. She was clean faced, without a
stitch of makeup; her eyes were shining. "Getting married was
just as good an excuse as any to quit high school," she'd chirped.

Jerry stepped so close to Arlan they could have kissed. But
Arlan didn't step back. His face was sullen and still; he stood as
if paralyzed.

"What's the matter, Arlan?" Jerry's breath was heavy on her
father's lips. "Your daughter's too young for me?"

Rosalie turned at the hint of a sneer in his voice. Though Jerry
was twenty-five, Arlan had been the same age when he married
nineteen-year-old Anna Marie.

"Don't do this, Rosalie," Arlan said.

With that Jerry turned and walked off towards a line of parked
cars, just out of earshot.

"Too late, you're gonna be a *grandpa*." She sang the last word,
motioning for Jerry to come back, but he stayed leaning against
someone's car in a triumphant way.

Arlan lowered his head. "It's my fault," he said to himself softly.
He touched the work glove to his face.

"Uh-h, Arlan." She chuckled nervously. "Technically it's—
uh-h—my fault." After her mother's death she started calling her
father by his first name. No one questioned it, not even Arlan.

"Don't do this, Rosalie."

She'd never seen her father like this. The desperate voice, the
request. She glanced back at Jerry. He seemed to be enjoying
himself. "I told you, it's too late. You're gonna be a grandpa." She
gestured holding a baby as if he couldn't figure it out.

"Not with him."

"Lotsa people don't like Jerry, but he's got a sweet side," she
insisted. "Nobody knows him; he's really sweet."

Her father wasn't listening. "What if I refuse consent?"

"Then we'll drive down to Iowa." She backed away. "I know you think I'm young—"

Arlan lowered his head. "It's not that—"

"Mom was barely older than me," she persisted.

So she went ahead, marrying Jerry for his thick, wavy honey-colored hair that she imagined brushing out for their daughters at bedtime. Reluctantly Arlan gave his written consent, and the disaster officially began. Just weeks into the pregnancy, she began bleeding.

"Sometimes people bleed," Lorraine advised, like she knew what the hell she was talking about. "Hey, you're young; freaky shit like this happens."

But later that evening Arlan drove her to the Emergency Room while Jerry arranged for someone to cover his shift. By the time he arrived, she'd been told on the examination table that she lost the baby. When Jerry heard the news, the two of them looked bleary-eyed at one another, as if they'd just been introduced.

"Damn dog," she muttered, deciding there was nothing she could do. But as she approached the junkyard, Smokey was tracing her path with his whole body from where he stood. His claim on her was like a whistle set to a frequency only she could hear. But instead of responding she turned her shoulder away. Maybe he'd leave her alone if she ignored him. But just as she turned away it felt like poison flooded her system. She turned back to the fence, but he was gone.

"Smokey." She walked up and grasped the chain link. The snow glowed with moonlight. He was hiding. A white paw was visible from between two fenders. She broke off a piece of the marshmallow pie hidden in her salon smock and tossed it. It hit the fence and bounced off, but he made no move. She stood there for several moments, sticking her nose through the kite-shaped metal wire.

Across the parking lot, Jerry slid open the aluminum ticket window to spit. He then paused, sticking out his good ear to listen. A cherry bomb had exploded near his right ear when he was ten, leaving him permanently deaf in that ear. *Shit.* She squatted onto her heels, holding the fence for balance. He kept a close eye on his buddy Kurt's junkyard after hours. "There's lotsa money in parts," he'd explain, nodding his head like someone in the know.

Jerry shut the ticket window. It made a *thunk* sound that was audible blocks away in the thin frigid air.

Something tickled her fingers. Smokey's pale eyes were within inches. She reached with the tip of her index finger through the chain link to touch his fur. He flinched and backed away, seeming to skim the surface before dropping down to crawl back under a junked car. Two long white furry paws stuck out, pointing towards her.

"Hey, Smokey." He scooted out to get the piece of cookie and she laughed out loud, stunned by the free sound of her own laughter. He gobbled it down. She passed the last of the cookie through the fence as he licked the sticky marshmallow off her fingers.

"Sorry, guy, that's all I got for now." He made another pass to graze along the chain link, eager for her touch as she dug into his coat, scratching him as much as the fence would permit. Through his thick pelt, the vertebrae felt like a line of stones. His fur was as light as air, so soft it barely registered. Though he flinched, he seemed to need her touch. Then he pulled back to sit, looking at her.

"I'm getting you out of here tonight," she promised. She looked at her hands. Grime from his coat had settled into the creases and grooves of her fingerprints and palms like elevation lines on some internal topo map. Then Rosalie marched across the parking lot and into the bus station to find Jerry. God only knows where she drummed up the nerve to ask if they could take Smokey as a pet.

.   .   .

"Now I *know* you're outta your fuckin' mind," Jerry said, study-ing her with a bemused little smirk. He was mopping out the men's room.

"Why not?" she asked.

He looked angry. "Because I fucking said so, that's why." He stared her down, not missing a beat as the mop clunked around the base of the toilet.

"I could start cleaning houses with Lorraine to cover his feed—she's got so many now," she offered eagerly.

"Good. Now you can make up lost pay after Marge fires your ass."

She tried to hide her surprise.

A wry smile spread across his face. "So you got fired again, did ya?" His neck was red. "Don't think I don't know what you're doing—don't be feedin' no dog. You ain't no fucking Saint Francis."

"I was just looking at the stupid thing."

"Yeah, well, don't look." He flipped his head back. His hair was getting too long for him to see.

"I can get a second job—"

"Didn't you hear what I just said?" He gritted his teeth, grunt-ing as he reached back behind the toilet with the mop. "You know nothing about the real world, wake the fuck up—"

"Kurt's gonna shoot him."

"And so what. He can charbroil and eat him for all I fucking care."

So she was right. She looked at her boots to hide her thoughts. Arlan was right. Everyone was right. She backed off.

"Okay, Jer, I'm sorry."

It was tough to hide her giddy sense of joy.

"Stop apologizing. It's fucking annoying."

"Ok-k-kay," she stuttered.

He turned to glare at her, but instead it made her laugh, espe-cially when he jammed his thumb against the side of the toilet tank.

"Okay, sorry," popped out of her mouth as she walked away.

. . .

She walked back out to the gate and pulled on one side. Eyeing the space, she estimated the width. Smokey joyously ran to greet her as she squatted, fingers stiff as she scratched his bony back. The bus would arrive from Fargo at eleven that evening. Jerry would be too distracted with passenger questions to keep track of what she was doing. Though the urge was to take Smokey immediately, she had to keep her wits about her.

"I'll be right back, good boy." He watched, bereft as she backed away into the shadows of the street. She had three hours to think of something. Time to call out the troops. She'd call Lorraine. Come up with a plan. Slip out of the stupid uniform and into some warm clothes.

Later, in the rawness of the cold night, Rosalie hid in the shadows of the decommissioned railroad trestle. Her hands in her pockets, she stood watching the bus station from across the street. It had stopped snowing. The stars rang true and the temperature was plummeting. Smokey stood at the bulge in the fence, watching. Right on schedule, the bus arrived from Fargo. Passengers filed off looking like baby birds at the edge of the nest. She could see Jerry's arms flailing about, pointing towards the restrooms, his hair shaking as he talked. She snagged a rope from inside the junkyard with a tree branch, fashioning it into a makeshift collar and leash. She approached the gate alongside the fence bulge. If she pulled on one side of the gate, Smokey's body might slip through.

Then Kurt drove up out of nowhere. She shrank back. The truck pulled in by his office at the gate on the other side. The door opened and Kurt hopped down. He stumbled in that telltale way only wasted people do. With the driver's side door left wide open, music blared as a giggling woman on the passenger's side—who seemed equally loaded—called to him as he opened the tailgate of the truck.

"Hey, Smo-o-okey," he called in a teasing way. "He-e-re, boy."

Rosalie ducked. Smokey looked towards the truck. *No, no, don't.* The dog watched Kurt unlock the padlocks on the gate near his office.

"Smo-o-o-key." Kurt's voice made her sick. The dog's ears perked as he peeked from behind a car fender. "Come he-e-ere," Kurt's voice mocked in a singsong. "Wanna treat?" The dog's ears perked at "treat." Then he looked confused. He watched as Kurt began to unwind the chain.

Smokey withdrew behind a fender and then looked at her as if for advice. She motioned to him to come. Just then Kurt walked towards the fender where Smokey was hiding. Kurt pulled him out by his leg. The dog yelped. Kurt lifted his bony body, tucking him under his arm, and dumped him in the back of the pickup.

Rosalie raced around the perimeter of the fenced yard towards the truck. Kurt climbed in. He shut the door and crept out of the driveway.

"No, you fucker," she hollered, and sprinted. The truck inched away the closer she got. She couldn't see the dog. "Smokey." Rosalie almost tripped and fell as the truck picked up speed. She bolted through the downtown street, frantic. People turned to look. Then Smokey's head peeped up.

"Smokey," she shouted. "Come." He looked frightened. She chased to close the gap. Just then Smokey stood; paws on the edge of the gate, he jumped out. He ran towards her as Kurt continued out to the highway.

"Good boy," she cried, feeling as if her heart would burst. He reached her and pressed his flank against her. She slipped the rope collar over his head.

"Let's go," she said. Together they ran as if they'd always been free. Around the back of the bus station, she led him up the stairs to the apartment. She planned to run across the highway and up through the woods to Eagle Bluff, where Lorraine had agreed to meet them. He'd be safe with her; no one on the Reservation would talk. They'd hide him until she could figure out what to do next.

In the kitchen, Rosalie held on to the Crock-Pot Jerry's mother, Joyce, had given them as a wedding present; Smokey wolfed down the last of the beef stew. The dog stopped cold. He stared at the door, ears sprung at the sound of a key. Jerry's form filled the doorway.

"Oh, this is real cute," he said with a twisted smile. "What are you doing, Rosalie?" His voice was as quiet as death. "You know that Kurt just called the County Sheriff."

She said nothing.

"You're just something special, aren't you?" Hands on hips, Jerry walked over to her. Smokey was still.

"Give me the rope."

She didn't move.

"I'm not gonna ask you again."

She tucked the end of the rope under her knee. "No."

"God fucking damn it." He grabbed the collar of her sweater, swinging her into the breakfast nook. He started kicking her where she lay on the floor. He grunted the words with each kick. "I'm taking him back," he yelled.

"No," she screamed. Blind wrath dissolved her fear. Scrambling, she raced him for the leash, kicking with her foot to reach it.

Smokey's jaws latched on to Jerry's forearm.

"Run," she shouted.

Then Jerry came at her. Her heart was beating in her ears. The dog dashed out the door; the white tip of his tail was the last thing she saw.

Hours later in Duluth General Hospital she woke up with Arlan's worried face at her side.

"I'm sorry," Arlan said like a prayer.

"Smokey?" was her first word. Tears streamed out of her swollen, crusted eyes, stinging as they oozed. Arlan nodded and touched her forearm, the only place that didn't hurt.

"He's okay. Lorraine's got him."

CHAPTER 5

The betrothal clothes were tucked under Jeaantaa's arm. She hid behind a twisted trunk of driftwood—Uptek shoulder to shoulder with Tariem—as sunrise prayers were finishing. The young hunters looked cocky, trading prideful looks.

Warmer currents had seeped up from Japan, clashing with arctic waters to create violent riptides. Skies crackled with explosive gusts, churning up the Bering Sea, a challenge to the most experienced hunters. Underwater clouds of shrimp lured back seals and walruses from rich Northern waters where they feasted all summer. Winter was coming early and with it the urgency to store up meat before the seas became too rough.

Uptek headed towards their umiak after the hunters dispersed. Tariem walked in the opposite direction towards the gear. Both spotted her and paused. Uptek started walking towards her, but she ran to Tariem instead. Uptek stopped and watched, puzzled.

Breathless and red-cheeked, she reached him. "Here." Tariem took the bundle, smiled and stepped closer.

"Give these to Uptek."

He was stunned. Then she ran off giggling, as if playing a child's game. Once at a safe distance, she hid behind a whale carcass, peeking out from behind a rib, her stomach a pinging ball of excitement.

Tariem looked down at the clothes as if not knowing what to do.

Uptek caught up with him, jokingly bumping into his older brother. He took the bundle and unfolded the anorak and boots. He looked at her.

She ducked, chewing her knuckles and laughing nervously.

He held the shirt against his frame, the top tucked under his chin, holding out the boots with his other hand. His white teeth flashed. Uptek slipped on the shirt, then the boots, and began showing them off. A hunter jabbed his shoulder. A few others tackled him on the beach, wrestling and shouting insults: "Jeaantaa must be blind."

Then Uptek stood. He slowly walked up the shoreline towards her, wearing the anorak and boots. She twitched, wanting to hide her face, but forced herself to stand fast. He reached her. On the bottom of the anorak, her mark of Avens flowers gleamed in the sun. Uptek's eyes were so deep she looked away.

"I will wear them. For luck."

"Let me check how the hood fits."

He bowed slightly towards her, his breath on her neck.

She reached over his shoulders, grasping the top, and pulled. She felt weak. Her eyelids fluttered as if struggling to stay open.

"There," she said. "It fits."

"Yes it does," Uptek said. "It fits."

Later that morning she went to a trading fair nearby, spreading news of her betrothal. She'd been negotiating an exchange of a flask of whale oil for several reindeer blankets. They would make walls for their own separate *yorongue* within the *yaranga*. It would be the place their children would be conceived and born.

"Jeaantaa." Gyrongav's voice touched her from the quiet space of a dream.

She turned. Her stomach twisted coldly.

They locked eyes. Gyrongav crashed though waves of people to reach her.

The two women stood without touching. Jeaantaa placed the flask of whale oil down. She lowered her head.

"Which one?" But she already knew. She dropped, sitting down in the middle of the crowd. Speechless, without tears, she tore at her hair with unbelief and a pain that would become embedded in the tissue of her heart.

Their boat had capsized; a walrus had gored Uptek. Tariem had thrashed about in the icy waters, diving repeatedly for his brother. Another umiak had steadied alongside, managing to haul Tariem up without capsizing. His body arched in desperation, like a dying fish, as he yelled, "Uptek," his face too frozen for anyone to understand what he was saying. Tariem shivered for days with fever and wouldn't speak, even when Cheyuga would come and sit with him.

At night when the village was sleeping, she'd walk down to the Cove. Her thick braid silent along her spine. She'd stand waiting. She was convinced that Uptek would pop up from the sea in his betrothal clothes, hold out his hand and lead her back under the waves where she belonged. Well into the time of heavy ice she'd drive her team out to the spot. Setting down the last tundra flowers, she'd remind him, "You left me. I'm waiting."

"Nothing bad ever comes from the sea," was what the Chukchi say. "The sea cleanses evil; there was a reason." But there was no reason. Nothing about Uptek had been evil; he'd been gentle and good. People shunned Jeaantaa, claiming, "She murdered our best hunter," and her betrothal clothes had been bad luck. "And now his brother is as good as dead."

Tariem refused to hunt. He hadn't left his *yaranga* since the accident. The burn of loss was too great. Tariem knew the truth. It was he, not Jeaantaa, who harbored evil. His jealousy had summoned the walrus. For months he'd loved and wanted her; he'd longed for her at night in his dreams. On purpose passing by the crescent stand of trees in hopes of seeing her, praying the dogs wouldn't howl to tip her off. When she handed the betrothal clothes to him, he thought he would faint. But disappointment turned to blinding hatred. No one could ease his burden, except maybe her.

Nosy onlookers would walk past, openly shouting insults: "I'm surprised the Guardians don't rip the flesh from her bones," before Cheyuga or Gyrangov could run out to shoo them away. "A virtuous woman would have died of grief," they openly taunted. "It's your duty to kill yourself, rid the village of your curse."

The village consensus was that the *keedle* spirits of her dead parents had left her with an unclean spirit. Shoreline prayers to Aquarvanguit hadn't protected Uptek, proving she was the greater evil. No young man would be her betrothed again. It was believed he'd surely die and she'd slaughter and eat all children born to them.

The village elders met concerning Uptek's death. They ordered Cheyuga to perform the ceremony of banishment, declaring her a creature of the underworld. She would then be turned out with no dogs or warm clothing, to die of exposure. Cheyuga and Gyrongav refused. "We will not turn out our blood," Gyrongav said. She used the word for "daughter" and not "relative."

"The reindeer bones said there was no evil," Cheyuga insisted after reading the markings in a sacrificed reindeer's shoulder "Uptek's death was an accident."

But no one believed him. "The old man's too weak to do what he should."

Tariem's fate had also been discussed. Meat was brought by villagers as a sign he'd been exonerated of any part of Uptek's death, but instead he brought it to Cheyuga's. And for this Tariem was shunned too—"under Jeaantaa's spell," "bewitched by her," they said.

"She won't come out," Gyrongav confided to Tariem. He followed her and Cheyuga into the crescent stand of trees, looking for her. "If she's not in the shed, she's in with the old dogs." The three of them walked around, looking for the girl who was wasting away to bone. She was curled up in a corner of the yard with Bakki tucked under her arm. Her nose buried in his fur, breathing his scent, surrounded in protective layers by the rest of the dogs.

Gynrongav lay down next to her. "You must eat, my little one," hand-feeding her niece like a sick reindeer calf. "Don't listen to them. There is only goodness in you."

When the seasons began their first repetition, Tariem drove a dog team down to the Cove. The sea ice heaved into shelves, he rode over a series of moguls before he spotted her. He stopped his team. Making the dogs lie down, he trudged towards her. Snow shifted like sand under his feet.

She turned her face away.

He sat down next to her, kicking granules with his heel. They sat in silence, watching wind scatter the tiny flowers in the moonlight.

"It's time to come home," he advised. "To marry." He held out his hand.

No one could love her like Uptek. Tariem was a good man; Cheyuga respected him. And though at first she tried, she could never be his.

CHAPTER 6

It was good to be home.

Smokey jumped up onto the coffee table the minute they entered the house. He stood surveying the cabin.

"What's he doing?" Arlan stood with hands on hips, watching the filthy dog—who, once inside, seemed even filthier.

"Just looking around," she spoke for him. The dog sniffed the air, studying the room as if he'd just gotten off a bus from Mars. "Doubt he's ever been in a house before."

"Don't look like it. Think he'll pee?"

"Yeah he'll pee, Arlan. He'll probably do everything."

Arlan winced. She snorted a chuckle.

Smokey knocked aside the ashtray and then stepped across a *National Geographic, Wool: Fabric of History.* The glossy cover slipped; he caught his balance. Then he stepped onto the sofa, tiptoeing up across the back as if he were a cat. He jumped down onto the side table, knocking the phone off. He darted, tail snaked under his rear, scurrying like a wild animal trapped in a house.

"Smokey."

"Smokey."

They began chasing him.

"Come here, guy." Each competed to win him over. He disappeared into her bedroom. She followed Arlan and peeked under the bed. A shivering pile of laundry tipped her off.

"There you are." She squatted and held out her hand for Smokey to sniff. "Be right back."

She scampered off and returned with flakes of smoked whitefish. His nose poked through the clothes. At first he sniffed weakly, but the oily smell of the smoked fish was too pungent to resist. Smokey flicked a few flakes with his tongue and then gobbled up the rest.

"Yeah, that's good, ain't it?" Arlan chuckled.

Their arms were rubber by evening. Finally the bathtub water ran clear. Towels lay in sodden heaps, wadded on the floor.

"Goddamn it, I swear I just blew a disc," Arlan said, bent over the tub. At the onset the water was dank, almost tarry with grime. Smokey had flinched with the first application of medicated flea shampoo that Noreen had dropped off. Patches of his skin were raw. He looked demoralized, ears akimbo, every inch of him saturated. Rosalie tried not to laugh.

"That's probably more washings than most dogs get in a lifetime," Arlan said.

She rubbed Smokey vigorously with the last dry towel. He shook. Droplets flew and soon everything was plastered with water and dog fur.

"That's it; you're free!" She released him into the living room. He stared back as if it were too good to be true. Then he took off scurrying through the cramped house in a goofy jig. Wide toothy wolf grin, tail tucked under his rump, he dove onto the couch—frantically digging into the cushions as if searching for a buried bone.

They burst out laughing. Smokey froze in a dramatic pose, darting side-glances at Rosalie, then Arlan. His two front canine teeth peeped out in a snaggletoothed smile inviting them to play. She clapped. He hopped down onto the floor, running excitedly throughout the rooms at a breakneck pace.

They brushed him until their hands cramped and they filled a garbage bag with fur. In some places his coat was so dense you couldn't part his fur to see skin. In others he was practically bald. But even those areas now looked healthier. His fur color changed as he air-dried. It was more ghostly silver, though brittle—like color-treated hair—from the strong shampoo.

Later, as Arlan lay snoring in the La-Z-Boy, Rosalie cuddled up with Smokey on the couch. He leaned his chin on her thigh and sighed as if it were all too good to be true. She fell asleep holding on to his back, breathing in his scent as they drifted off into the place of new dreams.

For the first few weeks they stayed close to home, walking on nearby trails. Under Noreen's advice Rosalie worked to leash train him. Smokey was like a newly roped rodeo calf. Throwing himself down, he tried to bite through the leash. But after a few walks and a lot of chicken treats, he resisted less and enjoyed more.

Staying close to home was also a way of not being a spectacle. That first week, she ventured out with Lorraine to gas up her truck. Standing on the opposite side of a gas pump, a snow-mobile tourist had blurted, "Whoa, ho, ho. Who'd *you* piss off, little lady?" Lorraine had tried to kid her out of it, insisting he was a member of the "more-snowmobiles-than-brains club," but that did it for her.

Locals were well versed in the Smokey saga. Some politely glanced to assess the fading bruises; others nodded in solidarity while buying groceries at Peterson's Foods. Dizziness from the concussion disappeared.

Even Smokey monitored her progress. His face was thoughtful as he'd perch and sniff to examine the healing. She was busy since being voted in as a Master Beader. Her signature "mark," a cluster of five bloodroot blossoms, was registered with the Guild.

Arlan leaned over to watch the dog from the La-Z-Boy. "Think he wants to lick the stitches?"

"Oh don't be disgusting." She frowned, though thinking the same thing.

"They do that, you know—he knows you been hurt."

She glared back.

"Maybe he thinks you're his puppy."

"Maybe he thinks you're nuts."

They began to roam down by Charlotte Eagle's place where the forest floor was wrinkled with gorges and steep ravines. Trees had grown so densely that it was practically dark during daylight hours. Birches and pines grew as tall as buildings on some of the steeper slopes. Snow would pile up in the canopies of white pines and junipers, often tumbling down on hikers in mini-avalanches when triggered by a shift of wind or the passage of a wolf.

Lake effect reigned supreme. Fluffy charcoal clouds hovered so low that with a good arm you could lob a snowball high enough to disappear. Snowflakes drifted like lint, covering windshields in a fine layer you could blow off like birthday candles on a cake.

So far just enough snow had fallen for the first appearance of snowmobiles. The first winter blast felt like minus three hundred. People dodged in and out of Peterson's Foods remarking on how no one "ever remembers it being so dang cold this early." Wind ripped through last year's winter coat like cheesecloth as people debated the effectiveness of mittens versus gloves.

As winter set in, Rosalie spent weeks thinking about Jerry; the stunning reality hit that what you can't take back must be endured. While her bruises faded into swirling paisleys of green, yellow and purple, no one saw the deeper wounds. She avoided her reflection as she brushed her teeth, clutching her collar closed.

They walked on trails she'd not been on since childhood. Lorraine and the others had run from tree to tree, giggling, finding the most excellent hiding places. Rosalie would lie in the sweet greenness of mosses and delicate spires of liverworts on the forest floor. Closing her eyes, she'd hide, hoping to escape September's chores. The familiar sting of iodine from her mother's hands, scolding her for bug bites and scratches she couldn't remember getting. But that all had stopped when being cool trumped the tickle of snowflakes on your nose, getting drunk more absorbing than velvet moss growing on birch bark.

Rosalie and Smokey walked past places in the woods where people had once lived. Long after sandstone foundations crumbled back into soil, there remained demarcations of flower gardens. Wives had once stood at the cliffs' edge, watching for the return of fishing vessels after a brutal November storm. Clumps of daffodils, telltale spires of purple and white lupines would poke up without fail. Annual shocks of ruffled orange poppies and borders of electric blue forget-me-nots proclaimed, *We were here; remember us.* Pushing up each spring, the flowers held their ground against native grasses and sapling trees. Stalwart little reminders of those who'd battled to hold on to the promise of spring. Imprinting the land forever—long after simple graves are shrouded in thickets and everyone who remembers is gone—the flowers continue to bear testament.

Rosalie's plantings grew on the sleeves of couture fashions. They crept up the bodices of stately gowns and meandered along the hems and lapels of cocktail dresses. Some circled collars and cuffs of sheer chiffon blouses like delicate frosted winter wreaths. The wearer would never know the origin of such beauty. When a product was completed Aunt Edie, who was everyone's toughest critic, would regard it in hushed amazement. "Wherever in that head of yours do you get these fresh designs?" She'd gently knock on Rosalie's head as if a door would open. And a shy smile of delight would spread across her face.

Noreen stopped by every few days to check on Smokey, although Rosalie suspected it was more to check on Arlan. The shelter never learned where Smokey had come from. There was some-thing wild and elusive about him, as if he'd never belonged to anyone. People made him uneasy. He seemed surprised to find people on trails, at the store, stopping by the house to visit.

Smokey had turned up one morning in August, rummaging through the garbage cans of Earl and Pearl, elderly friends of Arlan. The couple had been lounging in bed, disturbed by the unpleasant grinding sound of their metal garbage cans rolling down the blacktop.

"Sounds like your buddy again." Pearl nudged Earl to get up.

"Darn bear." Earl feigned irritation, tossing aside the com-forter and digging his feet into his slippers.

"Now you be careful," she'd warned. "Dorothy says they been getting kinda pushy."

"Oh, he runs the minute he sees me." There were more black bears than people in Bayfield County. He peeked out the blinds.

"Pearl. Quick. Get a load of this." Now "Pearl" and "quick" were not words that often sequenced. Pearl the one-ton-girl, she was affectionately called. "Looks like a wolf pup," he said. "Doubt he's even a year."

"Better call Franklin."

Concerned the dog would get hit by bustling vacation traffic for Bayfield's Apple Festival that weekend, Pearl jiggled out in her nightie waving a hunk of meat loaf stabbed onto the end of a fork.

"Looky, looky here what I got for you." Smokey was riveted, bouncing alongside on his back legs as if they'd become springs. He followed Pearl into the fenced yard just as Earl shut the gate.

An hour later, they'd almost given up. The two of them plus Franklin had chased as Smokey eluded pork chops, fish sticks, even peanut butter.

"I got him now," Franklin swore for the hundredth time. Serv-ing as Bayfield Dog Catcher, Franklin was armed with a humane grab leash. It was of no use until Pearl's angina kicked in and Franklin was too short of breath to continue. Just as they quit,

Smokey stopped too. Conceding that the game was over, he looked up at Franklin and walked towards the exhausted couple.

Apparently Mr. Junkyard filed a formal complaint against Rosalie. The complaint got "misfiled" with a plethora of public drunkenness citations. Jerry had also filed a complaint to have Smokey declared a "dangerous dog," pending a hearing; he wanted Smokey impounded and euthanized. All this from the cell—where he sat in the Bayfield County Jail—waiting to be arraigned on several counts of domestic assault and battery, not to mention being served with an accelerated petition for divorce.

Noreen and the Humane Society trumped everyone with charges of animal cruelty, aiding and abetting. It was ruled that "every animal has the right to defend itself" and Smokey had done just that. Rosalie was awarded permanent placement. Between signed affidavits of eyewitnesses and Franklin's photographs detailing the dog's condition while at Lorraine's, both Kurt and Jerry had the good sense to quit while behind.

Despite her new status as some sort of local hero, Rosalie was perpetually on guard. While out she'd stop at the slightest sound. Smokey would pause too, his pale eyes searching for confirmation. At the crunching sound of tire treads compressing snow the two of them would recede into the brush. She'd kick herself for not having slung Arlan's deer rifle over her shoulder. Hiding in the woods was useless. Fresh snow tracks, her bright blue parka easily spotted through the bare trees— who was she kidding? It would take ten seconds tops for either Kurt or Jerry to find them.

Her ear became tuned to trucks coasting down the driveway and footsteps under the windowsills. Smokey would be up at the window before she could say "boo." Varnish on the windowsills was already worn from his paws.

At dusk she'd swear she spotted an elbow pulled hastily behind a basswood or a birch trunk. She'd go outside to check.

"Now where the hell are you going?" Arlan would carp while standing over a pan of frying meat, watching her wrestle into the armholes of her coat. "Dinner's almost ready."

"He wants to go out."

"No he don't; look at 'em." Arlan gestured with the spatula to the dog, glued to the kitchen floor. Drool streamed from Smokey's lips, rapt from the smell of hamburger. Rosalie practically dragged him out. She'd circle the perimeter searching out fresh boot prints. Nothing ever turned up—only squirrel tracings and her boot prints from last time. But it was little comfort. Kurt or Jerry could pop up tomorrow, next week, five minutes from now.

When Arlan worked nights at the Mill, she sat holed up, TV sound off, dozing in the La-Z-Boy with Arlan's loaded rifle across her knees. Safety off, knowing she'd blast the first person to enter unannounced. "You're gonna shoot me with this." Arlan would wrestle the rifle away from her, smelling of sawdust from his shift. "Give me this goddamned thing." He'd lock the safety and unload the shells into his hand. She'd just smirk. He wondered what she found so funny. And more sadly, what had happened to his daughter.

Arlan's rifle use was limited to shots in the air to chase off overzealous black bears who wouldn't give up on the garbage can. He'd even cringe at Peterson's when a piece of beef looked too raw, vowing to turn vegetarian. "You think the poor thing knew it was up next at the slaughterhouse?"

While walking Smokey on the Brownstone Trail, she wondered if a distant, lumbering figure was Jerry hobbling along like Quasimodo in his stupid Wisconsin Department of Corrections ankle bracelet. It turned out to be a bear gathering a last meal before bedding down. It didn't matter how many restraining orders and injunctions were in effect. It was all just paper.

"I think I need a handgun," she announced.

"Just stay close to home," Arlan countered. But he went so far as to pull up to Rusty's Gun Shop. Engine running, he sat staring at the dashboard. Even the bravest dog's ferocity is no match for a bullet. But something stopped Arlan just shy of shutting off the engine. Instead he installed dead bolts on both front and back doors as Rosalie sat watching. He flipped the golden dead bolt back and forth several times and without comment handed over the key, as shiny as a piece of jewelry.

A month later at the attorney's office, Rosalie stifled a snicker when Jerry reached over to sign the petition for divorce. The cuff of his sweater pulled back to reveal a few raw-looking purple scars.

Arlan's elaborate plan to build Smokey a fenced-in yard was surprising. Typically he'd look around the cabin with disgust, "Goddamn, everywhere I look I see work," begrudgingly shoveling gravel into driveway ruts only after people complained of getting stuck.

But making a yard for Smokey excited him. He began planning at the kitchen table, sketching out a design on graph paper, counting off each square foot of backyard—where to locate gates and space the fence posts. Then he'd drag Rosalie out in the freezing cold to walk the yard as he explained his plan. He pounded bright orange stakes into the frozen ground so, when the heavy snows came, he could still see his markers from inside. Visualizing when the ground would be drained well enough to put a posthole digger to soil. Until then the rolls of chain link and posts he purchased on sale lay covered like mounds of snowy haystacks.

Arlan began his life in Stevens Point, four hours southeast of Bayfield. He was adopted at a young age by Lake Superior and the north woods. But whatever the boy tried to master, his father could only do it better. "I'd already gotten my first buck by the time I was ten," he muttered under his breath. With a buck in his sights, the boy couldn't bring himself to squeeze the trigger. Instead his father did. Cutting open the chest cavity, he plunged Arlan's hand deep inside, grasping the boy's forearm so he couldn't pull away. The heart was warm. His father's eyes glowed with a lust that made Arlan's bowels clench whenever he remembered.

His father pushed him out at fourteen, the assumption being there's only one stallion in the herd. By twenty-five Arlan alternated between working the giant ore tankers and logging with old man Isakson. The old logger still pulled logs from the forests using horses and chains. Tears wetted the old Norske's face as he'd wring his hands: "Goddamn it, Arlan, these trees are just too damn beautiful to pull down."

Over time he worked the entire north shore of Minnesota and Ontario, the Upper Peninsula and Northern Wisconsin. And then one day while on a job in Red Cliff with Isakson, he bumped into Anna Marie bringing her father his lunch. Thin, tall, taller even than him. Rosalie's young mom had the limber, almost sinewy body of so many Anishanabe—or Ojibwa, as they were called by the French, "those who step quietly."

He and Anna Marie bought fifty acres overlooking Sand Bay. They hunkered down in a camper until their cabin was finished, and afterwards kept the clearing around the house closely mowed. Ignore a white or red pine and its tenacious roots in a death grip with the red soil and before you'd know it, you're evicted.

The cabin's interior remained the same as when Anna Marie was alive, save Arlan's powder blue La-Z-Boy. The furnishings included a faux wood TV console from the furniture liquidator's in Duluth. Even the patchwork living room rug that warmed the floor Anna Marie had sewn together with upholstery thread from discontinued carpet samples. Controlling the temperature was impossible. They either froze or sweltered with the wood-burning stove. "Why put in a furnace when there's free fuel lying around in the woods rotting?" Arlan would reiterate each fall as they traipsed through the forest looking for downed trees.

"They're all dead," Arlan would dismiss questions about relatives. Rosalie knew he was lying. Her mother once mentioned his sister, Colleen, who, like Arlan, had run for cover.

CHAPTER 7

No one should have been surprised when the Red Army rolled into their village. At the ceremonial races of Keretkun, Russian fur traders and Evenek reindeer herders warned of army camps setting up near the shores of the Bering. The only thing preventing Stalin from controlling the far northeastern edges of the continent was wild Chukotka.

But it hadn't always been this way. For centuries the Chukchi lived in relative peace with the Imperial Russians. After some initial skirmishes, Russian explorers and fur traders mingled with locals. Functionaries spent their lifetimes mapping Imperial Russia with territorial borders that meant nothing to the Chukchi. Had it not been for local generosity—providing *yarangas,* provisions and dog teams—visitors would have perished in days. Interethnic brawls were common, as were mixed marriages.

After 1917, the newly minted Bolshevik government announced that native peoples, or Primitives as they were called, were to be "celebrated." The Revolutionary Council vowed not to interfere with "Primitives," and a "preservation" system was set up to protect this "museum culture." Aboriginal culture became all the rage. Classes in Primitive Studies were offered at universities in Moscow and Leningrad. Fashion reflected aboriginal themes on furniture, in fine painting, and on Paris runways. Hundreds of young people signed up to be Soldiers of Culture, many taking up residence in remote areas of the Siberian arctic.

But as Stalin rose to power, "celebration" was replaced by his programme of forced "civilization" and evacuation. "Refusniks" were gunned down along with guardian dogs and the bodies dumped into mass graves. Reindeer were confiscated, though suffering a much kinder fate as "State Commodities." Many Chukchi died. Others sacrificed Guardians and their children, before turning an antique flintlock muzzle loader onto themselves. Villages were torched along with clothing and walrus-hide *yarangas*, sleds, drums, boats, hunting implements—every vestige marking their existence as a people. Those who surrendered were deloused, issued Government clothing and crowded into wooden barracks where only Russian was to be spoken. No religious practice or hunting was permitted. The programme systematically snuffed out the soul of the Lygoravetlat.

Tariem noticed the reclusive Samoyed herdsmen moving their reindeer herds at the wrong time of year. Curious, he rode out to speak with them. They suggested he follow them southwest, towards the interior mountains where the Red Army would be sore pressed to reach. They relayed reports of huge gouges in the Forest Keeper's woods. Hills of burning slash spanned as far as a person could see. Even from the village, plumes of smoke could be seen like strange clouds from another world.

But as Tariem relayed their warning, the elders wrinkled their noses, "Eh, soldiers come and go," figuring it to be one more permutation of the same old story. "We are Chukchi; the Lygoravetlat we will always be." They spit tobacco to shame him back to his senses. "Look at you, hysterical like a woman. We'll make you wear beads," they said. "The Army wants to own the sea?" They laughed themselves silly. "Let them stuff it into their pockets. And while they're at it march across to Rochlit."

Their jeering angered Jeaantaa. It kindled memories of her treatment after Uptek's death. Though time had proven them wrong, she still seethed. "People outlive their stupidity; you must let them," Cheyuga said.

She began having premonitions that Tariem explained away

as someone's envy of her dogs. Hers were the fastest in all of Chukotka. People would journey across the Bering Sea to trade with her. She was very particular about with whom the Guardians went.

Last week as she was making pemmican, cutting up seal fat to mix in with fish roe, she paused. The wooden ladle she used every day felt different and unfamiliar in her hand. The ladle had been Gyrongav's. Jeaantaa listened. Was it her aunt's spirit? Slowly, Jeaantaa looked around the *yaranga*. She raised the ladle and touched it to her cheek. Though her sons were only steps away, sleeping in the *yorongue*, she felt alone. The *yaranga* was now a stranger's home and she'd never again stand there cutting seal fat, lifting the red clay bowl, hearing her children's dreams.

She looked up to where the birch poles wove together to form the chimney. Someone was there. Was it him? Jeaantaa listened. Though the fire was strong, she felt cold. The hair on her body prickled as if something brushed against her. She'd not mention these feelings. Not to Cheyuga and certainly not to Tariem. Sometimes it was hard to hide things from Cheyuga. He smiled in a way that told her he'd already seen her thoughts in a dream.

Maybe this was how Uptek had felt. Maybe he knew that he'd never touch the safety of the pebbly shore with the same foot that pushed off to sea. That wriggling into his betrothal clothes was the last he'd ever wear them. That he'd never feel her bare skin.

Keepers were known to belong more to their Keep than to the people who loved them. She hid this, not wanting Tariem to feel one more layer of separation.

Jeaantaa's sons were more like Tariem. Ankjem, the older, resembled his father and Tangek, the younger, resembled Uptek. Chukchi boys belonged to fathers, girls to mothers. The moment each of her sons was born she longed for a girl. Her love for them was tinged with a sadness she could never explain.

Sometimes while she was feeding the dogs, stray feelings whispered that she'd never see her sons as grown men. She pushed such thoughts away, figuring it was an envious spirit trying to scare her.

Later that evening tears came after she and Tariem made love. Tears streamed down to the roots of her hair, leaving a cold trail.

"What's wrong?" Tariem asked.

"Nothing."

Then Bakki shifted into a more comfortable position on the *yaranga* floor. The dog was strictly forbidden from sleeping in the *yorongue* with them. "He's more your man than me," Tariem complained the first week of their marriage. Only when Tariem was gone could the dog curl up and sleep in the *yorongue*. In Tariem's bitter moments he'd refer to Bakki and say, "Go ask your man," in a tone she tried to ignore.

She rolled over and sighed. Maybe bad air had gotten trapped behind her heart or was hiding under her liver. The more she pushed it away, the stronger it pulsed. It seeped into her armpits and down tingling into her fingers. Her black hair fanned out on the bed, now with a few silver threads. After a while she drifted to sleep. Tariem listened to her, memorizing the sound of her breath.

Outside Jeaantaa rearranged the *yaranga* walls in the brief respite between storms. Late last night the winds blew with a fury, as if wanting to clear the landscape to start anew. The internal birch poles swayed as precariously as a minutes-old reindeer calf staggering to find its footing.

The boys tumbled as they played. She hoped they'd burn off pent-up energy before the winds started again. Bakki and the older dogs lay around her, supervising as the boys brushed past her foot, engaged in battle, two walrus tusks as swords. Slipper, her favorite red pup, clamped down onto the pant leg of Tangek, growling—her frost blue eyes bulging as if they'd pop.

"Ama-a-a," Tangek called her, complaining in the way that seasoned mothers learn to ignore. "Stop it, Slipper," he whined louder, making the halfhearted pretense of swatting the puppy away.

"Baby, baby," Ankjem, the older boy, teased.

The adult dogs, tied in the crescent-shaped grove of trees, howled as they jumped into the air, pulling at their tethers. Right then the bad air shifted. It was hiding behind her heart. She turned.

"Forest Keeper?" She looked up to the crescent stand of trees.

Bakki glanced to see what had caught her attention. She sat and covered her face with her hands. The boys saw. Each tossed aside his tusk scurrying over.

"Ama-a?" Tangek squirmed into her lap, trying to wheedle between her arms to feel her warmth. But she didn't hug him back.

Even Ankjem started crying. "What's wrong?" He pulled her bangs trying to find her eyes.

She spied a tiny dog-shaped pebble lying in the snow. She picked it up, popping it into her breast pouch for protection against the People of the Red Flag. Maybe they were stealing her spirit. Or maybe it was time to leave a life to which she'd never belonged.

CHAPTER 8

Smokey stopped cold on the snowy trail. His whole body listened.

Rosalie's stomach fell. "What is it, Smokes?" She crouched low, sweating all the way down into her mittens. She'd been jogging for miles, holding on to the leash for dear life. With plummeting temperatures he dragged her as if late for an appointment.

The trail curved sharply; snow fell unbroken in clumps, sheltered by paper birches that obscured a clear view. The snowpack was already a respectable foot; by March it would be more than five. The woods had been silent except for Rosalie's running commentary on whose advice she should have taken regarding Jerry.

"Whatcha see?"

She hoped it was an animal. By Smokey's reaction, she guessed it was. She prayed she was right; people made him fidgety. Thanksgiving was always a weird day on the Reservation. It could be a family out with their dogs. Wrong time of year for bears; most snoozed in their earthen dens. Deer were a dime a dozen; wolves stared back through the cover of brush.

Smokey shuddered.

A charcoal mound of movement appeared. A silhouette of someone's head, shoulders preceded by a shorter pulsating mob. Smokey whined and paced excitedly. A sled. Shades of gray, black and brownish-red dogs strung together like the argyle patterned rows of a sweater. Syncopated bodies panted to jingling dog tags. They gripped and flicked the snowy ground as they propelled forward. Steamy breath frosted whiskers and chins into snowy beards. Smiling with broad toothy wolf grins, they trotted towards her. Some ran with a rocking horse gait; others trotted briskly like Smokey. There was a musky, earthy smell of warmth as they neared.

"On by," a man's voice instructed from the runners of the dogsled. "Fred. Harold," he corrected.

She was mesmerized, too transfixed to clear completely off the trail. She counted fourteen dogs. The two younger-looking ones craned towards Smokey.

"On by, Harold, Fred," the man repeated the correction. There was an obvious tug-of-war between burning curiosity and months of disciplined sled dog training.

Fred and Harold leaned into their harnesses and rushed by.

"Good job, guys," the man said. He nodded to Rosalie and waved woodenly as they passed. Rosalie mimicked the gesture. He pointed at Smokey, then gave a thumbs-up. The older, more experienced dogs sped by without a glance. The man's face was covered by dark amber-colored goggles. He wore a cobalt blue snow parka with fur lining the hood. A bright orange fleece muffler bunched around his neck and pulled up just above his chin. The bit of visible skin was tan. His thick arctic mitts looked like robot hands.

They vanished as quickly as they appeared. Smokey yelped as if she'd stepped on his foot. He lunged. Pain shot through her ribs as he gave chase.

"Heel," she commanded, trying to rein him in. "Okay, okay." She picked up the pace to a run but tripped over the toes of her snow boots and fell. He kept running, dragging her on her belly. "Whoa," she yelled, digging in with her toes and elbows. She eventually pulled him to a stop. Even then he stood on his hind legs and hopped, a circus puppy minus the tutu. Reaching towards the team with his front legs, he seemed to embrace their lingering scent.

· · ·

She couldn't get the dog team out of her mind.

The next day she and Smokey were out on the trail when he stopped again. Eyes focused, ears up, his face began to quiver.

"Is it them, Smokes?" She touched his head. He yanked it away; his irritation was amusing.

The dog team appeared. Smokey broke into his "dance of joy." His shoulders shrugged, front legs jigged in a goofy little dance. Just as before their walks he'd pace and circle as she gathered her hat, scarf, mittens. He could distinguish "going to the grocery store" movements from "going for a walk" movements. She hadn't faked him out yet.

The musher nodded deeply, acknowledging the second encounter. Another verbal correction was issued to the same two dogs as they passed. But Smokey didn't move. He stood watching from where they'd come.

"More?" She knelt down and watched.

A second team appeared. Smokey quivered. The team zoomed by as if there were no one on the trail. A woman on the sled runners smiled and waved as they whooshed by. Then Smokey lunged. Rosalie sat, her deadweight anchoring him, waiting until there was enough distance to control him.

The following day she was in Peterson's Foods rifling through a refrigerated bin of smoked whitefish, looking for the fattest ones. The metal drum smokers of Buffalo Bay Fisheries ran continuously out back. Buck, her mother's first cousin, ran the small Reservation grocery store on Highway 13. He stocked it with your standard groceries, as well as state-of-the-art munchies, guns and ammo, cheese curds, antiques, tobacco, chain-saw oil, soda, film and animal feed.

A woman in a bright orange down vest paused and tapped Rosalie's arm.

"Weren't you on the trail yesterday? The one with the husky out by Scheffel Road?"

Rosalie looked up. It was the woman from the second sled. Rosalie nudged up her scarf to hide the yellow and green discoloration on her bruised cheeks. But the woman had already seen.

The woman had that kind of white-blond hair you often see in the north, only a few shades away from platinum, tidily braided into one thick rope down her back. The woman's skin looked weather-beaten for about thirty. She wore a Scandinavian black-and-white wool cardigan with carved silver closures. A brand-name down vest like the ones tourists bought from the outfitters in Bayfield. Diamond stud earrings twinkled under the fluorescent lighting of Buck's store. Her wedding ring freighted a diamond the size of a cherry. Headlights, Lorraine called them. Lorraine often said that despite bitchy posturing, jewelry tells the truth.

"Possibly," Rosalie said.

She filled her mouth with cubes of a new beer cheese that Buck cut into samples. Buck had already stuffed a brick of the mottled cheddar into her purse to thank Arlan for fixing ". . . that bastard toilet." He'd also just opened a tab to take them through winter in exchange for Arlan fixing the store's three larger refrigeration units. When cash was scarce people bartered. Arlan always prided himself, "If a man made it, I can fix it."

". . . passed you with our dog teams," the woman continued.

"Yeah, my dog went nuts," Rosalie admitted. She chuckled remembering Smokey dragging her.

"Is he even a year?" the woman asked.

Rosalie shrugged. "Not sure. He was a stray." Noreen estimated that Smokey was a year, give or take a month. "Teeth and eyes tell age," Noreen said. His nails had been worn to the quick, classic signs of a wanderer. No collar or matted fur around the neck to indicate he'd ever worn a collar.

"Good," the woman said, and nodded slowly.

Rosalie furrowed her brow. *Why would that be good or bad?* The woman's crystal blue eyes were lined with white eyelashes.

"You get him from Bayfield Pound?" The woman gave her a look. She was smiling when she asked, though Rosalie felt herself clench. It was nosy and prying. She clutched the packages of whitefish to her chest.

"I know Noreen," the woman said. "You get him from Noreen?" she asked.

Rosalie tightened and pulled away. Did she know about Jerry too? "Um-m-m—sort of." She looked away. It was a long story that was none of her business anyway. Rosalie turned her back and bent over to forage for another package of whitefish. Reaching in the bin, she hoped the woman would take the hint.

Rumor had it Arlan's layoff might last until Christmas. So close to the holiday everyone was on edge. Only whitefish and a Packer game broke his funk. He'd loaf around bored and grumpy. If lucky, he might pick up odd jobs. Last week he sanded and primed the exterior window ledges for Max's Desolation Tavern during a freak warm spell. Max was just as broke. He opened a generous bar tab in exchange, always a dangerous thing going into the holidays. She made her final selection of whitefish. The woman was still there.

"Isn't Buck's the best?" Rosalie said, smiling sheepishly.

The woman smiled reflectively, as if noting the way her question had gone unanswered. "Yeah, it's great," she confirmed. "We always take some home to Grand Marais. For our folks. We moved here this past spring. Friendly Valley Road, know where it is?"

Of course she did.

"Just started a racing kennel. Finally." The woman rolled her eyes. "Sled dogs. We're getting ready for the Beargrease."

"Oh." Rosalie nodded eagerly like she knew what it was.

The woman piled cans of soup into her shopping cart. "You interested in running dogs?"

Rosalie stared blankly, not sure what was being asked.

"You like being around them?" the woman followed up.

Rosalie looked away. "I like *my* dog." Her eyes fixed on to the potato chip aisle. There was a long pause. She didn't know what to say. She stepped sideways towards the register.

"I don't mean to be pushy—." The woman unfolded her arms. "But we're looking to hire a handler. You seem really good with your dog."

Rosalie looked at the floor. She blushed and then felt embarrassed. "So—uh—what's the job?" she asked, more to be polite.

The woman didn't blink. "Part-time, mostly mornings, more during race season. Scooping poop, feeding, health checks, puppy training—Dave and I'll train you. Dave's my husband. We have a converted garage; you're welcome to live there. Free. Kathleen, the previous handler, did. She got married, moved back to the Cities. All meals included." She held out her hand. "I'm Jan, by the way."

"Rosalie." She extended her hand as if reaching into a small animal's cage.

"Dave mentioned when he saw you on the trail. Then when we saw you yesterday."

"Uh-h-h—no thanks. I live at home—with my father."

"That would be okay too," Jan said.

Rosalie took another step towards the register.

"You could bring your dog too—sorry, what's his name?"

Why would Jan be sorry? Rosalie hesitated saying his name. "Smokey."

"Smokey. Cool," Jan replied. "Are you busy tomorrow?"

Rosalie looked blankly back.

"I mean—if you're not—you're welcome to stop by. I can show you around, show you what's involved. Bring Smokey too. Anytime after one, after my show." She smiled shyly. "You can meet the dogs."

"Guiding Light?"

Jan seemed embarrassed. Rosalie looked more closely at the woman; she was starting to like her. "Yeah . . . ," Jan slowly admitted. "My husband teases me." Jan laughed, her cheeks turning deep pink.

"What for?"

"'Cause it's a soap." Jan seemed uncomfortable.

What a funny thing to be embarrassed about. Everyone watched *Guiding Light*. From twelve to one Buck might as well close the store. You could steal anything but the TV. The staff huddled around the set, smoking. A person could grow old and die waiting to get checked out. "Don't you people have more shopping to do?" one of the cashiers would invariably carp, annoyed that customers, especially tourists, hadn't the sensitivity to time their purchases during commercial breaks. Even Buck craned to watch from back in the storeroom as he checked in deliveries.

Maybe watching soaps wasn't high class enough. Jan's speech, her jewelry, their gear, they seemed classy right down to the expensive parkas. Hell, even their dogs looked well dressed, color-coordinated harnesses and collars—red for one team, blue for the other. Where on earth did one even get a sled?

Jan smiled at her. "We're probably the only two who'd admit it." She winked, as if taking Rosalie into confidence.

"Lots of people do," Rosalie countered. She was sorry the instant she said it—sounding like a child pleading a case before Santa. She fiddled with the Styrofoam bottom of the packaged whitefish, pinching it between her fingernails as if it would help her decide.

"Well . . . I have a puppy team I'm going to harness break tomorrow. If you'd like I can run Smokey."

"With your team?"

"Yep."

"I-I-I don't have any stuff—"

"Don't need any. Just come with Smokey. Dress warm." Jan waited to unload her groceries onto the checkout counter.

"But he's never run like—how will he know?"

"Oh, he'll know." Her face opened into a full smile.

Rosalie handed the packages to the cashier. Jan's ease made her shrink. The ugly mirror of comparison began reflecting images. The woman had the bearing of someone cherished and sheltered by those around her, a protective barrier against all things bad. Never in a million years would such an open, trusting face have taken a man's fist. Jan oozed with the wisdom and confidence that comes from having a base, one that makes it possible for women to see through men like Jerry in a blink. What life must be like from such a place of safety—to be so free of things to hide, with a clean past, without that panicky feeling that comes from having to police your thoughts. In the two minutes it took to meet Jan, Rosalie's eighteen years felt heavy, tainted and burdensome.

"Well, thanks but." Rosalie backed towards the door. "I-I-I'm not looking for a job."

"Hey, Buck," Jan greeted as she pushed her cart up next.

"How's it going, Jan?" He nodded. "Your dog feed's in."

"Mind reader. I just invited Rosalie out to meet the dogs. We're looking for a new handler. Kathleen's due in February."

"Good people, Roz." Buck held her eye and winked. "And I've known this one"—he reached over, wrestling Rosalie into a head lock before releasing her and pulling on her ponytail—"since she was a kid."

"I'm a pretty good judge of character," Jan said. She paused and gave Rosalie a searching look. "Hey—take my number. If you change your mind—just show up." She tore a piece off the envelope and jotted down her phone and fire number. "Maybe we'll see ya soon?" She laid a hand gently on Rosalie's shoulder before handing her the note.

"Yeah, well, see ya." She stuffed it into her pocket. She couldn't get out fast enough. Tripping over a wrinkle in the rubber mat by the front door, she caught herself. She felt Jan wave but pretended not to see.

Outside, Smokey's face searched for her through the driver's side windshield. He twitched with delight the instant she appeared. "Hey, guy." She climbed in and guided him to the passenger side. She closed the door and hugged him so tight his shoulder bones pressed together. It felt so good. He didn't wriggle free. She buried her nose in his pelt, breathing his sweet scent.

Jan walked out carrying grocery sacks. Smokey wrestled free and watched. He followed her trajectory across the parking lot to a berry red truck as shiny and new as a freshly painted fingernail. *Stormwatch Kennel* was stenciled on the door with the profile of a husky.

That night Arlan tipped back his chair after finishing dinner. Balancing against the wall, he perched as if clearing the quickest path through his intestines.

"So Buck tells me you got a job offer today," he said, watching the local TV news.

She stopped chewing her grilled cheese sandwich. *Wasn't anything private in this town?* "Uh-h—not really."

"'Not really'?" He turned to her.

She felt his eyes but kept eating. She was tempted to pass the sandwich off to Smokey, who drooled in anticipation under the table.

"Sounds like an opportunity—"

"I already have a job."

"—for getting out of the house."

"I get out of the house." Their eyes met.

"You can make money—"

"I already make money." She was earning twice as much beading as she'd ever earned at Marge's.

"That's not what I mean. Just sitting around moping—" His voice rose in frustration.

"I'm not moping."

"You coulda fooled me." They sat in a tense silence.

"Be good for you," he continued. "Make new friends."

"I have friends."

"You told Lorraine you're not going to next week's Holiday Dance."

She always went; the whole town practically did. She sighed loudly. *Jesus, now Lorraine too?*

"Hey—we're trying to help you." He raised his hands.

"Help me?" Her face twisted into a grimace. "Help me what?" She practically spit the words. She pushed out from the table. Grabbing her coat, she snapped the leash on Smokey.

"Don't walk out when I'm talking—," Arlan yelled.

"Stop yelling," she shouted back. Hot, angry tears broke the instant the frigid air hit her face. A thin strip of red sunlight was fading to violet over the distant Minnesota shoreline. Arlan never cared what she did before. Why now?

After Anna Marie had died, Arlan seemed to forget he still had a daughter. He spent a good three, maybe four, years intoxicated and going through jobs like water. Opening a can of SpaghettiOs, he'd hand it to young Rosalie with a spoon. Often stumbling home to find her curled up asleep on the floor as if trying to leach warmth out of the TV. Scattered bits of bark and twigs, evidence the girl had traipsed out to dig logs from the snow-drifted woodpile and drag in what she could carry. So lost in his own pain, he hadn't realized that she had lost a mother too. It was then Rosalie started calling him by his first name.

By the time Arlan began working steadily at Consolidated Paper, Rosalie was in high school—too late for him to begin asserting fatherly authority.

She veered off the road towards the Lake, following a narrow path half a mile through the woods. Scrambling down the frozen red sandy cliff to the shoreline dock, she hiked out onto the fast ice, the strip that freezes first and attaches to the shoreline. Underneath, frozen ice floes gurgled and belched as the evening temperatures plunged.

Smokey sniffed stray pieces of driftwood, cigarette butts and crushed beer cans as they climbed up onto what was left of the old dock: huge hand-hewn logs pierced together with centuries-old rusted bolts and rivets. She sat down and leaned over, her face hanging between her knees.

Smokey leaned his flank across her back, curving around her. The pressure from his body made her cry.

CHAPTER 9

It was their blindness she hated the most. Had Lena not been visiting, Jeaantaa would have left after the preparations—especially after the Great One's warning. Strange markings appeared in a sacrificed reindeer's shoulder blade, constellations no one had ever seen.

Despite the scent from nearby army bonfires, the warnings went unheeded. Like dominoes, villages along the Bering coast fell one after the other. The Red Army had advanced near Cape Dezhnev where steep cliffs dropped hundreds of feet to the sea. At the bottom on the small "neck" of sandbar lay the improbable village of Uelen. Straight-line winds would scream across the narrow strip of land. Only fifty-five miles of Bering Sea separated Uelen and Nome, Alaska.

The annual Festival of Keretkun was held in their *yaranga*. Earlier, Jeaantaa and Lena hurried to prepare the ceremonial shoulder blade for Cheyuga's interpretation. Voices of the drunken elders traveled into the back room where the two women worked. The men sat huddled around the inside fire on piles of walrus skins. Drinking vodka and strong Russian tea, they traded joking insults. The tips of Jeaantaa's ears burned just listening. The burly men were slick with layers of soot and sweat. Stripped from the waist up, they laughed loudly, waiting for guidance on hunting and reindeer migration patterns.

"Look," Tariem joked. He mimicked Cheyuga making a prediction. "Omryn will lose his nuts." The women glanced out from the skin partition, fearing a fight. Lena's husband, Omryn, didn't like being teased. But Tariem mimicked Cheyuga so well, pointing exaggeratedly to his crotch, Omryn was amused. "Hunting accident," Tariem whispered. "'Nutless' will be his new name." It triggered fits of laughter.

Despite the jokes, Tariem's voice was strained. That tinny, insecure timbre Jeaantaa would hear when he addressed the elders. Why he vied for their approval—something they granted to no one—she never understood. The skin around his eyes was pinched.

"Why wait to call him that?" another yelled. It made Jeaantaa laugh. She looked at Lena, who would only look at her hands.

Omryn hurled back an insult but was too drunk to be understood. The rest of them were so close to being in that state themselves that everyone found it hilarious. Many laughed until they were crying. Jeaantaa peeked out at the spectacle and shook her head, watching the men rolling on the floor as they held their sides. She sighed.

Tomorrow, after the ceremony, Omryn and Lena would leave. It was always hard. Jeaantaa and Lena were like sisters. With the Season-of-the-Fresh-Air-Going-Out, Jeaantaa prayed they'd make the journey. For weeks she searched the horizon for signs of travelers and reindeer. But the month-long visit flew. And while she and Tariem would venture inland every summer, she didn't like the ways of the reindeer people or how they treated dogs. Even more, she disliked seeing how Omryn treated his gentle-spirited wife, Lena.

"Why don't you speak up?" Jeaantaa asked Tariem on one of their visits. The two of them had been out alone gathering firewood. "Are you afraid of him too?" she taunted, a twist of accusation in her voice.

"There are different ways of doing things," Tariem said, trying to back away from hurt feelings. "One needn't leave a trail of blood and teeth to get people to change," he said. "Omryn calms when we're here."

"When we're here," she said. "Then it's back to the same old Omryn before we're even packed and gone."

"I've spoken to the Old Ones, asked Cheyuga for guidance," he said. "We've prayed for Omryn."

Jeaantaa glared at him.

"Things take time," he said.

She couldn't believe what she was hearing and lifted her hands up to her face. "Maybe I'm the answer to your prayer," she challenged, her anger rising. "Maybe the Old Ones told me to speak up. Call him outside; make him stop."

"Rather than being angry," Tariem said, "maybe you should ask the Old Ones to help Omryn."

"The only help Omryn needs is a hard kick when he mistreats his wife," Jeaantaa muttered, bending over to gather a piece of stray wood.

As she stood, Tariem looked stunned.

"What?" Her eyes were angry.

"Nothing." It was exactly what his brother would have said. "We all have our ways of doing things," Tariem spoke softly. "Sometimes patience is the best way."

She crossed her arms and walked back to the camp alone, not sure if Omryn or Tariem disgusted her more.

Before departures, the two women would sob for days. For Lena, it was particularly bittersweet. Each visit was her respite. Once Tariem's moderating influence was gone, it would be back to the bruises, harshness and false accusations.

The reindeer shoulder was ready. Jeaantaa signaled through the skin partition.

Cheyuga stood. He picked up the drum and closed his eyes. Everyone quieted. They sat up sober, eager for good news. The old man began to drum and sing; spirits were invited. Everyone's skin prickled. Then he set the drum down. He grasped the clay lantern suspended from a long gut line and lit a fresh wick of moss floating in whale oil.

Jeaantaa and Lena carried out a birch bark basket containing the prepared shoulder. They averted their eyes out of respect. Cheyuga grasped the shoulder blade and drew it towards the lamp. Jeaantaa studied her uncle's face. His reaction bothered her. His features lost emotion as if his soul had left. The old man's movements were rigid. Lena noticed too and the women clasped hands.

The men waited for Cheyuga's furrowed brow to soften. For the corners of his mouth to turn upwards into his wry little crooked smile, indicating good news. It was taking too long. Good news came fast. Complications took longer, but never this long. Cheyuga let go of the lamp. It swung like a pendulum, distorting shadows with its sway. He arched away from the shoulder blade, sighing deeply. Men darted glances at each other. No one dared break the silence. Jeaantaa lowered her head. Lena was crying.

The old man lifted his drum. He held it close, waiting. Then he began to play and sing the Chukchi dirge for lost souls. It was never sung at ceremony but reserved for the lost and doomed who wander in confusion. Those never to be greeted by clear-eyed dogs to lead them through the Labyrinth of Darkness—those fated to be cornered by vicious dogs in clay huts who'd tear them apart. There was no fast trail to the Land of the Living on the other side of the sun. Cheyuga began to shudder, stricken with the violence of a sudden fever.

Each man's skull was visible as he scanned the room.

"We are crushed under the rolling machines of the bloody star," Cheyuga said. "The Old Ones predicted."

But no one believed they would see the fulfillment of catastrophe.

"You're drunk." Omryn grabbed the old man, risking bad luck by touching a shaman in ceremony. He shook Cheyuga's bat-like frame until his few remaining teeth chattered.

Jeaantaa guided Lena into the *yorongue* with the sleeping children.

"Drunken bastard," another scream erupted.

"Tariem," Jeaantaa shrieked for him to stop them.

It exploded like a dogfight. Everyone dove onto the old man. Cheyuga submitted. He made no move to block the blows. "I'm sorry," was all he said, his voice muffled beneath the pile of slippery bodies.

"Stop it," Jeaantaa screamed at them. "Tariem. Help him," she yelled. Tariem was in a stupor. She slapped him across the chest to wake him. "Do something," she yelled. But her husband cowered, crouching down against a wall.

"Ach," she yelled in disgust, and dove onto the pile, scratching at their skin, kicking and pulling their hair. "Stop it," she shrieked. "Stop it, all of you." She grabbed Omryn's slick limbs, pulling him. He swatted her away. She flew against the center pole.

Finally Tariem moved. He reached to pull them off and they turned on him. "It's you. Your cursed wife," voices accused.

Omryn pushed open the walrus-flap door. He shoved Cheyuga past the outer ring and into the snow where Bakki was sleeping with the old Guardians. The dogs looked up in a breath of surprise. "Sober up, old man." Omryn turned to walk inside. "Now—the real ceremony."

Cheyuga pushed up onto a naked elbow. "There's no forgiveness for false testimony."

"This from a drunken shaman." Omryn waved disgustedly.

"Go wash your face," another said, shoving Cheyuga's face into the gritty snow.

"Listen to me." Cheyuga ignored the salty taste of blood from his nose.

The men piled back in, tying the outside door flap behind them. Lena hid in the *yorongue*. Jeaantaa scurried past them, outside to find Cheyuga.

"Let's start the reading," they began to murmur. Omryn picked up Cheyuga's drum. No one touches a shaman's drum. The sound of Omryn playing made her want to set their *yaranga* on fire.

The room became stifling, yet their hands were bloodless. Each fashioned an interpretation. As they egged each other on, it became all the more fanciful with additional vodka. How the People of the Red Flag would come to no good end at the hands of the Great One. Because they were the People of One Fire, the Chukchi, and always would be. Their mouths were cotton; pores oozed with panic and strong Russian tea. Bragging as to how many litters of fast dogs would be born and how many reindeer would be calved. Tariem quietly crushed more dried willow twigs in the palm of his hand and boiled more water for tea.

He should have stopped them. Jeaantaa helped Cheyuga to his feet, walking her uncle over to the crescent stand of trees.

The men swallowed the bitter brew all night.

CHAPTER 10

A strange truck pulled in.

"Who is it?" Rosalie asked without looking up from where she sat beading. As long as it wasn't Jerry.

Arlan and Smokey were already up at the front window. "Don't know." Arlan's voice was gentle.

She didn't recognize the engine. Needle poised in her hand, she listened, and then looked up, watching the backs of their heads.

The petals of a beaded rose were more troubling. They wouldn't lie flat without puckering the dupioni silk of someone's wedding dress. Fingering the petals, she sighed. Despite the cross-stitching beneath, the damn thing still wouldn't lie flat.

"Think it's for you."

"What?" No one visited her. Lorraine was off in the Twin Cities with another Mr. "I gotta feeling this is the one."

Arlan took hold of Smokey's collar and cracked open the door. "Hi, I'm Jan."

She looked up. *Oh shit.* Jan's white-blond head glowed with sunlight.

"I'm Arlan." He waved his "come on in" arm. The door squeaked as it opened.

"Sorry to pop in like this." The woman stomped off snow. Jan smiled. "Hey, Roz."

Roz?

"Missed you guys on the trail. Thought I'd stop by, see if everything's okay." Smokey jumped up. Jan knelt to pet him. "Hey, Smokster."

She had nicknamed him too. Ears flat back, his tongue flicked blissfully. He sniffed the soles of her boots.

"You think any more about running him with our yearling team?" Jan asked while petting Smokey. "Or the handler job?"

"Uh-h-h, not really." She looked quickly but didn't get up. "I'm pretty busy right now." She held up the fabric as proof.

Arlan glared at her rudeness. *Okay.* She stabbed the needle into the pincushion and stood. Tucking her hands in her jeans pockets, she rocked back on her heels. She stifled a yawn.

"Hey, just come out with us. You'd have a great time," Jan coaxed.

"Go on, missy. Smokey'd have a ball." She heard the effort it took not to make it sound like an order.

"Meet the dogs," Jan suggested. "Decide if you want the job—or just hang out. We could watch *Guiding Light*—it'll be fun."

Rosalie stepped back. It was clear they'd talked.

"Hey, no strings." The woman held up both hands. "Charlie Gokee, our kennel vet, will be there all week."

"Oh sure, we know Charlie." Arlan folded his arms. "They moved back some years ago from Alaska." He looked at Rosalie. "He's your ma's second cousin."

Rosalie knew but nodded anyway.

"Haven't been in touch," Arlan said. "I work third shift, but I see them around here and there."

"Yeah, he told me. He's finishing health histories for the dog-sled race in January, the Beargrease."

"Look, I don't know anything about dogs—," Rosalie said.

Jan nodded slowly to herself. "You have good animal sense. Your heart's in it. But I bet you don't know that."

She flushed as Jan said it. "Right. Like you saw that in two seconds?"

Arlan's scornful gaze enveloped her.

"Yeah, I did." The woman paused. "Dave did too." It was an awkward silence. "Well—we'll be there," Jan said.

Arlan unfolded his arms, either relaxing or giving up. Jan backed towards the door and Arlan saw her out.

Rosalie swore she'd never work for anyone again. With beading, deadlines were the only boss. So why heap one more humiliating experience onto the accumulated pile? Every first day on the job was the same, plopped on a toilet seat, face in hands, crying off mascara in some sacred rosary repetition of, "God, I hate this job. . . ." Aside from a string of daylong stints and a month at the Frosty Tip being the longest, she had lasted a week at Scooters Truck Stop outside of Ashland. Stuck behind the counter in a fifty-nine-dollar cocktail-style butter cream–colored uniform she was required to purchase. Lorraine had threatened to snap a photo. At least in the end Rosalie had the satisfaction of burning it in the wood stove. She lugged heavy porcelain coffee mugs, wiped pie crumbs off the lunch counter and fended off truckers trying to convince her to follow them out back to the free showers. A week at Scooters had been life without parole.

At Scooter's last words: "Hey, do me a favor—act like you actually give a shit," she gave him the finger and walked. Hiking out to Highway 2, she stuck out her thumb.

In a small town you quickly run out of options. But to her credit, Rosalie had learned to stop fighting for things she didn't want.

All that next week she bumped into Jan. As Rosalie pulled into Peterson's Foods, there was Jan's truck. At the sight of Jan's white-blond head at the gas pump Rosalie drove on. Praying the old truck had enough tank space to make it eight more miles to the next gas station.

She changed Smokey's walk schedule to avoid them, but he wasn't so compliant. He knew the timing was off. Looking longingly down the trail, he sniffed furiously where the teams had passed. When she bribed him with chicken, he left it untouched.

"You really wanna see them?"

That week Aunt Edie dropped off a seven-hundred-dollar check, reflecting the promotion to Master Beader. Arlan stumbled up the steps that night, tired from his shift. His boots smelled like freshly cut lumber.

"Look." Rosalie steered him to the kitchen table, pointing to the check. "See?"

He glanced at the check. His whiskers bristled as he rubbed his face, tired from more than just work.

"Yep," he acknowledged. "It's money all right."

Days later she waved a ticket to Bayfield's Holiday Dance in his face. She'd no intention of going, only he didn't know it.

"Happy now?"

He grunted in return, glued to a Packer game.

The dance was Saturday in the Pavilion down by the dock. She bubbled on like an idiot but then toned it down, thinking he'd get suspicious. Lorraine's cardinal rule about lying: simple is believable. Getting dressed in the pink party dress, Rosalie frowned in the mirror. It was the only one in the resale shop that fit. "Shit." She burned a finger while maneuvering the curling iron.

"Take your key," Arlan reminded.

"Got it," she chirped before shutting the front door, trying not to slam it in anger. "Stupid-ass dance," she sighed. Funny how she'd always looked forward to it. The heels of her pumps spiked into packed snow. She teetered towards her truck—how to kill time? After all this, she might as well just go. She was tired and queasy. The burn on her finger stung. Besides, Jerry might be there. Lorraine heard him talking down at Desolation Tavern. Eventually she'd have to face him; they could have one last dance. She laughed bitterly.

Instead she drove to the end of Eagle Bay Road and parked. The Overlook was popular among tourists. Every spring people flocked to the pullout, straining for glimpses of nesting eagles and their hideous offspring. Hiking towards the Lake with huge binoculars, wide-brimmed hats, brown safari vests stuffed with God-knows-what to enhance the experience. They'd step gingerly, as if the ground would crack. As kids, she and her cousins threw rocks at dive-bombing eagles that targeted their sandwiches on the summer beach.

The truck idled. Reaching behind the seat, she pulled out the sleeping bag she had stashed earlier. Kicking off those idiotic shoes that had already scored a painful dent in her arch, she yawned and checked her watch. The dance had started. She checked the burn on her finger. Crawling in, she zipped the sleeping bag to her chin like an earthworm and shuddered. Warmth collected in the bottom by her feet.

Lorraine's lighter and cigarettes lay on the seat. Rosalie wriggled out an arm, cracked the window and smoked until her head ached. Flicking out each butt, she listened for the satisfaction of its sizzle. The silent inky void of the freezing lake was so much darker than solid ground. Turning the engine off, she started to doze.

At once she was in a dream. Shoulder to shoulder she stood with the Indian-looking woman. Her profile was quiet as soil. On top of the cliffs they gazed towards a narrow outcropping of land. Sadness wove through the ventricles in Rosalie's heart. The woman's long black hair circled as weightless as a dark halo, the scent of pine resin all around her. "This is the direction we turn," the woman said. Rosalie was aware of grasping a wooden bar as if to steady herself. A dog was asleep next to her foot, curled up like a snowy wreath on branches from a fir tree. "East. The place where new life begins." It felt good to turn her face towards the warmth of the sun, although blindingly bright.

.   .   .

The cold woke her with a start.

Her fingers throbbed. "Oh shit." She drew her hands from the sleeping bag and managed to turn the key. She checked her watch. Already eleven thirty. The engine turned over. "Oh thank God." Icy air blasted from the vents. She held up her hands in the blue dashboard light. Frozen like last time. She tucked them into her armpits. Fighting the urge to pull away, she held them there.

She glanced in the rearview mirror—disheveled hair, weary face. She'd lost an earring. *Damn.* Searching around the seat, she knew she'd never find it. She pulled out the other dangle with stiff fingers. What a lot of trouble. She should have just gone. So what if Jerry was there? Her hands felt like foreign objects; this wasn't normal.

Inside the cab her breath crystallized into frosty swirls on the windshield. It was so dark out past the trees, as if the earth dropped off into nothing.

Rosalie parked next to Arlan's truck. She rehearsed her story while negotiating the icy stairs in heels. But Arlan turned full face to look at her the moment she entered. He was standing in the middle of the kitchen floor with his coat on, as if trying to remember something he'd forgotten.

"Hi," she said, tossing her keys on the kitchen table.

He looked at her strangely. His cheeks were scarlet with cold.

"Oh—so you went out?" She tried to sound casual. Draping her coat over a kitchen chair, she nervously smoothed wrinkles from the dress.

His brow was tense. An odd smile twisted his lips. "How was the dance?" His voice was hushed.

"Okay, I guess." She stepped over to the sink. Turning on the faucet, she leaned, waiting for it to warm. Holding her fingers under, she flexed each digit for blood to return. Smokey pressed against her leg like a cat.

"What's wrong with your hands?"

"Nothing." She sloughed it off. "Just cold."

Arlan hadn't moved, his coat still on.

"Met some new peo—," she broke the silence.

"Who?" His quick answer cut off her last word. His voice was toneless.

She turned to face him. "No one in particular." His eyes fixed on her. She couldn't lower hers though she wanted to. "Everything okay?" she meekly asked.

"No." He focused with a strange watchfulness. "Lorraine called just as you left. Was going to talk you into coming, I said you were on your way."

Her heart beat against her ribs. He knew everything. For a moment she couldn't breathe.

"Called an hour later saying you still hadn't shown, and then an hour after that."

She looked down at the floor. Why had she been so stupid? Blood drained from her. Her gaze fell off into nothing. She closed her eyes for a second.

"Been driving around, looking for you. Franklin too. Lorraine." His voice was so gentle, she would have rather he hollered. "Wondering if you were in a ditch somewhere—you don't just go off like that after all that's happened."

She cast down her eyes and clenched her aching hands.

"They're both still out looking, Edie too. Swung by to see if you'd come home."

Silence. She couldn't say "sorry." Instead she walked into her room, shoved aside shoes and socks and closed the door. Sitting on the bed, she felt nothing. She looked at her fingers. One thing was certain—she was a total idiot.

Smokey scratched the door. It opened quickly. He scampered in and hopped onto the bed. The door shut: Arlan's way of letting her "stew in her own juice." The dog curled up and settled. Eyes wide and round, Smokey glanced at the closed door, sensing that something had happened. She lay down in her party dress. It was getting cold with the door shut. Tomorrow she'd go to Stormwatch Kennel—Arlan's peace offering. She'd call Lorraine. Aunt Edie would understand.

Arlan was creeping about. The phone rang twice—probably Franklin and Lorraine. Soon the TV went silent. The bathroom sink ran. It stopped. The floorboards squeaked as Arlan climbed into bed. She waited a few more minutes to ensure the coast was clear and pulled out her sewing box. Jan seemed nice, Dave too. Maybe it wouldn't be so bad. It was sort of exciting, but excitement jinxes everything. "Expect nothing and you won't be disappointed," Lorraine would say.

"Get some sleep, missy," Arlan croaked from the bedroom. "You'll be dead tired."

"Yeah, I know," she said back as an apology. She concentrated on beading another rose petal.

It was a six-mile trip to Jan and Dave's. Rosalie drove through cherry and apple orchards into old Iron Range, one of the oldest mountain ranges in North America. Though worn down like an old dog's teeth, it still boasted hills steep enough to give you a run for your money. Passing the old fish hatchery, she slowed. Smokey sniffed intently at the open window. A wooden sign announced: *Stormwatch Kennel*—carved into the profile of a husky. Chain link gleamed through the bare trees like silver bracelets.

Rosalie turned in the driveway and paused. She rubbed the space between her brows, looking down a driveway that snaked through the woods. Her stomach was a knot. Smokey put his paws up on the window's edge. Thoughts tangled like heaps of embroidery thread. What the hell was she doing? She shifted into reverse. Fishtailing back onto the highway, she tore out towards home. She'd make it up to Arlan some other way.

Smokey looked at her, and then behind them towards the Kennel.

"Sorry, good boy." She watched him. "We'll go for a really,

really long walk," she bargained. Her indecision was excruciating. She veered off onto the icy shoulder and braked. Her arm buffered Smokey's flight into the dashboard as they stopped. One long angry blast issued from the car behind her. Her cheeks were hot.

So many emotions fired at once, each vying to be heard. Why couldn't she make up her mind? Like the Frosty Tip, another disaster in the making. Hair was exciting for the first thirty seconds. "Follow your heart," everyone said. But where was her heart? It clutched with Smokey. Jan was right.

Hell, show up once. Shut Arlan up. It didn't mean she was taking the job. Smokey reached and clawed her sleeve. He'd never done that before.

"Quit it." She pulled away. His nails left marks. He pawed again. "Stop it," she raised her voice. "You're wrecking my coat."

He sniffed her bangs, and then sharply bopped her head with his nose. He'd never done that either.

"Look," she said. "Maybe I'm not who you think I am."

The driveway curved past stands of stark paper birches. Except for their coal black hieroglyphic eyes, the trees vanished against the snow. Fence posts glistened in the sun. She reflected on how much her own little bundles of chain link cost. She and Arlan had agreed upon birthday and Christmas presents for years to come.

Stormwatch was newly constructed. Two huge fenced areas, loaded with free-running huskies, surrounded by clusters of metal outbuildings. The dogs rushed from side to side as she pulled in. The howling was deafening. Even with the windows rolled up, the walls of her chest vibrated. Smokey's eyes darted. She'd never seen him so agitated. A deep, low croaking sound like a chicken came from his throat.

"You okay?" Maybe it was too much. The sound of the mailbox door at home made him cower.

Then he broke into a low howl, returning fire.

Dave appeared from one of the outbuildings. He waved and pointed to where she should park. She hadn't seen him without the headgear. His features were sharp, almost handsome, eyes deeply set, shadowy. That tired look you see in people used to chronic sleep loss. His hair was the nondescript color common in Midwesterners, except for scatters of silver.

She pulled alongside Charlie Gokee's light brown truck with *Dreamcatcher Veterinary Clinic* stenciled on the door. She'd seen it around. The local paper ran a story about Charlie traipsing through woods looking for sick coyotes and wolves, another suspected Parvovirus outbreak.

"They're excited," Dave explained as she hopped down. He was much shorter than she remembered. "They think you're here for a run." He pointed over to their double-decker dog trucks, both retrofitted with stacked compartments for each dog. Each had its own little door with a window cut out to accommodate a dog's head.

Jan came bounding out of their log home. "Hey, Roz." She bent to greet Smokey. "Glad you guys made it." Her platinum hair was braided and pinned up like the girl on Swiss Miss. She wore a navy-colored cable-knit wool sweater, down vest and tall rubber boots.

Charlie Gokee followed, wearing a blaze orange down vest. A stack of files was clutched against his chest; his face was deeply scarred by acne pockmarks. Salt-and-pepper hair pulled back into a ponytail. Some parts more pepper than salt, others almost pure white. He was tall and willowy, like her mother's people.

"So *you're* the one who took Kurt's dog?" Charlie said, like an open-ended question. He looked at her sharply. It made her feel like she'd done something wrong. She shrank. He scanned her fading yellow bruises, learning what she told no one. He then glanced at Smokey. "You're a pretty lucky guy, I'd say." Charlie knelt to get a better look. Smokey jumped up. Charlie sat the dog and parted Smokey's lips and teeth. "Just a pup. Looks like a cage biter, though," he said gravely, looking into the dog's mouth.

"I-I don't cage him," Rosalie said defensively.

He didn't answer. "Bottom ones worn too for such a young kid."

"Is that bad?" she asked.

He still didn't answer. Charlie's thick glasses made his eyes look huge. Running his hands along Smokey's flanks, he stood. He pressed on Smokey's hips. "Hips are good." He stretched Smokey's back leg, checking for range of motion. "Damn good."

He then stepped back, taking in the overall picture. He sighed deeply, the way people do when they're disgusted. "Well, he's in one piece, all right." He turned to study her with a smile she couldn't read. "What about you?"

She wanted to cry. Her eyes wandered around the yard. How foolish. Jan and Dave were watching.

"Goddamned good-looking dog, though," Charlie said. He nodded slowly in surprise. The tension began to ease. They all stood, looking at the dog. Smokey's coat was clean and brushed. His eyes clear and bright, free of the gunk that had stained his face. Even the scabbed, bald areas were healed. Tiny new shoots of fur had sprouted. She choked with tears, so proud of him.

"What's he eating?" Charlie asked without looking at her.

"Puppy Chow."

"Uch," he said with disgust. "It's probably helping him shit. Dave'll give you something better." She felt Dave take a step towards her. "Meat and supplements too."

Charlie turned to leave, hurrying towards his truck. "Hey, Rosalie—"

She was surprised by her name.

"You and your dad should stop by." He didn't look back. It was more like sound advice than an invitation. "Helen'll call." He carried a tub stuffed with syringes and stethoscopes. He waved over his head. "How's Arlan doing anyway?" He didn't wait for a reply.

Jan caught her studying their log home. "Yah," she mimicked a Swedish accent, "it's a big pig, all right."

"Some wealthy Chicago businessman's dream house or, as Dave calls it, Wet Dream House." She paused as if testing the waters. When Rosalie laughed, Dave did too. "Built it to sneak girlfriends up here," Jan said. She looked distracted, thinking of something else. "The wife found out. Put him in the doghouse, got soaked in a nasty divorce."

"We got it cheap," Dave said, looking it over as a buyer mulls over a purchase. "Then we turned it into a *real* doghouse."

"Face it, Dave, we're rich brats," she said.

Their candor put Rosalie at ease, though she couldn't take her eyes off their shiny new trucks. No mechanic dared put Rosalie's truck up on the lift lest the rusted frame snap. Arlan had pieced it together with parts from the Blueberry Road junkyard on the Rez. Its floor so rusted the road was visible, slush splattered through. She lined the bottom with highway signs taken out by the plow.

"Wedding money from our folks. Both our dads are docs, Dave's a thoracic surgeon," Jan explained.

Rosalie nodded politely.

"Just finished his residency in the Twin Cities—" Jan gestured.

Dave lifted his hands as if guilty as charged.

"—got the job at Duluth General and here we are. I majored in English lit—," she explained.

"Code for 'unemployable.'" He pretended to hide the comment with his hand.

"Shut up," she said lightly. "Dave's a jerk. You can work for me." She winked at her. "Dogs are my career. We got bit by the mushing bug on our honeymoon in Alaska, six years ago," she explained.

"Ruined us for life," he said.

"Speak for yourself."

"Disappointed our folks."

"So, we started building our own kennel—with our own racing huskies—and here we are." Jan opened her arms wide. "Want the grand tour?"

Rosalie shrugged. "I guess." Smokey was beside himself with excitement.

"Down the hill to the left—the converted garage I mentioned," Jan said. "That's where Kathleen, your predecessor, lived."

She'd ask Arlan what that was.

"Left 'cause she got pregnant," Jan explained.

"The Beargrease runners are in these two yards." Dave pointed to the two yards Rosalie had driven past. "Dogs are free to dig, play and chase each other. They're only tied when pulling a sled."

Fourteen sets of eyes watched from where they stood, lined up inside the fence. Silent but curious, they began pushing each other aside before Jan reached the gate. A few placed their front paws up on the fence to stand taller. Some circled and whined, straining to see.

"This is *my* team." Jan unlatched the gate and stepped in.

Rosalie didn't move.

"Come in—they won't bite," Jan said.

Dave took Smokey's leash. Rosalie hesitated.

"Go on," he encouraged.

She mustered the courage to slip inside where the pack pressed in against her. Panic rose in her throat. Her hands rose up to her armpits. Hair prickled on the back of her neck. She fought the urge to bolt. The sea of hues and textures as well as the warmth of their musky scent was overwhelming. Wet noses sniffed her shoes, inspected her jacket and poked her crotch.

"Yikes."

"Some of them are goosers," Dave warned.

She laughed.

"Relax. Let your hands down," Dave gently instructed. "Let them sniff. They're just curious."

Jan pointed to the top of each head. "This is Teeny, Mitzi, Stella,

Stinko, George, Sweetie, Angel, Nico, Missile." Each pair of ears perked at the name. "Just to name a few—"

"There's a quiz after," Dave said.

"Great," Rosalie said. Nothing about school was ever funny.

Rosalie lowered her hands. "Gosh," she remarked. "They're so sweet." They licked her fingers. She found herself smiling.

"What did you expect?" Jan asked.

"I don't know," she said. "They're just like Smokey."

"Mitzi's *my* lead dog," Jan said to Dave. He rolled his eyes. "He's always trying to steal her."

Rosalie had seen Mitzi that day on the trail. Her fur was chinchilla colored, with the knock-kneed, rangy legs of a wolf.

"Mitzi's an awesome leader," Dave said.

"See—*I told you,*" Jan whispered. Rosalie laughed.

Jan recited dogsled commands. "'Gee,' 'Haw,' commands for right and left. 'Gee over' is to pull the team over to the right, 'Haw over' to the left. 'On by' is to pass another team on the trail. 'Easy' the command for slow. Mitzi's the brain and cruise control. She could lead you through rush-hour traffic."

"How do you remember all their names?" Rosalie asked.

"How do you remember your friends' names?" Dave faintly smiled. "Their voices?"

"Their voices?" She looked at him, searching for a punch line.

"They have unique voices," Dave said.

Rosalie stared back, her mouth open. She hadn't thought of Smokey having a voice.

Jan sat down in the middle of the pack. "Puppy pile," she said. Mounds of fur engulfed her. Only the white-blond top of her head was visible.

"Let's go meet Dave's team." Jan stood up, brushing off bits of straw. She smoothed strands of her hair.

"How many total?" Rosalie asked.

Jan opened the gate to Dave's dogs, showing her how to secure each gate. "Forty-eight. Thirty-two Beargrease dogs in these two yards. Puppy teams over there." Jan pointed. "Old dogs are house pets now; they get the run of the joint."

"You always keep them separate?"

"In summer we mix them. Keeps 'em well socialized," Dave explained. "If mornings are cool, we run with the ATVs, sometimes until July. Hard to walk 'em all."

"Do they ever fight?"

"Sometimes. Huskies are team dogs, though—it's been bred into their genetics for hundreds of years. We rehab fighters."

"They learn to like each other?" Rosalie asked.

"Nah," Dave said. "They still hate each other; they just don't fight."

She liked that his voice was riddled with an ironic humor.

"Tempers can flare with the stress of racing. Old slights rekindle. But they also know"—he raised his eyebrows—"fighting is out."

"What if they still fight?" she asked.

"Then we find them another home," Jan said. "Sometimes they do better elsewhere."

"Has that happened?"

"Once," Dave said. His face was serious. She could tell it still bothered him.

"Do you ever get mad at them?"

Dave laughed out loud. "Mushers are the only people who can curse all day long at their dogs and not get mad.

"At night, we rotate the younger ones in the house with the old ones," he explained. "By the end of the week the whole kennel's spent a night inside."

"Do they like being inside?" Rosalie thought of how Smokey would cry at the end of the tie out. Once his business was done, he wanted nothing to do with it.

"You'd think they would," Jan said. "Most of them get too hot. Even with the thermostat cranked down, wood stove out, a window cracked open, they pant all night. Can't wait to get outside when we get up. But it's good socialization."

Jan opened the gate to Dave's team.

"Did Arlan ever tell you about Charlie's time in Alaska?" Dave asked.

She shook her head.

Jan began telling her of the fiftyish veterinarian born on the Red Cliff Reservation. Charlie and his wife, Helen, had moved to Milwaukee after vet school to practice in a clinic specializing in canine orthopedics. After five years, Helen missed the north woods and the smell of birch logs burning in people's wood-stoves. But instead of moving back, they left for Nome, Alaska. A supposed one-year stint as a sled dog veterinarian had turned into more than twenty.

"That's a pretty long year," Rosalie said.

"No kidding," Dave said. He went on explaining how Charlie worked with Robert Ramsay, his mentor and one of the founders of dog mushing in Alaska. Dave chuckled. "Ramsay is amazing—guy's in his eighties, still runs the Quest, Iditarod. Amazing." He looked at Rosalie as if she would get the significance but could tell she hadn't. "Ramsay's got tons of stories: helped smuggle a team of dogs out of Siberia in the thirties, got shot by the Russian Army. Charlie used that original stock—village dogs from Siberia—to build his own racing kennel."

"For years old Doc Hanson, Bayfield's only veterinarian, begged Charlie to come home," Jan explained. "So that the poor guy could finally retire in peace."

"And then six years ago after the last of Charlie's dogs died of old age," Dave explained, "he obliged and moved back."

"Are your dogs from that kennel?" Rosalie asked.

"Some are. Pinny is; so are Fred and Harold," Jan continued with the formal introductions.

Rosalie remembered them from the trail. She thought it so funny how they had people names. The black-and-white dogs who looked to be wearing tuxedos.

"How can you tell them apart?"

"Oh, I can." Dave snickered, as if they were always guilty of something.

Each catapulted to lick Rosalie's nose. It almost knocked her over.

"Watch it," Dave warned. "They're snot lickers."

"Gross."

"That's why they call 'em dogs," Jan said.

"Harold's the worst," Dave said. "Fred, his brother, goes along."

"Fred's easily led," Jan explained. "We almost named him Snotty."

"Didn't you eat snot as a kid?" Dave asked.

Rosalie stared him down. "No."

"Leave her alone, Dave," Jan said. "He never knows when to quit."

Lorraine was sort of like Harold. Maybe she was more like Fred.

"Hiding in the plastic blue barrel doghouse over there is Pinny," Dave announced.

"She's his lead dog," Jan explained. "Thirty-seven pounds. She's really tiny, 'thin-as-a-pin.'"

"Pinny's got two speeds—sleep and haul ass," Dave said. "Sets a smokin' pace. Like her ass is on fire. No team can catch her—"

"Except us," Jan said.

He rolled his eyes. "Pinny's scared of everything. Sometimes trees."

"Trees?" Rosalie's face scrunched up. Wait until she told Lorraine a dog was afraid of a tree.

"One of those screwball dogs." He looked at the blue barrel. Pinny's scrawny back leg hung out. Her face was hidden.

"Does she always stay in the barrel?"

"Nope. She's scared of you," Dave said.

"Of me?" Rosalie touched her hand to her chest.

"She'll get used to you," he said. "She's from Ramsay's kennel too. Pinny's a freak, but she's got some interesting lineage. Charlie'll tell you about it sometime."

"How do you keep track of everything?" Rosalie was feeling overwhelmed.

"The schedule," Jan said definitively. "Immunization records, medications, feeding schedule." She waved it off. "Next time. Sound good?"

Rosalie slowly nodded. Apparently showing up meant she'd taken the job.

She came back the next day to run Smokey. They strode towards the puppy teams. The yearlings charged the fence once they spotted Smokey. All were out of breath, the fur on their heads wet with saliva from play-wrestling. All took turns being prey, lying on their backs as others would drag them by the scruff, spinning them on the icy ground like a top.

"Go for a run?" Dave asked the yearlings. They stood rapt. His hands poised like a conductor's, he clapped. He seemed too young; she thought of doctors as old men. Something about him reminded her of Arlan.

"You take *your six*—" Jan gestured to six of them.

"Why are they *my six*?" Dave asked.

"Because they're big and dopey. I'll take mine plus Smokey." Jan winked at Rosalie.

"We want them to follow the lead dog, have fun, learn the commands," Dave explained.

"To pass wildlife without dragging you on a wild-goose chase," Jan said. "Back in Minnesota I had a young lead dog drag us after a huge bull standing in an adjacent field. Evidently, her plan was to take the thing down."

"What happened?"

"The bull looked at her as if to say, 'I've crapped bigger than you.' That ended it."

"Next fall we start training," Dave said. "It takes a good year to figure out who's got what. For now, light loads, fun."

Dave explained how sleds were secured with a "snub line" to a steel pillar that had been cemented into the ground. "When you're ready," he said, "you pull this loop—it's a quick release snap."

Jan showed her the iron snow hook also used to secure a team. The heavy hook was attached to the base of the sled by a long nylon rope. It was pounded into snowpack by foot to anchor the team.

"You need at least fourteen inches of packed snow. Otherwise, an eager team'll yank it out and bolt," Jan explained. "And Roz—be careful not to do this." Jan held the snow hook just over her hand, tracing a sickle-shaped scar that perfectly matched the curve of the hook. "Was in a hurry—six-month recovery to reattach the tendon."

"Do you guys say 'mush'?" Rosalie asked.

Dave frowned. "This ain't *Call of the Wild*. We just say 'go' or 'okay.' 'Mush' dates back to the French Voyagers. They'd say '*marche*,' which means 'walk.' Even 'husky' comes from Eskimo, 'Esky.'"

Dave opened the metal shed door and took out two sleds. The whole kennel burst out howling. It was deafening. They offered her earplugs and used hand signals with each other. Dave pointed to the rigging. He showed her how to attach the gangline to a shock absorber made of a bungee-type material. It protected the dogs' joints and tendons from jarring starts and stops.

Dave disappeared. Jan finished attaching ganglines. He returned with two older lead dogs. Jan took one. Each person clipped the loop at the back of the harness to the brass snaps at the front of each gangline.

Both lead dogs pulled out their respective ganglines as Dave called "up front" or "up tight" so the lead dog would stretch the line.

Jan tossed Rosalie a harness, motioning to Smokey. She held it up, looking at the straps, bewildered. She watched Jan and then held it out. Smokey slipped his head right through. Rosalie popped his legs through the armholes. Jan motioned. Smokey dragged her to the gangline. She hooked his collar ring to the brass snap of the neckline, designed to keep them facing forward. Rosalie reached for the back loop of his harness, at the base of his tail. Smokey pulled all ways. No sooner had she turned him forward than he twisted from excitement. She finally clipped the parachute loop to the brass snap on the tugline, the place from which they actually pulled.

Jan and Dave had hooked both teams in the time it took Rosalie to get Smokey situated. The yearlings cried and jumped over each other. A few tangled in the center line. It was chaos. To Rosalie's amazement, they suddenly slammed forward in unison, everyone in sync with the lead dog. All that controlled power made the sled lurch. The quick release line was pulled taut, looking as if it would snap.

Jan pointed to the basket; Rosalie hopped in, her stomach butterflies. She gripped the side rails and pressed her feet inside the front brush bow for stability. Her eye was on Smokey.

Dave and Jan each pulled their quick release.

"Let's go," they said in unison.

Each team took off. There was silence. They barreled down the trail. The whoosh of the runners was like nothing Rosalie ever felt—more exhilarating than any amusement park ride. The lead dogs raced to enter the trail system first.

"Wooow," Rosalie heard herself yelling. She gripped the wooden rails tighter as they flew.

"It gets loud," Jan said from where she stood behind on the runners.

"No shit." Rosalie's ears were still ringing.

"Living out in the boonies helps," Jan explained. "There's a few racing kennels out here. In Grand Marais and Ely, this is all you hear. Running up to the Boundary Waters. Happiest sound on earth."

Jan tapped her shoulder. She pointed to Smokey. "Look! He's awesome."

Smokey's back undulated, reminding Rosalie of tall grass moving in time with the wind. Her eyes stung with tears.

Jan and Dave slowed each team, using the steel claw brake bolted to the sled near the driver's feet. "Easy," Jan gave the command to slow. She braked again so the dogs would associate its sound and drag to the "Easy" command. Jan explained how she was switching to the second brake, a square of recycled snowmobile tread attached by two cables to the claw brake. She and Dave preferred this one since it didn't tear up the trail.

"You don't want them running too fast," Jan explained. "They still have those soft puppy bodies. Injuries at this age can become chronic. We work slowly. Each dog develops differently. Building muscle'll take another year."

Just then two yearlings stopped to pee and mark something on the side of the trail. "On by," Jan called. One looked back in defiance. Jan jumped off the runners and chased them. "On by," she repeated, shooing them back into line. She caught the sled handle and jumped back on.

"Can't they pee?"

"Nope. No pooping or peeing while running," Jan explained.

"Why not?" Rosalie asked.

"It's dangerous. Running twenty miles an hour in front of a heavily loaded sled, someone drops to poop, you plow right into them."

"So what do they do?"

"Hold it till we stop. Like being housebroken; they're getting harness broken."

They ran for a few miles.

"Whoa." The teams stopped to rest. The lead dogs instantly lay down at the command. A few of the yearlings followed.

Jan and Dave pounded in snow hooks. They walked down the gangline, putting each into a down-stay. Smokey and his teammate began to simultaneously lick slobber off each other's muzzles.

"You're a good boy, aren't you, Smokster?" Jan called to him. His ears perked with his name. Tongue hanging out, foamy saliva dotted his face.

"So whatcha think, Dave?" Jan called over to him.

"You two want a job?" Dave called over to Rosalie.

CHAPTER 11

The realization hit: they couldn't take every dog.

Tariem and Cheyuga stood up; neither would look at her. Jeaantaa couldn't breathe. Squatting close to the outside cook fire, she hugged her knees, rocking as she hid her face.

The old Guardians couldn't make it. Some wouldn't make it out of the village, much less a thousand miles. Hauling puppies and nursing mothers on a drag sled would tire the teams. Increasing each team to twenty-five would still leave puppies and the old ones.

Earlier the last of the drunken elders had straggled out of the village.

Tariem and her uncle were off to search for abandoned food caches. While Aquarvanguit was generous that spring, few saw the need to stockpile food. Searching nearby was risky. Local collaborators might report them.

"Ankjem, Tangek," Cheyuga called. He ushered the boys onto the sled, lifting little Tangek on top.

The air was heavy as they left. Why did it matter anyway? Die now or on the journey from grief and heartsickness. She couldn't live with the reindeer cousins. It sickened her to think of her boys becoming men like Omryn, or how her dogs would be mistreated. Tariem would never stand up for them. He hadn't so far, ever passive in the face of a bully.

She stood up and dragged the sleds closer to the two kettles, waiting for them to boil. There had to be a solution. Extra dogs could run loose alongside the sled, but the very young and very old would die along the way. She couldn't bear it.

There was a break between storms. She hoped it would last long enough to prepare the sleds. Panic hovered. Her thoughts were foggy from missed sleep. She haphazardly grabbed gear. With fumbling hands she checked ganglines for cracks.

The dogs were silent. All stood somberly, watching her.

"It'll be all right," she promised. "I will make it be."

She'd be the first to leave, as soon as the sleds were ready. Then Cheyuga with the boys, followed by Tariem. Leaving separately wouldn't rouse suspicion. Many of the neighboring families were accepting Government rations in exchange for information.

Jeaantaa made three piles of gear, one for each sled. She wrestled a third kettle onto the outside cook fire. An answer would come. The Forest Keeper was kind. Walking off with a long knife, she sliced a cube of snow and carried it over to pack into the kettle. Runners of the sturdier, heavier distance sleds would be dipped and boiled until saturated. It took hours, time they didn't have. Each needed to be set up on rocks to freeze. Frozen runners glide effortlessly, even while heavily loaded.

She thought she heard a truck; she stopped and looked up the hill towards the Cove. Bakki stepped slowly out of the *yaranga* to see what she was doing. He yipped in pain, limping at first; it took a few steps before his gait evened out. She squatted near him. He still wagged his tail for her. She looked deep into his curious blue eyes.

"I promise." She rested her forehead on his, inhaling his scent, feeling his trust.

The rushing sound of water spiraling into a rolling boil prompted her. Dipping in the first set of runners, she balanced them against the edge. She moved to the second. The sleds would be heavy with food. Working dogs burned fish and meat like dry pine logs in a hot fire. She feared there wouldn't be enough.

When Tariem and Cheyuga returned hours later, the boys weren't with them.

"Where are they?"

Each looked solemn as they sat down by the fire.

"You'll leave first," Tariem repeated the plan. She hated the sound of his voice. He was trying to sound wise and calm.

"And the Guardians?" She'd make him say it.

Cheyuga nodded with a finality that invited no discussion.

"You're going to murder them?" She purposely used the word for "murder" instead of "sacrifice." Anger gathered in her chest like a thundercloud.

"Why hide what you do?" she taunted. "If it's sacred, let our sons watch. Let them see your hands; let them see what you do."

Tariem wouldn't look at her.

"It's the Great One's law," Cheyuga reminded.

"There is no law."

Cheyuga slapped her. It was a reflex. He never hit her before. Ordinarily she'd have been devastated.

She glared at Tariem. "Say it," she goaded. "You're going to murder them. Look at me and say it." She grabbed his arm, but Tariem pulled away.

The two men dreaded coming back. To not sacrifice the dogs meant the Evil One would block safe passage to the next life. They knew she'd take it hard. Even if a dog was ill, she'd suffer with it. Maybe her soul was more dog than human.

"Why don't we cross to Rochlit?"

"Because it's not of the Lygoravetlat," Cheyuga dismissed.

"And this is?" She laughed.

Neither man believed what he was hearing.

"Rochlit is close," she insisted. "Bakki can make it. We all could."

"We are going to our cousins," Cheyuga concluded.

"The Army won't find you? Think the *brave Omryn* will fight them off?" She mocked, "'Let the Lygoravetlat go, the holy ones.'"

They'd never seen her like this. "Don't look at her," Cheyuga ordered. He shook with rage. "An evil spirit has taken her."

She snickered. They were as stupid as the elders. "You will not kill one dog." Jeaantaa wobbled with anger. She bent to grab a few small branches, continuing to feed the fire.

"You'll do what you're told—" Tariem grabbed her arms. She wrestled free—hating him with a new intensity.

"Don't talk to her," Cheyuga yelled.

"So now the Lygoravetlat murder puppies and old dogs?" she shouted. "Go join the soldiers; put on their scratchy cloth." Her eyes flashed angrily as her reindeer-skin hood fell back. Her long hair burst up in a gust of wind, floating in darkened streams.

Cheyuga walked off, leaving Tariem to handle his wife.

Black soot from the charred wood chalked over her lips as she touched them. A long silence passed.

"You think I want to kill our dogs?" Tariem asked. His voice was shaking.

He was trying to be calm, but she noticed his chest heaving.

"They belong to no one," she said curtly. Contempt rose in her throat like a foreign object.

"How can you?" His voice cracked. Tariem seized her so quickly she lost her balance. He trembled, his breath shallow and rapid. They'd only been that close making love. He'd always been so gentle. "It's decided." The enamel fronts of his teeth almost touched the tip of her nose.

She wrestled free.

"It is our law." He gripped her arms, twisting them, trying to make her obey.

"Let go—" She wrangled out of his grasp. Let him beat her to death. Cut off the tip of her nose as some husbands did. She shuddered, imagining the ceremonial spears piercing Slipper's soft puppy body. Or Bakki. "Start here if you're so brave," she goaded Tariem, tapping her sternum. Her voice was oddly calm.

He was afraid. It was her wildness—the part that Uptek had loved but Tariem always feared. The part of her that could never love him, that despised him; the part she kept hidden, veiled under a veneer of respect. Through the years he caught glimpses of this but would dismiss it, hoping he'd seen wrong.

She stormed past the *yaranga,* leaving the runners to boil, and raced towards the crescent of trees. The last of the neighbors scrambled to catch the end of the argument, peeking out the walrus-flap doors of their *yarangas.* They whispered, not wanting to miss a good fight.

Jeaantaa hooked Bakki and seven yearlings to a sled, taking off in fury towards the Forest Keeper's woods. There had to be another way. She cursed her people, hating them as much as she hated the Red Army.

Never again would anyone sacrifice her dogs. She vowed it last year when Tariem was forced to sacrifice his mother's two lead dogs, when—after years of complaining—the old woman finally died.

Each dog betrayed by hands that had offered nothing but food and gentleness. Terror as Tariem's spear pierced their breasts, bleeding out their lives. One watching his companion shriek knowing he was next. The old women sat nearby, singing ancient chants to ease each dog's suffering. But all Jeaantaa felt was disgust.

Jeaantaa was the maker of ceremonial harnesses for sacrifices. Carving and fashioning each with utmost care. Even tying ribbons on them before the dogs unknowingly ran off to their deaths. She stifled her impulse to defy and looked away. There was blood on her hands too. Dutifully holding out the harness as each dog willingly and trustingly looked into her eyes.

CHAPTER 12

"You're ducking her." Dave stared at Rosalie with the force of law.

"I'm not. I swear." Rosalie laughed at her own lie. After two weeks, she figured there'd be a breakthrough with Pinny long before Dave busted her.

"Oh yeah?"

She laughed in protest. Glad he hadn't bought it, yet relieved he wasn't angry that she tried to cover it up. He marched her off by the arm as if under arrest. The sight of Rosalie coming at her with a harness sent Pinny running for the safety of the blue barrel. The first few days Rosalie had climbed in after her. A few warning snaps later, Rosalie had backed off. Her burgeoning confidence was shaken.

"She can't be afraid of you," he admonished. "Soon you'll be lifting them into the trucks. Gotta win their trust, Roz. Dogs like Pinny are different."

The more she tried to supplicate Pinny in breathy baby voices, bribing her with offerings of salmon, the quicker Pinny's tail curved beneath her. Sometimes she'd pee in fear.

"She's more curious than scared," he explained. "So milk it."

So Rosalie employed "the treatment." Sitting on frozen ground, her back turned towards Pinny's barrel. She checked her watch. Willfully distancing her thoughts from the dog who wished she'd go away.

Forty-five minutes later, the seat of her jeans was frozen to the ground. She was about to throw in the towel. Then Pinny's nose tickled the back of her head. She held her breath. Though euphoric, she didn't move. Any jerky movement would hurl them back to where they started. Slowly she unfurled her hand, and Pinny sniffed her fingers. The dog licked Rosalie as she raised her index finger to scratch Pinny's chin.

Rosalie learned to harness a dog in seconds. She and Dave would race, and the two of them ended up scrambling and laughing so hard neither finished. Jan sighed, hands on hips, reminding them of just what idiots they were.

The work triggered daily aches and pains. Initially Rosalie figured that hanging on to a dogsled would be no sweat. Routinely lifting fourteen forty-five-pound dogs up into the cubbies of the dog truck left her arms like rubber by the end of the day. She gained a newfound respect for the physical toughness of Jan and Dave. They could run fifteen miles behind the sled over rough patches of trail in heavy boots and layers of arctic gear. Dave told of pushing a heavily loaded sled up a mountain pass in Montana during the Race to the Sky. This was not a sport for the wimpy or whiney. Her hands doubled in size in only a month, developing what Jan called Musher's Grip.

She became well versed in which type of sled to load onto the truck. Different conditions required specific equipment. Toboggans were for distance traveling and basket sleds for shorter trips. Sleds' fronts were rounded like the prow of a ship to cut through snow and brush. Though traditionally sleds were made of wood, the new ones were aluminum and polyvinyl plastic. Lighter, faster and easier to repair. The old wooden sleds were lashed with gut, the new ones assembled with pins. A bent aluminum stanchion could be repaired in under a minute. Basket sleds were more comfortable for passengers, but toboggans were the real workhorses.

She studied pictures of Inuit running dogs with what was called the Eskimo fan hitch. This formation consisted of dogs hooked independently in a fan shape, best for short distances and over rough terrain. Dave explained that modern sleddog racing used the Chukchi style. Dogs were hooked in tandem, sometimes with ganglines of twenty for long distances.

"You're ready now," Jan pronounced on Friday after they stowed the gear, fed and watered the younger dogs. "More than ready to run the yearlings by yourself."

A month had passed and Jan was pushing her to take on more responsibilities. For the first three weeks they ran teams together, which seemed more about training Rosalie than the yearlings.

"You think so?" Rosalie leaned against her truck before leaving for the day. Twisting and pulling her bangs, she considered it. Keys jingled in her pocket as Smokey sat on her foot.

"Training wheels gotta come off, Roz," Jan said. "Think about it over the weekend. You got my mom's number?"

She nodded. Sunday was Jan's birthday. Rosalie had made her a deerskin shawl beaded with her team of dogs. She worked in shells and porcupine quills in the traditional Anishinabe style, all bordered with blue and white flowers. In the background of the team was the face of Basha, Jan's first sled dog. Rosalie slipped the shawl to Dave on Friday. It would be presented to Jan on Sunday at the surprise thirtieth birthday party her family was throwing in Grand Marais. Rosalie was so excited at how beautiful it turned out that she carefully unwrapped the package to show Dave. His astonishment made her smile.

"Remember. Hay'll be in this Sunday. And food for the old ones."

"Yeah. I got the list."

"We'll be back late Sunday night. Monday . . ." Jan paused and held up her pointer finger. "New duties. You're more than ready."

But just last week, when Dave was on call, she had had to run his Beargrease team. Pinny ignored her commands. Fred and Harold acted up. A few dismissed her with an icy stare the instant she stepped onto the runners.

"Don't let them get away with it," Jan coached from her team. "It's *your* sled now; you own it."

It was humiliating. The team lost respect for her. They ended up chasing Jan's team home while Rosalie hung on for dear life.

"Well, I hope you're right," Rosalie said, the fiasco still fresh. The truck door squawked where the rusty hinge rubbed. Smokey hopped up onto the seat.

"Remember, Sunday," Jan reiterated. "Take my truck. You got the keys?"

Rosalie held them up.

"Good. Get twelve bales of hay. Count them. Don't let those Cenex guys give you any crap about there not being enough. I ordered twelve last week. Show them the receipt. You got it?"

Rosalie nodded. Hay was like gold up north since the growing season was so short. It had to be ordered and shipped. "Okay."

As Rosalie climbed into the truck, Jan seemed to decide something about her—something she couldn't take back. Rosalie's inner life was roiling like Superior after a furious summer storm. Churned up and red from the sandy bottom, it lay open like a raw wound.

She pulled into the Cenex on Sunday. Receipt in hand and ready to do battle, though hoping she could sweet-talk a cute attendant into loading the hay. As she was walking towards the glass door, a familiar voice stopped her.

"Well, well, well, so whose truck you driving now, Rosalie?" Jerry stood smirking, a Styrofoam coffee cup in each hand. He looked Jan's truck over and then stared at Rosalie with steady, unblinking eyes.

She was mute.

"What's the matter, Rosalie? Afraid you still like me?" His eyes gleamed with the joke. He traced the Stormwatch logo stenciled on the door with his pinky in round, circular motions as if touching her. "Figured we'd bump into each other sometime. It's a very small town, you know."

It was overcast and dreary, damp with charcoal gray clouds that softened the tops of the surrounding hills. Her eyes darted past him. Plenty of people scurried in the parking lot, tying Christmas trees to the roofs of their vehicles.

"You know you really made me out to be some kind of bastard." Jerry took a step towards her. "But you and I know the real story," he mock whispered, gesturing between them with his Styrofoam cup. His smile lingered as he looked her up and down. "Mm," he uttered. "Still look good."

A conditioned twitch of desire pulsed in her. Her teeth gritted in revulsion. He pursed his lips in a kiss before walking back and climbing into the Camaro. A woman's young face peered through the back window, studying her as the car drove off. Wasn't it just like Jerry to pick on the young and wounded? She watched long after they crested the hill.

Rosalie leaned against the side of Jan's truck, legs wobbling. She had rehearsed this hundreds of times. "You *lame mother fucker*," or some other cutting remark, but nothing had occurred to her. Like Pinny, she practically peed herself in fright. *Go. Get the hay later.* Grabbing the door handle, she scrambled in. She jabbed the electric lock button over and over, as if each jab would lock out the world.

She turned and drove off on Highway J. Her arms shivered as if controlled by someone else. She searched the rearview mirror and then each side one. Then, from out of nowhere, appeared the front grille of Jerry's Camaro. He flashed his lights. "Oh God." She cried. He followed so closely his headlights disappeared. The truck slid on the slushy roads. The temperature was dropping, the surface freezing to ice. *Drive to Franklin's.* The turn to Friendly Valley Road approached. She took it and the Camaro drove straight past and beeped twice. *Thank God.*

Rosalie pulled over and started to cry in spastic jolts, checking the mirrors. She turned into Stormwatch as quickly as she could without spinning out into the ravine. Once parked, she ran into their house, locked the front door and waited. The old dogs greeted her, toddling over, wagging their tails. She listened for the sound of tires; the whole kennel would cue her if someone was driving in.

He looked so ugly. Why had she clenched with desire? Less than five months ago she was desperate for his touch. It repulsed her to think of it. A time when he couldn't undo his pants fast enough for her, to feel him inside, welcoming the surging warmth.

A half hour passed. *Shit,* the hay, food for the old ones. Sitting at the kitchen table, she started to gain composure. Then a thought popped into her mind. Had she gotten her period? She counted back. October was cool. They had sex on her birthday the first week in November, days before the incident. Had it come at all since she'd been home? With everything happening she hadn't noticed. Now it was nearing Christmas. She'd missed one. It couldn't be true.

Arlan was startled to find her early Monday morning, bundled on the couch. She was usually gone by five. "You're still home."

Smokey paced at the window.

"Don't feel good."

"You call?"

"Yeah. They said stay home." Jan had gushed about the shawl when she phoned in early that morning. She went on about it being the most beautiful thing and was astounded at the work that had gone into it. "How did you know Basha's face?"

Dave had smuggled out a photo at Rosalie's request. She could hear him hammering. "We're hanging it in the front entrance in the great room by the fireplace," Jan said. "I want to see it every time I walk into the house."

"You gonna at least take him out?" Arlan asked.

"Already did." She rustled under the covers.

"So what's wrong with you?"

She didn't answer.

He lifted both hands, indicating, *So what?* Last month she was out running with Smokey sporting full-blown bronchitis after Arlan yelled at her to at least put on a hat. He was always a hard sell. He never called in sick. Even with pneumonia and a bad whisky hangover, he'd always muster up enough to show up at work. He towered over her, hands on hips, studying her motionless form.

She moved the covers and looked up. "What are you staring at?"

"You want some eggs?"

She shook her head.

"French toast?"

"I don't feel good." She conjured a meek sick voice.

"You gonna puke?"

It was like August when she'd first been pregnant. But sometimes she felt that way right before her period started. Then again, maybe the sore breasts and arms weren't from lifting dogs in and out of truck compartments.

Maybe she was Jerry's hostage now.

Arlan lingered with a strange watchfulness. She could tell he knew there was more to it. "Something happen?" he asked.

"Like what?" Her heart beat faster. He'd been so proud of her, it would break his heart. Disappointment crushed like broken glass. She shifted to face the wall. Kathleen, the last handler, had gotten pregnant and left. Maybe they had pushed her out.

"You should try and eat something," Arlan offered, though his voice was tentative. She did look washed out. He gave up and marched into the kitchen, hands on hips. "Got tons of stuff to do today. Can't be sitting around babysitting you."

Pots clanked as Arlan rummaged around. Then the comforting thunk of the iron skillet used for morning eggs and bacon on the front burner. She clung to the sounds, holding them to her heart. If only she could wake up and go back to the week before she met Jerry. Wipe the landscape clean. The toaster clicked. Two slices of the German pumpernickel bread Arlan could only get at Peterson's Foods. She lay, smelling the toasting bread, wondering how she could lose it all so fast.

She didn't move all day. Looking at the TV until her head throbbed, she hadn't watched a thing. It was almost two weeks late. She'd been late before; maybe it was just stress. Earlier she had contemplated driving to Walmart to get a pregnancy test. She knew the cashiers and a rumor like that would hit town before she got home. There was always driving to Duluth, though she hadn't enough money for gas.

Arlan's scrutiny tightened upon discovery of her the next morning, virtually unchanged, lying in the same position. "What happened?"

She pretended to be asleep.

Within the hour Jan's truck stormed up to the house. Arlan opened the front door. Jan sat opposite on the coffee table with her coat on. "What happened, Roz?"

She faced the back of the sofa, mouth under the quilt.

"Stop hiding under this stupid blanket." Jan pulled it back. "You didn't get hay on Sunday. They sold it to someone else." Her voice stern in a way usually reserved for Fred and Harold. "Something happen with Jerry?"

It was a long silence. Rosalie pulled the blanket back up.

"Well—Beargrease is two weeks away. Should I find a new handler?"

People like this didn't know. Jan lived with the confidence of one who chose wisely. So much for starting a new life, for waking excited with the whole day to look forward to. So much for being surprised at the end of the week when Dave handed her a paycheck. It hadn't felt like work at all.

"Gotta talk, Roz. You're so bottled up. This makes me sad. You can make me a treasure for my birthday, but you can't talk to me. You gotta trust people."

Jan sighed. Rosalie heard the front door open and close. The rock wall of Arlan's frustration came at her. At the sound of Jan's engine, she bolted up and ran out the door, leaving it wide open. The bottoms of her socks stuck to the snowy road as she sprinted.

"Jan, wait," she yelled. "Wait," she shrieked. The truck paused. Jan rolled down the window; Rosalie leaned on the side mirror. "I'm scared," she whispered.

"Of . . ."

"Running alone—"

"Bullshit," Jan cut her off. "I've seen you scared."

Rosalie wouldn't look up. "I can't."

"It's Jerry, isn't it," Jan said.

She didn't answer.

"You gotta talk. You hide everything, stuff it inside. Did he threaten you?"

She shook her head no. "But maybe I can't handle a team either. Maybe you guys overestimated me."

Jan looked over the steering wheel. "Don't think so."

"What if something really bad happens on the trail?"

"Something really bad *will* happen." Jan laughed in a slightly sinister way.

"What if one of the dogs gets hurt? Gets loose?"

"You figure it out, Roz." She turned to face her. "You think you're any different from the rest of us? It's not the end of the world. There's a whole universe of mistakes out there waiting to be made."

The two women looked at each other.

"Have a little trust."

"Why?"

"Because we care. People care."

Like who? They fired Kathleen because she was pregnant. Where was the caring there?

Jan put the truck in gear. "Be there tomorrow morning sharp or your ass is fired for sure," she said, stipulating with an index finger. "Think I'd let you out of the yard with *my* dogs if I didn't trust you?"

She gave up on sleep. Tiptoeing through the living room, she sat next to Smokey. He was snoring, belly-up, and didn't stir as she sat next to him.

She pulled out her mother's satin work box and caught her mother's scent of Cashmere Bouquet talc. In spring when the air was damp from melting snow Rosalie would catch the passing scent emanating from the box. "Mom," would slip out effortlessly from her lips. She'd sniffed its entire surface but could never locate its source. It was her mother's scent in the evenings after a bath, when they'd sit down to bead, her mother teaching Rosalie the stitches. "What should I do, Mom?" She held her breath, afraid of using up the rest of the scent molecules.

Often her mother's intuition would guide her hand to the proper design proportion, "Rosalie, that leaf is too long; shorten it up—looky here, that flower should be joined by another smaller bud for balance." As a girl she helped with gown panels once she was old enough to submit to a pair of white cotton gloves. She watched as her mother's hands brought assortments of glass beads and pearls to life in graceful bouquets of tulips and wildflowers, transforming ferns and fronds into colorful swirls. Standing out in subzero weather waiting for the school bus, Rosalie watched as blowing snowflakes glinted into patterns. Gathering to form momentary designs before dispersing, as the slightest of breezes cleared the canvas.

Rosalie was almost finished with the train of someone's wedding dress, beading the last swags of seed pearls and silver beads. Forget-me-nots bordered the hem of the fifteen-foot silken train to accompany the hopes of some young woman.

CHAPTER 13

Even her sons were instructed not to look at her. Though each snuck glances to see what was so dangerous about their mother.

Tariem and Cheyuga took the boys along to search for more food. They'd be gone well into the night, possibly though the next day. That spring the waters were thick with the bloodred bodies of salmon—river bottoms obscured as they lay their eggs. People remarked that it seemed you could step along a bridge of fish to walk across.

She took advantage of a break in the wind. Stepping outside, she angrily slashed to cut a walrus skin down from a wooden frame. It would make a storage bag for the third sled. As she gazed off into the horizon, a feeling of cold seeped into her. Lives were broken within the span of a few short breaths. Uptek's death. Now their home, the Guardians, swept away like a broom scatters dust. A world disappearing with the finality of a hunter breaking winter camp. Folding down a *yaranga,* burying the fire, clearing the land clean. What's left is a storyteller's bounty. A tale you tell strangers, as if the telling might help you to believe it yourself.

The walrus skin was frozen stiff. She'd have to thaw it before sewing. Slipper chased the remains of a walrus bone. The puppy dove onto her foot before repeating the game. Bakki basked in the dim light of low, thick storm clouds drifting in from the Cove.

Something caught the old dog's attention. Three figures approached. They looked to be pulling a drag sled loaded with items for trade, walking with purpose as if looking for someone. One of them she recognized—an Inuit guide from Rochlit. He spoke Chukchi well enough for trade. During the Month of New Leaves he'd appeared with someone she hadn't liked. He wanted to trade tobacco and wool blankets for fast dogs. She refused.

"Jeaantaa," the Inuit guide called to her.

She tucked the knife into her waistband and started towards them. Ordinarily she was more guarded; there were generations-long hostilities between Chukchi and Inuit. Her hair was matted in an uncomfortable sweaty ball by the nape of her neck. She slipped off her reindeer-skin anorak, tossing it aside like the discarded spleen of a walrus. Walking rapidly and then running, she caught up with Bakki. He could be protective to the point of vicious. Slipper toddled behind her dad, trying to keep up.

The first man removed his hat. Men from Rochlit always did this. He reminded her of Solokov, a Russian trapper, and of happier days. He was dark like the Inuit but taller, with the gangly arms and legs of a Russian. Poor Solokov once attempted to trade a head of cabbage for a good lead dog. He'd carefully cradled the cabbage in his black fur hat as he offered it, earning his nickname, Cabbage Head.

The second man had hair the color of dried grass. His eyes were the same blue as the Guardians', a Brother Spirit. She'd never seen a human with Guardian eyes. Jeaantaa grasped his sleeve.

"Come." She couldn't take her eyes off him. She tugged his sleeve, urging the Brother Spirit to follow.

The Inuit slapped her hand. "Let go, you whore." The guide shoved her. She shoved him back harder and Bakki bared his long snaggletoothed canines. His rumbling growl seemed to emanate from the center of the earth.

"What's she saying?" the Brother Spirit asked.

"Tell him to follow," she ordered the guide.

The guide seemed amused by her distress. "He wants dogs, not to see your filthy dump."

"He'll have plenty of dogs. Tell him to follow." She walked backwards, motioning with both arms.

The three men followed her to the crescent stand of trees. The dogs squealed as soon as Jeaantaa appeared. It was deafening. Walking into their midst, she clapped her hands, and the dogs quieted. She laughed with relief; she knew the Forest Keeper would help.

"Pleased to meet you, Miss Jeaantaa. I'm Robert Ramsay, of Nome." The Brother Spirit held out his hand to shake. She looked at it. Names meant nothing now. "My brother, Johnny," he introduced the gangly one. Ramsay motioned for the guide to translate. "I've heard of your dogs, ma'am. If you're interested . . ."

Yearlings and nursing mothers would easily make the fifty miles across the frozen Bering. She'd use the sacrifice sled, construct driftwood cages for puppies. That just left the old ones.

Tomorrow, before Tariem and Cheyuga returned, she'd sneak off a large team with the two brothers. She looked at the decorative sacrifice sled propped behind a tree. Women were forbidden from touching sacrificial objects. It would bring doom to a family. The sled was a sacred and dreaded object. The sight of it had clenched her heart since childhood. Now it just looked like a sled.

She reached an index finger, touching the runner. It was wood. She expected it to feel different, like flesh. Jeaantaa lifted the sled and set it upright on the ground. It was heavier than she thought. Maybe it too needed freedom from its burden. Tricking the Guardians and carrying their suffering for so long. She looked up into the trees, waiting for retribution. But above was only the quiet swishing of wind streaming though needled branches.

This was her sacrifice. The Brother Spirit would take this sled to

Rochlit, into another world. She couldn't guess what Tariem would do when he discovered the missing dogs. She hoped she'd be gone by then; there was still time to prepare. She set the runners to boil.

"Tell the Brother Spirit." She turned to the guide.

"There's no Brother Spirit, stupid whore." The guide shoved her. She fell against the salmon drying rack. Weathered slats collapsed, scattering on the snow.

Bakki lunged. He sank his canines into the man's arm. The dogs exploded into sharp barks. The Brother Spirit and the gangly one grabbed the guide, both yelling in their language.

"What's the hell's wrong with you—hitting a woman?" the Brother Spirit growled.

"That's a filthy animal, not a woman." The guide laughed in a nasty way. "Look how they live; their dogs live better—" He winced, touching where Bakki's teeth had punctured.

For the Chukchi, the outdoors was their home. They kept it pristine. Inside didn't matter. Ordinarily the ugliness of such behavior would have made her ashamed for having talked to men alone.

"Tell him tomorrow morning before the sun settles." Jeaantaa got up onto her feet, frantically tapping the guide's arm and pointing to Ramsay. "Tell him," she raised her voice.

"What did she say?" the Brother Spirit yelled. "Tell me now." He grabbed the guide by his collar again.

"Before the sun rises to twilight, tell him to be here," she explained. "I will have a team ready." Waving with her hands around the yard, to the sled, she then pointed to the Brother Spirit.

The guide translated. She and the Brother Spirit nodded.

"Miss Jeaantaa, how can I make the trade fair?" Ramsay gestured to the drag sled.

She smiled at such a question. Her eyes filled with tears; they were more than even. Jeaantaa looked at the items. She pointed to a large folded oilcloth tarp and then to a bag of candy canes. A rare treat.

Ramsay laid the tarp and bag of candy at her feet. He asked for her to choose more. She indicated with her hands the trade was even. He looked puzzled, either not understanding or suspecting there was some catch.

The Brother Spirit moved to touch her lip. "Ma'am, you're bleeding." He offered his handkerchief.

"She's scared out of her mind," the gangly one said in his language.

"No kidding," Ramsay said. He turned to the guide. "What's going on here?"

"Russians are killing 'em off." The guide answered as if it were a question about an item on the drag sled.

Ramsay looked at his brother, puzzled. "Why?" he asked.

The guide shrugged. He didn't know and couldn't care less.

"Do you need help?" the Brother Spirit asked. "Are you in trouble?"

She smiled sadly as the words were translated. She didn't answer.

"Remember, tomorrow when the sky is early, no later." She pointed to the ambiguous light skimming the horizon. "I will have one"—she held up a finger and pointed to the sacrifice sled—"team ready for you."

She held out both hands. The Brother Spirit grasped them. His hands were warm and certain; she didn't want to let go. She looked into the Brother Spirit's eyes without shame, like she'd once looked into Uptek's. Another twinge of fear tweaked her stomach. The Evil One was using trickery to scare and confuse her. The Brother Spirit leaned over and kissed her on the forehead. The guide turned away in disgust, making a noise.

"Ask her if she'd come with us," Ramsay said.

The guide translated.

She glanced quickly at the Brother Spirit and then looked at Bakki, smiling.

She scooped up Slipper and tucked the puppy under her arm.

Bakki followed as she swiftly walked back. She dragged the ceremonial sled behind her by a gut line darkened with the blood of generations. Hurrying towards the boiling kettles, she set the runners to boil.

CHAPTER 14

Snow crunched under her feet, a telltale sign that temperatures had fallen below zero. The first yearling team was set to go. Steam rose sluggishly from the chimneys at Jan and Dave's house. The whole kennel howled as the couple stood nodding in approval. Smokey was situated next to Porkchop, his buddy.

Rosalie stepped onto the sled runners. She kicked snow off the rubber tread—digging her feet nervously to reaffirm they were firmly planted. She looked back at Jan and Dave before reaching for the quick release line.

They burst out laughing.

"Gosh," Jan shouted over the roar. "You look like you're marching off to slaughter."

Dave rubbed his eyes, pretending to get choked up. Jan hit his shoulder. "Textbook perfect," Dave called, giving Rosalie the okay sign.

"Don't jinx me," she shouted.

"No such thing," Dave scolded with his index finger. "Just remember—," he called. He tipped his head as he always did when about to impart some critical information. Maybe this was the secret. The dogs yelped and slammed into their harnesses. The sled jerked forward. Her neck muscles were tight, shoulders up around her ears.

"Rule number one: hang on," he shouted over the howling. Rosalie hung her head at the familiar edict. "Rule number two?" He waited for her to repeat with him, "Don't let go."

She pulled the quick release. Instant silence as they became weightless, like stones skipping along Sand Bay. The team careened towards the trailhead where two thick posts marked the entrance to the Chequamegon Forest. She braked. *Too fast this early.* Jan's voice was in her head. There was a treacherous section of glare ice near the huge tree at the turn onto the forest trail.

"Gee." The command to turn right. The sled fishtailed. She braked as the team turned, but that only seemed to make it worse. *Shit.* The sled handle bashed against a tree trunk, her pinky stinging as it got clipped. Why hadn't she moved her hand? *Gotta think ahead, look down the trail,* Jan said constantly. *Accidents happen in seconds. Pay attention—anticipate what can go wrong before it does.* She winced, vigorously shaking out her hand. *Oh Jesus.* She'd screwed up already.

Heavy snow weighed the lower branches of pine trees into arcs like bows. *Maybe grab snow and pack it around the pinky.* But as she shifted her weight to reach for it, the dogs bolted. The team was still too hot. Gripping the handle, her pinky stung. She started to see stars and felt like she could pass out. It throbbed like nothing she felt before. But there was no way to turn back now. Let them run, burn it off. Snow kept icing up the rubber treads, faster than she could kick them clear.

The trail was the consistency of buttercream frosting. The dogs began settling into an even pace as she sighed in relief. Her back felt clammy; she popped open the top snaps of Jan's old vest. The first few miles of a run were always nerve-wracking as the dogs ran out of control. Even for Jan and Dave, the dogs heard little when they were fresh. With all that power the best you could hope for was to ride it out until they got through the initial surge and settled into a pace.

She'd try to pack her finger again.

"Whoa." They stopped, but it was more of a pause than a stop. They leaned into their harnesses, the gangline taut as a bowstring. A few glanced back in surprise. "Down." They were supposed to lie down automatically. No one did. Even Smokey glared back, which made her angry. *Maybe it's because they never stop so soon.* The sled jerked forward even with both feet depressing the brake.

"Whoa," she yelled. *My God, they're going to drag me!* "Whoa," she yelled again. Once should be enough. *The more you repeat, the less they hear.* Jan's voice again. Rosalie's finger throbbed in time with her heartbeat. How was she supposed to get the snow hook out without the team bolting? She started wobbling. One of the dogs nonchalantly shook, almost arrogantly so.

"Stay," she called, but the sled budged again, the dogs still leaning. *Tough luck. Make them stop now, whether they like it or not. Otherwise they win the battle.* She flipped the snow hook out of its holder, but it tumbled upside down onto the trail. Sweat trickled down her forehead into her eye.

Standing on the sled brake with one foot, she kicked the snow hook over with the other. Leaping onto it with all her weight, she pounded it in, praying it would hold. The dogs bolted to the end of the line, but the sled jerked to a stop. They turned back, a profile of faces and asses all the way down the gangline, looking surprised she had it in her.

Easing off the glove, she winced. The pinky was swollen. *Damn.* She packed the glove with snow and slowly eased it back on, though—once wet—the glove would be useless. As she stepped back onto the runners, something looked wrong. The snow hook was too far from the sled, out of her reach. She'd attached it wrong. How would she reach the hook without the dogs bolting?

She pulled the hook and then dove onto the runners, braced for the surge. No one moved; maybe they were learning to respect her. But all eight heads were distracted by something off in the woods.

"Okay," she gave the release command. Still no one moved. What were they watching? As she gazed into the woods, the sled lurched. As she grasped the handle, almost thrown by a momentary lapse in attention, the team charged three deer that had leapt onto the trail.

"Easy." She braked. They ignored her. It was too fast. "Easy," she shouted again. Frustration in her voice turned them deaf—another "Dave" axiom. "Slow down." She tried to sound more confident, braking with both feet as they charged.

But then, to her horror, they mutinied. Yanking the sled off the main trail, they dragged her into the woods in hot pursuit of the three deer. "No," she screamed, braking and leaning back. "Trail, whoa." As if that would make any difference. "Stop god-damn it." Her throat was raw, calves cramping as she pushed the brake to China. They heard nothing.

"Smokey." He'd already been co-opted. "Stop—stop, you fuck-ing assholes," she yelled, almost losing her footing. She leaned far back to counterbalance the sled as it bounced and tipped from side to side. As she bumped and bashed against ruts in the un-even trail, it was all she could do to hold on.

They were closing in on a deer. *Oh shit, what if they brought it down?* One time Mitzi, one of Jan's Beargrease lead dogs, caught a pheasant mid-flight and a dogfight ensued. But after one com-mand, "Drop it," from Jan, both the fight and pheasant were dropped in seconds. Rosalie didn't have that kind of clout.

Ducking heavy branches, she held out her hand to block smaller ones. They ricocheted off her parka, ripping her stock-ing hat, scratching her cheeks and poking her as she held on. But just as the deep snow began to slow them, a low sweeping branch bashed her forehead, knocking her flat onto her back.

She lay there with the wind knocked out of her. The team took off. Scrambling up, she ran after them. The sled tipped over, littering the woods with Jan's extra dog booties, a pair of sunglasses, first-aid gear. "Shit, shit, shit," was all Rosalie could yell. *What if one of them broke a leg, got an eye poked out? Are there any crossroads?*

Her chest heaved. The snow was waist deep and she couldn't run anymore. She leaned over her thighs to catch her breath. The jinx was back. She'd been so careful, tried so hard. She leaned back to sit, floating in the deep snow. *Why had I ever thought I could do this?* She pulled off her glove. The pinky was turning purple, but at least it was numb. All of her other fingers stung with cold.

Up along the ridge she heard sounds of dog cries. She squinted and spied the sled handle. They seemed to be stopped. She lifted one leg out of the deep snow, traipsing over, steeling herself for whatever horror she might find. "Oh shit, shit, shit." She winced, repeating it like some magical incantation.

But there was no deer. Smokey looked back at her in his darling way, but she ignored him. A downed tree limb had hooked through the curved front of the sled, the brush bow, stopping the team cold. "Oh thank God." She fell on her knees in the snow. Laughing and covering her face for a second, absorbing her good fortune. A few dogs whined softly after the deer.

"Oh shut up." She laughed, instantly forgiving them. Some began twisting in the gangline, trying to get free. Fifi and George tangled into each other's tug- and necklines. Soon the two of them were wound up tightly into a mass of nylon rope, fur and dog parts. No sooner had Rosalie untangled the two of them, having to unhook them and start over, than George tangled into Smokey's tugline. As George tried to get free, he dragged Fatty into it by winding into his neckline. They were all too inexperienced to keep the gangline taut and untangled, each holding their team position.

"No, stop." She untangled another one, but they wouldn't stand still. And rather than keeping the line up front, they seemed to panic and re-tangle. Fifi sheepishly looked for help. Morty began biting into the gangline, as if resolving to fix the situation himself.

Why were they doing this? They'd lost their minds and were compelled to twist only tighter the more Rosalie worked to get them free. Someone growled; she could swear it was Fatty. Past vendettas rose to the surface like bloated fish.

"Hey," she yelled at the growlers. They stopped. Then Fatty growled at her. The hair on her body stood, he'd pulled a loaded gun on her. She grabbed him in an instant and he cried out as she lifted him in the air, off balance. He whimpered, struggling against her. She held on to him until he stopped fighting and relaxed in submission.

"Don't you *ever* growl at me." She set him down. It seemed to break the spell for the rest. Fatty pawed her leg apologetically, ears flopping back. Continuing to unhook necklines, tuglines, she felt stupid yet grateful neither Jan nor Dave was there to witness such a spectacle.

Jan and Dave stood at the trailhead, waiting. Arms folded, legs crossed, Dave lifted his arm for an exaggerated glance at his watch as the team ran in.

"Nice gash," he remarked, looking at Rosalie's forehead. He grabbed the neckline of the lead dogs to park the sled as she walked down the gangline, petting them as they looked up to acknowledge her. "Lost 'em, huh?"

She grimly nodded, lowering her head. "It was so stupid," she yelled, and started to cry in frustration.

"Yeah, it always is," he acknowledged. "Everyone loses their team—even experienced mushers. Embarrassing as hell, but everyone does." He bent over to examine her forehead. "Let me butterfly that before you take the others."

"You're gonna let me take the others?"

"Well of course, you silly goose," Jan called over, guiding the mutinous lot back to the kennels.

"Dizzy?" he asked, tilting Rosalie's head up to the sunlight to examine her pupils. She didn't mention her finger. The packed snow had numbed it for now and she was overheated from running.

"Eh, you're fine." He released her. "Duck next time," he called as Rosalie walked to get the other yearlings.

"I did," she yelled back, feeling better already.

"Then duck lower."

CHAPTER 15

Jeaantaa stirred a porridge of fish roe, seal meat and walrus blubber for the dogs. It was the last time she'd feed them. Slipper jumped on her lap and curled up. She leaned on the puppy as she infused each stir with prayers so the Guardians would remember. Prayers that knowledge would be passed to successive generations, and with it a promise that her spirit would someday guide them home.

She startled to see Tariem. They were back early. His cautious footsteps crushed snow, snapping the branches beneath. He walked the team into the crescent area. It had just begun snowing, nothing serious yet, though a stronger storm was coming.

"You found more food?" She stood to unhook and feed the returning team. It was a good way to hide her bewilderment at seeing him.

"Who was he?"

She stiffened as he studied her face.

"They said an Inuit and someone named Ramsay were here."

She shrugged as if she hadn't noticed. He squatted next to the fire, holding out his hands.

"You're lying."

She wanted to glare back at him. "No I'm not; I forgot," she said, and began to unhook dogs.

"Why didn't you tell me?"

"Because you just got back." She laughed, trying to make him seem ridiculous. She fumbled, dropping the gangline.

Voices of Cheyuga and the children were by the *yaranga*.

"Inside there's warm food," she said. "Why don't you go eat?" She moved to bring the team closer to the yard.

He grabbed her arm and drew her close. Not able to meet his eyes, she looked at his hand and nudged the feeding troughs with her foot. The noise signaled the dogs. They burst out howling and shrieking with anticipation.

"What did they want?" he shouted over the noise. The fire sputtered, sap fizzling before it gave a final pop.

She pretended to be confused. "Directions," she said into his ear. "They were lost." She offered no resistance as he squeezed her arm, though it hurt.

He released her. Conviction made her a good liar, though her heart ached to see his face so tired and pale. For years he took on her enemies, saved her from whatever fate the village had cooked up for her supposed "murder" of their best hunter. In return, she resented him for surviving. Wishing he'd be cruel like Omryn so she could justly hate him. Yet for the most part he'd treated her politely, more like a guest of the family than his wife. The smell of his skin had never become familiar.

And while their nights were enjoyable, afterwards she felt more lonesome. What kind of weakness allows a man to live with a woman who loves his brother? Cheyuga saw Tariem as her savior whom she should love out of gratefulness. The Old Ones say we don't choose whom we love. But maybe we don't choose whom we can't either. For more than a decade she stayed busy by avoiding him as much as she could. Taking off to Chukchi fairs throughout the region, trading embroidered clothing and blankets made of seal and reindeer hides decorated with blue trade beads. Sometimes she stayed on for weeks at a time, squashing how bad she felt about Tariem and the boys missing her at home.

Tariem's expression softened as he watched Slipper's antics. "Take her with you when we leave," he said.

Oh, how he grants himself power over life and death. She smiled slyly.

"We found several caches," he offered with an almost chatty, conciliatory tone. "One of the sleds broke. There was too much," he continued. "We're going back now to get the rest; I hope we beat the storm. We'll be back before dawn. Don't leave before we get back."

"The boys must be tired," she said.

"They're coming along."

She hid her relief. That was the part she worried about, having them see her leave.

"Are the sleds packed for morning?" he asked.

She looked up at him. Was he trying to catch her in a lie? Had he seen the sacrifice sled being prepared?

"Yes, everything is set." She counted time. With the incoming storm, she doubted they'd get back before the Brother Spirit returned.

The sound of porridge hitting the birch troughs intensified the howling, blotting out any chance for conversation. Tariem studied her a few seconds too long. Feeling sorry, she watched his burly figure walk away pensively and slowly. Sorry for not having loved him, for not returning his kindness all these years and for planning deception on a scale he could have never imagined.

CHAPTER 16

"It's your daughter or we put him down."

Arlan and his work buddy Dan followed the man out to the parking lot after their shift. It was two days before New Year's Eve, the Hades between Holidays. Walking across the snowy red gravel, they spotted the haloed silhouette of a dog's head illuminated from behind by the industrial lights. The dog's ears reacted to highway noise from just beyond the plant.

"Told my son about your daughter, what she did to save that dog. Thought maybe she'd take this one too," the man explained. They walked towards the man's truck, getting a first look at the dog. His dark coat gleamed; two black spots inked each eye in sharp contrast to his white face. His eyes were swollen completely shut. Shoulders were bunched up, head low.

"Got rammed by a drunk snowmobiler going the wrong way up in Ely," the man explained. "A few days ago. Vet thinks he's blind. My son don't got no money for surgery. Dog's uncomfortable, that's for sure. The others turned on him yesterday, got him good in the neck there." The man pointed. Arlan looked over to see the dark matted clump of dried blood in the dog's fur.

"Was lead dog. Now they won't have him. Won't eat either."

"What's his name?" Arlan reached out with his fingertips, but the dog turned away.

"King," the man said. The dog's ears twitched. "Smarter than most people you'll meet." He sounded more sad than proud. "Young dog too, not yet three. Old Ramsay line. My son got him at a race in Nome when he was just a pup. Guy's got a kennel on the Bering Sea. Eighty-year-old still runs the Iditarod.

Distance dog. I'd keep him, but I can't be messing with no blind dog."

King delicately sniffed the air. A semitrailer loaded with sheep was paused at a red light.

"A bit standoffish, lived outside his whole life," the man explained. "My son won good money at the Beargrease with him last year."

"I'll get my truck," Arlan said.

He pulled alongside and parked. Lowering the tailgate, Arlan watched as the man untied King and led him over.

"Well, good luck to you." The man's voice cracked. He handed the rope to Arlan. The man stood for a few moments, memorizing the dog, and then turned and walked off. Climbing into the truck, he drove off without looking back.

"Well come on, King," Arlan coaxed. The dog wouldn't budge. Arlan tugged. "King," he called. The dog ignored him. "Come on; up, big guy." Arlan patted the open tailgate, but the dog stared at nothing.

"Maybe he's deaf too," Dan said sarcastically.

Arlan frowned and shook his head. He managed to drag King maybe half an inch. "Well, that's not gonna work." The dog lay down, head facing away.

"More than one way to skin . . ." Dan bent over, slipping his arms around the dog's middle to lift him.

King growled.

"Whoa." Dan jumped.

King stood up.

"Well, at least he got up," Dan said, embarrassed. But before he finished the thought, King let go a perfectly aimed stream of urine into the top of Dan's work boot. King then jumped effortlessly up onto the back of Arlan's truck.

"Shit," Dan yelled. "God damn—" He shook his foot.

Arlan laughed, slapping his thigh as he took in the one-footed dance.

"Asshole." Dan glared at the dog. "We're doing you a favor,

buddy boy, saving your life," he scolded, gesturing with his work glove. King looked unimpressed.

"Dan," Arlan said quietly. "He just got dumped in a god-damned parking lot, for Christ's sake. Have a little compassion."

Dan glowered.

"Jeez, he really got to you, didn't he, Danny boy." Arlan was surprised by Dan's anger.

"Yeah well, maybe he'll piss on you next," Dan said, hopping into Arlan's truck.

"Rosalie-e-e," Arlan hollered as they pulled up to the cabin.

What now? Truck doors were slamming outside. She looked up from where she sat beading black jet beads into a paisley design. She'd just marked it with her tiny cluster of bloodroot blossoms. It was to be someone's red-carpet dress, due back in Los Angeles A.S.A.P. Smokey's back pressed against her thigh as he slept. He lifted his head to listen. Then he jumped off the couch and was up at the door, sniffing at the doorjamb. Something out of the ordinary was going on.

The only time Arlan hollered for her after a night shift was when he needed help unloading a La-Z-Boy or some other item he'd scored from Larry's Furniture Liquidators in Duluth.

"Missy, get out here."

"Oh shit," she mumbled.

Arlan popped inside. "Hey, I got a surprise for you," his voice high and excited.

Jerry's balls on a platter? There were some things you didn't say to your father. His eyes were unusually bright. A twinge of excitement jumped in her.

"Put your stuff away and come out." He gestured with his arm, holding on to Smokey's collar with his other. "Come on."

Smokey sniffed Arlan's jacket and stared out intently towards the truck. He barked. Arlan gently pushed him back inside and shut the door.

"It's cold," she protested softly. Why risk breaking the chain of stitches?

"Get your ass out here," Arlan hollered back.

She exhaled deeply. There was no ignoring him once he took the bit into his mouth. Winding the thread around the needle, she secured the glass beads by weaving it into the fabric.

"All right already." She'd struggled with the fabric for hours. Organdy was the trickiest to work with. She'd finally conquered it and was making real progress. The black beaded paisleys looked vintage, almost Victorian. Holding up the piece to view it, she smiled. It was beautiful. She then tucked it into her sewing box.

All evening she felt queasy. It was getting worse at night. She wrestled into the sleeves of her coat and dug her feet into boots. Smokey sniffed at the door, slowly swishing his tail behind him like a wooden jointed snake. "Stay." She opened the door. Smokey poked out his head, trying to see past her. She tucked him in and closed the door. He whined forlornly.

The first porch step made the usual pop when the temp fell below zero. "Loud enough to wake the dead," people would complain. "Gotta fix that thing," Arlan would say every time. She'd just roll her eyes, wondering why he bothered to waste his breath.

Dan was far younger than she'd imagined—closer to her age than Arlan's. Not the crusty geezer from years of "Dan" stories. She'd seen him around. Once at a tractor pull in Cable. Again that past Fourth of July Pow-wow at Red Cliff. She stood behind him at the venison burger stand the night she got together with Jerry. Dan's hair was the color of crow feathers and his eyes aquamarine. A testament to the French and Ojibwa blood that flowed through many Northerners, regardless of which box they checked for ethnicity on the U.S. Census form.

Then she saw the dog.

"Huh!" she exclaimed, and walked away from the two men. "Where'd you . . ." She slowly approached the pickup as Arlan filled her in on the details.

"Well hi, you." She held out her hand. King sniffed it and gave one short staccato lick. More like a velvet panda bear. He yelped when she petted his shoulder. "I'm sorry." She held up both palms as an apology and got one more lick.

"Now would you look at that. . . ." Arlan turned to Dan, gesturing as if she were patron saint of the lost and damaged.

Dan looked away. Arlan chuckled.

"He's mad 'cause King pissed on his foot." Arlan thumbed over his shoulder. Dan glared nervously at her, which amused Arlan all the more. "Well, you two kids figure out how to get 'em down; I'll get you clean socks and something to wipe out that boot, sonny boy." He patted Dan's shoulder and handed the leash to Rosalie. Arlan listed a bit to the left as he walked. His foot was hurting again.

Rosalie untied the rope and let down the tailgate. The dog jumped down.

"Well hi there." She bent eye-level to scratch gently under his chin. He nudged her lips with his dry nose. His eyes were crusty and swollen shut. His ears lay back; he touched her lips again as his tail swished once.

"Watch it—he growled at me before," Dan warned, tucking his hands into his armpits.

"Maybe he don't like you." Injured and sick dogs often became protective. She'd seen it at Stormwatch. Rosalie tried to remember the last time she'd washed her hair.

"Man says he's lived on the end of a chain all his life," Dan said.

"Yeah well, that makes two of us," she said to the dog. She petted him the way Jan had shown. "Good boy." Rosalie used her open hand, applying a bit of pressure as mother dogs do to comfort their puppies. King shrugged his shoulders and pawed her awkwardly, not wanting her to stop.

Dan wrinkled his brow. He shoved his hands into the pockets of his brown work coat. "Still belongs there if you ask me."

"I didn't, did I?" She stood and leaned over the dog, another thing Jan did to calm distressed dogs, and King leaned back against her. She then lowered her face towards King's and rested her forehead on his. The pressure of his skull was so familial, it made her drowsy.

"You're *way* too close," Dan warned.

She stood up and smirked. "Here." She tossed him the rope. Dan reflexively caught it. His arm was rigid as if he'd been handed a chained alligator. She snickered just watching him.

"I'm getting you a snack," she said in a goofy doggie voice. King's ears twitched, knowing something good was coming. He sauntered to the end of the rope. The dog sniffed and listened as the front door opened and shut, awaiting her return.

King moved slowly with the confidence of a dominant dog who'd long lost the need to challenge. Unlike Smokey, there was nothing skittish about King. He moved slowly and with deliberation. Noble, yet resigned, with a sensuality that was cat-like.

Rosalie appeared with a hunk of chicken.

"Better to chain him out tonight," Dan advised.

She frowned at the unsolicited advice, thinking he didn't know what he was talking about. "Only if I get to chain you first," she said, joking in a singsong voice. He was so easy to tease that it almost felt mean.

"What?" Dan recoiled, not sure he heard right. "I meant your other dog might want to fight."

"Right." She laughed at the thought of Smokey challenging any dog.

Dan seemed flustered by how his intention to be helpful had turned on him.

Rosalie felt bad. "You're right, it's always good to be cautious," she kowtowed, as a bit of an apology.

Arlan finally reappeared. Her father tossed Dan a roll of paper towels and a bottle of Pine-Sol. King wolfed down the chicken, frantically sniffing for more.

"Wanna meet Smokey?" she asked in the goofy voice. She stood and began to guide the dog up the porch. He didn't startle at the loud pop. King let her help him over the threshold to where Smokey waited inside. The dogs touched noses. Smokey gently sniffed King's swollen eyes. The dog lowered his face to allow it.

King sniffed deeply into the house. Walking cautiously, he scooted his nose along the edges of the TV console and chair legs. Bumping into the coffee table, he paused to gain composure and correct his path. Venturing slowly into the bedroom, the kitchen and the wonders of the bathroom. He paused at Smokey's food bowl. King turned deliberatively towards Smokey, who watched. Then he ambled into the corner.

The refrigerator compressor clicked on. King turned, momentarily distracted as he listened. He registered the sound of Arlan's spoon hitting the counter where he'd been dishing up three huge bowls of ice cream. King then tottered back to Smokey and Rosalie.

"I'll call Charlie first thing," Rosalie said.

After King eased himself down next to Rosalie's foot, his head sank to rest on his white front paws. He sighed with deep resignation, knowing this was his final stop.

Arlan placed a smaller bowl of ice cream in front of each dog.

CHAPTER 17

It was early twilight. Jeaantaa watched for the outline of the team; all was set to go.

The yearlings and nursing mothers were harnessed and ready. Wild with excitement, they jumped and tried to break free. Pups were groggy and sleeping in the cage on the sacrifice sled. She was ready. Her sled bag contained the tarp and several pine branches.

Jeaantaa began to pace, afraid to look away and miss their approach. The red puppy paraded with her. Slipper cuddled onto her foot and she stroked the puppy's velvety ears. She picked up the soft little body, burying her face into Slipper's fur, inhaling the garlicky puppy smell. If only life could stop at this second. Red sparks popped and flew like angry fireflies from the fire, chasing and spinning in a whirlwind towards the lower branches of the trees.

For the last time she walked into the storage hut. She set Slipper down and the puppy began sniffing the ground with great interest. Kneeling, Jeaantaa pressed her cheek against the reindeer-skin floor. So many Guardian lives had begun here. Arching their little backs, they had taken the first breaths to inflate their lungs, breaking the membrane that separates two worlds. This was her place. And just because she'd never be here again wouldn't make it any less so.

She tucked Slipper under her arm like a pillow and walked outside. It was with bitter tears she'd leave her sons. Hidden between the trees were three tiny *yarangas* that contained the dried afterbirth from each boy and the mummified body of her baby girl. The daughter was born alive but died soon after.

Jeaantaa had tended each since their birth. Gently lifting the two small sealskin pouches, she wrapped them together and tucked them under the branches in her sled bag.

A dog team was approaching. By their outlines and gait she could tell it was a team of Eskimo dogs.

The Brother Spirit waved at her silhouetted figure by the fire. She waved back. Setting Slipper down, she positioned the sacrifice sled east towards Rochlit. Frantically, she began to hook up her dogs. Only a few were harness broken. She hoped they'd chase the Eskimo team to Rochlit.

"Up," she commanded. The front dogs didn't understand and kept tangling.

The Brother Spirit was out of the sled and running before it stopped. "Hold them." She motioned to pull the gangline tight.

The gangly one stayed with the Eskimo team. She noticed a rifle balanced on his forearm. He scanned beyond the trees.

The yearlings were uncontrollable. It took all her might to wrestle each into place. She scooped up Slipper, tucked the puppy into the cage and fastened the ivory toggle. Slipper's blue eyes glared through the twigs of the cage wall. Jeaantaa hurried away before she changed her mind.

"Go." She motioned for Ramsay to get onto the sled. The team faced east. The direction old dogs turn before they die so their souls can enter the place of the sun. New life begins in the east from the place of eternal warmth.

"Go now." She waved him off. "Go quickly."

"Come with us." He gestured. "They're going to kill you,"

She heard him step onto the runners. The Eskimo dogs began to stir. Creaking leather harnesses, the jingling of metal buckles, then the command to go. She turned briefly to see. The young dogs took off, chasing the Eskimo team out onto the frozen Bering. The thumping of their feet on packed snow quickly tapered off to nothing. Only the whooshing of the runners.

Jeaantaa turned to hook up the last of the old ones. Her sled was ready to go.

CHAPTER 18

It was a frigid New Year's Eve morning. Wind whooshed through the needled branches of the sheltering white pines at Storm-watch.

By 6 a.m. the Kennel's lights had long been blaring. The early appearance of Rosalie's truck now triggered paroxysms of howling. Dave's truck was warming for his early hospital rounds in Duluth. He waved his arm like a windshield wiper once Rosalie pulled in. She returned the wave.

The buzzing alarm clock had been particularly brutal. She was tired; last night was a late one. After Charlie's referral, she and Jan had driven to the veterinary ophthalmology clinic at the U of M in Minneapolis. There King would remain until a week following the Beargrease. It was a relief that the stoic dog was getting care, though it about killed her when the surgeon gestured to hand over the leash. King began to back out of his collar. "Go now," the vet had ordered her out of the examination room. "We'll call." King's mournful cry filled the hallway.

She and Jan began the five-hour trek north with weighty hearts. "Oh, he'll be fine," Jan tried to shake it off. "He's getting the best medical care on the planet, right?" Neither would look at the other. "When they're that bad off you don't get to see them," Jan explained. "They need to be still." It had taken all Rosalie's will not to make Jan pull over.

Dave's taillights glowed through the bare trees, visible out to the road. Rosalie deposited Smokey into the yearling yard and then hurried towards the heated outbuilding to begin the morning feeding. Inside, she began warming the mix in huge iron kettles on the old restaurant stove. This close to the race, they'd switched to Dave's secret diet. Yesterday she helped Dave mix batches of venison, raccoon and salmon along with olive oil and red cell powder to boost iron production. He swore her to secrecy. "Who'd I tell, Dave?" She chuckled at his paranoia. They packed the mixture into blue plastic tubs, storing them in an industrial refrigerator he'd scored at a farm auction. This time he swore he'd gotten the formula right.

Mushers were a secretive lot. Their dogs usually ate better and received better medical care than their families. All knew their vet's phone number by heart.

The food mixture was warm. She scooped it into a thermal cooler set on a plastic drag sled. She'd pull it between yards, stopping at each. A few inches of downy lake-effect snow had fallen overnight; the flakes tumbled aside with the toes of her boots. The dogs began jumping as if their back legs were springs.

"Okay, okay," she joked, "I can't feed you all at once."

Kennel protocol was that certain dogs were fed in reverse order of dominance. Rosalie followed instructions. Some of the bossier ones were made to sit alone, their "noses out of joint." "Status reduction builds character." Dave had winked.

She unlatched the kennel door to Dave's Beargrease team and pulled in the drag sled. The dogs pressed around her. "Back, back." She motioned. "Sit." All were rapt; tails swished the feathery powder.

"Pinny," she called. Pinny always ate first. The scrawny dog skulked out of the blue barrel. Rosalie set down her bowl. After a few furtive glances, Pinny gobbled the wet food as frantically as she lived her life. The practice was repeated with each dog. Two bowls were left.

"Harold. Fred." She looked around. They always ate together. Strange how neither had been jockeying to bully someone out of their food. "Hey, goofballs, where are you guys?"

The pinging of dog tags against stainless bowls began to lessen.

"Harold," she called. "You playing tricks?"

She froze. In the corner of the yard Harold lay on his side. The sheen of the black ridge of spine faced her. How curious. Fred looked up the moment she noticed them. His one blue eye shone in the kennel lights. He appeared to be in a down-stay, as if keeping vigil, his paws towards his brother. That side of the dog yard was flush with woods. It smelled of fresh pine sap even in winter. Harold faced east, towards the trees.

"Hey, buddy." Her voice tentative, she slowly approached, holding the two food bowls. "Something the matter with your brother?" Rosalie placed down the bowls. She leaned over Harold in the dim light. The dog's face was blank.

A few dogs began to sniff and circle the food bowls.

"No." She barked for them to back off. A few filed by the body. A quick read of Harold's face and they walked away. Rosalie touched the dog's cheek. It was warm. She pushed on his shoulder. It was pliant, yet he didn't respond. His black lips were flat, a death mask. "Oh God." She clicked her tongue. "Oh my, good boy. Oh my, you poor thing."

Rosalie lifted the two food bowls lest there be a free-for-all. She backed away, watching for Harold to get up and startle her, trickster that he was. His personality had dominated the yard. She left Fred attending to him and walked towards the gate; her nylon wind pants swished. Latching the gate behind her, she ran towards the house.

"Jan, Jan," she cried out, gasping as she ran. Wet food sloshed in the stainless-steel bowls, spilling onto the front of her coat. Flying up the icy porch steps, she knocked on the door. "Jan," she called. "Jan."

The door opened. "What's wrong?" The older dogs circled, sniffing up at Rosalie.

"It's Harold. Something's wrong. It's like he's *dead*." She whispered the word.

Jan looked at her.

"He's just lying there, Jan; he's not moving." Rosalie started shivering.

Jan stepped into her boots and ran outside. The two women raced towards the kennel. The dogs met them at the gate; they parted as Jan walked through.

"There by the fence."

Jan knelt beside Fred. "Hey, good boy." She touched Fred on the top of the head; his tail rustled once. He looked at her and then back at the body. Jan touched Harold's flank.

"Oh my. Oh, Harold." Her voice was hushed. "He's still warm." She felt for a pulse. "Must have just died."

Rosalie had never seen a dead dog.

"Stay here. I'll go call," Jan said.

Rosalie smoothed the fur on Harold's face. She leaned over to press her cheek to his.

Charlie pulled in within the hour.

"Now you didn't see them getting into anything did you?" he asked the obvious, walking the yard, bent at the waist, scouring for anything that didn't belong.

Rosalie shook her head.

"You leave any meds lying around?" He looked sharply at Rosalie. She shook her head again. "Any of that deicer stuff you guys use?"

Both shook their heads.

"What do you think happened?" Rosalie shivered though she wasn't cold.

Charlie looked over the rims of his glasses. "Ah-h—he died?"

She looked down at her boots. He liked to make her feel foolish.

"He seemed fine yesterday." Jan folded her arms into her parka and started to cry.

They both turned to look at her. Neither had ever seen Jan cry. Charlie seemed particularly flustered. He circled her with his arm.

"His appetite, stools were fine." Jan wiped her nose with her sleeve, looking to Rosalie, who nodded in confirmation. "Did a long run yesterday, he seemed okay."

Charlie checked his watch. "I'll take him, Jan, but tell Dave the necropsy's gotta wait. Nine hours to Chicago and Helen'll bludgeon me if I'm not home in thirty minutes like I promised." He looked at his watch again. "Everything'll keep a few days till we're back. Labs are closed anyway until after New Year's. Blood and liver samples'll just sit with Uncle Sam anyway."

He looked at Rosalie. "Did they all sniff him?"

"I think so," Rosalie said.

"Make sure and call 'em over. They're smarter than us. If they don't see he's gone, they'll always look for him."

No sooner had Charlie spoken than a few more filed by Harold. They sniffed his face and his body; a few cocked their heads, solving the riddle. Jan ran inside to get a blanket. She and Charlie then wrapped Harold and carried him out of the yard to Charlie's truck. Rosalie latched the gate and followed slowly. The finality of it choked her.

Harold's teammates lined up along the fence. As Charlie laid the body in the truck, the entire kennel broke out howling in long, mournful cries.

Getting through the day was tough. Feeding, scooping poop, she took the yearlings out. But death's blunt force was everywhere. It lurked in the corners of every yard and streamed alongside her cheek as they ran the trail. Harold's silent face knotted in her throat. It was like the day a red granite marker was placed on her mother's grave on the tribal burial grounds. For weeks spots in the house seemed like air was displaced by ozone, vacuums of spirit. The stillness of Harold's lips drew Rosalie back.

Aside from animals killed in the road, she'd never seen a dead thing up close. She'd harnessed him dozens of times. Fed and scolded him, dropped down into a play bow to chase him and Fred.

By late afternoon, the mood of the dogs was still subdued, except for the yearlings who continued to chase and play. Fred lay atop the doghouse. He and his brother had slept together since they were puppies. Fred's face rested on his front paws. Rosalie offered him the afternoon meal, but he didn't move.

Dave came home early. Jan held him and the two of them swayed for some time. Then Dave straightened and wiped his eyes. Rosalie helped hook up the two Beargrease teams. Dave harnessed Clara, another of Fred's littermates, who was cut weeks earlier from the starting team. He put her in Harold's place. It was a short ride to boost morale and integrate Clara. Rosalie watched as they entered the trailhead. Harold's royal blue harness hung on a peg, his name scrawled across the back strap in indelible black ink.

She pulled out of Stormwatch at four that afternoon, glad to have no plans for New Year's Eve. Lorraine was out of town. Even Smokey was quiet. Curled up in the passenger seat, he napped as Rosalie passed through the birch grove. It was getting dark; snow was falling heavily. She turned after a County snowplow onto Friendly Valley Road. In a flash of peripheral vision she spotted the Camaro, parked along a bend.

"What?" She took her foot off the gas and checked the side mirror. Maybe she'd imagined it. Between lost sleep and Harold, it was possible. The plow kicked up a cloud of blowing snow.

By the time she managed to turn around, there was nothing there. Her stomach lurched. She crept along, peering down several driveways until conditions started to deteriorate. There was a good chance she'd get stuck if she didn't head home. Jerry didn't know a soul out this way.

Her truck was floating; she slowed to a crawl. The Camaro was even worse in the snow.

. . .

By the time Arlan came home at ten, she'd wandered restlessly throughout the house. She'd had it with beading for the night and sealed off two long peach silk charmeuse sleeves. She rummaged through kitchen cabinets looking for something to eat before shutting them in disgust. Smokey watched her pace. She landed next to him on the couch, stroking his fur. She tried to get into a made-for-TV movie about a flight attendant with two husbands who didn't know about each other.

Finally, Arlan's truck pulled up. She met him on the porch.

"Harold died."

"Harold?" He kicked the snow off his boots as he petted Smokey. "How?" He peeled off his coat and threw it on the couch.

"I found him. First thing this morning." She broke down unexpectedly, thinking she'd already had her cry. She then filled him in on the toxicology tests and the necropsy that would have to wait until Charlie returned.

"So far the others are okay."

Arlan looked at her funny and squinted.

Now and then you'd hear of people throwing poison meat over a fence. Angry landlords, disputes over property lines, such was the stuff of petty revenge. It would be just like Jerry. She wouldn't put such a thing past him. If meat was involved, Harold would have fought for the lion share.

"How are Dave and Jan?"

"Broken up."

"Sorry, missy."

She glared at the floor before speaking. "I think it was Jerry. He poisoned him," she whispered.

"Did Charlie say he was poisoned?"

"No, but I know."

"Oh, so now you're a vet too." He put his hands on his hips.

"Why would a perfectly healthy two-year-old sled dog just die?" Her voice had gotten louder.

"You're upset—"

Angry tears stung her throat. She forced out the words. "I saw his fucking car," she almost whispered. "Parked along the road when I left."

"Missy." Arlan reached to touch her. She yanked her arm away.

"Why won't he leave me alone? He killed an innocent thing, Dad."

"You don't know that—"

"I know I saw him. Maybe I should leave town—"

"No one's going anywhere. Come to Buck's party at the casino tonight. They're having a band. Forget about all this."

She looked at him in disbelief. Harold was dead in Charlie's cooler and tomorrow another dog might turn up dead. So far the New Year was ringing in as shitty as the old. She waited in agony. For her period to start, for Charlie to perform the necropsy and now for the hours to pass before she could search for another dead dog.

———

The kennel lights gleamed brightly the next morning, shining out onto the snowy road. They seemed brighter than usual, but then again she wasn't sleeping well.

Dave was usually out warming his truck by now.

Snow crunched under her boots as Smokey yanked on the leash, eager to be let into the yearling yard. She unlatched the gate, let him loose and proceeded to walk around. The snowy ground was bright enough to make out shapes. She searched for lifeless dogs. Someone was down in the far side of the yard near the hay bales. *Oh no.* Her stomach rushed. It was Sweetie. She rushed over. Sweetie then bolted up, jumping to lick Rosalie's nostrils.

"Oh thank God." She squeezed Sweetie in relief until the dog wriggled free. They were all up now, going through the ceremonial greeting and sniffing, ensuring that Smokey wasn't an imposter. Once satisfied, they crowded Rosalie, looking for breakfast.

"Just wait. I'll be right back." She eased out and latched the gate. She searched each yard, behind doghouses and bales of hay. Especially those flush against the woods. She'd expect a commotion if someone was lurking in the trees, lobbing a hunk of poison meat over the eight-foot fence. Something stopped her from telling Jan and Dave about the Camaro. It wasn't fair that her mess spill into their lives.

Dave announced that New Year's Day would be "Shoveling-Out-Dog-Yard Day." He was paying double time. The more packed the snow became, the higher the ground and lower the fence. An eight-foot fence became four. He'd also enlisted several local high school students.

Later when Dave called a break, Rosalie phoned the vet school. Still no word on King. She sat entering run times into the computer that Dave had shown her how to use. Admiring her shawl hanging in the space above the stone fireplace, she picked up a copy of the veterinary pharmacology book. Leafing through the section on toxicology, she looked for symptoms of poisoning.

"Hey, any word on King?" Jan popped in.

Rosalie startled and shut the book.

"You okay?" Jan touched her shoulder.

"I guess I'm still jumpy from yesterday. No calls yet."

"They'll call. Dave's pager's on." Jan sat facing her. "He's destroyed. Looked at puppy pictures all night, going over Harold stories. Neither of us slept."

"Me neither," Rosalie said. "Thank God the rest are fine. I checked first thing."

Jan looked at her funny. "Of course they're fine."

Rosalie cast down her eyes.

"Are you worried?" Jan asked.

"Just want to be sure."

"Well—Charlie and Helen'll be back tomorrow," Jan said. "They're funny. Such a long drive just for one night, but they miss Shannon. Nine hours is nothing for as many times as they've driven to Nome to visit their old friend Robert Ramsay. Once we rode along to the Yukon Quest up in the Territories. Charlie yakked the whole way; my head was killing me by the border.

"Maybe you and Arlan can come over when they get back from Chicago. Robert Ramsay's planning a visit. His wife died and this is the first year he decided not to run the Iditarod."

Jan could tell Rosalie wasn't listening.

"You think things'll be okay?" Rosalie asked. Her face was pale, her green eyes dull and troubled.

Jan studied the bewildered young woman. She always seemed to worry several paces in advance of everyone else. "Why wouldn't they, Roz?" Jan pushed her shoulder. "You're such a silly goose."

Rosalie smiled. She looked into her lap. "Sometimes I get scared."

"Have a little faith in the future." Jan stood up. "Come on— let's get out of here. I'm sick of shoveling. He's such a damned slave driver, let him finish it. Buck's is open until three; let's go get some smoked whitefish."

"Aren't you at all worried?" Rosalie looked at her.

"About what?"

"About the others? Fred still hasn't eaten." Rosalie looked at her. "He refused a second feeding."

"Of course he has. He's grieving. We all are. He'll grieve until he's done. It was Harold's fate not to grow old. Fred accepts this. Now we have to. When Fred's done, he'll turn to good things, like Clara cuddling up to him in his doghouse. She knows he's sad. Last night I saw her pawing to get him to play. Just because sad things happened doesn't mean that good things won't. Dogs know."

It was dusk by the time Rosalie came home. Franklin's sheriff's car was parked in the driveway. Arlan's wasn't. Her uncle walked out in uniform, both hands up as if surrendering.

"Relax; nobody's dead," Franklin called out.

She grabbed Smokey's leash and stepped down onto the driveway. "Franklin, what are you talking about?" Her mother's brother could be so melodramatic. It was usually funny, but Rosalie was in no mood.

"Tried to catch you at Dave's. Jan said you'd already left. Arlan's in the ER."

"What?"

"He's okay. A bit banged up. Has a slight concussion. They're keeping him. Fell down the stairs at the bus station."

"The bus station?"

"Mixed it up with Jerry about the dead dog at Stormwatch Kennel." He pursed his lips, which reminded Rosalie of her mother.

"Jerry? Oh shit."

"Let me drive; I'll explain."

"No." She bounded past him to let Smokey in. "I'll drive myself." She jogged towards her truck. Franklin followed.

"You're not going to do something whacky like go see Jerry—?"

She frowned. "I'm going to see my father, Franklin." The truck was still warm and started right up.

"You sure about that?"

"Fine, Franklin." She glared. "Follow me."

"That I will," he said, in an official way that made her roll her eyes.

It was dark by the time they got to Ashland. Arlan was already in a private room. His nose was swollen, eye blackened. A two-inch-long centipede-like line of stitches along his cheek.

She leaned over the bed to get a better look. "What did you do?"

He moved his arms with masculine verve in the Anishinabe way of announcing that a score is even.

"Cut the bullshit, Arlan." She raised her voice and placed both hands on her hips.

Franklin left the room.

She cringed thinking of Arlan going against Jerry.

"Jan and Dave's dog—man-to-man."

"What the hell are you talking about? He beat the crap out of you, Arlan. Have you looked at yourself in the mirror?"

"Man-to-man—," he repeated.

"I'm not listening to this," she muttered, and slung the strap of her purse over her shoulder. "Fine. Get yourself killed. I'm not hanging around to watch." She fished for her keys, sauntering towards the door.

"There's things I never told you." His voice changed. The gravity of it made her stop.

Arlan began to tell the story.

"After your mom died, I had a hard time." He looked at her. "I spent a lot of time in the taverns." He poured a glass of water from the plastic hospital pitcher and sipped. "I picked up with a local woman named Joyce, who spent a lot of time at Max's Desolation Tavern."

A nurse came into the room. Arlan stopped talking while his blood pressure was being taken. The nurse marked it on his chart and left.

"Joyce's husband worked on a tanker, gone for long spells at a time. After her two kids were in bed, Joyce would also go out to the taverns looking for company." The affair had gone on fast and furious for less than six months. "I'd drive home blind drunk, dodging long strings of foraging deer running across the highway in early morning." Other times he'd bolt up in Joyce's bed with a start. "I'd be scrambling to make it home before the sky lightened, before you woke up and realized that I wasn't there."

Several times as he'd tiptoe towards the front door, an adolescent boy's face watched him lace up his boots. Not long after, he heard that Joyce and her husband had separated. Years later, the boy now a man, Jerry, would stare him down.

"I'd see Jerry in taverns, he'd knock over my drink. 'Oops,

Arlan, you spilled,' Kurt along with his other shitty buddies would guffaw. The day I saw you coming down towards the dock arm in arm with Jerry, I about died on the spot."

Rosalie was silent. Rage bubbled. "So my mother's body is barely cold and you're fucking Jerry's mother?"

"Don't."

"Don't what, Arlan?" she hollered. "Care that you left me alone? Jesus Christ, I was just a little kid, Arlan, just a little kid. All alone. You know how scared I was? Wondering if you were dead on the highway? Hauling in logs that were almost as heavy as me."

"I'm sorry."

"Oh, that makes it all better."

"Please—"

"The whole town knows, don't they? Jerry knocked me up to get even. And you didn't even warn me."

A nurse popped in to check on the noise.

There was nothing to say, no salve to ease it. Nothing like the truth to stab you sick. Rosalie staggered out of the room. She pushed the elevator button once, and then jabbed it several times, "Come on, God fucking damn it."

Franklin rounded a corner and strode towards her. She ran towards the *exit* sign, pushed open the heavy fire door and raced down three flights of stairs. Out to the parking lot and towards the safety of her truck. The door groaned as it swung open. Frost covered the inside windshield like dried paste, sparkling into diamonds from the headlights of passing cars. Thicker than she could scrape off by the time Franklin would reach her.

She left the truck idling and ran. Across the rush-hour traffic of Main Street, dodging cars. She climbed the snowbank that lined Highway 13 to head down to Superior. Get to the Lake. She raced down the frozen snow-crusted beach, her feet punching through. It was pitch-black. A flock of turkey vultures startled. The span of their huge wings grazed her cheeks and eyes. She shrieked and tripped over the roadkill deer they'd been feasting on. She stepped over knife-sharp heaves and pressure ridges out onto the Lake, and collapsed into a heap.

CHAPTER 19

Her hands fumbled.

"Bakki," Jeaantaa called for the dog to pull the gangline tight as she hooked up the last few elderly dogs. She placed the three who could no longer run into the sled bag, on top of the tarp and pine boughs. They were ready.

Sudden commotion. The rest of the Guardians began squealing.

Tariem and Cheyuga were returning with the boys, followed closely by the sounds and sharp smells of an army truck. She panicked and dashed towards her sled—before Tariem noticed the missing dogs, the old ones, before he could stop her.

The empty spaces of the yard stuck out like dark patches of open water.

"Where are they?" Tariem hollered, jumping off his moving sled to chase her.

"No," she shrieked. "They're gone," she shouted in defiance, running towards her sled runners.

"Where is he?" he shouted, enraged, more angered than worried about the truck. "I knew it—," he screamed. "You're leaving with him." He caught the corner of her skin shirt, pulling her down. The whole kennel broke out into a howl.

He slapped her and she hit him back as hard as she could. Tangek screamed, "Ama-a, Ama-a." Ankjem clutched Cheyuga.

"Stop it, Tariem," the old man yelled. Prying off the boys, he rushed towards the couple. But Tariem heard no one. Jeaantaa held up both forearms to block his blows, until she fell. She scrambled on all fours towards her sled; then she grabbed the stake securing the team and yanked it out.

"Bakki, run," The dog took off before her foot was firmly planted. She grabbed the sled handle to gain a foothold. They surged like a team of wild yearlings in their prime, accelerating as she pulled herself onto the runners.

Tariem ran after her but fell forward, catching only air. Scrambling to his feet, he watched as she grew smaller against the darkening sky.

Tariem closed his eyes. His head fell back and the palms of his hands faced the evening stars. Yelling, cursing and crying out for her. Tangek and Ankjem were sobbing. But she was long past the crescent of trees, their *yaranga* and the familiarity of their lives.

Cheyuga walked over to crouch beside Tariem. The truck engine was growing louder. The old man sighed deeply, looking for answers in the creases of his hands.

She was gone. The bushes were still springing from her passage on the path to the Cove. Tariem slumped to his side, clutching his ribs as if punched.

The army truck stopped abruptly on the other side of the *yaranga*.

Cheyuga turned. The metal-on-metal grinding sound of rifles they'd come to associate with death. Two young soldiers hurried around past the *yaranga* once they'd spotted Tariem.

"Get up." One of them kicked him in the back.

His back arched in pain. The boys stiffened, their bodies clinging to Cheyuga.

"Get up, savage." Both soldiers raised him to his feet, shoving him towards the truck with the butts of their rifles. Tariem fell.

Cheyuga asked, "Where's he going?"

"Shut up, old man." The soldier moved to shove him too, but something stopped him.

Their neighbors must have seen Jeaantaa readying the sleds. A pit of fire burned his stomach. He watched them push Tariem

towards the truck, purposely making him fall so they could jeer
at him, kicking him in the rear to make it even more difficult to
stand. Cheyuga looked down at the boys. Why hadn't they been
taken too? Maybe the Forest Keeper had made the sleds invisible.

The remaining dogs stood quietly watching.

The men's voices shrieked with laughter from the other side of
the *yaranga*. The engine started. Cheyuga waited for the sound
of wheels rolling and crunching snow. He listened for the sound
to lessen and for the acrid bluish smoke to scatter into nothing.

Once the truck sounded far enough away, Cheyuga looked at
his sled and sighed. "Boys." He crouched down, looking at them.
Their bodies were stiff with fear. Sad, chubby faces. Tangek's red
cheeks spilled out of his hat. The boys climbed into the deep sled
without looking up. They sat on the bags of peppermint candy
that Jeaantaa had placed for them to find.

Cheyuga quickly transferred the dogs onto the prepared sled.
He pulled out the stake. "Ke, ke."

Heavy snow had begun to fall.

Neither boy looked back. Heads lowered, they took off into
the storm.

CHAPTER 20

"Thanks for letting me move in on such short notice," Rosalie said in her upbeat voice.

Jan unlocked the door of the converted garage and handed her the key. The place smelled of crackling fire, new carpet and freshly split wood. "I told you the place sits empty," Jan said. Though her face was impassive, her tone polite, Rosalie guessed the timing was suspicious.

Clutching the black lawn-leaf bag containing her beading and sewing box, she looked around for a safe place. She was up against a tight deadline. She placed the sewing box atop the pillows at the head of the bed. Dirt and grime were ever present in places you'd think clean. White and ivory silks could be ruined in one careless instant.

"Yeah, well thanks anyway." Rosalie hated being labeled the "troubled" girl. After her mother died, kids at school expected Rosalie to do something creepy. It hadn't helped that she wore the same clothes days on end. It added to her "cootie" status. "Her mother's *dead*," they whispered louder than their natural speaking voices.

"It'll save gas and travel time." She nodded sensibly. But as Jan stood with arms folded, Rosalie guessed the woman knew more.

"Well, hope the place is warm enough." Jan paused. "I ran down here after you called to start the woodstove."

"It's fine, Jan, really."

Rosalie looked around. There was no garage door, as she'd expected, and the interior was drywalled. Nothing about it looked like a "converted" garage. Smokey stood by her side. Jan demonstrated the trick to lighting the stove's temperamental burners and how to stop the toilet's running in the world's tiniest bathroom. The woodpile was located just outside under a green tarp, wood splitter next to it. A narrow closet was packed with piles of fresh sheets, towels, blankets and a tiny dresser.

"So—eh, what did Arlan say about you moving out?" Jan asked after a pause.

Rosalie shrugged. "I left him a note." She felt herself grow pale.

"You left him a note?" Jan raised her eyebrows.

"Well—the place looks cozy," Rosalie said after a long pause.

"He's got a concussion, Roz." Jan's eyes were fixed on her. "Don't you think he might need some help?"

Rosalie squirmed with discomfort.

"I know it's none of my business, but you should call, Roz. At least tell him you're here."

She looked at Jan quickly but said nothing.

"You're welcome to use the phone up at the house anytime."

"Thanks."

The women looked at each other. Rosalie looked away first.

"Well, holler if you need anything," Jan said. She looked around one last time. "Warm chili's up on the stove. Dave'll be home any minute. You hungry?"

"No thanks, already ate."

"Need help with your stuff?"

"Nope. Just got my clothes, Smokey's bed."

"Okay, then, I'll be leaving you guys. Tomorrow we leave by five. Four-hour drive to the Boundary Waters. They had a good storm yesterday. Alarm clock's on the nightstand." Jan bent to pet Smokey on the way out.

Rosalie sighed in relief after the door shut. Sitting down on the edge of the bed, she then sprawled out and watched Smokey drag his leash around the room. He sniffed the carpet and the curtains.

It felt good to lie down. The bed was comfortable. Across the room sat a green plaid couch, a maple end table with lamp, and a kitchenette. A pair of old wooden and gut snowshoes criss-crossed on the wall over the bed. They looked large enough for Bigfoot. The bedspread was the red wool Hudson Bay blanket with black stripes that Jan had mentioned picking up in Thunder Bay. Neatly folded at the foot of the bed was a poofy blue goose down comforter. The padded Berber carpeting felt luxurious.

She got up and rummaged through the kitchenette's cabinets: packages of instant noodles, Campbell soup, round cylinders of Kool-Aid and boxes of tea. Tea sounded good. She filled the kettle from the sink and started one of the burners. Throwing another log into the stove, she stoked it up with a black metal poker.

She wrapped herself in the down comforter as she waited for the kettle to boil. Smokey had sniffed every inch of the place. She patted the bed next to her. He jumped right up, turning twice before he settled. She snapped off the leash and dropped it.

"This is home for now," she explained. The kettle started to whistle. Cinnamon spice released with the boiling water. She settled back down onto the bed, cupping the ceramic mug to warm her hands.

"What do you think?"

Smokey's ears swiveled at the playfulness in her voice. His eyes fixed on her and then sniffed steam from her mug. She placed it on the maple nightstand to cool. The sewing box with her beading called to be finished. Instead she curled up. Warmth accumulated in downy swirls.

She admitted that she'd never loved Jerry. When "I love you" flew out of her mouth, she knew it was a lie. It felt obligatory. Especially with him being her first, the occasion warranted such a claim—a declaration of magnitude. Little had she known that her body was a practical joke. One he probably let his buddies in on the minute it was over. "Hey, Kurt—guess whose cherry I just popped." How revolting to remember his grunts, his face, laboring on top of her.

She also knew that Jerry didn't love her either. The words sounded just as fake coming from him. "Love you too," he'd say back. A hint of a sneer following every declaration. Playing house in his apartment above the bus station with all the pretentiousness of "honey this," or "honey that," it smacked of phony. Days after the civil ceremony, his sweetness evaporated. Her mother's words, "What a liar reaps a liar sows," gnawed at Rosalie. It was a hard truth. A brutal and public lesson.

Having Smokey was the one true thing she'd known. Dogs were what they were and every day was a fresh start.

"Hey, good boy." His eyes were clear, holding so little from his troubled past. Her voice triggered a playful paw. Then he rolled onto his back, wriggling into the newness of the bed. She began to doze, remembering her clothes outside in the truck bed. The plastic bags were open. In a rush she'd neglected to cinch them shut. It was only snow; snow was water. Water dries clear. Tomorrow she'd brush off whatever flakes had fallen.

For the first time ever, it felt good to be expecting no one.

The alarm went off at four the next morning. She awoke to cramps and her period. She rolled over and opened her eyes, and then bolted to the bathroom to make sure.

Oh thank God. She crouched on the floor, weak with relief. Grateful tears flooded her; she'd dodged a lifetime tied to Jerry. A child who might have grown to become like him. She swore to God that she'd never again be so stupid. Her life was back in her own court. Maybe the universe had decided it would have been too cruel a fate, even for her.

The outside kennel lights were stadium bright and the dog

trucks were warming. Rosalie slipped into her boots and coat, snapped a leash onto Smokey and ran outside.

"Hey, sleepyhead—," Dave joked, surprised by her bouncy, elated demeanor.

She smiled at him and shrugged mysteriously.

"Now there's the Rosalie we know and love," he teased. "Got news about King."

"Tell me." She could tell by Dave's voice something had gone well. She ran over to help fasten the second tier of dog boxes onto his truck.

"Jim called about two. Jan wanted to wake you; I told her to let you sleep." Jim was Charlie's friend who graciously agreed to slip King into the surgery schedule. "Looks like you have a sighted lead dog now."

Rosalie squealed and jumped, thumping her leather mittens together. She didn't think she could be happier.

"They reattached the retina in one eye; the other had to be removed—too much damage. I know Charlie hoped to save it. They're keeping him quiet until it fully reattaches and heals. But he's comfortable now."

King would come home after the Beargrease. All she had to do was get through the race to see him again.

The days leading up to the race were an exhausting grind. Each night she stumbled into the converted garage, beat from training runs in the Boundary Waters. She'd throw a goodly share of wood into the stove before collapsing onto the bed. Too tired to unlace her boots. She'd bundle in the down comforter and lose consciousness in an instant. The alarm always went off too soon.

They drove to different locales in search of fresh snow. Huskies grew bored doubling back over familiar terrain, run after run. They hated long, flat surfaces where the trail was visible ahead for miles. Winding, hilly tree-lined trails were their favorite; they lived in anticipation of what might be around the next bend. Each day Rosalie dropped off both teams at a cross-road and met them twenty miles ahead. She often strained to decipher the sketchy Forest Service maps. Fresh trails kept the dogs' enthusiasm high. Curiosity made them run harder. And the better their morale, the stronger they'd become.

These Boundary Waters runs taught her how to care for dogs under wilderness conditions. She found it ironic that the colder the temperature, the greater the threat of dehydration. While most dogs scooped snow as they ran, keeping their hydration relatively balanced, others were less efficient. Rosalie had become skilled at baiting them to drink. She'd lace water with chunks of salmon. For the ones who turned their noses away, she discovered that a pinch of the kitchenette's leftover Kool-Aid powder on the surface of freshwater made them drink like crazy. They greedily licked the bowl and then looked to her for more.

Charlie taught her how to test for signs of dehydration and respiratory trouble. Checking a dog's gums for color, pressing the tissue with a finger. Pink meant they were oxygenating. A pale color meant they were becoming anemic from either exhaustion or pneumonia. For dehydration, she'd softly pinch the skin, pull and then let go, testing for elasticity. If it sprang back quickly, hydration was good. If it didn't, you needed to get water into them fast.

During the race Rosalie would follow both teams in Jan's truck, driving the entire 410-mile loop from Duluth to the Canadian border and back. That meant meeting them at each checkpoint, if necessary being snowmobiled into the more remote parts of the trail. She'd camp out with the team at the mandatory rest stops, laying down fresh hay for the dogs during layovers and then cleaning up after. Providing freshwater, feed, snacks, and if there were any dogs to be dropped she was to haul them to the nearest vet station.

After they pulled in from their last evening of training, dogs were fed and bedded down. The three of them sat with beer and

pizza to anayze each dog's attitude, speed and endurance over
the past few weeks. While they were fairly certain of the lineup
for each team, the final runners were selected that evening.
Medical records had to be submitted the next day to the race officials in Duluth. No substitutions were permitted. All dogs
would be checked against the roster and their fur painted with
bright pink, orange and green markers.

Charlie was Chief Beargrease Veterinarian. He'd worked the
race ever since he moved back from Alaska. And every year in
March he flew up to work as one of the Chief Veterinarians for the
Iditarod and spend time with Bob Ramsay. Veterinarians from all
over worked the race circuit every year. They followed the dog
teams. Passing information from checkpoint to checkpoint about
dogs to be watched and team conditions. Sometimes vets or techs
were dispatched by snowmobiles to the more remote areas.

An army of volunteers worked the starting chute and staffed
each checkpoint, delivering musher "drop bags" of food and
bales of hay. Some camped out in storms and bitter cold to staff
the more remote wilderness areas. Others worked the busier
crossroads, forming human chains for passing teams.

Jan knocked at the door. It was the day before the race, and team
medical records, food bundles and hay bales had to be checked
into the Race Headquarters in Duluth by five.

"Come in." Rosalie was sitting with the windows propped
open, woodstove akin to an inferno, wrapped in the blanket, all
to smoke a celebratory cigarette. She managed to finish the bodice of the wedding dress in stolen moments. It was sealed in the
FedEx mailer and placed outside before she lit up.

Jan stepped in, holding up the FedEx package. "This yours?"

"Yeah, just leave it," Rosalie said. The Guild had a no smoking
policy. Who wants to pay a small fortune to smell like an ashtray?

She'd drop it off at the FedEx office that afternoon in Duluth.

Jan frowned as she entered, waving at the blue swirls of smoke. "Golly, Roz, it's like a tavern in here."

"Yeah, sorry." She chuckled.

"What's with the open windows? It's minus eleven."

"Sorry. Didn't want to stink up the place."

"Wouldn't it just be easier to go outside?"

"It's cold out there," she joked. She was in high spirits. They both laughed. The cigarette had burned down to her knuckle. She periodically flicked ashes into a jelly jar cap she held with the other hand.

"I'm celebrating."

"King?" Jan asked.

"And finishing this dress among other things."

"Like what?" Jan pushed.

"Other stuff."

"Always the enigma, Roz, the mystery," she said, and they both laughed.

"My period started."

"Oh. So that's what it was." Jan nodded slowly.

Rosalie nodded.

"I sort of guessed."

"I also finished that bodice with time to spare." Rosalie motioned with her cigarette towards the door and laughed in relief.

"Did I mention that Dave's dad died of lung cancer last year?"

"Oh. Sorry." Rosalie unfolded her legs and placed her feet flat on the floor. She sat up straight, holding the cap of the jelly jar. She glanced with apprehension at what was left of the cigarette. "I didn't know. I *am* cutting back."

"Man never smoked a cigarette his entire life. Was quite an aggressive jerk about not breathing other people's smoke either."

"Weird."

"It is. It's true, though." Jan nodded and then looked at the pack of Camels lying on the bed next to Rosalie. "Goddamn it, toss me one of them there coffin nails."

Rosalie laughed. She tossed the pack and Jan caught it. Tapping it against her hand, she placed a cigarette between her lips. Rosalie was surprised how Jan's demeanor relaxed into the cigarette.

"Don't have a lighter, sorry." Rosalie pointed to the stove.

"You breathe a word of this," Jan warned with the cigarette poised between her fingers, "you're a dead woman."

Rosalie laughed out loud at the seriousness of the big-sister face.

Jan flipped on the front burner and leaned over to light the tip.

"Don't set your hair on fire—," Rosalie warned.

Jan's shoulders jerked, as she laughed and choked at the same time, waving at Rosalie to knock it off.

"Explain *that one* to Dr. Dave," Rosalie said.

"Had my first cigarette in eighth grade," Jan said as she exhaled.

"Damn," Rosalie said. "I thought *I* started young."

"I was a wild girl," Jan said. The way she held the cigarette with her wrist cocked left no doubt.

"At fifteen, I hung out with *Scott*," Jan said. Her eyebrows rose when she said the name. "Twenty-one-year-old troublemaker. Smoked, drank and ran around. Life in a small town, growing up flawed in the perfect family, can be tough. Sometimes tougher than being in a flawed one."

She inhaled deeply before going on.

"Got pregnant. Wanted to abort it. Mom made me have it."

"*You had a baby?*" Rosalie didn't want her surprise to come off as insulting.

Jan was silent.

"What happened to it?"

"She's fifteen now. Born June 16. Lives in the Twin Cities. They took her from me before she'd taken her first breath."

Jan was quiet for a long time. The cigarette burned slowly into white ashes.

Rosalie sat in shock. "Did you want to keep it?"

She shook her head. "I would've been the world's crummiest

fifteen-year-old mother." She chuckled sadly. "In college I looked them up. Parked near their house to see her. She looks just like Scott."

"Did Dave know?"

"He knew. We both grew up in Grand Marais. It's nosier than Bayfield, if you can imagine that."

The two of them laughed.

"But it bothered me for many years. Like I had a stain that everyone could see. Except for dogs—they're blind to things like that. Dogs and Dave."

"Have you met her?"

Jan turned the cigarette in her hand, observing it. "Not sure what it would add to her life. I think of her, though. More often as I get older. It bothers me for different reasons now. Not that it was the wrong decision or anything. Maybe more because we're talking about starting a family after the Iditarod."

"God, Jan, she's fifteen. *I* just turned eighteen," Rosalie joked as she thought about it. "You could almost be *my* mother."

"Not quite." She swatted at Rosalie and laughed. Jan walked towards the wood-burning stove. "Something about a drink and a cigarette at a college party. Mr. Healthy made me quit."

They were quiet for a while.

"Wow." Jan laughed nervously, a bit embarrassed. She stood looking out the window as if gathering her thoughts. "All this from one stupid cigarette. Guess maybe I needed to tell someone," Jan whispered, and sat down on the love seat. They sat quietly for a few minutes. Rosalie recalibrated what she knew of Jan as they absorbed the gravity of what was shared.

Jan looked around the room. "So how is this place?"

Rosalie took another look around. "It's okay I guess," she said in a noncommittal way.

"I never asked Kathleen—she was too polite to tell the truth anyway."

"Why did she leave?" Rosalie wanted to hear Jan say it.

"Kathleen? She left to marry Craig."

"Did she want to leave?"

"I'd tried to get her to stay, but Craig didn't want her working. Even offered more money—what I'm paying you now. But once Craig digs his heels in, that's it. They offered to stay here this weekend for the race."

So she hadn't been fired. How could she have been so off base about Jan?

"Well—it's pretty cozy in here now," Rosalie said more as a secret apology. She looked down at the carpeting, missing Arlan's cabin in the woods and wondering how he was doing. The butt burned down to the end. Rosalie mashed what was left of it into the jelly cap.

Jan stood up. She brushed off her lap to kill any evidence.

"The real reason I came down here." Jan tossed the rest of the cigarette into the sink, dousing it under the faucet, and then reached up to close the windows. "Charlie called. The toxicology panel was clean. Necropsy revealed a congenital heart defect." Jan pressed her eyes with her thumb and index finger. She tried to smile, but her lips were stiff. "'The dog would have died had he been living on someone's couch.' Said it's amazing he lived as long as he did."

"Poor guy." Rosalie thought about it for a moment. "Wouldn't his heart have sounded weird through the stethoscope? Or his EEG?"

Jan looked up, surprised by the astute comment. Rosalie surprised herself too.

"I asked the same thing," Jan said. "Charlie says they're only detectable postmortem."

"Poor Harold," Rosalie said, and looked away. She thought of Arlan and Jerry.

"You talk to Arlan?" Jan asked.

Rosalie knew she'd ask. "Not yet."

"You guys have a fight?" Jan asked.

There was a long pause. Rosalie stared at the fire and then sighed deeply. "Sort of." She pictured Arlan lumbering around the house. He'd probably announced to the town mothers and fathers that he was "giving her space."

"Well—looks like the sun just came out." Jan moved towards the door. "Shall we finish and go to Duluth?"

Jan was funny about gear bags. She didn't trust Dave.

"He says he already went over the checklist."

Jan shook her head and frowned. "Never believe him—Dave forgets."

It was too cold inside the shed, even with the space heaters full blast, to hold a pen without mittens. Rosalie stood with the clipboard checking off mandatory gear as Jan called it off. If a musher was missing even one item at the start, it meant immediate disqualification. They needed two working headlamps for each team with a beam powerful enough to see past sixteen dogs. A knife, sleeping bag appropriate to the temperatures, as well as a pair of snowshoes, an axe, and dog booties to protect their feet in rough conditions. They had a vet log for each checkpoint and dozens of items related to dog safety and first aid.

"You know, Roz . . ." Jan paused. She gave Rosalie a long look as if wrestling with herself. "No relationship is perfect. Haven't you ever done things that now you can kick yourself over?"

She knew where Jan was going. She looked at the clipboard, feeling cornered.

"Hell, since it's True Confession Day." Jan stopped. "Shit, didn't we just see this episode of *Guiding Light* over lunch yesterday?"

Rosalie laughed and looked up at her. They were almost at the end of the checklist.

"I've never told a soul this either." Jan began, poking around in Dave's gear bag, searching for a particular item. "But Dave went out on me once."

"You mean he cheated on you?" Rosalie was astonished. She realized her mouth was gaping open and quickly shut it.

"Towards the end of med school. We weren't married yet, not

that it made it okay. Was sort of a strange time—for both of us. I sort of knew it too. It's like an atmosphere."

Rosalie felt embarrassed, peeking through a crack in the door to their marriage. "I thought you guys had the perfect relationship."

"No such thing." Jan straightened up and stretched out her lower back.

"So you got married anyway?" Rosalie said.

"Yup."

"Who was it?"

"Doesn't matter."

Rosalie looked away.

"Did lots of soul-searching. Strange, but it did make us stronger, like the cliché says. What you can't take back sometimes has to be forgiven."

She didn't know what to say; so many questions popped up. It was none of her business.

"Yet in a weird way I was sort of glad."

"Glad?" Rosalie asked.

"Yeah. Sort of like we were even." Jan laughed in a sinister way. "Here he'd been this saint, saving 'the fallen woman.' The girl with problems."

She stood stunned, as if Jan had read her thoughts. She always thought she was alone in her shame.

"After that Dave seemed real. Human like me. Ironically, it made me trust him more."

Rosalie held the pen in her mitten. Her mouth hung open.

"Catch a fly." Jan reached over and tapped her jaw.

How could anyone forgive? But then again it was Dave. Always so patient, so caring, so quick with a word to let you know he was on your side.

"Hard to believe, eh?"

Rosalie dropped her eyes.

"I could have dumped him, or married him anyway and have it poison everything. Maybe outlived it to the point where I'd no longer remembered what I'd let ruin my life. But I chose to forgive."

"You make it sound so easy."

"Forgiving him was easy. Forgiving myself at fifteen was not."

Something in Rosalie unclenched with those words. Perhaps it was acknowledgment that the random distribution of trouble was often just that, and that so far she'd done no more, no less, to earn her fate than Jan.

"What woman hasn't been humiliated at the hands of some man—a husband, boyfriend or father?" Jan laughed in a nasty way. "Rise above it." She winked. "We're a lot tougher than they tell us."

Rosalie looked back to the clipboard.

"Hey—" Jan looked up and caught Rosalie's eye. "Don't get me wrong. He ever does it again, he knows I'm a better shot."

CHAPTER 21

JANUARY 1993–DULUTH, MINNESOTA, LAKE SUPERIOR

It was early Saturday morning and the Beargrease start time was noon. She followed Jan, driving Dave's truck. He'd been called away to an emergency at one that morning but was leaving the hospital. He sounded cranky on the phone. Going into a dog-sled race sleep-deprived was not advisable; it would only get worse in the days to come.

Rosalie hadn't slept that great either. All night, shocks of adrenaline woke her. Her mind raced over checkpoint protocol. The day was really here.

Arlan's truck approached in her rearview mirror outside the city of Superior. He beeped and waved as he passed, trying to catch her eye. She honked and waved back. Weeks before, Arlan had volunteered his truck to pick up dropped dogs and deliver supplies to veterinarians along the trail. He built cubbies for injured, lame or exhausted dogs. "Races are won by the dogs you leave behind," an old racing adage Dave had etched into her thoughts. "You're only as fast as your slowest dog." Though it was all volunteer labor, people would tip, and Arlan had pledged all proceeds to King's eye surgery fund. This combined with Rosalie's stack of paychecks from the Northern Workers Beading Guild. Jan and Dave also pledged to match her overtime pay and donate it to King's recovery.

Earlier Lorraine had rocketed by, beeping as if sending off a bride and groom. Rolling down the window in minus eighteen degrees, Lorraine waved frantically in a show of support.

Rosalie missed Smokey already; the cuffs of her parka smelled of his fur. She'd hugged him tightly before she left. This would be the longest she'd be away from him since he came into her life. Kathleen, the former handler, was staying at Stormwatch until the race was over. Smokey was only too happy to spend time romping with his yearling team.

Low-hanging clouds frosted trees along the highway. They shimmered in the low light like the beaded bodices of bridal gowns. Rosalie remembered the first time she noticed such beauty. As a child, she made the connection that quality beadwork should mimic nature.

As she crested the bridge, the mist softened a tangled industrial skyline. She remembered how, when she was a young child, these structures frightened her. Ducking down on the back floor of the family car, she hid from the jumbled knotted pipes of grain elevators and ore docks. Once believing them to be the bleached bone yards of monsters. Now they held a grotesque sort of beauty, much of it defunct, sitting abandoned and left to rust.

The Nemadji, Pokegama and St. Louis rivers flowed northward, forming miles of tributary wetlands that replenished the largest body of freshwater in the world. Sadly, most had been polluted long before she was born. "Too bad," Franklin used to lament. "Probably good fishing there too. Fry a fish betcha the damn thing'll explode right there in the frying pan."

She glanced over the side rail of the bridge. Below braided arteries of railroad track twisted through the Nemadji's tributaries. From there overseas containers were off-loaded and disbursed to America's northern tier, restocking countless shelves and warehouses. Everything was imported. Even "handmade" Bayfield summer souvenirs—lighthouse key chains and T-shirts—were brought in from Indonesia, Mexico and the Philippines.

The twin ports of Superior-Duluth were working docks, not built to be picturesque backdrops for vacation photos. Less than a generation ago, ore pellets from the surrounding Mesabi iron range were shipped to Detroit, Chicago, Cleveland or down the St. Lawrence Seaway to the Atlantic. Workers once blasted ore from the red granite mountains of the Mesabi Range. But cheap Chinese ore put everyone out of business. They still spoke of the massive, thundering crash that granite rock makes when crushed into fine powder. Industrial drums as tall as buildings reduced mountains to peanut-sized pellets of iron ore. The men's faces turned a burnished red from the dust. They inhaled a stench they could never rid from their nostrils, a smell that would ooze from their pores whenever they sweat.

Ore docks stood silently rusting like scars on the wetlands. Boarded-up downtowns and dwindling elementary school enrollments. In a Northern diaspora, children and grandchildren scattered in search of that moving target called a livelihood.

Eighty dog teams, more than a thousand dogs, were packed into the parking lot of an unassuming Midwestern middle school. For the past twenty Januarys, Ordean Middle School's athletic field had transformed into the starting chute for the longest and most rugged dogsled race outside of Alaska's Iditarod.

It was not 7 a.m. and already traffic was heavy. Police officers directed the glut of dog trucks and cars jockeying for the closest parking spaces. A *Beargrease 1993* banner spanned the entrance. Ropes of Crayola-colored plastic flags wove through the chain-link fencing. Media trucks with satellite dishes jammed the outer ring. Local reporters sauntered through the teams; they held up microphones, interviewing the local favorites.

A sponsoring car dealer's sky blue Subaru was parked alongside their booth. Someone dressed in a husky costume danced to country music and gave away candy canes. Kiosks sold emblemized coffee cups, T-shirts and baseball caps. Steaming peppermint chocolate warmed the hands of spectators. It seemed more like a North Pole State Fair than a dogsled race.

The lot was wallpapered with trucks and dog teams. Rosalie hopped down from the truck. Surrounding mushers and handlers fussed with last-minute adjustments. Coils of replacement nylon sled runners lay on the snowy ground, duct-taped in color-coded circles for temperature. "You can't have too many spare runners," Jan had said. "That granite will tear them up." Gouges and ruts added drag, making more work for the dogs.

Teams were required to bring a spare sled for handlers to have ready at all times. Aluminum sleds crumpled and wooden stanchions snapped like matchsticks. In remote areas, snowmobiles would tow replacement sleds to stranded teams. Dave said that many mushers scratched after the spare sled broke as well.

At 410 miles, the Beargrease was the longest and toughest race in the lower forty-eight. It combined the difficult elements of the Iditarod into less than half the distance, boasting one of the highest "scratch rates." Big-name national and international competitors were frequently humbled.

Over a beer the day before, Dave had explained the legend of John Beargrease. The son of an Ojibwa chief, Beargrease delivered mail and supplies up the North Shore during the later part of the nineteenth century. The race was a commemorative tribute. Before each race an opening prayer paid homage to the man's unbeatable spirit.

Rosalie began to unload Dave's gear. She attached cable lines to the truck so the dogs could be unloaded and secured until the start. Hay was spread for bedding. License plates from Montana, Washington, Wyoming, Massachusetts, New Hampshire, even Alaska surrounded the Stormwatch trucks.

Some of the more experienced teams lounged on straw. More than happy to conserve their energy and let the young and inexperienced yell their heads off.

Three people were chatting with Jan.

"Roz," Jan called. "Come over; meet my folks and Dave's mom."

Just then Lorraine grabbed Rosalie's arm.

"Hey," Lorraine said. "This is so fucking cool I can't stand it," she squealed. "So many cute guys walking around, holy Christ." Lorraine's head bobbed from face to face.

Rosalie smiled at her friend.

"Hey, looks like you're busy." Lorraine looked at Jan's parents. "Why don't I catch you later?"

Rosalie nodded. Lorraine flipped her bangs into coquette position and disappeared into the crowd.

Rosalie was introduced as the new "Kathleen." She took off her mitten to shake hands.

"So nice to finally meet you," Jan's mom said. "Heard glowing things about you, Rosalie." The woman squeezed her arm. "From Jan that's something. She's a pretty tough customer. What do you make of my crazy daughter and son-in-law?" Jan's mother laughed as she teased. "Nuts, isn't it?" Rosalie smiled. Soon the three of them walked off in search of the hot peppermint chocolate stand.

First she lifted Fred, fastening his collar to cable line; he shook off and looked around excitedly. He'd bunked with Clara on the ride over. "Hey, good boy." Fred and Harold had had the same sweet smell. Fred looked in her eyes. "You're gonna be fine. You know he's running with you." Harold would have been a lunatic from all the excitement.

She unloaded the rest of the dogs. Other mushers sorted through harnesses and tangled ganglines. Stormwatch gear had been sorted like clockwork. All they had to do was load sled bags, harness, attach ganglines and go. Rosalie surged with pride. How much she'd learned in under two months. How quickly she'd come to belong in this world.

She climbed up the back bumper and unhooked Dave's aluminum sled from the roof. It was so light she could practically lift it with one hand.

"Dave'll be here any minute." Jan walked over, hands on hips. "When he gets here, go look around; there's tons to see. You've probably never seen so many dogs in one place in your life."

"I think you're probably right," Rosalie said, looking over the dozens of teams in their immediate area.

People strolled in brightly patterned hats and scarves. Some wore colored stocking caps shaped like dragons. Spectators had watched her setting up Dave's sled and asked questions about the dogs. A small crowd formed as she demonstrated how the shock absorber protects dog joints from abrupt starts and stops. Dave's words, "Always remember, we're ambassadors for the sport," had her explaining patiently as he'd always done for her.

"Would you snap a photo of us with your team?" a man asked, showing her how to work the camera.

Just as she made the final check of brass snaps, to make sure none had frozen, Dave appeared.

"Well done, Roz." He looked over his team. "I timed it so you'd have all the hard work done." He winked at her and hugged Jan, kissing the side of her head. She laughed from excitement; her breath steamed. Dave stepped into his blue down overalls and grabbed his arctic parka.

"Go look around while we get checked in," Jan said.

Rosalie didn't know where to look first and opted to follow the race officials. They sorted through each musher's sled bag, checking off the mandatory gear. A few trucks with Alaska license plates were as rusted out and beaten up as hers; you could tell every penny went into their dogs. Crudely constructed wooden dog boxes were bolted to the backs of their trucks. Each compartment door had a circle cut out, just large enough to accommodate a husky head.

Other rigs were all showbiz. Trailers and RVs were airbrushed with images of dog teams spanning their length. Murals of howling wolves or dramatic scenes of Alaska's Mt. McKinley. It was the Life, as Jan called it. Many racers lived in their campers from December through March, following the race circuit. Dogs also loved traveling. No end to new places and people, racecourses and landscapes, not to mention an endless array of smells. It was Jan and Dave's goal to qualify for the Iditarod and

Yukon Quest races. Their dream was to live the "husky life" from December through March. To race to their hearts' content.

"Charlie," Rosalie called. He stood in front of a team, checking off forms on a clipboard.

Recognizing the voice, he turned. His face lit up. That alone pleased her.

"Hey, Rozzie, you busy?" he asked.

She shook her head.

"You wanna come give me a hand, we're down one tech."

Four hours until start time. She held a dog while Charlie flexed wrist joints, elbows and back legs.

The veterinarian medical team wore identical forest green parkas with fur-lined hoods. Most were covered with race patches from Yukon Quest, Race to the Sky and the Iditarod. Charlie worked quickly; the dogs were typically in better shape than their drivers. But in one case he stopped. The dogs were too thin. He looked at Rosalie, catching her eye with an expression she'd now come to understand.

"These dogs are half-starved. You're withdrawn," he said, jotting notes on the clipboard.

Rosalie ran her hands over the flanks and along the spine of a dog. Smokey had been like that when she took him. Jan always kept the dogs at a good weight. "Thin dogs are mean dogs," she always said.

Charlie glared at the mushers, a couple in down overalls.

"I'd like to talk to your boss," the wife demanded.

Rosalie and a few other vet techs snickered.

"*I am* the boss," he said quietly. The woman continued threatening him, going on about how they'd traveled all the way from Vermont.

"Lady, I don't give a rat's ass if you touched down from Mars. Those dogs are too thin. You're withdrawn. I'm calling the Vermont authorities." Charlie looked right at her. "Looks like you spend plenty of money on gear. Spend a little more on feed."

Charlie turned his back and smiled at Rosalie. He didn't seem angry. "Come on, Rozzie, lots more teams to check in."

The veterinary team's clipboards held detailed medical information for each dog, including bloodwork, hip X-rays, results of cardiograms. The vet team flexed joints, checked shoulders, wrists, knees and hips. They scrutinized the pads of each dog's feet, consulting with the musher about injuries that would need to be watched. Full disclosure was the rule. Then each dog was cross-checked and its fur marked with a line of bright marker—Day-Glo pink for 410 miles and blaze orange for the mid-distance of 150. Each team was required to carry a waterproof pouch with the veterinarian's log at all times. The vet team made notes at each checkpoint. Losing the log was grounds for immediate disqualification. The word of the medical team was law on the trail.

The thirty-minute warning sounded. Rosalie checked her wrist-watch, astonished. It hadn't felt like three hours.

Charlie motioned with his head. "You'd better get back. They're gonna need an extra pair of hands."

Rosalie hurried to the Stormwatch trucks. They scrambled to harness the dogs. She secured both sleds to the frames of the trucks with snub lines. Then she helped Jan and Dave tie their race bibs. Charlie finally made his way to the Stormwatch dogs as the fifteen-minute warning sounded. He nodded in acknowledgment and checked over Jan and Dave's dogs.

"They look fine. Anything to report?" You could tell he'd asked the question eighty times. Charlie initialed their vet log and moved on.

Race starts were spaced in five-minute increments. Fifteen volunteers would descend on each team in order. They'd lift and carry the sled; others—including the musher's family and friends—would hold on to the gangline for dear life, guiding the frenzied team into the starting chute. A crowd of volunteers marched through the parking lot in search of the starting team. The dogs went ballistic. It was electric, the energy primal and eerily familiar.

After more than forty-five minutes' worth of departures, Jan's team was up. She was followed immediately by Dave. Rosalie had bootied up both teams for the start, making the Velcro around the dogs' ankles tight enough so they wouldn't throw them in the takeoff.

The crowd of volunteers came bounding towards her.

"I think you're next," Rosalie shouted to Jan over the howling.

"I think you're right," Jan shouted back. She pulled up the hood of her red parka, fastening it under her chin. Her mother and father hugged her. Rosalie looked around again for signs of Arlan.

Two volunteers lifted Jan's sled; others grasped the gangline. Rosalie grabbed the neckline attaching Mitzi as they marched towards the starting chute. The explosive roar of the crowd and announcer became louder. The volunteers placed the sled beneath the starting banner. Jan kicked in the snow hook. Volunteers held on to the strong dogs. Rosalie guided Mitzi into position and held the dog's collar. The bleachers were packed. People lined the track, four and five deep, packed all the way down the field towards the entrance to the Gunflint Trail. Both sides of the chute were mobbed. Camera flashes popped from the bleachers. Local stations were set up on either side, sending live feed.

The dogs lunged as the bright digital clock counted down. An official at the start line held Jan's sled handle to make sure there was no false start. Jan stepped onto the footpads and peered down the trail. The dogs were slamming in their harnesses. It was a level of frenzy Rosalie had never seen.

Jan straightened her white plastic bib. Number 15. Her mother stepped out in front of the team; her camera flashed.

"Be my good girl," Rosalie whispered to Mitzi. The dog was not so frenzied that she couldn't lick Rosalie's nostrils. "Win for your mama."

The announcer began. "Jan Andersson of Stormwatch Kennel, Bayfield, Wisconsin." The crowd roared. "Another husband and wife team. And Rosalie MacKenzie from Red Cliff, chief handler at Stormwatch Kennels."

It was shocking to hear her own name over the P.A. The official lifted the snow hook and handed it to Jan. She slid it into the holder. The crowd began to count. Volunteers gripped the gangline. Jan kept her eye on the official, waiting for his cue. The crowd began to count in unison with the electronic clock.

"Five-four-three-two-one-go!" The start gun prompted a lunge.

Rosalie let go of Mitzi. The volunteers sprang back. Jan's team blasted out of the chute. An explosive roar rose from the crowd with the team's burst of enthusiasm. They flew around the first bend, which was lined with bales of hay. The dogs shoulder checked each other as if trying to get out in front. Rosalie stood for several moments in a stupor. She watched them rocket down the tree-lined trail as if she'd never seen dogs run before.

Dave's team. She shook out the stupor and ran. She checked the Velcro fasteners on their booties. The volunteers descended. Dave suddenly gripped her, hugging her so tightly that sharp pains shot through her mending ribs. They hadn't hurt in a month. But the pain was nothing compared with her exhilaration.

"You're gonna be great," she yelled over the dogs, surprised at Dave's rush of emotion. Mr. Dial Tone, Jan called him.

He had tears in his eyes. "Thanks, Roz. You're a pro."

Volunteers lifted the sled. Rosalie released the team from the truck. The volunteers grabbed hold of the gangline and escorted the dogs to the chute. Clara and Fred were jumping over each other in a crazed way. Rosalie escorted Pinny into starting position. But Pinny was in the nutcase zone, as Dave called it. She was aware of nothing except the trail before her.

"Dave Andersson, Jan's other half from Stormwatch Kennel. And we won't say which half—" People snickered and cheered.

"—from Bayfield, Wisconsin. Rosalie MacKenzie again, of Red Cliff, chief handler from Stormwatch, doing double duty."

The crowd roared again. Jan's mother stepped out to snap more photos.

Dave fidgeted with the compass bolted on the top of his sled handle. His dogs lunged in unison as the seconds ticked down.

"Five-four-three-two-one-go!" The starting gun sounded.

She released Pinny and they took off. Pinny ran as if her ass were on fire. They barreled down the chute.

Lorraine ran out and grabbed Rosalie's arm. "Good job, kiddo! Did you hear? You're a celebrity."

"Yeah, right, I'm a celebrity."

She pulled off the Stormwatch baseball cap and peeled up her damp bangs. Her ponytail had matted around the nape of her neck. She stuffed it all back into the cap and clipped on a pair of earmuffs to keep the hat in place.

"Hey—let me ride to the checkpoints with you," Lorraine said. "I got nothing better going on."

Rosalie frowned and gave her the finger through her mitten.

Lorraine flipped it back.

"I'll be out there about two days, maybe three," Rosalie qualified. "But someone'll give you a ride back to Duluth."

"Hey—maybe we'll meet those cute guys on the trail," she kidded. "You never know."

"Let's go; Highway Two checkpoint's a ninety-minute drive."

They drove to meet the Stormwatch teams all the way up to the Canadian border until Lorraine screamed, "You see one doggie butt, you've seen 'em all." They were at the midpoint, where the Gunflint Trail looped back the last two hundred miles to Duluth. They'd been sitting at a checkpoint in the kennel's portable chairs when Lorraine sat up. She smacked Rosalie's shoulder.

"Hey, isn't that Arlan? Look. Standing across the road?"

It was. He was straining to lift a dropped dog into the back of his truck. Arlan looked older and more bent than she recalled. A stoop was forming between his shoulders that she'd never noticed.

"Dad." He turned, looking at her in surprise.

Just then Dan Villieux climbed out of the passenger side. Thick black hair, five o'clock shadow, she could tell it was him by the way he moved. He awkwardly waved. She wondered whether to reciprocate but waved back nonetheless.

"Oh shit," Rosalie said in disgust.

Lorraine poked her shoulder. "Hh-h-h—isn't that Dan Villieux?"

Rosalie could think of nothing to say.

"God, I can't believe you know Dan Villieux," Lorraine said.

"I don't," Rosalie qualified. "He works with Arlan."

"Um-hum." Telltale sounds of Lorraine staking territory. She'd heard it hundreds of times at parties and bars. "Now that's someone I'd love to go out with."

Rosalie looked at her and blinked. "Tell me you're kidding."

"Him." Lorraine pointed with a lit cigarette. "That guy right there."

"We can't be talking about the same person."

Lorraine grasped Rosalie's head by the earmuffs, cigarette between her fingers, and manually turned it. "Look. That's Dan Villieux."

"Lor—he's a meatball."

"My high school fantasy." Lorraine drew on her cigarette as it glowed. "Knew his sister. I think he dropped out before it was legal—like in ninth grade or something."

Lorraine usually had better sense about men.

"Introduce me."

"I got stuff to do."

"Like what?" Lorraine exclaimed. She opened her arms, her giddy laugh fueled by the sudden shot glass of adrenaline.

Judging by the latest update, it would be at least another hour, possibly longer, before the front-runners even showed. All day the handlers sat bundled up in their chairs until their clothes smelled like campfire smoke. The race workers had already chatted through life stories, their involvement with every dog since childhood. A few nursed petty resentments after tiffs about politics, finally settling like old married people who were all talked out.

"Oh shit, don't look." Lorraine pitched the cigarette and pushed back her hood; her black permed hair tumbled out. "They're coming over." She rummaged through her purse. Pulling out a tube of mascara and a comb, she rushed behind the pickups to a parked snowmobile and darkened her lashes in its side mirror.

Rosalie snickered.

"Shut up," Lorraine sniped. She fished in her purse for lip gloss. "If you had any brains this would be you."

The last thing Rosalie wanted was to worry what she looked like. Not a stitch of makeup, and hair wadded up into a Storm-watch Kennel cap.

Lorraine pinched her cheeks and tore a comb through her hair. "Will you ask Arlan?" Lorraine cast anxious glances to where the two men had been stalled, chatting with volunteers.

"Ask him what? For a ride back to Duluth?" She knew what Lorraine was fishing for.

"That too," Lorraine said.

"Then what?" Rosalie teased.

"You know." Lorraine's eyes sparkled with whimsy. Wet mascara dotted the skin beneath her eyes. "If he's seeing anyone."

"No way." God forbid he think she was asking on her own behalf.

"Why not?"

"Because I don't think it's a good idea, Lor." Rosalie frowned. The two men were still talking with the trail workers.

Lorraine gave her a look that Rosalie hated. "I'd ask for you."

Rosalie sighed. *Shit.* Of course she would. Lorraine had taken Smokey that night, hid him as Jerry and Kurt were prowling the Reservation. She'd risked mixing it up with them as she waited for Franklin to arrive.

"Well, if it comes up."

"Make it come up. When you see Dan, get him talking."

"I don't see Dan; besides, he doesn't talk."

"I like quiet guys."

"You're impossible."

"You know I do," Lorraine insisted. The pitch of the last few words rose with a girly whine.

"I told you, he's a meatball."

Dan looked down as he approached. Lorraine made the same "doggie butt" joke after she asked Arlan for a ride. She then turned towards Dan; she cocked her head to the side and flipped her hair. *Good,* Rosalie thought. *Keep him occupied.* Dan was oblivious. Rosalie felt embarrassed as Lorraine kept chatting—a disproportionate investment of effort with pitiful return. Dan seemed like Pinny. A nervous but dominant dog who looks at everything other than what is before him.

Rosalie smiled, realizing how awful she looked and how little she cared. Puffy down jacket and bib snow pants like she wore when she was a kid. There was something honest about working with dogs. Times, hydration, heart rates, this was the stuff she craved. Knowing her job and doing it gave her a satisfaction she'd never felt before.

"Hi, Arlan," Rosalie greeted him.

"How are you?" Arlan asked.

They smiled at each other, both a bit embarrassed.

"I'm good. And you?"

He nodded.

"I miss you," Rosalie said.

"Me too."

They stepped towards each other and then hugged.

"I'm sorry I said those things," she said into his coat sleeve. Neither released their grip.

"I'm so sorry, missy."

"I know," she said. They released. "King's coming home this week; he can see."

"I know; Dave told me."

It felt good to smile for real. Her stomach rushed with excitement.

"Can I come home too?"

"Always."

"Thanks, Arlan."

He looked around to the other handlers.

"Anybody radio with dropped dogs?"

"Nope. Not that we've heard," someone called back.

"Okay . . . we're moving on then." Arlan signaled Dan. "Come on, Lorraine, you ready?"

The two men walked back towards the truck, Lorraine hurrying to catch their stride. Rosalie watched the three of them— Lorraine chatting as her hair flounced and hit the shoulder of Dan's coat. Then Dan turned. He glanced once over his shoulder at Rosalie in a way that made her flush.

It was 3 a.m. at the finish line. Rosalie leaned under the banner, waiting for the Stormwatch teams to cross into the parking lot at Billy's Bar. Finish times were clocked when the noses of the lead dogs crossed. In the event that a driverless team crossed the finish line, which was not uncommon, the finish time was calculated when the nose of the driver crossed.

Heavy snowflakes began falling. The clouds thick and low, pinkish in the glow cast from a lone streetlight. She looked for signs of her teams. Arlan said he'd be there, but most likely he slept through the alarm.

Earlier she was dozing inside Billy's Bar when the owner shook her arm. "Rosalie, they just clocked your Stormwatch teams right outside of town."

Outside it was silent. No traffic. Just Rosalie and the race official, who stood ready to clock finish times. They were both in a stupor from lost sleep. She spotted two headlamps softly glowing down the trail. Mounds of moving dogs were coming closer. She waved but didn't know if they could see her. The dogs' eyes reflected the solitary streetlight in ghostly blue and red glowing retinal orbs. Then came the tinkling of their dog tags as they trotted closer. The dogs spotted her and sped up, running towards her as she squatted, arms out to greet them.

The dogs had icicles dangling from their whiskers and chins, Dave and Jan crusted ice on the gaitors around their necks.

Such a peaceable finish, so unlike the frenzied start. Just people and dogs working together—no money, no glory. Just love of the dogs and the rush of watching them do what they love.

The race official checked his watch. He jotted down their times and took an official finish photo. Rosalie took out the Stormwatch camera and shot photos as Jan pulled her sled up next to Dave's team. Both Jan and Dave set their snow hooks more out of habit than imminent threat of a runaway team. Each moved slowly, their gestures heavy with fatigue.

"You guys look tired," Rosalie said. She crouched down as both teams surrounded her. They licked her face, nostrils. "The trucks are right here." She motioned to the lot. "Arlan helped me move them."

"Thanks," Jan said.

"Why don't you guys just go on inside," Rosalie said. "I'll get the dogs all set." She grabbed the gangline of Dave's team and led them over towards his truck.

"Thanks," Dave said.

The dogs looked too tired to eat. They seemed to long for their fresh straw–filled cubbies and sleep. She started to unhook them and watched Dave and Jan lumber towards each other in their heavy gear and boots, like astronauts taking their first few steps. They kissed and ambled towards Billy's Bar and the pancake breakfast no one was ever too tired to eat.

Here she was. Free of lingering doubts and fears. Jerry and the Frosty Tip all seemed so alien, as if having belonged to someone else's little miniseries drama. The future was open. With her first race behind her, she'd done everything they asked and more. At each checkpoint Jan and Dave had greeted her in a way that said they were pleased. They could count on her. And now soon she'd be home with Smokey. King too would be home in a matter of days. Just for an instant, her life lay before her like some bright beautiful thing.

CHAPTER 22

Arlan coaxed her with a breakfast of honey bacon and eggs, but she wasn't hungry. She sat at the kitchen table in her coat waiting for Jan. King was ready to come home.

Arlan's National Weather Service radio blared from the table.

"Tanker's caught in the ice," Arlan repeated as if she couldn't hear it herself. "Hull's crumpling." He mimicked the steel with his hand. "Seventy miles off Saxon Harbor."

Smokey sat in begging position under the table.

"First you see flaking paint." Arlan's green eyes pulsed. "Even before a dent." Arlan grasped the table as if steadying himself aboard the doomed ship, his half-eaten meal in front of him.

"Good thing we don't live on a houseboat."

He frowned at her lack of compassion.

"Betcha it's foreign—no one's out this time of year."

Usually the deeper waters of Superior remained open, though every twenty years or so the whole thing froze. Experienced captains knew how to read the signs.

"How come Dan keeps coming around for dinner?"

She'd lost Arlan to the unfolding maritime drama.

"Past few nights he shows up like some stray," she pushed.

"So what."

"He gives me the creeps."

Arlan made a face.

"How come he's never come over before?"

He turned his ear to the radio, hungry for details.

"Why now?

"Play-offs."

"Can't he watch them somewhere else? He's gotta eat over too?"

"You buying groceries or something?" Arlan peered at her sharply, irritated by the interruption.

She looked out the window. "It's just weird all of a sudden, that's all."

"It's nice having people around." He looked at her. "You don't hear me bellyaching about Lorraine showing up for meals."

"Lorraine's family." Not to mention calling in a favor. As promised, Rosalie had phoned on the sly at Dan sightings.

The clipped military style of the weather announcer's speech warned of another Alberta Clipper, an arctic front. Arlan brushed aside the gritty mix of salt and tiny white seed pearls scattered on the blue-checked plastic tablecloth.

"He's just weird." She squirmed. "Just sits there, doesn't even talk, like a ghost or something. He's so still—it's spooky."

"He's a good man," Arlan said in a compensatory way.

"What's that supposed to mean?" She glared back.

"Hey." He turned and raised his voice. "None of us comes gift wrapped."

He stared her down as if to end the debate.

"My ride's here." She stood, relieved at Jan's truck creeping towards the house.

It was almost dark that afternoon when Jan dropped them off. All the way from Minneapolis, King had tried to scratch; only shredded chicken distracted him. His entire face had been shaved and was itching like crazy.

Smokey greeted him; their tails swished. King lowered his face and Smokey sniffed thoughtfully. He took particular interest in the missing eye and sewn-together lids. Once satisfied, Smokey hopped back up onto the couch in his spot. King jumped up onto the other end.

"Look at you!" she exclaimed, and squatted to eye-level.

King's ears pinched back in a cheeky grin. He awkwardly tromped in circles, stepping high before settling. Husky feet were legendary. They could feel down through to the bottom of a trail to determine if it was solid. King mirrored Smokey as if they'd been doing so for decades.

"*Now* where am I gonna sit?" she said in a funny voice, delighted that King made himself at home. "You guys are bookends."

He rubbed his face on the cushion and sniffed—luxuriating in the comfort of familiar smells. Stretching his nose towards Rosalie, he peered at her with his one eye. He was a different animal.

Arlan's truck pulled up followed by another. Smokey and King sprang up, paws on the windowsill, each silently on guard.

"Whoa." Arlan stepped inside chuckling. "You'd be nuts to break into this place now. Impressive to see both of 'em up at the window like that." Arlan smelled of the cold. He pulled off his hat and held the door for Dan, who carried a monster-sized tub of KFC and a white bag of condiments.

"Dan brought dinner tonight," Arlan announced.

"Hi." She looked down to hide her smile.

Dan breezed past.

"So where's Lorraine?" Arlan asked.

"Working." It was her late day, otherwise she'd be draped on the La-Z-Boy. She'd get a kick out of the KFC.

"Dan brought enough for a crowd," Arlan said. Dan gazed at the window.

"She'll be here soon."

Arlan knelt. "Hey you." He peered into King's eye as he scratched the dog's chin. "He can really see."

"Yep."

"Kinda scary how he looks right into you, don't he though?" Arlan turned to Rosalie. She raised her eyebrows and slowly nodded. "Looks like he's winking." Arlan chuckled.

Dan crouched too. He held out his hand. King looked away. "Asshole." Dan stood, shaking his head.

"You two gents got a 'thing.'" Arlan shook his head, remembering the parking lot. "Bumped into Noreen filling up the truck—"

"Don't tell me—" She held out her hands. "Another husky, right?"

Arlan looked stunned. "She called?"

"Nope." Rosalie laughed mysteriously. "There's a lot I know," she teased.

Dan's eyes were on her face. She never knew a person to be so still, like he'd stopped breathing. Everyone's jeans were permanently soiled from outside work, where Dan's were crisply blue with a crease. Who wore jeans with a crease? Calluses were infused with eternal grime that resisted all manner of scrubbing. Dan's hands and nails were startlingly well groomed, even more so than Dave's.

She checked her watch. Time for King's meds. Lifting a bottle of eyedrops, she moved towards the dog.

"Need help?" Arlan asked.

She was done before he finished the question.

"Jeez." Arlan pulled back. "You're good at that."

"I do it all the time at Stormwatch. The old ones."

Dan was watching. Hard to believe he worked the same job as Arlan. Even harder to figure out why Arlan thought so highly of Dan. He was so out of place standing in their cluttered kitchen. She moved quickly to clear off the counter, only dishes were already piled to the faucet. The garbage smelled. She was annoyed with Arlan for not cleaning up. The living room seemed shabbier than just this morning. The couch rattier along with the living room rug. Towers of Arlan's old *National Geographics*. How shameful to be embarrassed of one's home. It made her dislike Dan even more.

"Noreen says it's a young female." Arlan was as eager as a kid. "She also says they're full." They both knew what that meant. "We could just look."

"Oh right, Arlan." She glanced at Dan, offering him a chance to poke fun at her father. He didn't take it.

She loved it when Arlan looked sheepish. The gentle way he'd totter over to Smokey and fork over half his dinner and then later scold her for doing the same. Talking to Smokey like some grandpa. Ever since the race, it was clear just how lonely he was.

"We don't *have* to take her—"

"Oh hush, Arlan." Smokey bumped her thigh with his nose, hurrying to the back door. The whites of his eyes reeled as if to say, "Hurry."

She tied him out and then came back in. Getting the fence up in spring would be heaven. The snowy bundles of chain link lay dormant. The yard still delineated by Arlan's bright markers. Everything, save the season, was set to go. She dreamed of Smokey and King chasing each other and not just cabled to a foundation post to "do their business." And though still cold, the winds smelled of change. Fresh air on her face the past few mornings was a sign that winter was breaking.

"Figured you'd want your own team and all," Arlan offered.

She smiled and said nothing. It was *he* who wanted the dog.

Arlan pointed. "You wouldn't smile like that if it wasn't true." He counted on her saying yes.

The truth was she had everything she wanted. Not one spare minute left each day after Stormwatch and beading. Tired like Smokey after a good, hard run. Waking up with purpose, a place to go each morning, somewhere she belonged. The two of them climbed into the truck and were off. Soon King would join them. At this point they could get the dog or not. She didn't want to see the husky euthanized, but there were hundreds of dogs out there. She couldn't take them all.

"Go ahead and blame me—you're such a softy," she said.

As he smiled she noticed his wrinkles were deeper than most men his age. It had hurt his pride when he was no longer able to work the pulp boiler on the main floor, his spine in full rebellion against that kind of abuse. After hobbling home for months on end, sleeping on two strategically placed heating pads, he finally relented and transferred to packing and shipping. She'd watched as he developed that "bent-over look" that comes from a life-time of the wrong type of work—the kind that wears you out long before you're old.

Smokey signaled with one sharp bark. She opened the door.

"Do you need to call Noreen?" she asked.

Arlan smirked and raised the hand with his Timex.

"Oh—so she's waiting." She laughed, shaking her head.

He turned to Dan. Keys jingled from his pocket like a question mark. She winced as if bracing for a balloon to burst. *Don't ask him.*

"You up for this?" Arlan asked.

"Sure," Dan confirmed.

Damn Lorraine for having to work late. They could have left the lovebirds together and gone to get the dog.

Smokey and King sat at attention before the KFC on the counter. They concentrated as if it were possible to command a chicken part into their mouths through the sheer power of will. One long string of drool streamed like a silken thread from Smokey's lips, so fine it was barely noticeable.

"You guys want a sister?"

They looked eager, convinced it was all about a drumstick.

"Thanks for bringing food, Dan," she said.

She wasn't sure he heard.

Smokey and King looked bereft as she moved the tub of chicken safely on top of the refrigerator.

"Dan?" she said. "Thanks."

She snapped her fingers under his nose. "Da-a-n?" she said in singsong. As she neared, a jolt of sexual heat rushed through her. Her stomach fluttered. The skin on the side of his neck looked warm; she could have pressed her lips to it. Pulling back, she snuck a glance at Arlan, hoping he hadn't seen.

"Earth to Dan." She meant it to be funny, but it came out mean.

She felt Arlan's disapproval from where he stood by the door. Her face felt hot. How embarrassing to be flirting in front of her father.

Dan blinked several times, seemingly perplexed. He shrugged, as if to indicate the KFC was no big deal.

"Be right back," she assured the dogs. Both were more stricken by the disappearance of the chicken bucket than her departure. She took full advantage to slip on King's plastic Elizabethan collar, relieved she didn't have to chase him around the room.

Noreen met them at the door in blue scrubs, stethoscope hooked like a necklace.

"Gosh, Arlan." Noreen laughed once she unlocked the shelter door. She winked. "Now *that* was fast." Noreen gestured to a row of mismatched padded kitchen chairs. Pieces of yellow foam protruded from the corners.

"I'll get Bella."

"Bella," Rosalie repeated the name to herself.

Noreen's closely cropped blond hair looked freshly dyed from a recent trip to the Frosty Tip. Rosalie wished that she and Arlan would get together—same age, good friends. Thursday mornings they'd meet at the Log Cabin for the town meeting and then later for bingo and a pork-chop dinner at the Isle Vista Casino in Red Cliff. The two would sit chatting, long after the others left. They never seemed to run out of things to say as they'd sit drinking coffee. Noreen doted on him, adding just the right amount of cream. Arlan soaked it up like a dry sponge.

Index cards and signs were pinned to a bulletin board—lost cats, dogs and a missing turtle that most likely had scrambled back into the Lake.

Noreen reappeared with a tall, well-marked gray and white husky who immediately sought their attention. The dog had one brightly pigmented blue eye and another amber colored. Bi-eyed, it was called. Tufts of fur spiked off her shoulders like molting feathers. Her top line and back legs looked ragged, comically so. The dog was blowing her winter coat though it was only February.

"This is Bella."

"Bella," Rosalie repeated. The dog looked squarely at her. Bella was like a ballerina with long white prancing legs, a beautiful graceful stride, and a lovely guileless smile. "Hey, girlie, whatcha here for?" she asked. The dog licked Rosalie's nostrils and began to rapidly sniff her clothing. Bella's pupils dilated as she took a particularly keen interest in the soles of Rosalie's boots.

"'Chewed vinyl siding off the back of the owner's house,'" Noreen began to read the owner surrender form, the Rap Sheet, as she called it. Bella just smiled brightly and swished her tail. "'Ate off the top layer of linoleum when confined to the kitchen.'"

"Dog sounds hungry." Arlan was smitten. "We got tons of chicken waiting, Bella." The sound of her name prompted a wag. Bella had a happy-go-lucky resilience. Unlike the shy, sensitive Smokey and the dignified, reserved King, who'd never learned how to play. Bella was carefree.

Dan crouched. Bella looked up adoringly.

"Looks like she likes you," Rosalie remarked.

Dan smiled and scratched Bella's chin. "Yeah, maybe," he said.

"It's good *someone* does," she poked fun, her voice softer this time.

By his gentle smile she guessed he'd gotten the joke, though he didn't volley back or acknowledge.

Another frown of disapproval shot from Arlan. She batted her eyes in an exaggerated way and shrugged "just kidding."

A wide mask surrounded Bella's eyes; copper shading marked her hind legs and front shoulders. Each eye was outlined with what looked like black eyeliner.

"Ran away so many times they surrendered her," Noreen continued. "With chronic runners or repeat offenders as we call 'em, fines can get steep." Noreen smiled as she looked at the dog. "Their ten-year-old's all broken up. Keeps calling, wants to make sure we find her a home."

They watched the dog walking about.

"Lots of Northern dogs named Houdini. It's getting harder to place them 'cause they run. It's too bad too. Most are just good old souls." She looked at Bella and sighed. If only cars and roads didn't exist. Or the tempting smells of domestic livestock, not to mention the propensity of rural residents to shoot strays.

Arlan lifted his green plastic checkbook.

Noreen nodded. "She's not spayed now, Arlan, so it's an extra seventy-five. Bring me her spay certificate from Charlie next week, you'll get it back."

"Fair enough."

Lorraine's truck was parked at an angle when they got back. Smokey and King greeted Bella at the door. After all the obligatory sniffing, Bella dropped down into a play bow. Her front paws splayed out, hindquarters up in the air. Smokey reciprocated. The two of them romped through the tiny cabin until the coat-rack crashed against the front door. Smokey darted into Rosalie's bedroom. Bella chased after him and licked his face. He flipped over, submitting as if he were her puppy.

King was not so effusive. He stood rigid and reared back a bit, his front legs stiff. Tail straight up, wagging stiffly, he was skeptical of this ingénue. He strove to be nonchalant as Bella sniffed his shaved face, missing eye and then every part of his manhood. His ears lay flat as if rubber-banded into a ponytail. He growled as she sniffed his lips. His resistance egged her on. She nibbled deeply into his thick chest fur, showering him with wolf kisses. He glanced at Rosalie, seemingly for help. Bella clamped down on his tail. She shook it furiously, trying to get him to play. He finally snapped back. She dodged, dancing millimeters beyond his reach. The sound of his teeth snapping was chilling.

"Whoa ho." Arlan chuckled with a newfound respect. "Don't be getting him angry."

It was totally engaging. There was a loud crunch as Arlan attacked a chicken thigh, wiping grease off his lips. Dan tipped back an amber-colored bottle of beer, allowing it to pour down his gullet.

"I swear she's flirting," Lorraine said. She fixed her eyes on Rosalie as if she'd better do something. "Did Noreen say anything about her going into heat?"

Rosalie shook her head. "Don't you think she would have mentioned it?"

"Maybe she missed it," Lorraine interrupted.

"Noreen doesn't miss things like that," Rosalie said.

"Maybe you should call her, Arlan." Lorraine looked at him.

So now Lorraine knew everything about dogs. Rosalie was getting angry.

"Hey—fine." Lorraine crossed her arms. "Have a litter of puppies, see if I care."

Lorraine looked away. She leaned on the counter mirroring Dan, pushing her elbow against his. Rosalie caught the gesture. Her chest tightened. It felt like anger but more confusing.

"Next week we're getting her spayed," Arlan broke the silence.

"Next week'll be too late once she's knocked up, Arlan." Lorraine looked at Rosalie. "Okay, so now you're the 'dog woman'; I get it," she conceded as if washing her hands of the whole thing. "I'm not telling you what to do. I've just been around enough dogs to know something's up."

Bella hopped on King and started humping.

The room was electric. Rosalie tried to catch Lorraine's eye to call a truce but couldn't. The men glanced at each other as they picked their teeth.

"Another beer, Dan?" Arlan stepped away to fish out two bottles from the refrigerator. He grabbed the magnetic can opener from the door. Bottle caps pinged on the countertop in rapid succession.

Lorraine took a chicken thigh out of the bucket. The dogs were too preoccupied with each other to even beg.

King looked mortally embarrassed as Bella wouldn't leave him alone.

"Good," Dan muttered. He smiled in a lazy way after he took a sip of his beer. Reveling at seeing the arrogant dog knocked down a few pegs by this flirty wisp of a girl.

King sought refuge behind Dan's leg, but he hopped out of the way.

"Oh no, buddy boy," Dan said. "You're on your own with her, pal." Bella continued in her playful ministrations to Smokey and unrelenting in her teasing pursuit of King.

Late that night sharp cries made Rosalie bolt up onto her feet. *Detached retina. Damn.* The surgeon had warned of the risk; cage rest was mandated. She should have borrowed Jan's cage, but she'd been confident she could keep him quiet. All the excitement with Bella was too much. She should have known better; they should have waited to get Bella. Noreen would have understood.

Rosalie raced to the kitchen, expecting to find him pawing his face in agony. Where could she take him this time of night? She'd call Charlie at home. Jan had his number. Start a morphine drip to dull it. Drive back down to Minneapolis early that next morning.

She flipped on the light. To her horror, Bella and King were tied together in a mating—plastic Elizabethan collar and all. Any residual post-operative discomfort hadn't deterred him from doing the deed, as Arlan called it. Rosalie stood, mortified. Arlan appeared beside her.

"Guess Lorraine was right," he said. The words stung.

"Holy shit, holy shit," she cried, pulling on the skin of her face, prancing around the kitchen.

Lorraine had called it first, though she'd seen it too. This was her stubbornness of not wanting to be shown up in front of Dan—now wait until they both found out.

Jan warned to be on the lookout for silent heats. Each female's cycle was tracked so they could be separated before an accidental breeding occurred. Breeding was carefully planned; there were never enough homes and the fate of dogs hung in the balance. She should have cordoned off Bella in her bedroom, called Noreen like Lorraine said. At Stormwatch she could have been fired for such an oversight.

It took fifteen minutes for the dogs to separate.

"Guess we'll need a bigger yard now," Arlan kidded. "You okay?" She didn't answer. Her hands still covered her face. She remained frozen since the initial shock. "Nothing you can do now," he said. "Might as well get some sleep." He gave up and headed back to bed.

What stupidity had stopped her from agreeing with Lorraine? Lorraine—her unwavering friend since second grade. The day after Anna Marie had been killed, seven-year-old Lorraine hiked three miles through woods and steep ravines to console her friend. She knocked on the door to ask in a child's universal gesture of comfort, "Wanna play?" Why would she think that Lorraine would sabotage her life? It seemed crazy now, yet only hours ago it felt so real. And then the dirty secret rose up. She was jealous.

Noreen couldn't apologize enough about the "silent heat." She refunded the seventy-five dollars and offered to take the dog back. Arlan would have none of it but accepted a home-cooked meal as consolation.

CHAPTER 23

"Charlie wants to talk," Dave called over the hum of his warming truck.

"About what?" she called back. It was two days after the accidental breeding. It couldn't be good.

"I'll let Charlie tell you."

She knew Charlie was coming that morning to check on Mitzi's lameness.

"He'll be here any minute." Dave glanced at his watch. His face was serious, not his usual jovial self. Dressed for morning hospital rounds, he wore mushing boots with his dress pants.

"Is it bad?" she called.

But he'd already climbed into his truck. The backup lights lit the ground.

She pulled on her bangs, twisting a section as she began to ruminate. Maybe they'd lost confidence after she fessed up about the accidental breeding. She prefaced it by insisting that she *had* recognized Bella's behavior.

"And you didn't separate the dogs because . . . ?" Jan asked pointedly, waiting for a good answer.

"Because I'm an idiot?" She laughed bitterly.

"Beating yourself up won't help." Jan hadn't thought it funny. "The more you act on intuition the stronger it gets. Someday it might save your life." Jan looked at the dogs. "They're born listening. So are we. But we have to remember."

Getting reprimanded by Charlie, or even fired, might be the price for having gotten cocky.

Only yesterday Fred had wriggled loose and bolted. Chasing

him across the highway, she hadn't even looked for cars. She tackled him in a field of winter wheat after he stopped to pee. The week before, she failed to break up a fight. Sweetie's ear got shredded. She'd noted the eerie way Stinko had moved but didn't act to stop him.

Waiting for Charlie was torture. At least he'd get right to the point. Dave usually did too; it was odd how he left her dangling like that. Her stomach squeezed beneath her ribs. Jan was out of earshot on the far side of the kennel, letting out the old dogs. Rosalie paced and darted looks at the driveway, then immersed herself in the morning feeding.

A thin strip of red sky ignited the hills. Entering the out-building, she mixed food, loaded it onto the drag sled and began pulling it to the yards. Her wind pants swished as she walked. The last group of dogs finished just as the Dreamcatcher truck pulled in. She tossed the empty bowls onto the sled and latched the gate. The empty bowls clinked together.

Charlie called as soon as he saw her.

"Hey, you wanna go grab Mitzi for me?" He lowered himself carefully down from the truck. "Bring her out here," he barked. "My back's killing me." She was too nervous to divine anything except he was grumpier than usual.

She rushed back and clipped a leash on Mitzi. A few others howled with jealousy. It wasn't fair that Mitzi got to have all the fun.

Charlie motioned to set the dog on the picnic table so he wouldn't have to bend. She cleared off a gangline with broken snaps, lifted and set Mitzi down. She restrained the dog but leaned away as if Charlie might bite.

He touched Mitzi's elbow. The dog squirmed away. Charlie stepped back, hands on hips. "What the hell's with you today?" he groused. "You gonna hold the dog or not?" He looked sharply over the rims of his glasses.

"Sorry." She adjusted so that Mitzi had no room to wriggle. She began owning up to the accidental breeding, thinking it might soften his reproach.

"Big deal," Charlie cut her off before she had the satisfaction of a full confession. "You make it sound like she got hit by a truck, for Christ sakes," he said in his quit-your-whining voice. "So she'll have a litter of puppies in sixty-three days—it's not the end of the goddamned world."

Now she was confused. Not the reaction she'd thought.

"You learned. Right?" He looked at her.

She nodded.

"Okay—so what's the problem?" Charlie had no tolerance for histrionics. "Sometimes breedings don't take anyway."

"Really?" She hadn't known.

"*What are you, deaf?*" He glared over his glasses.

"When would I know?"

"Maybe next month. Maybe the night she whelps."

"Great," she muttered.

"It varies."

"By what?"

"By dog," he said to the ground. He stood, delicately feeling the bones in Mitzi's rear paw.

"Okay." He signaled for them to change places. She clipped Mitzi's leash to the table, and he grabbed the dog's collar. She began to examine the next paw. Charlie instructed her on how each bone should feel. The week before he lent her one of his veterinary anatomy books. She'd begun memorizing the bones in a dog's foot. She named each bone and joint as she touched it. He nodded in approval, correcting the few she reversed or mispronounced. It was amazing how such delicate bones, like handles of fine china teacups, could be so strong.

Charlie was impossible to read. He had infinite patience for showing how to give injections or fluids under the skin. Anything personal and he turned a deaf ear; she'd asked Dave if maybe Charlie needed a hearing aid.

"Start checking your own dogs," his voice softened. "With this litter, you can immunize them. Next year start running your own team."

Why did everyone think that was such a great idea? Smokey had fun with the Stormwatch dogs. He'd become a contender for one of next year's Beargrease teams. As soon as she got an okay from the surgeon, King would take over as lead dog to train the yearlings. He was used to running seventy-five-mile legs during a race. Good lead dogs tolerated no monkey business on the trail. She could picture him giving the icicle eye at the slightest whiff of insubordination.

She mustered the courage to ask.

"Dave said you, uh, wanted to talk to me?" Her voice creaked as she braced for impact.

"Oh yeah. How 'bout riding along with me on afternoon calls?" Charlie blurted out.

"Uh-h-h—ride along?" she stammered, not sure what was being asked.

He motioned for them to switch back so he could finish examining Mitzi. "I'll match what Jan and Dave pay."

It was more like an order than a job offer.

"Hey, you want a job or not?" he gruffed.

Mitzi yelped just as he located the tender spot in her elbow. He glared over his glasses.

"Uh-h-h—I guess." With the race season winding down, she was finished with kennel duties by noon.

"You guess. Rozzie, which is it?" He let go of the dog and watched Rosalie's expression. His eyes gleamed. "You need cash for more dog food, I need a good assistant."

A good assistant.

"I mean, yes. I want the job."

"Holy God—try and get a straight answer out of you." His voice was brusque, but his eyes were smiling.

She looked down at Mitzi's paw.

"Start next week. Give your Social to Helen; she'll put you on the payroll. I'll pick you up here, Monday through Friday, after you're done for the day. Leave Smokey and King; you can get them after we're done," he explained. Then he turned. "Hey, Jan," he called over to where Jan was shoveling off the front steps. "Your handler's working afternoons with me."

Jan paused and shrugged like "she's all yours."

"Mitzi's got a bit of tendonitis," he called to her. "Right elbow, like you thought. Rest her a week. It should clear up."

Jan nodded.

Rushing to gather up his stethoscope, Charlie crammed gear into his vet carrier. He forced the compartments to snap shut. "Son of a bitch," he cursed.

As she made sense of the job offer, Rosalie squealed, "Oh thank you, thank you and thank you!" Jumping up and down, she tapped Charlie's sleeve but then stifled it as he frowned in annoyance.

Another new job had fallen into Rosalie's lap. She had butterflies in her stomach. The makings of a new world were taking shape.

She set Mitzi down. The dog began trying to drag the table.

"Arlan working tonight?"

She shook her head.

"Why don't you two come over for dinner?" he said as he hurried off. "Meet a good friend of mine. Jan'll tell you more about it. They're coming over too. About six."

She smiled at the invitation. "Okay."

"And tell that damn father of yours to bring some decent beer for a change. None of that Pabst crap." She studied his face. Since when had Arlan been to Charlie's? She watched him load gear and then rushed to help, shutting the tailgate of his truck. He climbed in and drove off without as much as a wave. This time it didn't even hurt her feelings.

Jan began to cook them breakfast. She filled Rosalie in on Charlie's long, distinguished mushing career. He'd bred and raced several generations of his own dogs; mixing them with

Siberian village dogs he inherited from his longtime mentor and buddy, Bob Ramsay. Together, the two men bred a line of dogs that were virtually unbeatable.

Charlie supported his "habit," through his vet practice—spaying, neutering, annual shots, squeezing anal glands. Helen worked as a bookkeeper for a local fish-processing plant on the shore of the Bering Sea. They'd scrimp and save, any sacrifice to eke out a living and come up with money for dog food and race entry fees. Living in a remote area on the shore; Helen claimed she didn't mind. Charlie thought it a mystery that she stayed. But Helen was no fool. Who wants a husband who's grounded at a desk job? Though only in her early thirties at the time, she had the good sense to know there are some loves against which a person can't compete.

"They moved back six years ago after the last of his dogs died." Jan set a plate of eggs down on the counter in front of Rosalie.

"Thanks, Jan."

"No prob. So back they moved," Jan continued. "For the past six years the Dreamcatcher Veterinary Clinic has been the only vet within sixty miles of Bayfield. Helen manages the clinic with an iron fist, but Charlie's a sap."

It was hard to think of Charlie as a sap. Rosalie tried to imagine it as she shook pepper on her eggs.

"He drives thirty miles one way to examine an elderly lady's fifteen-year-old cat with a urinary tract infection," Jan explained. "Knowing full well he'd never recoup gas money, much less the cost of the meds. It's what Helen loves about him yet wants to wring his neck at the same time."

She went on to announce that, for the first time, Robert Ramsay was coming to visit. Dave and Jan met him in Alaska the year before. Ramsay was a legend in Alaskan mushing circles, having helped organize the first Iditarod, Yukon Quest and many other great distance races. Ramsay's wife died that past summer. Charlie finally talked him into visiting after the Yukon Quest. This would be the first Iditarod Ramsay would sit out since its inception. At eighty-five, he was cutting back.

When she relayed Charlie's message about the beer Arlan had a good laugh.

It was dark by six. The carton of Pabst Blue Ribbon resting on her thighs made her cold. Snowflakes were cotton in the headlights. She'd never been inside Charlie's log home. It was on the same property as the Dreamcatcher clinic, only a short walk across a field. At the time they purchased the practice from old Doc Hanson, Charlie thought the location ideal. Helen thought it too ideal, afraid he'd always be working. She was right.

"Haven't been to their new place since they moved back," Arlan said as they turned into the clinic driveway. Jan and Dave were already there. "They used to have a place on Blueberry Road. Your ma and I used to go over all the time," he said. She looked at him. "You were little, probably don't remember."

Arlan looked younger, sadder and different after he said it. He rarely mentioned Anna Marie. Whenever he did it made Rosalie sad, not so much for herself but for the life her father could never seem to regenerate.

A fire roared in Charlie's fireplace, a rock wall all the way up to the ceiling. Post and beam construction overhead. Drawings of hawks and horses were framed on the walls, mostly gifts from owners, Helen explained. Hangings of feathers and strips of leather, also gifts from potlatch ceremonies and grateful owners.

Rosalie vowed right then to make a beaded wall hanging for Charlie and Helen as a "giveaway" to thank them. She pictured it hanging up on the rock wall. At Jan's house Charlie would stop and comment on the one she'd given Jan. In a flash, she got the whole design—an eagle in flight with beaded and quill wings. She had time between Guild projects. She'd finish it and present it to him that first Monday on the job. She smiled— imagining Charlie's face when he'd open the bundle.

Two mismatched love seats and chairs formed a semi-circle around the fire. In the kitchen, the table was covered with dishes of venison, wild rice and cranberry casserole. A large salad was identifiably Jan's along with a couple of her uncut pies.

Arlan set the six-pack of Pabst onto the table in a way as to attract Charlie's attention.

"Uch, Arlan." Charlie laughed in disgust. "Get with the program."

Then with his other hand, Arlan set a six-pack of Leinenkugel onto the counter.

"Now you're talking, old man." Charlie got up and went over.

It was the first time Rosalie remembered meeting Helen. The woman handed her a plate and gestured to the table.

"Last time I saw you, you were this big." Helen held a hand to her hip to illustrate.

Rosalie smiled and shrugged.

"I grew up with your mom. In the same class through high school." Helen moved to hug her.

Rosalie shyly hugged back.

"You look so much like her," Helen said. "We were in Alaska when she passed. Always felt so sad about that. We hadn't a cent back then. I'm so happy you agreed to work with Charlie."

"Me too," Rosalie said.

"He's never had an assistant." She motioned towards him with her head.

"No one can stand him," an older man Rosalie assumed was Bob Ramsay called from the couch. Everyone laughed.

"True," Helen said, and they all snickered, including Charlie. "But it's high time he admits he needs help."

Rosalie began loading up her plate.

"Don't take any crap from him," Ramsay warned.

Charlie smirked from where he sat, smiling into the fire.

"Look at him." Ramsay gestured. "He knows it too."

Ramsay's skin looked like animal hide crinkled into diamond shape. His cheeks and nose were red from windburn. He'd just come off of ten days on the Yukon Quest trail, he explained. His white hair was scant and his eyes a pale watery blue. So kind, so open. His hands were crusty and callused, the tops wrinkled and spotted. His fingers twisted like savannah oak limbs from arthritis. Yet as he walked over to sit next to her, she was struck by how Ramsay moved with the energy and agility of a much younger man.

"So tell me about yourself, Rosalie. I wanna see if Charlie's lying." Ramsay said it loud enough to elicit another smirk.

She laughed, immediately at ease, and began eating. Dave joined in, giving a full account of her facility with dogs and mushing.

"We're hoping she'll join us in Alaska next March," Dave said. Everyone looked at her. "We qualified."

Rosalie's mouth dropped.

Jan nodded and smiled.

"If you're willing to come and work as our official handler, that is," Dave said.

"Hell, I'd do it for free," she said. She looked at Arlan.

Charlie perked up. "She said she'd work for free; you're all witnesses."

"Sh-h-h." Ramsay held a finger to his lips. "Never say you'll work for free," he joked. "He's one cheap bastard."

Rosalie told him about Smokey and Bella. As soon as she mentioned King, Ramsay stopped eating.

"Charlie told me about that dog. Bet you a beer it's one of mine. Think I sold the guy a pup three years back at a Quest," Ramsay said, studying her face. "Small world, eh?" He looked at Charlie. "I remember the litter. Bred that line full circle. Mind if I come have a look?"

Rosalie nodded.

"Watch he doesn't try to steal the dog back," Charlie ribbed. "He's done that."

Ramsay watched as Rosalie began to eat.

"So Bob, why don't you tell Rosalie the story of how you came into dogs?" Jan suggested as they all sat eating.

He began telling of how he and his brother moved to Alaska from Cincinnati when neither was quite twenty. "Was my mother's fault, you know," Ramsay started. "Made us read Jack London books all summer to keep us from stealing neighborhood bikes and getting into all kinds of shit."

"Talk about a failed strategy," Charlie muttered.

"Mom became a schoolteacher after my father died in the First World War. Johnny and I left high school, headed west to see the ocean." He switched his seat, moving away from the fire. "Broke Mom's heart, she had such high hopes. Camped on the beach in California for months, worked and saved every penny. People used to do that, just camp," he explained to Rosalie. "Once we made carfare, we took the train up north. Mountains, ocean—we were done for. We got into shitloads of trouble in Anchorage. Mostly fighting."

Charlie raised his beer to toast.

Ramsay continued. "We watched our first Alaskan Sweepstakes and were hooked. Bribed a bush pilot with bootleg alcohol to fly us in since property on the Bering Sea was free if you survived the first winter." The brothers figured: what better way to get oceanfront property?

"Everyone was saying that the best dogs came from Siberia, so we paid an Inuit guide to take us sixty miles across to where we'd heard you could trade for a couple of fast lead dogs."

Ramsay paused, thinking before he spoke.

"So in '29 we crossed with two of his dog teams. He brought us to a village and a Siberian woman. Name was Jeaantaa." He paused. "She gave us a whole team plus young pups. Wasn't a long trip."

Rosalie looked up from her plate to see him overcome with emotion. He looked embarrassed.

"Sorry," he whispered. He held his fist up to his mouth and coughed. He cleared his throat several times. Rosalie watched as he worked to calm himself.

The joking subsided. His voice was serious and soft as he began to tell the story. "So this young woman tells us to come back next morning. So we hide. Russkies all over the place. Poor young, miserable bastards." He laughed with a generosity that time affords.

"Cold, thin, they had this dazed look. I can see them like it was yesterday," he said. "Felt sorrier for them than anything else. Then the Inuit guide ditched us."

"He ditched you?" Rosalie asked.

"Um-hum," Ramsay said. "Left us a team to get back."

"Why'd he ditch you?" she demanded.

"Got spooked, all the killing."

"Killing?" she asked.

"Figured maybe they couldn't tell him apart."

"Who?" she asked.

Ramsay looked at her with a funny expression. "Aren't we sitting on Indian land? Russians were doing the same thing to these people, just like they did here. Especially there, right across the Bering from the U.S."

"True," she said.

Jan stood up to cut the pies and begin serving.

"So we show up the next day. She gives us, including pups, thirty dogs hooked and loaded on the most beautiful sled. I still have the thing," Ramsay said, and looked at Rosalie. "You come to Nome I'll show it to you."

"It's incredible," Jan said. "Belongs in a natural history museum."

They all nodded.

"So the Army chases us, but those dogs run like crazy." He gestured, like he still can't believe it. His watery eyes were blazing.

"Bastards shot me." He patted the back of his shoulder as a point of pride. "Son of a bitch's still in there. Whole shoulder blade aches when it rains."

He stopped and looked at Rosalie. "You know that one-eyed dog you got?"

She nodded.

"He's a descendant," Ramsay said. "That woman's face. Shook me to the core. Here Johnny and me are joyriding on this adventure, looking for a couple of fast dogs, and we stumble on this woman who's running for her life."

He sat thinking for a few moments. "I tell you one thing—it killed her to give away her dogs." He paused and leaned forward to rest his elbows on his knees. "I might have been a young knucklehead at the time, but a person knows such things. Might as well have given me her heart."

He looked down. "And her hands. She was so tiny, yet I remember those hands." He held up his hands. "Strong. How a woman like that, small as a child, can handle those dogs . . ."

They'd all finished eating, balancing empty plates on their knees.

Rosalie looked at the floor. Her face flushed.

Ramsay shook his head. "Offered to take her with us." It seemed his voice would break. He paused and tipped back an amber beer bottle. "Guess that's not what she wanted. But I tell you one thing." He paused and looked around at all of them. "*That* woman was the face of courage."

No one spoke. Only the fire crackled. Charlie stood and threw in another log. They waited for Ramsay.

"What did she look like?" Rosalie asked. Her voice seemed to startle them as a log popped and sputtered.

"Gosh, Roz." Jan chuckled in surprise. "You say that like you just bumped into her at the Kwik Trip ten minutes ago."

They laughed.

Ramsay described her without taking his eyes off of Rosalie. She was quiet for a while. "It's just a coincidence"—she looked around as if having second thoughts—"but I swear I've seen her in dreams."

"I have too," Ramsay said. Their eyes met.

The room was still. Rosalie didn't know where to rest her eyes. She looked at her plate and then at the fire. Her eyes settled on Ramsay. He smiled.

"Maybe she's trying to tell you something," Charlie said.

She looked at him, surprised. If it wasn't science to Charlie, it was "voo-doo."

"Those dogs straightened me out," Ramsay said. "Alaska was a wild place back then. Knew more than a few guys who got killed." He pointed to a facial scar. "Never thought we'd come back from Siberia with a kennel of dogs. No time for trouble after that, it was like inheriting a whole kindergarten class that never goes home." He smiled, remembering. "Grew me up real fast. Dogs do that to a person."

He looked at Rosalie. "Gave me a livelihood. Met my wife, the best friends a person could ever have." Ramsay gestured to Charlie and Helen. "I always wished there was some way to pay that Siberian woman back."

Ramsay shrugged. "One of her pups even saved my life," he began. The Army had chased him as far as the pressure ridges, but not before they fired several rounds. The Eskimo dog team got spooked and bolted, dragging Johnny along. Robert was knocked off after he was hit. The Chukchi sled flipped as the dogs bolted. A red-colored pup fell out of the cage. The team took off, chasing Johnny. The sled then hit a mogul and flipped upright.

The red pup stayed with him. Just as he felt himself going into shock, the pup took off running, dragging his glove in her mouth in the direction of the sled. Hours later, Johnny found him.

"That pup lived to be seventeen," Ramsay said. "Called her 'Sassy.' Never left my side. She threw plenty of winning lead dogs. That King you got there is a descendant. Every red dog that shows up in one of my lines, I keep it. Figure it's Sassy coming back to keep an eye on me."

"God knows someone's got to," Charlie said.

The story seemed to have tired Ramsay. Helen moved to gather the plates and Jan stood to lend a hand with the cleanup. He excused himself, citing the long flight from Alaska. He waved good night to Rosalie and headed towards the guest room.

Rosalie heard the phone ringing out in the living room.

"Rosalie-e-e," Arlan called over the booming TV.

The Frozen Four hockey play-offs had just begun. She'd been sequestered in her room since early that morning. Arlan's refrigerator-sized buddies, including Dan and Franklin, arrived before nine to take over the house for the weekend.

"Pearl's got another one," Arlan announced, holding the telephone receiver over his head. Rosalie seized the phone with contempt, likewise regarding his lingering buddies. The house was like a dirty bathrobe—too much bean dip and unwashed hair. Men with unbrushed teeth wearing clothes they probably slept in.

Bella's puppies were due the next day. The dog lay panting beneath the front window; nine weeks of gestation had passed in a snap. It was the end of March. Though spring officially had arrived, no one had tipped off Mother Nature. Last night Charlie had examined Bella. "Two for sure. Feel 'em." Rosalie cupped their bodies. Two wasn't so bad. But then Charlie the mind reader grinned. "That's not to say two or three more aren't stuck up there somewhere."

"Hi, Pearl," she said.

"Rosalie—my God." Pearl sounded out of breath. "Just caught her. Husky's about to drop a litter in my yard, I swear it," the woman puffed.

"I see." Rosalie sighed and pulled on her bangs.

The men looked at her. More were on the way, hauling their

own ringside chairs for the weekend hockey orgy. The windows had fogged up from boiling brats.

"Poor thing—don't want to call Franklin," Pearl said.

Rosalie glanced at her uncle's rear end from where he was bent over, rummaging in the fridge for more bratwurst.

"Figured you'd know what to do," Pearl said. "Poor thing's half-starved, Rosalie. Been setting out cooked noodles. Gobbles 'em up. Reminds me of your Smokey."

Rosalie stepped over and turned down the volume, the phone cord stretched across the screen.

"So?" Arlan asked. Everyone watched her.

She covered the receiver with her hand and nodded. She could've screamed from frustration. Her chin dropped.

"Sure, Pearl," she murmured. "I'll be right over." It was hard enough to walk three dogs. Although Arlan helped, he wheezed and hobbled by the end of the driveway. Floor space was already scarce. Bella's pups would be contained in a green kiddie pool crammed in Rosalie's bedroom. It would hold them for five weeks. After that she prayed the fence would be up.

"Pearl's been feeding her noodles," Rosalie reported.

"Noodles?" Arlan's chin pulled back in consternation.

Like that was the point.

"Hey—it's better than a bullet in the head," Rosalie raised her voice.

They all paused to look at her. She sounded more like Charlie every day.

"Christ, that's harsh," Buck said. He shifted on the couch and grabbed a handful of Doritos. The others remained non-committal. Franklin tipped up his beer bottle and looked at her.

Arlan looked to Dan. He was up in a ready way, sensing opportunity.

"You two kids go on over," Arlan suggested.

"Aren't you going to—"

"I got a house full of company," Arlan cut her off.

Dan pulled keys from his jean jacket. Examining each one, he listened, waiting for her to make up her mind.

"Go on, missy," Arlan said. "We'll make do. That fence'll be up in a weekend." He glanced at Dan.

Oh great. So now Dan was building the fence, too.

"Go on. Go get that Noodle dog."

They drove twelve miles to Pearl's in complete silence. Rosalie grasped the door handle with the iron grip she'd developed from holding the collars of strong dogs.

She'd only seen him briefly since the night they got Bella, and met his comings and goings strictly with a nod. Several times while watching a game with Arlan, Dan would look for an opening to talk, to move closer on the couch. But Rosalie pretended to be lost in beading and would put her feet up on the cushion to block all inroads. And while congratulating herself on just how tough she could be, the minute she heard his truck leaving she was sorry. Standing up by the window to watch the Bronco pull away, she wondered if she was punishing him for the sins of another man

Pearl's driveway was marked by two whitewashed whisky barrel planters, stenciled with colorful designs of Norwegian rosemaling. During the summer, flowers would cascade over the edges. Dan pulled the Bronco just inside the long gravel driveway and parked. The early spring air had a damp bite.

Rosalie carried a leash, a chain collar and two of Arlan's bratwurst she thought to grab as bait. In the backseat of Dan's Bronco she'd thrown her sleeping bag.

Pearl's house was dark; she'd mentioned they'd be at a card game that evening at St. John's Methodist church in town. They lived on the other side of Buffalo Bay in a tidy A-frame perched on a hill overlooking Madeline Island. The steep slope afforded them a wide panoramic view of Superior and Madeline Islands.

Rosalie approached the gate. The dog stood watching; the set of her ears, shape of skull and length of leg were all similar to Smokey. Black wolf color with a charcoal undercoat, even the insides of her ears were black. Blue eyes and a white keyhole mask circled her black nose. The dog's brows were furrowed. She began to pace as Rosalie neared the fence.

Rosalie tore off a piece of the brat to toss it over.

"Hey, good girl." The brat was cold and greasy between her fingers.

The dog stopped.

"What is she?" Dan caught up, standing beside the gate.

"A husky."

"Doesn't look like one."

"It's the old face; I've never seen it." She recognized it from old photos in books at Jan and Dave's. "Jan says show breeders bred it out. They thought it ugly," she said, mesmerized. "It's in racing huskies. No one cares what they look like."

The dog's legs were so thin she looked as if she were standing on stilts. Her front feet turned out like a moose calf, huge swollen belly like Bella's. The dog kept a fixed eye on the brat.

"Looks worried," Dan said.

"Wouldn't you be?" she sniped. "No safe place to whelp puppies."

Rosalie and the stray searched each other's faces. She tossed another piece of brat over the fence. The dog still didn't move.

Rosalie made a kiss sound. "Come on, Mama Noodle." Unlatching the gate, she stepped inside and closed it.

Dan leaned against the fence, watching.

The stray held her ground, lowering her head with each of Rosalie's steps.

Rosalie crouched. She broke off another piece and held it out.

The Noodle began to pace. Sniffing the fence line, the dog circled, searching for a way out.

Rosalie sat on the snowy ground and averted her eyes.

Dan scratched his nose. His movement startled the dog. The Noodle looked at him, then back at Rosalie as if confused.

"Don't move," she said softly.

They sat for what seemed like twenty minutes. It was getting dark. The Noodle sniffed the farthest piece of brat. She then backed away, watching to see if Rosalie would move. Once satisfied, the Noodle nudged it with her nose and then ate it. She walked towards Rosalie. Slowly, Rosalie opened her hand. A piece of brat lay on her palm. The dog sniffed it.

"Here, Mama Noodle," she said in her gentlest voice. "Take it." She held the collar and leash in her other hand. As the dog took the piece, Rosalie slipped the collar over her head.

The Noodle shrieked and jerked backwards to the end of the leash, spinning and yelping to get free.

"Sh-h, sh-h, sh-hh-h. It's okay," Rosalie assured.

The dog's eyes bulged. But then the Noodle eased, as though weighing her odds.

Rosalie sat motionless for several more minutes.

The dog stepped towards Rosalie's open hand. They'd both forgotten about Dan. The dog began to lick the grease off her palm. Rosalie reciprocated with an index finger to scratch under the dog's chin and into the fur on her neck.

"Come on, Mama Noodle." Rosalie slowly stood.

With no further resistance they walked back to the truck. Dan lifted the dog, placing her onto the sleeping bag. The Noodle circled several times and settled with a loud sigh. She rubbed her soiled face in the flannel fabric.

"God, Pearl was right about the pregnancy," Rosalie said.

They started to ride back in silence. She felt Dan studying her profile in the moonlight. It was one of those clear-as-a-bell nights. The stars were like diamonds, clustering together in clouds.

She turned sideways to keep an eye on the Noodle and peeked at Dan's profile in the oncoming headlights. Suddenly the dog grunted.

Rosalie and Dan looked straight at each other. She unhooked her seat belt and reached up, feeling for the dome light.

"Holy shit, Dan, she's having them."

"You're kidding."

"Better pull off somewhere," she advised. They were still a good ten miles from the cabin.

A wet baby seal–like form was partially tucked inside the Noodle's rear leg. She dutifully cleaned her baby. The dog paused and lowered her head. She looked full faced at Rosalie. It was an odd look. Not a challenge or even a warning, but rather a declaration. *These are mine.*

"I think we're gonna be here awhile," Rosalie said.

Dan pulled into the driveway of an empty vacation home. They both leaned through the bucket seats, watching as the Noodle began to grunt again.

"So much for a first date," he chided.

Rosalie snorted a laugh. "Is that what you think this is?"

The Noodle looked up at the change in Rosalie's tone. She then scooted her puppy closer with her snout. The pup angrily fought back—tearing deaf and blind at the sleeping bag—like a newly hatched turtle making its way down the beach. It fought folds in the fabric as if competitors for the Noodle's nipple.

Carefully, Rosalie reached between the seats, testing. She rubbed the Noodle's spine as the dog rested between whelps.

Dan leaned over Rosalie and covered her back with his chest, his face resting against the side of her head.

"I love you, Rosalie," Dan said.

She couldn't breathe. The nakedness of his words had found her out. She fought spastic sobs that were as embarrassing as they were impossible to control. She turned and he held her for what seemed like months. At last, the Noodle whelped the last of her five puppies.

CHAPTER 24

Tariem was sure this was the window, even in the dark. The reindeer stopped on his command and Tariem kicked in the stake. Cheyuga stayed outside keeping watch with the sleds.

He hoped the boys were still in the same dorm room. At first the State School had separated them by age. But Tangek had cried so hard he kept vomiting. Sharp weight loss prompted concessions. So many children would die. It was agreed he could bunk with Ankjem and the older boys until his adjustment was complete. That was two years ago. And as of Tariem's last visit, the arrangement was still in effect.

Cheyuga signaled "clear." No teachers or State Officials milling about. The world had grown many sets of eyes and ears. He and Tariem would be shot if caught—a passing thought not strong enough to deter either of them.

Tariem crept up to the window. The same one the boys peered out after the last Family Visiting Day. Both had drooped despite promising to be brave. But then Tariem had drooped too as they were loaded back into the Army truck to leave.

He shook his head remembering. Now he'd broken the promise about being strong and making the best of it. But there was too much missing—the sea, the land near Uelen and most of all his sons. As "Primitives," the State deemed them archaic. He'd rather be obsolete with his sons by the sea. Not seeing big water every day was suffocating.

Their departure from Bilibino was as secret as it was spontaneous. By morning their tracks would be blown over and no one would know where they'd gone. Besides, soldiers wouldn't chase into the steep valleys of the Ush Urekchen Mountains. Only Omryn and Lena would notice, and they had enough troubles of their own.

The bright moon cast bluish light inside the children's sleeping quarters. Tariem could make out cots with sleeping bundles. How to find them without risking a disturbance? Cheyuga crept up and peered over Tariem's shoulder. He nudged him, pointing to a cot with two sleeping bundles.

Tariem pushed on the window frame. It was locked, maybe frozen.

The old man crept around to the side door. He pushed. The door budged open a thumb's width. They glanced at each other, surprised by their good luck. Tariem knifed in sideways. The smell of disinfectant blanched the membranes of his nose. It was the same sharp stench as the barracks.

Looking both ways down the hall, they saw soft light from an oil lamp sitting on a table. Floorboards squeaked under his weight as he entered the boys' room, though his reindeer-skin boots made no sound. He knelt beside them. Tangek's cheek was as round as when he was a baby. The boy had always seemed breakable. Even the feel of his skull was different from Ankjem's. Thinner, more brittle, like a bird's egg. The boy coughed.

Tangek's eyes opened and Tariem covered his mouth. The boy struggled, then calmed once his father's features made sense. Ankjem woke. Tariem held a finger to his lips. The boy recognized his father's breathing. He motioned to get ready. A few boys stirred, but no one moved to speak.

The boys pulled on wool pants, coats and army boots. Tariem gestured towards the door. They were noticeably taller. The hems of Ankjem's pants touched the tops of his boots. Tariem lifted Tangek and carried him. As he rested his face on the boy's neck, the sweet scent of Tangek's sleepy skin was the smell of home.

Tariem closed the side door carefully, making sure the latch clicked.

"Are we going to Rochlit to get Mommy?" Tangek asked in Russian.

Tariem held a quick finger to his lips. His heart fluttered at the sound of his son's voice but hardened with the mention of Jeaantaa. Outside, he set Tangek down. The boy immediately ran towards the sleds, searching for his mother's form, "Ama?" he whispered, hoping for a surprise.

It angered Tariem. After all that had happened, this was the first thing Tangek wanted.

Cheyuga patted the top of the sled for them to come. Both boys climbed up to sit on piles of reindeer blankets and provisions. They started to shiver. He covered them with reindeer blankets to fight off the wind's greediness.

Tariem looked to the moon and stars for reassurance. The sky was clear. Breathing in the freshness cleaned out the dormitory smell. The aurora borealis built to a green crescendo and then exploded into red. He said a prayer to the spirits that lived in the twenty-six directions of the wind. When he tapped the beasts with a long tree branch he'd fashioned into a prompt, the sled jerked and then glided. He looked over at Ankjem, the older boy. The familiar forms of his sons were silhouetted by moonlight against the inky sky. Tariem's heart thumped against his ribs. Everything was back in place.

"We're going back home," Tariem whispered in Chukchi. Tangek turned and looked at his father, not understanding a word.

"She won't be home either," Ankjem whispered to his brother in Russian, anticipating the next question. "She's gone."

While they'd been discussing and planning an escape for a year, their exit was marked by what Cheyuga came to call the-Night-of-Having-Had-Enough, an impromptu execution of an old man and his son. Though it was strictly prohibited by the State, the old Nenets reindeer shaman performed a traditional ceremony out near the Brigade's winter camp deep in the woods. As was customary, the old man sacrificed a yearling reindeer calf to ensure the herd's health for the following year. He knifed it through the heart, killing it instantly, and then smeared its blood and marrow over a wooden figure he kept hidden in the trees. And while penalties for such ceremonies could be severe, violators usually received no more than three days in isolation with corresponding loss of food rations.

The shaman and his son were arrested upon returning to town. Bound at the wrists, they were lined up and summarily executed against the wall of a building. No explanation was offered to screaming wives and family, who were then ordered to dispose of the corpses.

This prompted Tariem and Cheyuga to begin stealing frozen reindeer meat from the "People's Stores." Cheyuga snatched provisions from where he worked in the People's Commissary. The old man also helped himself to a Winchester rifle and boxes of ammunition.

Tariem collected branches. Using rope, he bound them to create three sleds.

"We don't need three sleds," Cheyuga said.

"What about the boys?"

"They're too young to handle reindeer," the old man said. "Take it far into the taiga and burn it," Cheyuga instructed. "It has a spirit. It's calling to someone."

But they were in a hurry. No time for the old man's magic. Tariem was due to report back to the Brigade the next day. Why waste time hiking out into the taiga? Flames and the smell of burning larch might alert the Red Guard. Instead he stashed the sled in a small grove of saplings behind one of the housing barracks.

Opportunity came by nightfall. The soldiers were drinking and being entertained by Ukrainian prostitutes. Tariem snuck out six of the "People's reindeer," harnessed them and left.

"You burned it?" Cheyuga asked.

Tariem nodded. The old man knew he was lying but was too weary to challenge him.

Jeaantaa had been right. In no time the Red Army had reached the reindeer cousins. The sting of her words stayed as fresh as the day they were uttered. Tariem seared with jealousy, imagining her life in Rochlit with Ramsay, imagining him touching her.

Once the Army settled in Bilibino, forced collectivization began. Everything was destroyed except for reindeer. They were declared "State Commodities." The practice of traditional beliefs was forbidden under threat of imprisonment or execution. This time, though, Tariem could tell the Red Army lacked the same fervor. They were worn down and broken by a climate that fought back with more savagery than Moscow could have imagined. Bilibino was staffed by the young and eager; older officers knew better than to get stuck in the winter death trap. Soldiers frequently didn't return from routine patrols. Vehicles would break down, their comrades' bodies brought back as rigid as sea ice. But rather than raging at Moscow, many took their anger and grief out on the "Primitives."

Bilibino became a veritable ghost town. Children ages five to seventeen were shipped to state boarding schools for "modernization" until reaching age seventeen, completing eleventh grade or dying from influenza—whichever came first. Families were granted two one-day visits a year. Schools reserved the right to cancel "Family Visiting Day" with no warning or explanation.

Impromptu visits from heartsick parents were denied. Officials would remind them that if the modernization process was to be successful, parental influence had to be minimized.

Only Russian was spoken. Children's sleeping quarters fell silent. All caught speaking anything else were sent into isolation. Sitting in cold, dark chambers, they were to reflect on the inferiority of their primitiveness. Yet even as they became fluent, many still said nothing—the private agony of homesickness buried deep within the hushed folds of their hearts. Awakening to morning whistles, they stood like good comrades at attention. In the dining room they waited for the final signal to lift their spoons.

Earlier that spring, Ukrainians drifted into Bilibino looking for work. Rumors of jobs in the State-run reindeer meat processing plants and fur farms lured them in. Tariem was fascinated by the many combinations of unfamiliar facial features and body types. He'd stare intently just as they studied him back with the same naked curiosity.

For two years he and Cheyuga were assigned to the Reindeer Brigade. Tariem was a hunter on the ice, a fisherman on the water; a herdsman he was not. Reindeer were different. But they provided one thing that he was hungry for—solitude.

Herds blanketed the hilly tundra into the horizon. Some twenty thousand thundering hooves made the ground rumble. When something spooked a few it could trigger the entire herd. At first Tariem had dropped down, grasping rocks, dwarf tundra willows, anything to hold on. He was frightened that those million heartbeats could shake him loose. Bounce him high in an unbreakable trajectory towards the moon.

State Officials explained that everybody, and nobody, owned reindeer—they belonged to the "People." "Who are these People?" Tariem asked. "All of us," he was told. Even his clothes and shoes, he was told, belonged to everyone.

Tariem preferred being out, saddled to a reindeer. For almost a year the sight of others had sickened him. Isolation was soothing. While others returned weekly for provisions, Tariem would take enough to stay out for weeks. Even in winter he preferred to sleep rough on a bedroll. Only vodka calmed him. And—though it made him ill—it brought him to a place of forgetting.

Memories of Jeaantaa running across the tundra with the boys would break through the membrane of memory. Many times he'd wake, gasping for breath—drowning in despair. Once, during an influenza epidemic, he lay shivering with fever on the edge of the herd, thinking Jeaantaa was just in the other room of their *yaranga*. Swearing he heard her voice. Her face red and sweaty from running behind the sled all the way from a trade fair, excited as she breathlessly explained, "Too many reindeer skins, no room for me."

Towards the end of those years Tariem's solitude was interrupted. After the snowmelt, People of the Red Star came with horse-drawn wagons. They set up strange camps. Horses struggled through the permafrost, hauling canvas tents and gear he'd never seen before. The people appeared to dig randomly as if searching for a lost object. Many holes were drilled until black tarry liquid oozed out. Once it did they seemed to immediately lose interest, turning their attention to drilling another close by. The crude seeped out, leaching into miles of tundra and forest until it poisoned the conifers.

CHAPTER 25

Dan's lovely and strange admission was turning into an even odder courtship. She'd not met any of his friends and wondered if Arlan was his only one. Dan scared up every excuse in the world not to go out with her friends. Dating consisted of grabbing a bite to eat in downtown Bayfield, watching TV and playing cards with Arlan. "Let's go to your house," she suggested, and Dan would yes her to death, though nothing came of it.

Rosalie finally managed to lure Dan out with Lorraine and friends for the play-offs of the Minnesota versus Wisconsin Adult Hockey Leagues. It was the ultimate in rivalry and Rosalie guessed that he wouldn't say no. He showed up wearing the beaded buckskin vest she'd made him—two hawks in flight on either side.

They all agreed to meet at Bub's Steak House in Duluth, the gathering place for raucous hockey fans. Lorraine and Russell, the new boyfriend, plus their friends from on and off the Reservation were bringing tickets. A table had already been commandeered by the time Rosalie and Dan arrived.

Large round tables with red tablecloths crammed the dining room and people had to slide through sideways to get to their spots. Overhead a life-sized wagon-wheel chandelier with tiny red lampshades was set over each table, and a full wall was lined with a quarter-mile salad bar. The steaks were as large as a grown man's head, served by a gum-snapping, wisecracking waitstaff—dressed in western attire—who'd heard and said it all.

Pitchers of dark ale and tall clear glasses along with steer-shaped menus the color of raw meat were deposited at the table.

Her friends badgered each other, lobbying for what they believed to be the best on the menu. Lorraine maneuvered hers with new red acrylic nails. "Frosty Tip's got a new nail gal." She waved her fingers and then pretended to claw "porno-style" at Russell's shoulder until he told her to quit, feigning embarrassment.

Dan quietly nursed a beer. He seemed sullen and indifferent. His menu lay closed as the server worked her way around taking orders

"Hey, Dan," Russell called from across the table.

The table focused on Dan.

"Looks like you got that whole menu memorized."

Russell had red hair, red beard, pink skin and a big mouth. Rosalie looked at Dan. They waited for a comeback from the razor's edge of male rivalry.

"You okay?" she asked quietly, placing her hand on Dan's thigh. Ordinarily, he'd cover it with his. It had become their trademark relationship move. But he didn't.

Russell was a known asshole with a couple of children from different mothers, but for now Lorraine didn't seem to mind.

Dan touched the menu, as if thinking about opening it, but then withdrew. The waitress had made her way around the table to Rosalie.

"I'll have the New York Strip."

"Make that two," Dan said, and handed the menu back to the cowgirl server. It was another endearing trademark. Whenever he and Rosalie went out, he ordered what she did without bothering to check the overhead counter menu or those on the table.

Rosalie nudged him in an exaggerated way to joke him out of the mood.

"Copycat," she teased. Everyone laughed.

"You gonna take that shit, Dan?" Russell egged, his arm draped in a proprietary manner across the back of Lorraine's chair.

They waited for a retort. Instead Dan stood and walked off brusquely. All eyebrows rose. Quick glances and split-second confirmations passed between good friends.

Rosalie's cheeks burned.

Mercifully, buckets of onion rings arrived. Conversation seemed to rekindle as the table made strides towards a full recovery.

She stared at the red cloth napkin before her, folded into a fan. What had just happened? She glanced towards the front of the restaurant. Replaying her words, she searched for culpability. Then she was struck with a sudden thought: *Had he left?*

Her stomach was stone. She'd been showing off to them, so proud to have Dan in her life. Slipping between tables up front, she practically bumped into him as he exited the men's room. Cold air rushed in as someone held open the door.

"Dan." She touched his forearm. "What happened?"

He didn't answer. Neither could she read his face; his eyes were hollow, almost hateful.

"I was kidding—it was a joke," she offered. "Are you mad?"

"Let's go back." He steered her through the crowded room by the elbow. The table remained tense despite the chitchat.

"I'm sorry," she whispered near his ear. He didn't respond. She watched for his features to soften, his shy smile to break, some sign to release her. She felt Lorraine's eyes the entire meal but couldn't meet them.

"Ladies' room?" Lorraine asked, indicating a meeting was in order.

"No, I'm fine," Rosalie said. She didn't want to talk about it. It took all her self-control not to cry.

Once they were in the university hockey stadium, the gladiator-like atmosphere broke the evening's spell. She began to censor her words, no longer rattling off whatever crossed her mind. The realization hit that she knew far less of him than she thought.

Lorraine called early the next morning. "I'm coming over at ten; be ready."

Rosalie waited outside on the steps, soaking in the warm sun on the last day of April. Lorraine pulled in driving her father, Bennett's, truck. She leaned out the window, grinning.

"What's up with your dad's truck?" Rosalie wrinkled her nose.

"So, what's Dan up to today?" Lorraine asked.

"They're working in Two Harbors till noon, then coming here to finish the fence."

"Perfect."

"For what?"

"A little surveillance. Especially after that performance last night," Lorraine said as she reached to open the passenger's side door. The outside handle had been broken for decades. "Time we dig deeper with Mr. Dan. He don't know old Bennett's truck, so what the hey." Rosalie's friend was smiling wryly.

Rosalie climbed in and shut the door. "You don't think I said something—"

"Shit. Stop it, stop it, stop it." Lorraine hit the steering wheel with her hands. "I knew you'd do this," she half-scolded. "Stop second-guessing yourself."

Rosalie looked out the window.

"You were nothing but cute, funny and loving," Lorraine assured. "He was out of line. Everybody thought so."

They deconstructed the night's events as they drove towards Dan's house.

"So you've never been inside?" Lorraine asked.

She shook her head.

"Have you asked?"

"Of course I've asked; what do you think I'm stupid?"

"Well . . ." Lorraine paused. "It's still sorta cold out, so where are you guys doing it?"

They both chuckled.

"Here and there."

They were quiet as they watched the Lake; the darkening ice indicated it was getting thin.

"Has Arlan been in his house?"

Rosalie shook her head.

"Are you kidding me?" Lorraine's mouth opened so wide Rosalie could see her dental fillings. "Arlan's never been inside?"

She shrugged.

"All those years of the two of 'em working together?"

Rosalie slowly nodded.

"Oh—there's something there." Lorraine was playing with her lower lip. "He's hiding something. Maybe bodies stacked inside."

"Shut up." Rosalie hit her arm. "You always think the worst."

"Yeah, well—welcome to my world," Lorraine said.

They sat with their own thoughts for the last few miles. *Welcome to Cornucopia, pop. 231.*

"So what are we looking for anyway?" Rosalie asked, looking out the window.

"Who knows," Lorraine said as they neared the turn to Dan's house. "Just eyeballing the place for now."

Corny's claim to fame was being Wisconsin's most northerly zip code. The whole town was two blocks. The main thoroughfare along the Lake was lined with tiny shoe-box vacation cottages. During a good summer, when it wasn't too cold and rainy, there were more vacationers than town residents. Dan's Bronco was nowhere in sight.

"Perfect. Be ready to duck anyway," Lorraine said.

Rosalie's chest was tight. She'd die a million deaths should Dan catch her and think she was spying. She cleared a space, shoving Bennett's tools off to one side of the floor, prepared to hide.

"He always seems sort of mysterious, distant."

"Oh, like Russell."

"Fuck you." Lorraine laughed out loud. "Don't knock it— Russell's a good time." Lorraine seemed pensive. "Dan seems to really like you."

"You think so?"

"Yeah. I do."

"How can you tell?" Rosalie asked.

"Uh-h-h—the way he looks at you." Lorraine's voice softened.

"Dan looks at me?" She laughed in unbelief. The observation struck her as uncanny. Dan didn't look at her. She'd jokingly imagined him walking right past her in downtown Bayfield.

"Yeah. When you're talking, he sneaks these little peeks," Lorraine said.

She braked at the turnoff to Dan's house.

"It's sort of sweet. I noticed it last night a couple of times," she said.

Rosalie smiled, thinking of Dan looking at her.

"Yeah, well don't bask in it too much. Last night was really weird." Lorraine raised her eyebrows. "Everyone's still talking about it."

Lorraine proceeded to share the little she knew. The Villieux family moved back from Massachusetts during Dan's freshman year of high school. "His dad was a skin, born here. Mom was a bitch, younger sister too. From over in the Fox Valley—a big-time paper money family."

"Were they rich?"

"Mm-m—probably more like comfortable, as old Bennett says," Lorraine qualified. "His mom had the money. Old man Villieux grew up poor as dirt, God rest his soul. Was a real looker, like Dan."

Lorraine lit a cigarette and drew deeply. "You wouldn't think he'd have this 'society type' mom."

"I would," Rosalie said. It explained a lot.

"Everything on Madeline Island's named after her. 'The Louise Graham Villieux Center for the Arts' and all that shit. Yet that's where old man Villieux's blood's from—you'd think she'd at least mention him."

Rosalie had seen the plaques.

"Probably made Dan even more ashamed of being a dropout. I remember in the girls' bathroom, his sister saying he was a loser like his dad." Lorraine braked, looking around, not sure where to turn.

"It's that way." Rosalie pointed.

"Kinda bad to say shit like that about your own brother even if it's true."

"Maybe he's married or something," Rosalie said as they pulled up in front. "Wouldn't that just suck."

Lorraine laughed. "*That* Arlan would know." The truck stopped. "Holy shit, look at this place," Lorraine whispered. They were both awestruck. "I've seen this house since I was a kid." Her voice was hushed. "Used to pretend to myself it was mine. Had no idea *he* lived here."

It was a huge gabled structure covered with gray weathered shingles and white shutters. Large picture windows and a wrap-around porch surrounded the first floor. The house looked abandoned. Dan's rusting snowplow sat off to the side of the driveway. His backyard was Lake Superior. Waves were frozen in twisted heaves as if having thrown themselves in one last fling of resistance. The sun still lacked sufficient heat to melt the last of the lingering fast ice.

"His dad was an ore tanker captain," Lorraine said softly as if the house could hear. "Died after they moved back. Think they came home for that. Mom hated it here—didn't want her kids to be skins. She died about two years ago, though I seriously doubt it was from a broken heart." Lorraine laughed in a nasty way. "His sister married some fancy-ass lawyer from the Twin Cities."

Her cigarette glowed like an angry firefly. Residual smoke twirled from her nostrils as it mixed with the moisture of her breath.

There were gaps in the gray weathered exterior where many shingles were missing. The angle of the roof, elaborate returns around the roofline, added up to a sea captain's house.

"Yeah. It does look kind of sad," Lorraine conceded. "Felice says he inherited it two years after *Mama*"—she faked a French accent—"died."

Remnants of a small cherry and apple grove surrounded the house, overtaken by wiry scrub trees. Old wooden whisky barrel planters marked the driveway entrance. Rotted and collapsing, their rusting rings sat lopsided.

"He mentioned marriage."

Lorraine turned abruptly. "No fucking way."

Rosalie was silent, taking in the house.

"Tell me you said no."

Rosalie sighed. "I didn't say anything."

"What's wrong with 'no'? 'Not now, maybe never'?"

"I think he really wants to marry Arlan."

Lorraine laughed.

"Or get adopted," Rosalie said. "You know, the father he never had, son *he* never had."

"You don't even know him." Lorraine turned serious. "Shit, no one does. Think 'Jerry.' Remember how you rushed into that."

"I was pregnant."

"So what. That's no reason to get married anymore." Lorraine looked at the house, as if it might have an opinion.

Wise enough words, though there's nothing like hormones to turn a person deaf. At times Dan was kin, the next moment a stranger who'd wandered into her living room.

Lorraine looked up. Something got her attention in the rearview mirror.

"Oops—incoming Bronco. Thought you said they're working till noon."

Lorraine put the truck in gear.

The moment Dan was out the door it felt like he no longer existed. Not that continuity of warmth that lingers when people become attached. Rosalie ached with a grief that was impossible to explain. Each parting became more difficult. Sometimes she phoned him, but Dan wasn't one for the phone. His belabored monosyllabic grunts only intensified her distress. Then loneliness would wrench her, like the weeks following her mother's death. The finality that she would never again enter the house to see her mother standing at the sink, washing dishes. Holding a puppy helped. And then Smokey, Noodle, King and Bella would gather. They'd circle her as she sat on the couch beading.

The nights Arlan met Noreen for dinner and bridge at the casino in Red Cliff, Rosalie and Dan would make love with ferocity in her childhood bed. But mostly they pulled off onto forest roads when neither could wait. Her insides tugged with a desire from which she thought she'd die. His glacial eyes drew her into their fluorescent aqua as his heat pounded through her. Her back would arch, nipples painfully constricted in their desperation for the wet of his mouth. And after the storm of their lovemaking, lying back in the Bronco seat, she'd stare at the lacey patterns of frost on a windshield iced over from their heat. Even as he stood outside, scraping, she half-expected another face to be revealed in the glass.

Perhaps Dan was the flip side of Jerry's molten core. Maybe he'd melt with time, or else freeze her beneath the underworld of his icy surface.

It had been a cold and wet spring. Mother Nature walloped them until the bitter end with a series of freaky snowstorms, as if to remind everyone who was boss. Steamy clouds tumbled into the contours of surrounding hills. Trees were finally leafing into a glowing green. Graceful wisps of steam, like stray ribbons, twirled over slopes and hills. They veiled the spiky tops of white pines in the distance, changing shape before merging into Superior's morning fog.

Seagulls vanished into a patch of mist and disappeared.

Scented wet sand, sweet grass and ferns filled the house and the dog yard. Bracken ferns popped up all over, their unfurling fronds like the brown wrinkled fists of newborns.

Noodle's five puppies had grown from deaf, blind sausages—their eyes and ears sealed—to motoring, grunting piglets. Their bellies dragged on crooked legs, tearing around the green plastic kiddie pool. They grew into toddlers, biting and dragging each other round by the tails. And soon they were leggy adolescents.

"How do you come up with all these names?" she'd asked Dave.

"Whatever name pops into your head. It's a stream-of-consciousness thing."

She looked at him. "What if Jan doesn't agree?"

"She always agrees."

Rosalie enunciated her words, "No she doesn't."

"Then we arm wrestle for it."

Rosalie looked at him through hooded eyes. It was always fun to gang up on Dave and he seemed to enjoy it.

He gave her a look. "Okay, so take Burpie."

Rosalie looked at the dog.

"Pet her. Go ahead. Pet her," Dave said. "I triple dog dare you."

It was a setup and she knew it. As she petted Burpie's head, the dog belched loudly. Rosalie bent over chuckling. Dave won this round.

He opened his arms. "Ta-da."

"So you never repeat names?" she asked.

"Never." He was suddenly serious. "Names are sacred memories."

Peculiar words. Rosalie guessed they came from a place inside that was still hurting.

One of the Noodle's puppies resembled Smokey and was named Junior. The Noodle's clone was named Kicky, since she kicked the others away to nurse. Another was named Goofy, the jokester who never tired of egging everyone on to play. Then

Panda, a large placid boy, the last to be born. His body was charcoal black like the Noodle, with piercing blue eyes and a sweet
disposition like Smokey. Flyer, a particularly active female,
never tired of flying off the tops of furniture.

Bella's two puppies, Clowny and Rascal, were born three days
later. They stayed in the wooden whelping box that Arlan nailed
together at Jan's direction. As promised, the fence was up before
May and a doggie door was installed. Though it was odd to go
from one dog in November to ten by June, the pack provided
endless entertainment. Half slept like a furry wagon train circling the couch where Rosalie sat beading. The others camped
around the La-Z-Boy where Arlan snored, missing yet another
movie ending. She'd have to update him in the morning, and
then he'd argue with her, like she wrote the script.

Smokey and the Noodle had yelped loudly at first sight. Both
dropped into a familiar play bow and ran around the living
room with excitement. Despite her newborn puppies and the
sometimes protectiveness of a mother dog, the Noodle nuzzled
Smokey's face. They had the same conformation. Maybe they'd
been littermates. Dave and Jan speculated that the two might
have run off together, gotten separated, and perhaps the Noodle
tracked him to Pearl's yard. No one could know.

For the first four weeks, the Noodle rarely left her puppies
except for trips outside. Rosalie would try to sneak one to hold,
only to get busted the instant the dog raced in. The Noodle
would walk up with the same expression as the night she'd
given birth in Dan's truck.

"I just want to hold him."

The Noodle stood firm.

"Okay, okay. Jesus." Rosalie would return the puppy to the
kiddie pool, knowing the Noodle would not back down. Once
the dog stepped back into the kiddie pool and lay down on her
side, the puppies would waddle over to nurse. She'd scoot each
one with her nose as if taking attendance. Once the puppies
were firmly latched on and feeding, the Noodle would lift their

bodies with her nose as they ate, consumed by the task of per-petually counting and recounting. Then, after they were stuffed and groggy, they'd offer up their faces, eyes and mouths closed, as she methodically cleaned.

"Cleanest faces and asses in all of Bayfield County," Arlan would remark.

Clowny and Rascal were Bella and King's two pups. At about four weeks, Clowny—a red husky, also the smallest—was the first to escape from the whelping box. She explored the house and introduced herself to the other dogs. A red-colored Napole-onic female, she earned the nickname Peanut from Arlan. Feet firmly planted, Clowny was too intelligent for her own good. She became incensed when treated like just another dog. Her wolf gray littermate, Rascal, would cry mournfully after her sister. Clowny would then turn back as if to say, "Come on." But Rascal didn't quite have the oomph needed to haul her fat body up over the walls of the whelping box.

Smokey and King still came along to Stormwatch, running the new crop of puppy teams. King led each team and Smokey ran in point position immediately behind him. Some of the yearlings were promoted to competitive teams for the upcom-ing winter; others went to live with other mushers.

Afternoons Rosalie worked closely with Charlie. She switched off with Jan and Dave on surgery mornings to help assist in the clinic.

Initially the puppies were very little work. Both moms fed, bathed and cleaned up after them until they were mobile enough to walk. Once the puppies were five weeks old, Smokey tumbled with them as if he were just a kid himself. King politely ignored them, sometimes flashing an icy stare, other times a warning growl.

Bella herded the puppies with purpose and conviction. Ex-cept for Clowny, they all gathered in the kiddie pool with the Noodle, sleeping in one collective heap. They grew—filling the kiddie pool to overflowing—a sea of multicolored bodies rising and falling as they breathed.

Clowny followed Arlan to bed every night. They slept face-to-face, conversing in snores. When it got too late for Dan to drive home, he'd crawl into Rosalie's cramped bed. Smokey would sleep alongside on the floor. The couple quietly making love to the unbroken sound of Arlan and Clowny's snoring in the other room.

Once tall enough to reach the doggie door, the puppies would run in and out a million times a day. Webbed furry paws thumped across the living room, crashing against the couch in a perpetual tumble of play. They embroiled in play fights that sometimes turned real. Usually because someone failed to exercise proper restraint and would bite too hard.

The Noodle ran in and out along with them, dashing with happy anticipation. Panda, her Baby Huey, as Arlan called him, "runs in like you got money for him."

The Noodle's greedy little opportunists were only too happy to nurse her into the ground. Just a bag of bones, she was bald in places, her pink skin visible through what was left of her coat. They couldn't get enough of Mama's milk, neither could she say no. Noodle surrendered everything. When Rosalie would slip her high-fat treats, the dog dutifully marched to drop them center stage for her little maximizers.

Rosalie would then softly scold her, "Noody, it's for you." She tried barricading the Noodle in her bedroom, but as the door closed the dog began clawing and shrieking. She wouldn't be separated from her puppies. Awestruck by the power of instinct, Rosalie thought the Noodle's tie with her pups seemed stronger than that to her own life.

Upon Jan's urging, Rosalie intervened. Especially as their sharp little milk teeth chewed into the Noodle's sensitive underbelly, she needed to recover by allowing them to eat puppy food.

Bella, on the other hand, was quite a different story. By three weeks she was already growling and snapping at Clowny and Rascal—making it clear it was time to get a life. By four weeks Bella lost interest and by five they were completely weaned. But just as Bella was no fool, neither were Clowny and Racal. Rosalie caught the two of them sneaking into the kiddie pool to seek comfort from the Noodle. She had to separate them all so the Noodle could finally dry out and begin to regain her strength.

It was a fascinating crash course in parenthood. Bullies were swiftly and firmly chastised by their parents for misdeeds. The Noodle flipped aggressors over onto their backs, holding them down until they gave up and surrendered. Bella would clamp the jaws of the offender shut with her own, the puppy's head surrendering limp to her authority.

CHAPTER 26

MARCH 1931—USH UREKCHEN MOUNTAIN RANGE, CENTRAL CHUKOTKA

They knew someone was following, but nobody said a word.

"You should have burned the sled like I told you," Cheyuga raised his voice when they stopped to make camp. It was the first stop after two days of traveling; they wanted to put as much distance between them and Bilibino as they could. With an incoming storm, the protected valley was a good place to camp. Mountains were on one side and the taiga forest on the other.

"Why did you lie?" Tariem's father-in-law hollered.

Tariem hadn't the stamina to deny. He sighed and rubbed the accumulated ice off his spiky mustache.

The old man stood scouring the horizon. Tipping his head, Cheyuga pointed his large hairy ear, listening to the wind.

"I warned you it had a spirit," the old man continued.

Both boys listened, their eyes round. They looked from father to grandfather.

"That sled summoned 'the-one-who-follows.'"

Tariem sighed. He was sick of magic talk. There was so much to do before they could make camp.

Gusts of wind boomed randomly as the storm front approached. Even the reindeer were faltering. Tired and hungry, they refused to plow one step farther into the headwinds. Tariem tied them together and staked them so they wouldn't wander.

Cheyuga and Tangek watched as Tariem unhooked and situated the six reindeer.

"Are we going to eat them, Daddy?" six-year-old Tangek asked, half in Chukchi and half in Russian.

Cheyuga chuckled.

Tariem looked sharply at the boy. What foolishness were they teaching children in the State School?

"Think," Tariem said sternly, and pointed to the boy's head. "If we eat them who will pull the sled? You? Your brother?"

Tangek lowered his head and Tariem was instantly sorry.

Reindeer had long, spindly legs and fat, meaty bodies. It seemed impossible they'd be so swift and strong. While in repose their stocky faces sometimes looked to be smiling. A tall tangle of antlers—like tree branches—scattered above them. Their fur was indeed magic; reindeer hide made for blankets under which you could sleep naked at minus fifty-five. They'd been the foundation material for *yarangas, yorongues,* boots and clothing for eons. Each individual hair shaft was hollow, with the capacity to trap warmth—a factor that made for buoyancy, as reindeer were excellent swimmers. You'd see huge herds take to the freezing arctic waters at the sight of a polar bear, outswimming the bear and then some. It was believed a person wearing reindeer-hide clothing would never drown.

Tariem watched as one of the reindeer struck the frozen tundra with his front hoof. He broke through the crust, his meaty nose sniffing in loud steamy puffs, searching for twigs and lichen from the Season-of-the-Fresh-Air-Going-Out.

"See how hungry they are," Tariem said. "They need food."

The creatures rooted about unsuccessfully. Tariem looked up to the taiga. The forest would be full of fresh budding branches.

"Let's hurry," Tariem urged. "Here." He handed Ankjem the canvas tent to unfold and then looked to Cheyuga.

"I'll get the fire going," The old man set down kettles and firewood they had collected along the way. Tangek helped to arrange branches and twigs in layers to make a fire.

There was a Chukchi saying about firewood, "take it when you see it or be cold and sorry later." Cheyuga had turned wood gathering into a game. Each boy was appointed as a lookout.

Once spotting a branch, they had to fetch and hide it in the sled so the Snow Walker wouldn't steal it to make his own fire.

Tangek sat packing snow into one of the kettles. Once the kettles were boiling they'd cook a slab of frozen reindeer meat. The boy looked up.

"Maybe Ama's following," Tangek said in Russian, still thinking about "the-one-who-follows."

Cheyuga raised his eyebrows.

"Maybe Ama's *coming*," Tangek corrected in Chukchi. The boy reached up, pretending to catch Chukchi words like floating clouds.

"That's so much better." Cheyuga nodded with the satisfaction of a man sucking marrow from a cracked bone. "We will name this a new Chukchi season. The 'Season-of-Remembering-Words,'" the old man announced, not answering the boy's question.

"Maybe Ama's looking for us—," Tangek insisted. He looked to Tariem, risking the anger of his father. "Maybe—"

His brother flashed him a look to stop.

"Maybe nothing—" Tariem cut him off. He gave Cheyuga a sharp look to stop encouraging such talk. "No one's coming." Tariem's voice was harsh.

Tariem folded his arms and sighed. He looked up at the incoming low, dark clouds. He had no more patience.

Yet he also felt someone's eyes not far behind. He'd not wanted to whip up the old man's superstitions or alarm his sons. But he knew it wasn't her; that would be impossible. It was the kind of naked and baseless hope that twisted people inside out. It wasn't soldiers either—unlikely that he and Cheyuga would warrant a two-day search party.

"No one is following," Tariem said softly to Tangek as an apology. He squatted and touched the young boy's shoulder.

Tears rimmed the boy's eyes. "Ama's not coming," Tangek confirmed with a fake smile. "Because—now she lives with Slipper and Bakki in Rochlit, right?"

Anger shot through Tariem. He squelched it, though the boy could see his eyes.

"It's not Ama," Cheyuga said, and touched the boy's back. "Look." He pointed to the clouds. "See? Only the storm is following."

After the provisions were unpacked, the boys sat listening. Their grandfather interpreted shifts in blowing snow, reciting the names of the twenty-six spirits scattered in the directions of the wind.

"Boys, let's go," Tariem called. "Grab the other axe." He watched them. "Come—" He started to tromp up the incline towards the edge of the taiga. "No one eats before reindeer."

Only Ankjem stood, expending his last reserve of energy to catch up. They hiked into tall spires of boreal forests as dense as thickets. Tariem began hacking down dried, dead branches from lower portions of tree trunks. It was a good place for firewood; they'd come back to load up before they left. He showed the boy how to use the axe and handed him one.

Ankjem's stomach cramped with hunger. He hadn't realized how hungry he was yet knew better than to complain.

Tariem talked as he worked. "Cut branches with thick, fresh new growth on the tips"—he pointed to an example—"keeps reindeer strong." In the Season-of-Extending-Days, fresh, spongy new growth was everywhere. It would hold the reindeer for several days of travel.

Back in Bilibino, Tariem bumped into several people from Uelen relocated to work in the factories. Maritime residents were moved to Bilibino and Anadyr, living in barracks and working in the fur collectives. The few who spotted him asked about Jeaantaa. He tensed up and turned away without acknowledging them. They backed off, afraid of getting him angrier. "Oh, I'm sorry," they said, curious about the mix of bitterness and sorrow. Not one of them was untouched by loss.

He and Cheyuga had decided to head towards the newly constructed port city of Anadyr on the Bering Sea. Some of the Ukrainian workers mentioned there was plenty of work.

But it was strange for the Chukchi to live in Anadyr. For reasons that were mysterious, the region was known as the Place of Death. No Chukchi ever lived there; only Russians and non-Chukchi dared make settlements. Now it was being developed as the capital port of Chukotka. The Ukranians also spoke of the Government's plan to dredge the harbor to accommodate larger cargo ships. There would be plenty of jobs. At least they'd be by the sea, albeit it in the Place of Death. He shucked the old thinking. Everywhere was the place of death.

Ankjem was cutting branches when he looked to his father.

"Is this enough?"

"That's good," Tariem said. "But they're hungry. Cut this much more." He cupped his arms together, touching fingertips to show the boy.

"But I already cut." Ankjem pointed. He started crying from exhaustion.

"Come, we'll cut together," Tariem said. It seemed the school had taught them that fully cooked meals dropped from the sky.

Ankjem stopped crying.

"Each reindeer eats several armfuls," Tariem coached.

"Why isn't Tangek helping?"

"Because he's not strong like you."

The last days of their journey would cover the barren northern tundra. "Tomorrow or when the storm quits, we'll cut more," Tariem explained. "We'll load it on the sleds. It will make our shelter and be their food."

"Look." Ankjem pointed. Not far away were many green buds. The boy seemed emboldened and ran through deep snow, swinging the axe as he tromped, proud of being entrusted with such an important task.

After they cut enough for all six reindeer, they dragged it to a pile near the edge of the forest. Ankjem sat down in the snow.

"It's all down now," Tariem said. "The easy part," he encouraged.

They began dragging branches down the hillside.

"Cheyuga," Tariem called, trying to get the old man to come help. The sight of the fire roaring filled Tariem with unexpected hope. The sky was growing dark, almost too dim to distinguish sky from land.

"Tangek," he called, but neither budged.

Instead the two of them sat on the edge of the sled, scanning the horizon. Tariem could see Cheyuga's arms waving, as if speculating about "the-one-who-follows."

The two moving specks in the valley stopped. Lena strained to see from atop a mountain ridge in the Ush. For two days she followed, trying to catch up.

Memories of how they traveled every year—guided by familiar mountain passes, valleys and rivers—en route to Uelen for the Festival of Keretkun. Even after two years in Bilibino, Lena still expected to see Jeaantaa playing with the boys, her hair loose and wild. When she saw a Maritime Chukchi she'd ask, convinced Jeaantaa was looking for them.

Lena was reluctant to stop. But as she watched them unload, it was clear they were setting up camp. At least for now the gap between them wouldn't grow wider; the impending storm would make sure of that. She'd taken only small bites of a loaf of bread, figuring she'd have stumbled upon them by now.

The reindeer stopped. They were in need of rest and food. The untrained animals had not faltered, following in the tracks of the others. The animals began to strike the crusty snow, munching on dwarf willows. There was much good food on the ridge.

Spotting the two sleds was comforting. By the direction of their tracks, she guessed they were headed south to Anadyr.

Lena also left Bilibino on the spur of the moment. Late at night and she was lying in the square room with cement walls. She no longer slept at night, though the vodka made her do so all day long.

Drinking vodka was the idea of the mothers. They said it helped to ease the loneliness of missing their children. The first drink seared her insides, but she ignored it since the liquid stopped her feelings. Afternoons were longest, working in the kill pen at the State reindeer processing plant. Drinking vodka was supposed to make that easier too. It had for the others. Working twelve-hour shifts, up to her elbows in reindeer blood and guts, she watched as the creatures darted in fear. She was sickened at how the workers laughed and joked at the animals' suffering as they were slaughtered; some took pleasure in prolonging the agony. Lena had been a Keeper of the reindeer. In the old ways, animals were taken sparingly—only what was needed to survive. Even then they asked forgiveness as the animal was led away to be killed instantly. The processing factories became carnivals of gore. Supervisors yelled for them to move faster, kill more. She couldn't take it a day longer.

Someone in the plant always passed around a bottle. That afternoon drink started it all. Later, it was followed by a sundown drink. Soon Lena drank all the time.

But then she bolted up at the whoosh of sled runners out the apartment window. It was the sound of home. She crept up to the glass. There went Tariem and Cheyuga, long after curfew, each riding a reindeer-pulled sled like the old days.

She quickly stepped outside in slippers. Walking down the snowy road, she followed their tracks. Her pace quickened as she entered the edge of the woods. The snow stung her bare legs up past the knees. The tracks ended in a dense grove of larch saplings. There, tipped on its side, wedged between the saplings—looking as if someone had hastily tried to hide it—was a sled.

She lifted and set the sled upright, stunningly clearheaded for the first time in months. It was light enough to carry. Light like they used to make them. She balanced it on her hip under one arm, carrying it back to the apartment. Setting it down in the middle of the floor, Lena sat cross-legged in front of the sled. She watched it, waiting for it to speak.

Hours before the morning's first siren, Lena was fully packed. She slipped into the kill pen and took four reindeer who, in a matter of hours, would have been ground meat.

It was good to be free. Free of Bilibino. Free of Omryn. For the past two days she'd not thought of vodka. Bilibino was someone else's stupor, somebody else's nightmare. Better to die in the maze of the Ush, surrounded by the world, than imprisoned in concrete walls.

Her drinking angered Omryn, though he'd scarcely been sober a day. He stopped sleeping with her. Claimed the smell of her skin had changed and that she looked old. Then he turned her out. She'd become disgusting and useless. Before long he moved into another apartment building with her younger sister. Her sister—who spent her time flirting and sleeping with soldiers for cigarettes—took her place beside Omryn. "You're no use to anyone," he accused while her sister stood behind his shoulder, nodding sanctimoniously. "Even your children are ashamed. They don't want to see you."

So often she wished the six-month span between Family Visiting Days could be crumpled like paper and burned in the fire. Each visit came so slowly and passed so quickly. She could hardly believe it when the bell would signal—time to climb back into the army trucks.

And last month she missed Family Visiting Day. She'd been passed out and didn't hear the last call for the fifty-mile truck ride to school. She awoke soaked in her own sweat, knowing she'd missed the ride, wanting to die. Why would her daughters love her?

Then she was dismissed from the processing plant. She couldn't look into another pair of kindly eyes and kill. She'd rather turn the knife on her wrists. Upon gathering her things that last day, she took a small butcher's knife for that purpose. That had been her plan until the whoosh of the runners called her away.

The Ush was an endless maze like veins branching out on a cloudberry leaf. It was as stunningly beautiful as it was terrifying. On long journeys, they formed winter camps, sometimes staying for weeks. Breaking ice from rivers to fish, they waited for children to be born, reindeer to calf, and for storm fronts to bring new seasons. Life went on between the long legs of travel. They never rushed. Time was not something to be counted.

Lena tipped the sled on its side to block the wind. She began to prepare her own camp. Crushing small twigs and dry branches, she started a fire with the matches she'd taken from home. Cupping the flames with her hands, she protected them until the fire crackled. Once satisfied it wouldn't blow out, she scooped snow into a kettle. She staggered a bit as she stood, dizzy from dehydration. Strange thoughts crept in; maybe she'd died and was just realizing it? She shook her head and placed the kettle on the fire for tea. Crunching ice between her teeth, she watched the fire below in the valley. Where could Jeaantaa be? Lena never believed the things Tariem said about her.

The reindeer nosed up lichens, snorting as they chewed.

"You're having a good meal?" she asked.

Lena laughed at their steamy breath. She walked over and stroked the ruff of fur under one of their necks. On the male, she petted the extra fold of fur by his throat, the inflatable pouch used to bellow during rutting season. They were getting used to her touch, learning she wasn't to be feared. One met her eyes and wagged its stubby tail.

"Yes, it's good, isn't it?" She pined for the cycles of the reindeer. October's rutting, calving in spring, moving all winter with the herd. How funny the newly born calves looked while running, testing their speed. Through play they practiced and rehearsed running from predators. The ones who became family pets would step into the *yaranga* just like a person, looking around for something to eat. In so short a time the Evil One had crushed them. Under the rolling machines of a bloody star, just as Cheyuga had predicted.

Days after their arrival in Anadyr, Lena pulled into the center square of the city. She looked at the three-story apartment buildings that sat above the permafrost on pilings. How would she find them? She held the halter of the lead reindeer. "Tariem," she began to call. Her voice echoed off the cement buildings.

Tangek was alone in their newly issued apartment, hiding so he wouldn't be taken away to the boarding school. The sound of his father's name woke him. He thought he was dreaming until he sat up. Then the boy stepped out, carefully looking to see if it was a trap.

The men headed down to the dock. Ankjem tagged along, garnering suspicious stares at why a boy his age wasn't off in the state boarding school. They were told the Government was hiring. The ports and docks were to be built and completed by spring. Once the sea opened, the next phase of dredging the harbor would begin.

By the end of the day, the two men and the boy stumbled home, dead tired and cold. They were shocked to find Lena sitting on the concrete bench with Tangek inside the building's vestibule. The neighbor's cat sat in her lap as she chatted in that reindeer click-clack way his cousins had of speaking. The boy leaned against her as he listened.

Within days Lena settled into their life; her round and familiar face softened the angles of the rooms. But Tariem didn't like the suspicious way Cheyuga regarded her. The old man searched for clues as to her sudden appearance. While Tariem and the boys relaxed into her softness, Cheyuga kept to himself. He sensed a deep hollowness within Lena. With shaman eyes he cautioned Tariem, but the observation was met with anger.

"Be careful," the old man warned. "She has a deep well of pain of which I can't see the bottom."

Tariem looked away, guarding the contents of his thoughts.

"Dangerous for her, for the boys," Cheyuga said. "False love is a trick." The old man turned and gazed deeply into Tariem. "It comforts, but deceives."

Tariem left, slamming the metal door behind him. Its echo sounded loudly in the empty cement stairwell. The words stuck to him in ways Cheyuga probably hadn't meant—all those years ago when he fetched Jeaantaa from the ice.

Having Lena puttering about made him smile. Tangek would worm into her lap, accidentally calling her Ama. Lena had not moved to correct him. Yet Tariem felt a twinge of betrayal each time. Why would Cheyuga begrudge them such little comfort? Tariem admired the sweet woman who cooked, laundered and asked for nothing in return.

She'd hug Tangek, holding him far longer than the boy wanted. He'd protest and struggle to get free. After he pushed away, Lena would sit, sullen. Gradually the euphoria of reunion began to wane. Lena disappeared, sometimes for hours in the evening. The men would come home to an empty apartment. No dinner. No sign of where she went or when she'd be back. Cheyuga would look to Tariem. On cue he'd get up and go looking for her. Knocking on doors, he wondered if she went to one of the abandoned lots where people stood drinking. These meeting places were scattered throughout Anadyr. They were congregating places for those without enough money to go to the taverns. They passed bottles, sometimes falling asleep in piles. Some wouldn't wake.

Tariem would be angry when she came home. Lena even angrier that he was upset. But instead of standing up to him, she crumpled, repeating, "I'm bad, I'm bad." Life in Anadyr was not suited to any of them, but for Lena even less so. Tariem smelled vodka. He scoured the apartment, looking for a bottle, but found nothing. Then Lena began staying out all night. She drifted away, her absence as palpable as a bruise.

In less than a month she was gone as suddenly as she appeared. Everyone combed the city for her. Neighbors, people they knew from Uelen, scoured the outskirts of town. Maybe she'd ignored their warnings about polar bears. On occasion the animals would storm through parts of the city. Those who had rifles took shots at them; others threw metal garbage cans.

Sadly, it was Tangek who found Lena. She was frozen and curled up under their apartment building, lying in the four-foot space formed by the sagging permafrost. Cheyuga bent and crawled under the building, lifting her light frame and stroking her matted black hair. He clicked his tongue and shook his head before whispering the Chukchi prayer for the dead into Lena's ear. He laid her on the ground. Tangek and Ankjem stared wide-eyed, their hands tucked into the pockets of their coats. Everyone else bowed their heads and whispered Cheyuga's prayer. They hoped no soldiers were watching.

CHAPTER 27

Fall came quickly. Sugar maples fired in furious reds along the surrounding hills.

The puppies turned six months old, ready to be harness broken. It was a crisp morning, quarter to six, cold enough to see your breath. Arlan and Dan wheeled the contraption they spent the summer building into place for its inaugural run. Rosalie folded her arms, staring at the little Frankenstein.

"I'm running only half," she said.

It was a tripod design—ATV front wheel, two car tires on back, platform for passengers and a wire basket for gear just behind the front wheel.

"Throw 'em all on." Arlan motioned with his arm.

Smokey and King watched at the fence.

"Half," she insisted.

Once the two dogs spotted the gangline in Rosalie's hand, they yelped. It triggered a deafening roar, though most didn't have a clue what for.

"It's three-fifty." He looked to Dan, who predictably nodded. "No way they'll drag her."

She hadn't known it was a girl.

"You'd be surprised," she shouted over the howling.

All summer long Arlan was welding and slathered with axle grease. The dogs watched lazily through the fence. Some curious, most couldn't have cared less except for Arlan's outbursts of profanity and occasional flying wrench. Clowny kept an eye on him; he'd scratch his head, groin, and then look to her. "I don't know, Peanut."

"Oh, don't be a party pooper," Arlan called.

"Eleven dogs have a lot of power."

The rig was built with scavenged parts from the Blueberry Road junkyard. She'd saved enough to buy a used ATV, but Arlan carped, "Pay *me* if you wanna flush money down the toilet." He checked out books on vehicle stability from the Bayfield Library. "First library card of my life," he bragged to anyone who'd listen. The hundred-year-old floor creaked as he strolled through the shelves in wonder. His face mesmerized like a boy who stumbles upon an undiscovered forest.

Since June he'd pored over the engineering, intent on building a dog rig the likes of which the world had never seen. He discussed prototypes with Dave and visited racing kennels on his way home from Two Harbors.

Dave was excited. He stopped by almost daily and the two of them would commiserate. Rosalie figured he was humoring Arlan. But then to her dismay, Dave issued a professional seal of approval. "Well done, Arlan," he pronounced. "As sound as anything I've run dogs on." She was horrified.

"Dave says it's sound," he protested.

Great. Use Dave.

Arlan kicked the two back car tires as if that was supposed to inspire confidence. It made her laugh.

"Think I'd let you on something not safe?"

She realized she'd hurt his feelings.

"You gotta trust me."

"It's about control, Arlan," she called, and hopped onto the metal platform. The howling intensified. "Brakes, steering."

Arlan jumped on and gently shoved her aside. "It's got brakes." He pumped the foot pedal. "Hydraulic brakes—they're real sensitive." Arlan wore the nutty expression you see on small-time inventors. "Just tap 'em or you'll go flying." He shook the frame and watched her face carefully, looking for confirmation.

"Solid, ain't she?" He said it with such conviction, it was hard not to laugh. "Ain't nobody's gonna roll this puppy."

It had a wide axle from an old trailer frame for stability; she'd give him that.

"Great, Arlan. I'm still only taking half." She disassembled the gangline into a five-dog.

Running the whole team on an untried piece of equipment was reckless. *Rule one of a first run:* expect something to go wrong. *Rule two:* what goes wrong will never be what you think. But her resolve weakened. He had a way of wearing her down. She reattached the second five-dog section of gangline.

"Atta girl," Arlan congratulated her as if she just passed the Iditarod finish line in Nome.

"Should have my head examined," she muttered, weaving the additional section back into the line. "Dad?" She gestured for Arlan to stay on board for the inaugural run. Instead he hopped off, gesturing for Dan to step up.

"Too scared, are ya?" she shouted.

"Just not sure my life insurance is paid."

"Hypocrite."

All summer long she'd harnessed the growing dogs to a heavy tire. It was the first step in strength training and promoting their natural instincts as working dogs.

She slipped them into the old Stormwatch harnesses Jan palmed off on her at the end of the season. "What else are we going to do with this old crap?" Jan insisted, shoving their older gear into Rosalie's truck. The equipment wasn't *that* old and she knew it. Another instance of their chronic overgenerosity, for which she stood perpetually at their service.

Rosalie attached the rig to the bumper of her truck. Arlan tapped her shoulder.

"That damn thing's half rusted off," he yelled over the dogs. "The tree. Use the tree." He motioned to the tall white pine along the driveway.

Rosalie wheeled the rig into place, locking the brake and securing it to the tree with the snub line. Dave once told of how they hooked their first team to the front of their porch in Minnesota.

Not only had the enthusiastic team yanked out a support beam, but they also had dragged off a significant portion of the porch roof before Jan was able to stop the runaway team.

First Rosalie brought King. He was hopping on his rear legs as if ready to fly over to the rig. He'd never been so uncontrollable. Maybe it was the combination of inaugural run, newness of the rig, running as a whole pack—all the stuff of excitement.

She looked to Dan. He rushed to grab the dog's collar. Once hooked to the gangline King jumped and slammed forward in his harness. Arlan's 350-pound creation, locked brake and all, pulled to the end of the snub line like it was nothing. King took on the old-growth white pine as a personal challenge.

Arlan eyed the tree trunk as if having second thoughts.

King emitted a pitiful cry she'd never heard.

"Is he in pain?" She worried about pressure in his eye.

"Nah—more like heaven," Dan shouted with a sly smile, as if understanding King better in that moment.

She hooked Smokey next to King in co-lead since they were experienced. King looked instantly grumpy. Smokey was wide-eyed and oblivious, always just happy to be alive. He suffered from having no earthly ambition whatsoever and ran happily in any position. Dave dubbed King as a "single-lead kinda guy."

They quickly hooked up Bella, Flyer, and Noodle behind the leaders. Then Kicky and Goofy, then Clowny and Rascal. Last they hooked Junior and Panda—the biggest boys—in wheel position, their brawn needed closest to the rig. Rosalie hopped up onto the platform behind the steering bar. The rig vibrated and jerked as the yelping, leaping dogs slammed in unison at King's cue into their harnesses.

"Hope the brakes work," she hollered to Arlan.

Arlan lifted his hands like, "Me too."

"Ready?" she called to King, who lunged to acknowledge the command.

But as she reached for the quick release, her stomach clenched.

She couldn't. Dan tapped her arm, motioning for her to pull the release snap.

"I can't," she whispered, suddenly hostage to herself.

"Do it," he yelled. She was frozen. Darkness shadowed her sight as if a shade had been pulled. Dan reached behind her and released the team. They took off, dragging the rig sideways.

"The brake." He tapped her foot with his. "Let it up."

She lifted her foot. The rig straightened out. The dogs lined up and barreled down the driveway towards Ridge Road. There was utter silence except for the tinkling of eleven sets of ID tags.

Dan slipped his arm around her shoulders and squeezed her tight, kissing the side of her head.

"Haw," she called. King turned left onto Ridge Road. Barreling down the hill felt like a free fall. Her stomach rushed. The rig gained momentum; Panda glanced back as it were rolling faster than they could run.

She braked. What would she have done without Dan's weight?

The aqua jewel of liquid horizon spanned out before them, the cliff's edge immediately ahead. Her mouth was cottony. Timing was everything; King held their lives.

"Gee," she called. King anticipated the right turn. Like clockwork the rig steered. The force about threw them, like a roller coaster broken free. The physics of it were so new, the awkwardness of unfamiliar dance partners coming together for a first song.

Dan gave her a look. She could barely breathe. Thankful they made it onto Scheffel and the level trail.

The team was airborne. It was hard to see where their feet were making contact. Tall grass slowed them; heavy dew drenched her boots and pants. Electric yellow leaves littered the trail like ticker-tape confetti. Burnished orange ferns and dried stalks of wildflowers flicked dewdrops off the dogs' coats, sparkling like sequins in the early autumn sunlight.

They'd fallen into a good pace when Clowny began to drag the team off to the side.

"What's she doing?" Rosalie watched the dog accelerate. She tried to pass Goofy, the dog in front of her.

Dan shrugged.

Clowny dragged Rascal, to whom she was tethered, along with two wheel dogs behind her. She pulled the rig lopsided, breaking the team's momentum. Rascal took a swipe at her to knock it off, but the smaller red dog continued to drag the team sideways.

"Clowny!" Rosalie called, trying to get her attention. "Clowny!" The dog heard nothing.

King glanced back. Clowny surged and bit her neckline as if trying to chew herself free. Both spotted the pattern at the same time.

"She's chasing him," Dan said. Rosalie nodded.

Split-second messages passed between the two. Clowny—like a stray copper penny amid a pile of loose quarters—her back undulated to ape ahead of her teammates out in front.

A rabbit scurried across the trail. King's pace remained unaltered.

"Look at King," she remarked. "My God, he's just like Mitzi."

King was clearly grumpy. To no avail he tried to egg Smokey on to race, but Clowny had taken the bait.

"He's a running machine all right." This was Dan's first chance to experience sled dog focus and power.

Tall black seed pods of wild lupines filled the meadow openings along the trail. Beds of swirling grass flattened like crop circles. Signs of sleeping deer that might have been nuzzled together—moments before they sprang off to avoid the charging team. The beds looked like they'd still be warm.

"Whoa." Rosalie braked. The rig stopped cold, almost throwing the two of them over the steering bar.

"Jesus," Dan complained. His sternum hit the metal frame, practically knocking the wind out of him.

"Sorry. I guess the brakes *do* work." She smiled sheepishly.

"Damn right they do."

"I'll get used to them."

King looked back at her.

"Gee, come," she gave the command. King reversed the whole team, turning them back around without a single tangle. She locked the brake. Walking up the gangline, she kissed and petted each dog. Their faces were dotted with foamy saliva, their eyes wild. Clowny's eyes looked as if they'd pop out of her head.

"I'm switching Smokey and Clowny."

"Good idea," Dan said from the platform where he stayed to secure the rig. She unhooked Smokey and walked him back to Clowny's position.

"Look at Panda's face." She stopped to laugh out loud. His pitch-black face was plastered with white cottony seed puffs from the surrounding wildflowers. He looked tarred and feathered as he smiled brightly at her.

The instant she hooked Clowny next to King their shoulders pressed together. They pulled the gangline tight, satisfied at the fair fight. King seemed pleased with the more respectable rival of his daughter. Clowny gave every indication she was up to the challenge.

"You okay?" Dan asked. Rosalie stepped back on the platform. He grabbed her shoulders, jokingly shaking them to relax them. "Thought I'd have to hijack this thing up there."

"Oh shut up." She laughed, pinching the flesh beneath his jean jacket. "Tell me you weren't freaked."

"I wasn't freaked."

"You lie." Grateful tears filled her eyes. "Thanks for helping Arlan—it meant so much to him. I think I'll take only half when I'm alone."

He winked in agreement.

"Team A: Clowny." Rosalie pointed out the members. "Team B: King."

Dan put his arm around her. "You really love this, don't you?" She nodded shyly, leaning her head on his shoulder.

"I'm glad," he said, cradling her for a moment. "I'll help you run them together when I have time."

She kissed him. The rig lurched even with the brake locked. King glanced back impatiently. Rosalie hadn't seen Clowny as a lead dog, so much smaller than the rest. But dog mushing is a funny business. Often the bossiest, most dominant of the yard will shirk when up front with the pressure on. Who wouldn't be intimidated by a pack of gaining wolves tearing for the chance to bite you in the ass?

"Okay. Let's go," Rosalie gave the command.

The dogs jumped into their harnesses. Rosalie released the brake. King and Clowny leapt with delight as they took off, racing each other towards some mythic finish line.

"My God, Dan, just look at 'em go."

CHAPTER 28

It had been the lightest of days. The Chukchi believe that when the spirit is bright and open the gate to another world is left unguarded. When one is in that state—through either happiness or sadness—evil *keedle* spirits are drawn towards the opening. They are lonely and attracted to such lightness. Ready to take a person with them for company.

Tangek's second wife, Katerina, had just given birth to a son. It was particularly bittersweet since, nine years earlier, his first wife died giving birth to their second daughter. At the time he'd been sick with grief and disappeared, leaving his two baby daughters. Tariem had tracked him south where the Eveneks used to herd their reindeer. He brought Tangek home, explaining that "it is not good for daughters to lose both parents."

After his young wife's death, Tangek swore to never remarry. The prospect of enduring such pain again was unimaginable. It was a promise he kept for nine years, until Katerina barged into his life. During that span of time he had more than his share of lovers: Chukchi, Russian and Ukranian. The young women named him "the-one-whose-heart-has-been-lost," though it hadn't stopped many from trying.

Tangek was taller than Tariem, with many of Jeaantaa's good looks. He had lived in the same government-issue apartment, along with other family members, since the day the reindeer stepped into the City of Death.

They met on Katerina's first day working in the People's Commissary. She made a point of scolding Tangek for using the wrong ration tickets that month. It became the story of legend, at least in her own mind. She'd beam with its recounting, thinking it endeared her to everyone. Little did she know that family members cringed, wondering how Tangek missed so serious a warning about her character.

She was an older woman, though that in itself had no consequence. There were so many other things about Katerina they found puzzling—not at all who they hoped to be the "one-to-find-Tangek's-heart." But love has its ways. Only weeks after they met, she quit her job and declared, "It is time to marry."

Days later the cement walls of the apartment stairwell echoed with every possible sound a human with blind determination could make.

"What's that noise?" Cheyuga sat up. Several grandchildren stepped into the hallway. Duffel bags filled with Katerina's personal belongings bashed against the walls. The metal banister reverberated with each hit, all the way up to their third-floor apartment.

"Come help me," she hollered. There was a loud crash. "Can't you see I'm struggling?" she scolded. "I'm your new family."

While no one recognized the face or the voice, its demanding quality made them ignore it all the more. The tiny apartment would be stretched even further. Tangek, his two daughters, Ankjem, his wife and three children, Tariem, Cheyuga plus several assorted relatives from Uelen—no one was sure how or if they were related. Katerina elbowed her way into their family with a voracity seldom seen.

Just as everyone agreed that they couldn't hate her more, Tangek announced her pregnancy. Katerina beamed coquettishly, looking to garner their adoration. Stone faces met her procuring glance. "Too bad," Ankjem's five-year-old son whispered loudly. "Now we're stuck with her." Katerina trembled with rage.

"The only one she's got charmed is Tangek," Ankjem's wife complained under her breath. It was always Katerina's way. Challengers were bullied or forced to endure her endless theatrics.

Soon Tangek's daughters were pushed into the margins as Katerina's needs came to eclipse all others.

She, like Lena, had come from reindeer country. Both her parents drowned during the Season-of-Extending-Days when lake ice proved too thin for travel. They were riding to another camp by reindeer sled when one of the animals yawned. A yawning reindeer was a very bad omen. Her mother shrieked and demanded they turn back. But just as they did, the ice gave way. Only Katerina survived. The seven-year-old swam to shore, robust enough to make it back to camp. She told the story to everyone in Anadyr, adding skepticism about her present fragility. There were so many sad stories, but as Tangek's daughters guessed, Katerina used hers as a ploy to get out of household work. "No, no, don't ask me; I'm unlucky," she'd say. "I have bad reindeer luck." She'd turn her face towards her shoulder to hide the bad luck. As if it were a cold she didn't want anyone to catch. Yet Tangek's daughters both swore she was hiding a smile.

During the nine months of Katerina's confinement, she travailed well in advance of labor. "You'd think that in all of the history of the earth, a woman had never been pregnant," Cheyuga griped. Everyone looked at him. The old man never spoke ill of a soul. For the last few months of his life, Cheyuga preferred to accompany the men to the gold mines, rather than stay home listening to Katerina. Each morning he'd leave with Tariem and his sons. The old man collected garbage, swept and did whatever he could to add to the much-needed income. The teetering government owed workers two months' back wages. Ankjem, Tangek and Tariem covered for him so the comrade at arms wouldn't ask the old man not to come back.

After twelve- and fourteen-hour shifts the men straggled in dead tired. Katerina would be waiting for Tangek to collect her foot massage. "He listens how to do it right." And to everyone's horror, Tangek immediately attended to her swollen feet. Listening as she went on about what a hard day she'd had and how nobody liked her.

She did no work around the house, even to collect her own dishes. "I am so weak from bad reindeer luck." Her feet were perpetually up in the air, propped up on some object. Her toes became fat sausages, much like the rest of her, in so short a time. The children marveled at her rapidly expanding size, her legs like stumps. "Too bad she hadn't kept them crossed and on the floor in front of her," sniped the woman in the downstairs apartment.

The whole family was baffled. How had Tangek gotten roped and tied like a reindeer calf during a Government demonstration?

The men drove bulldozers in the open-pit gold mine, hauling boulders of black shale to the processing tables. The mine, located just outside of Anadyr, was believed to contain the second-largest gold reserves in all of Russia. The mining operation stripped away mountains, leaving craters that rivaled their actual height. Many of these were topped off to form poisonous lakes. Sulfides were used to lift off yellow flakes of metal growing like lichens into the black rock. Surrounding hills were blanketed with discarded metal drums as far as a person could see.

Because the terrain of Chukotka was either permafrost or impassable mountains, railroads could not be built. The last stop for the trans-Siberian railway ended twelve hundred miles west of Anadyr. Materials were hauled forty miles overland to the port of Anadyr and loaded onto barges. It was a mad dash to the sea since the waters were open only a few short months. The mine was worked round the clock. Corners were cut, equipment was substandard, time frames unrealistic and the ratio of lives lost to mine activity the highest in the world.

The unstable nature of permafrost also made building roads to Anadyr impossible. Thus the arduous task of hauling shale was left to trucks with caterpillar-like metal tracks. Drivers took a new route each trip since previous tracks rendered the land impassable. They tore across the uneven tundra, permanently damaging the *yagel,* or deer moss, that blanketed and stabilized the delicate topsoil. Nothing would grow. Erosion pockmarked the surface and chemicals accumulated from the sulfide wash, rendering the tundra a dead zone.

The day Katerina gave birth to their son, Tangek bounced rather than walked in the open-pit mine. He talked of dreams. How his son would go to school and become educated so he wouldn't have to work in the mine. Coworkers teased Tangek, saying if that was the case the baby must be someone else's child. Yet as he spoke, everyone saw his words weaving a future—where hope alone was enough to create a life. To Tangek, everything was possible. Until one of the huge dump trucks began to back up as he stood talking.

Something prompted Tariem to glance across the open pit. He was helping Cheyuga. Tangek's movements were alarming. He was not paying attention; he was drunk with joy. Tariem had driven enough trucks to see that Tangek was in the blind spot. Dashing as fast as he could, Tariem yelled and waved his arms.

The hospital had been too far away. There was no working X-ray machine or certified doctor. The evil *keedle* spirits took Tangek's breath. Tariem couldn't move; how could he have failed to protect his son? He'd left Tangek unguarded. He'd left Jeaantaa's breakable son unprotected in his joy, so alone in the light of his happiness. Tariem had forgotten the old ways. He forgot that sorrow so often rides on the heels of happiness. Now it was too late. From then on Tariem wondered what the magnitude might be of all he had forgotten.

CHAPTER 29

"Helen and Charlie think I should get my GED."

"What for?" Dan asked sharply.

"I guess they think it's good to finish." Rosalie stooped to open the grate of the wood-burning stove. The room was chilly. There were a few more days until Halloween. She poked the coals and ashes.

Dan sat with his coat on, sampling a bowl of her chicken soup as he waited for Arlan. He softly blew to cool each spoonful.

She closed the grate and stepped to the wood bin. Leaning over, she sorted through what was left of the driest ones. Blood rushed to her face as she straightened, cradling a shaggy paper birch log like an infant.

"I'd be the first." She smiled in a bashful way.

She watched as Dan stared absentmindedly at the salt- and pepper shakers in front of the bowl.

"They already pay you, right?" he asked in a measured way that made her think he meant something else. His voice was neutral. Its indifference bothered her. His features were tranquil, yet he seemed agitated. She had the impression he was waiting for a right answer.

"Well . . . yeah—of course they pay me."

Dan turned and looked at her. "Okay." His voice was condescending. "So—what do you need it for?"

His impatience surprised her. Like he was annoyed at having to explain what she should know by now. What a relief when he resumed eating.

"They think I could go on to Indianhead Tech. . . ." She

paused. An unexpected stab of fear pierced her stomach. Her mouth dried, hands cold. Then a familiar drowsiness settled in, tempting her to space out, let it go, not create a fuss. But something new nudged her to finish the thought.

"—to get certified as a vet tech."

"Sounds like a colossal waste of time and money if you ask me,"

Opening the grate, she pitched in the log, watching the shaggy paper ringlets and spiral curls ignite. Spinning and sizzling like fireworks, they popped into flames, disappearing into nothing but energy. Sparks flew out and landed on the stone slab hearth before she shut the grate. It filled her with peaceful satisfaction. She warmed her hands.

"Well, maybe so—" She was hypnotized by the glow. The flames drew her as she surrendered. Fire had its own language. "—but I think I want to anyway."

"*You* think—or does *Charlie* think?" Dan snickered with the aggression of counting coup on an enemy.

She looked in surprise. His voice was different. Gravelly, as if someone had borrowed his mouth. Why paint her as someone incapable of independent thought? And then it dawned on her. She smiled slightly, realizing what he was fishing for.

"What do you mean?" She softened her tone. She'd make him say it.

Folding her arms, she waited.

His silence turned angry. It was disquieting, like tension between two rival dogs. She braced. The seductive urge to back down chipped away. Just nuzzle into his lap. Twist the whole thing into one big joke. But then Jan's words: "Courage doesn't mean you're not afraid; it means you do it anyway."

"You're still not saying why you don't want me to do it." Rosalie's voice was steadier than she felt. "It's what *I* want, Dan." She touched her sternum.

He set down the spoon and pushed out his chair. The oak legs rubbed the wood floor. "You seem awfully worried what Charlie and Helen think." He chuckled as if confirming he'd been right about her all along. Shaking his head, he bent over to lace up his work boot.

Who was this person who'd just eaten her soup?

"They're my friends," she said.

"Your friends, Rosalie?" He looked up. "They pay you." His eyebrows rose in mock surprise. "Friends don't pay each other."

"They *are* my friends."

Anger rose in her chest like a thundercloud. She pulled her hands out of her pockets. It had all the potential for a "yes-they-are," "no-they're-not" seventh-grade lunchroom brawl.

"They want to see me get somewhere—" She grabbed and tossed the soup bowl into the sink. It clunked, the few remaining spoonfuls splattered on the counter.

"What's with you?" She raised her voice. "Like working in that stupid-ass mill is so fucking great—don't you want better? I've started memorizing morphologies of wild canids from Charlie's anatomy books."

"Well, good for you." The chair flew out as Dan stood. He walked towards the door.

She could barely breathe. Why didn't he care about what she'd grown to love? During the long drives between calls, Charlie explained how the canine circulatory system works. She sat rapt, visualizing how blood oxygenates differently in working dogs, ingesting information with a hunger she never imagined. It burned with the intensity of heartache. For months she watched as Clowny, Panda and the rest practically inhaled their food, the kibble being muscled down into their fat little bellies through peristalsis. She pictured nutrients synthesized into bone material and nervous system development. Listened to their stomachs with the brand-new stethoscope Helen and Charlie gave her during a potlatch ceremony. The thumping of the dogs' growing hearts, the whooshing sound of blood rushing through arteries. Listening through the soft folds of puppy fat never seemed to get old. Each would flip over, gently pawing her face, as if she were the most delicate thing on earth.

"Why are you being like this?" She tromped after Dan. "We could take classes together, Dan; it could be fun."

Nothing about Dan was obvious. Like the outsider circling the pack, the gentleman dodger, it seemed Dan ran reconnaissance. He offered compensatory niceness rather than the quiet trust born from finally admitting yourself to another.

"Tell your father I'm out in the truck."

Your father?

Dan opened the front door to end the conversation. She followed down the porch steps wearing moccasin slippers that had been her mother's.

"We could get better jobs, Dan, have a future—"

She picked after him like a crow after a meal.

"Charlie said he knows the people at the vet tech program—"

"Yeah well, good for you and Charlie." He rushed ahead, but she followed him to the Bronco.

"Why are you being such a baby?"

He climbed into the truck and started the engine. She continued talking after he shut the door.

"Dan." She tapped the window, thinking he'd roll it down.

Instead he stared into the blue of the instrument panel. His face was expressionless, illuminated by the aqua-colored light.

"Dan." She was more puzzled than angry. She pulled the door handle. It was locked.

The cabin door opened as Arlan emerged. Lunch box in one hand, coat draped over his forearm. He had a funny look on his face.

"You kids okay?"

She stormed past without answering.

No word from Dan the entire weekend. Neither did he pop in to watch TV. An odd sort of disappointment set in. Like discovering the first round of delphinium blossoms shriveled in an unexpected late freeze.

"What were you fighting about anyway?" Arlan folded the Sunday paper in half.

"You tell me." She didn't look up from beading frosty tendrils of a fern onto the back skirt of a wedding dress.

The house had been noticeably quiet that weekend. Arlan kept letting out long sighs, glancing at the clock and then rather pointedly at her. She wasn't sure what she wanted from Dan. Maybe she'd barged into a part of him he hadn't wanted her to see, one of the parts we hide because *we* hate them ourselves. And when love cracks open the door to peek in, we swear our days are numbered.

With dogs you can push the line of their fears, test their drive and endurance, even their bite threshold to win their trust. They can't hide.

She wondered when she'd see him again as the weekend passed. She ran the dogs alone in two halves and mentioned nothing to Arlan about the GED program. There was something about education that seemed to make everyone unhappy.

Arlan pulled back into the driveway after it seemed he'd just left.

Something was wrong. She lifted her head to listen.

A stream of dogs dashed out the doggie door. Squealing and jumping, they lined up along the fence to welcome him. Then they raced back, vying for the spot closest to the front door.

She was rushing to finish the elaborate bodice of a "red-carpet" gown for a celebrity, or so she was told. A deadline was a deadline and money was money no matter whose sweat would stain the armpits. She'd already ripped the design out twice and couldn't afford another screwup for fear of scarring the fabric. The last two deadlines had been very tight. A peach-colored chiffon dress for the First Lady of Kansas and now this.

The dogs yipped with excitement.

She slipped the movie star's bodice into her sewing box and crept to the window.

Layoffs were always announced at the end of a shift. The Bronco pulled in. They hadn't spoken; she'd called a few times but chickened out after the first few rings.

She smoothed back her hair and took a deep breath to calm down. Maybe he wouldn't come in. She glanced down at her chest, *oh shit*, dried crusty splashes of tomato soup from lunch. She briefly entertaining the idea of sucking it out.

The porch step cracked noisily. Arlan's footsteps sounded heavier than usual. No kicking aside of pinecones, broken twigs and accumulated needles.

"What happened?" she asked as he stepped inside.

Dan was quickly on her father's heels. The dogs jumped at the reunion.

"Plant's closed." Arlan plopped onto the sofa, immediately buried under the deluge of fur. "We're locked out." He pulled off his hat and tossed it. Smokey jumped up beside the hat, sniffing inside.

Clowny dove into his lap, knocking him back against the couch. Her hind end wagged as she reclaimed him with a face wash. Arlan closed his mouth and submitted. "No sense fighting City Hall," he'd always say.

"Locked out?" she repeated.

"Gates are chained shut—thanks for telling us," Arlan reported. He closed his mouth against Clowny's French kiss. "Sign's posted." He quickly shut his mouth as Clowny continued. "Two Harbors Mill Closed," he said. "Hauling out furniture, machines—like burglars." The dog jumped down. "Bastards don't waste any time." He laughed bitterly. "Clay said they soldered shut the east gate."

For years the company had cried poverty. Last year management mustered the testicular fortitude to demand that the town of Two Harbors build them a new plant. After the town's refusal, a sizeable pay increase along with stock options was afforded to executives. The rank and file were forced to shoulder an even larger portion of health insurance premiums. Now, one year later, the company made good on the threat.

Dan strode to the kitchen table and sat down with his coat on. Folding his hands, he stared past them into nothing.

"Sure they're not just weaseling out of the Christmas bonus again?"

Neither responded. She guessed they weren't. Yet it felt as if the neighborhood bully had moved away for good.

Arlan parted the sea of dogs to hoist himself up. He walked to the fridge. Fishing out two cold beers, he popped both tops with the magnetic opener on the door. Sitting across from Dan, he slid the bottle over.

"Well, Danny boy, it's not like we didn't see it coming," Arlan muttered.

"Foundry's hiring; I saw the sign," Rosalie said. "Felice says the Forest Service is too." She looked at Dan. "You know trees so well, Dan."

There was a tense silence between the two men. Neither took a sip of beer. Arlan sat curved over his, elbows on the table, chin in his palm.

"Why not go down there now before everyone else does?" she urged as if Dan hadn't heard the first time. "You just have to take the stupid State of Wisconsin exam. Felice did; she said it was like second grade—the Noodle could pass it."

The dog looked up at the sound of her name, ready and willing to take any exam for Rosalie.

Dan stood up. He paused as if about to speak, and then walked out—quietly closing the front door. The Bronco started. They listened as it backed up and drove towards the road.

Arlan sighed loudly, rubbing his face with his hands as his whiskers made scratching noises.

She sat down in Dan's place and grabbed his beer. She took a sip.

Arlan sighed even louder. A preamble to a much longer conversation he didn't want to have. "See." He shifted in his chair. "Dan's got this problem."

She waited for him to go on. Yet somehow she knew what he was about to say.

"Can't read well or write."

"But the state exam's easy—"

"Easy ain't even closer," he cut her off. He looked long into her eyes, the same color green as his. "There's something wrong with him. He can barely write. Doesn't read well either. I've watched him for years—it's painful to see. Even filling his time card out each week." Arlan replicated the spiky tracings of Dan's writing in the air. "You'd think it'd get easier, never has."

They sat in silence.

"Funny how he . . ." Arlan paused.

"How he what?"

He motioned with his hand to forget it. "Maybe we can get some work with one of the local loggers come spring."

Then she saw it all in an instant. Arlan, the Guardian Angel, covering for Dan all those years. Reading instructions out loud in that nonchalant way he has of understanding and not embarrassing—every new piece of equipment, new safety instructions. Her father was a true friend to Dan and a loyal coworker. Maintaining his secret and dignity without acknowledging there were secrets or dignity to protect.

"Doesn't his family have tons of money?"

"Ha!" Arlan laughed in a bitter way that made his head dip back. "It all got donated to Louise's causes—those hoity-toity Purple Ladies of the American Revolution or whatever-the-hell on Madeline Island."

He stepped to reach an open bag of Doritos from atop the fridge.

"Built that stupid-ass Theatre for the Arts for rich people who don't live here—brass plaques all over the place. 'Her cultural legacy.'" He made a face he thought a cultured person might make. "Five years later people ask, 'Louise who?'"

He pushed the Doritos towards her. "Leaves her own son with all his problems to hang out to dry like that." He shook his head.

"He's got that big house," she said.

"You can't eat a house, Rosalie."

"He could sell it."

"Now who the hell's gonna buy something like that up here?" Arlan stared her down as if it were all her fault.

She lifted both hands to concede.

"Her 'Beautiful Bayfield County Flower' trust fund. Ever wonder why there's so many goddamned flowers all over the place during tourist season? Dan's inheritance growing in sheep shit."

"What's he gonna do?"

Arlan closed his eyes, covered his face with his hand and shook his head.

CHAPTER 30

Tariem sat across the table, dressed in half Soviet garb, half Chukchi. Waist up in sealskin shirts he constructed as best he could remembering Jeaantaa's method. Waist down in government-issue snow pants, hems frayed from dragging the ground. Last year he pulled them through a broken window of an abandoned Soviet commissary along with a pair of rubber boots that were too large.

It was cold in the Council Room of the People's Community Center. The power had just come back on after being out for the night. The space heater smelled like burning hair as it labored to make up for lost time. Ice coated the inside windowpanes, condensation trickling in crooked streams. More overhead fluorescent lights were out than working. A few buzzed and flickered on a death march into silence.

The three-person contingent of Alaskan Natives from Nome sat down. They scooted chairs closer to the gray Formica table. Bundled in hats, gloves and coats—their breath steamed. Eyeglasses fogged as they took stock of the bare room. Voices echoed off peeling plaster walls. It was cold even for them.

"I'm Gracie," a middle-aged woman who seemed in charge introduced herself. "This is Gregory, one of our elders, and Thomas, who's in our youth program and speaks Russian."

The adolescent relayed the information. Tariem nodded.

Tariem was filled with questions and requests but first let them talk about the Glory of God and whatever they wanted. Their green pocket-sized Russian Bibles were stacked up on the table like booty. One of the few conditions of the humanitarian exchange. A pile of chocolate bars that Tariem kept his eye on set beside them. Help was contingent upon listening about Jesus. He figured after sixty years of being force-fed Soviet ideologies in exchange for nothing it was worth a gamble.

"We need hunters to come teach our young men to get food once again from the sea," he interrupted. "For so long they didn't let us that the memories are forgotten."

The contingent agreed to send whale and other mammal hunters from Alaskan villages to Uelen as soon as the waters opened in July. They'd teach young Chukchi men how to fish, maneuver boats and hunt the large mammals. For more than six decades Native hunting and fishing was prohibited by the Soviet law. Government-sanctioned hunting—if you could call it that—consisted of Soviet gunboats with anti-tank artillery blowing bowhead whales to smithereens. Carcass parts were then retrieved and sent to State mink and fox collectives to be used as feed. This as the Maritime Chukchi watched, sentenced to a lifetime of canned Soviet rations.

None of the young men knew how to get food from pack ice or navigate the rough currents to hunt. As the old ones died, so did the knowledge. Tariem was one of the last, though he lacked the strength to teach out in the seas. Hunting wasn't taught from shore by telling old stories. You had to feel the boat. Conquer the stomach-squeezing fear of free-falling in an umiak once it crests over a swell and let terror turn to exhilaration. Having your boat tossed up by a huge mammalian tail. Learning to steer and navigate the primordial dance of whale and umiak. As Tariem would relay stories, the young men of Uelen looked at the sea with fear and not desire. The old man would crumple to sit on the pebbly shore, wishing again for his youth. To feel the ocean spray on your face and take what Aquarvanguit had promised would always be there. Watching as families gathered on the shore, standing ready with knives, as they waited for the whale to be towed to shore. Celebrating and welcoming the hunters back as heroes, giving thanks and taking what was needed. Whale meat spoiled quickly. Villages from the entire region would show up, picking a carcass clean in days. Every part was eaten or used. Ribs and vertebrae served as building materials. Taking more than needed was a sin, but even worse was waste. The animal gave its life so all could live. To waste was to disrespect. And to disrespect brought bad luck and evil.

"I also would like for you to find Robert Ramsay?" Tariem asked. "He knows where my wife is and he has my dogs."

They found the question funny but didn't glance at each other out of respect.

"Your wife," Gracie stated.

"Yes, she lives with him," Tariem said.

They all frowned, not knowing what he meant. Ramsay was well-known in Nome.

"My goodness." Gracie started making small talk as they waited for a bus to come pick them up. All airplanes were grounded for a few hours because of wind. A sudden break in the storm front was their chance to get out; otherwise they'd be staying overnight.

"God has blessed you with such a long life," she changed the subject. Her face shone with foregone conclusions about God's gift of longevity.

Dabbing a leaky nostril with crinkled white tissues, a gloved hand tried to hurry the translation along. Young Thomas was more intent on accuracy than speed. Tall, too thin, a sincere pimply face, he looked about the same age as Yevgheni—Tariem's thirteen-year-old great-great-grandson—who by now was on his way to pick him up. Tariem tried to guess the age of the other two. It was tough with people from Rochlit. They looked like spring's new buds, even when old. In Chukotka, old age pulled up a chair and sat down early.

Gracie looked vaguely familiar. He studied her face as the boy doled out words. But after ninety-one years Tariem had seen just about every combination of nose, eyes and cheeks. His stomach growled louder than Thomas' voice. Before they left Uelen for the meeting in Anadyr, Tariem had not had time to find more seal meat and fish. They'd rushed to make it to Anadyr before the contingent had left. It was a day's travel from Uelen by snowmobile. Earlier he handed the last chunk of meat to his grandson. There was little food in the Place of Death, though his grandson was looking for some before the return trip. Tariem was told the residents were owed two years of back wages. He wouldn't eat canned rations again. His hunger would wait. They'd start home after the meeting, making camp halfway in the Valley of Flowers. Break ice in the River of Bears and fish.

Gracie waited for Tariem to acknowledge God's blessing.

Tariem's eyes darted as if the woman were crazy. He frowned and turned to Thomas, gathering his thoughts. What blessing was there in watching grandchildren die from hunger? With no hope—the indiscriminant dollop of heartbreak that seemed to be no respecter of persons. Spending decades second-guessing and wondering if different actions would have yielded different results. Forty was old, fifty dead. He was antediluvian by Chukotka standards. Nothing seemed to kill him.

"Why don't you die, Grandfather?" one of the grandchildren asked.

"Because I'm not alive," Tariem said. "Like the wind, the *yagel* moss." The children regarded him with skepticism; the elders just regarded him. For too many death had come early. Hunger, malnutrition-related illness. The population shrank. Pneumonia killed children in hours as parents watched helplessly. There were few doctors and less medicine, even if you had dump trucks full of money. The one ingredient there always seemed to be an abundance of was alcohol.

After the breakup of the Soviet Union, the government dropped Chukotka like a hot potato. Soviet officials and non-Chukchi workers practically tripped over each other, scrambling to get out before the ice locked them in for another year. Everything tasted bitter. Many like Lena killed their taste buds with vodka, brawls and early death. Once taken, there was no road back from the-place-of-despair. Decades' worth of lives were wiped out by the impersonal tsunamis of change.

"Tell her." Tariem paused to study Gracie's face.

The woman looked away.

His eyes made her uncomfortable. He'd not meant to offend. Tariem crooked his finger for the young Thomas to listen carefully.

"It's just as easy to punish with so long a life as it is to bless."

Thomas relayed the words to Gracie. She looked down at her hands and shook her head.

"No." Gracie looked at Tariem. In her eyes were flecks of gold. Her voice softened. "God doesn't punish."

Tariem shifted his gaze onto the stacks of Bibles as if to put her at ease.

"Maybe we're your answer to prayer," she said.

Tariem looked up at her. If he could learn about Jeaantaa, find the Guardians. He spent so many decades poisoned with an anger that had finally burned itself out. He hoped her life had been a happy one, and was now more curious than anything.

His stomach growled again. They were too embarrassed to ask—he too proud to tell. Somewhere down by the docks in the Place of Death, Yevgheni was siphoning gasoline from abandoned Soviet trucks. Enough to fill the extra petrol cans to get them back to Uelen.

Tariem leaned towards Thomas. "Perhaps you are," he said.

Thomas clasped his hands and smiled. These people smiled at everything. Either life was truly wonderful in Rochlit or they were idiots. The youth waited with the same trained patience Tariem had seen in the young Soldiers of Culture generations ago.

"Thank you for agreeing to return this summer," Tariem confirmed.

"You said you have your own boats?" Thomas conveyed Gregory the elder's question.

Tariem nodded once.

That past fall he'd instructed Yevgheni how to build the first umiak in more than sixty years. A walrus-rib frame lashed together and covered with hide just as he and Uptek would build lifetimes ago. So far, Tariem and his grandson had produced three. By spring, when the Alaskan hunters from Nome arrived, they were hoping to have six more—their own fleet of hunting boats to be launched from the Cove.

"The ice opens in July," Thomas confirmed.

Tariem nodded. "And thank you for finding the Guardians."

"We'll do what we can," Gracie qualified.

"Now that we're back in Uelen," Tariem explained, "the Guardians can return." This had been their first winter in a reconstructed *yaranga* at the crescent stand of trees.

"You have his name—R-o-b-e-r-t R-a-m-s-a-y?" Tariem clarified.

Thomas waved the piece of torn envelope that Yevgheni had written on, as proof.

"And the phone number where you can find us?" Tariem asked.

Thomas waved the envelope again.

"He knows my wife," Tariem confirmed. The possiblility of ever seeing Jeaantaa again choked him up. There are some hatreds and loves that outlive their hurt. "He knows her, this Robert Ramsay," he insisted. "He knows where she went."

They shot quick glances at each other.

"Forty years ago, she left with—Robert Ramsay." He said the name as clearly as possible. Even though he'd begun forgetting some of the grandchildren's names, this one rang clear.

Gracie nodded, not sure she was understanding, but pointed to the phone number anyway. "Is this where you live?"

"No. But they will come get us," Tariem explained.

Yevgheni's friend Uri lived in an apartment building in Uelen. Uri was a few years older; he owned a truck and had agreed to make the short trip up the ridge to their *yaranga*. Uelen was so far east only American TV and radio came through. They'd all crowd into Uri's family apartment to watch American basketball games.

Gracie moved the stack of Bibles across the table towards Tariem as a reminder.

Tariem used the table for leverage to push up to his feet. He nodded to her, indicating their purpose was complete. They watched him maneuver around the chair.

"Would you like help with these?" Thomas touched one of the stacks.

Tariem looked at them. He stuffed all of the chocolate bars into his pocket. Then he began stuffing as many of the Bibles as he could into the deep pockets of his pants. They'd be quick fire starters when he made camp.

"We'll come back for the rest," Tariem said.

Gracie lifted the box they'd brought. As she began repacking it, Tariem pointed to the corner.

"Will they be safe?" she asked, eyeing the dried water stain on the ceiling.

Tariem nodded.

"Will you be locked out?" Thomas relayed her query.

Tariem shook his head and smiled. No one carried keys in Chukotka. If you stole something, everyone knew. Thieving was for short-term use. Items often reappeared as mysteriously as they had vanished.

Tariem noticed how worried Gracie seemed. He blinked twice in a deliberate way and grinned.

She blushed.

Tariem nodded deeply towards the woman, almost bowing. Emotion flooded the gesture. He awkwardly waved.

"We'll call you about Ramsay," young Thomas relayed. "And we'll see you this summer."

For now weather and sea ice were the only powers granting permission to cross the Bering Sea.

"Thank you for finding Ramsay and the Guardians," Tariem repeated, leaving them with no room to back out of their promise.

Gregory said something to Gracie. Doubt shadowed her eyes, but it didn't worry Tariem.

"We'll do our best," Thomas acknowledged.

Tariem winked at Gracie and raised his eyebrows twice in quick succession. She flushed, looking embarrassed yet flattered. Tariem shuffled towards the door to go wait for Yevgheni.

"Ask if he needs help." Gracie tapped Thomas on the shoulder.

"Are you okay by yourself?" Thomas asked.

"My grandson is coming." Tariem motioned towards the door. He studied the woman's face for the last time. "Just come back like you promised. Teach our young men about the sea," Tariem said. "And bring the Guardians home." He looked at Thomas. "That will be our blessing."

Tariem then shuffled out; his feet dragged in the rubber boots. Still too big even with the toes stuffed with balls of old newspaper. Outside his nostril hairs froze. The frigid air felt clean. Those buildings always felt like a sick person's breath.

Two thin-coated stray dogs huddled against the exposed hot-water pipes that lined the streets. One dog looked up.

"The Guardians are coming home," he said to them in Chukchi. Their ears moved with the lilt of his voice. The other lifted its head to see if he had food. They lost interest once they saw he didn't, and tucked their noses back underneath their scrawny tails.

Weather was the preeminent power, defeating an empire with a climate they couldn't outgun, outman or civilize. Impassable mountains year-round cut Chukotka off from the rest of Russia and Siberia. It was a struggle to keep Chukotka stocked with fuel and food since an approach from the sea was impossible most of the year. Violent shifting wind made landing even the most stalwart of aircrafts dicey.

Industrial society cried uncle in Chukotka. The promise of rich tungsten and gold reserves, oil stores within deep bedrock beneath the sea, all remained a pipe dream. Four years earlier, a wry smile spread across Tariem's face as he watched the then

Soviet Governor. Standing on the dock, shaking his fist at the sea ice, he ordered the ports to stay open as sea ice formed more quickly than he could spit out the words. Anything but this godforsaken place for another season.

Maybe the Old Ones had been right after all. "Ignore the soldiers; they will go. We are Chukchi; we will always be." But it had been a long, bitter war of attrition.

As he stood waiting for Yevgheni, their old apartment building stood across the street. In all the years they lived there, it was always a stranger's home. Hot-water faucets in first-floor apartments gushed around the clock in winter. All to prevent connecting water mains from freezing. Boarded-up windows, others simply jammed with cardboard, had frozen solid.

Tariem spied the top of Yevgheni's head cresting over the rise into town. The tip of his rifle peeped up from where it was slung over the boy's shoulder. The familiar hysterical whine of his snowmobile engine called to Tariem.

The thirteen-year-old rose on his seat and waved his whole arm once he spotted Tariem. He stopped to help the old man climb into the attached drag sled. Tariem touched the edge to steady himself, hoisting one leg over the side, then the other as he plopped down onto the pile of walrus blankets.

"So what did they say?" Yevgheni's eyes gleamed.

"They'll come back this spring with hunters."

"And the Guardians? What about the Guardians?"

"They will try to find them," Tariem said.

The gleam lessened.

"Hey, Yevska," calling him by his nickname, "it's okay," Tariem bopped Yevgheni sharply on the shoulder to shake out his disappointment. "Look. Look what I got you." Tariem pulled out a few of the chocolate bars from his sealskin anorak and handed them over.

Yevgheni nodded in a gesture of thanks before hanging his head.

"Yevska." Tariem bopped him again on the shoulder. "We'll

wait for now. Soon it will be too bad for travel from Rochlit anyway. Spring brings new things."

Yevgheni's disappointment showed in his shoulders. It was
like Jeaantaa, like Tangek. Maybe that's why he loved the boy so
much.

He covered Tariem with reindeer blankets, tucking them in
around the old man's body, and then climbed onto the pile he'd
tied to the snowmobile in place of the missing seat. It would be
a fifteen-hour ride back to the Cove.

The previous March marked another "Day-of-Having-Enough."
Tariem had enough of both fear and Anadyr. The continuous
rumbling of children's stomachs became unbearable. Immediately following the breakup of the Soviet Union, food supplies
were cut off. Within weeks commissaries were empty. Moscow
promised emergency airdrops of food and supplies. Daily they
drove out to the tundra, scouring the cloudless skies. They
waited in minus forty, letting their trucks idle, afraid of running out of gas and getting stranded. At sunset they drove back
for the night, only to return the next morning. After weeks of
hoping and signaling for help, they gave up—just as it seemed
the world had given up on them.

Days after, Tariem stormed out of the apartment leaving the
door open behind him. Hurrying down three flights and out to
the street, he rushed through the square towards the loading
docks. Tall cranes were secured for winter; cargo ships frozen
into the harbor for the duration. He stood looking out. Damn it,
the sea was rich with seals, walrus, whales and dozens of variet-
ies of fish just beneath the pack ice. In his mind's eye they swam
layer upon layer, twirling about as they chased each other. He
salivated at the memory of their sweet meats.

Tariem worked on the docks long enough to know there were
several well-stocked toolsheds in each slip. He rushed to one,

then the other; both had been thoroughly looted. Then he hurried down the snowy pier to the last slip. As he approached, he spotted the last shed by a cargo ship on the far side. The door was broken, shattered into what looked like triangle nautical flags. Gusts off the Bering slammed the remaining shreds of wood into the glaciated doorjamb.

Tariem stepped inside anyway, rummaging through piles of rusted cans. He kicked them loose, rolled away truck tires and tossed layers of old pipe and fan belts aside. Then he spotted it—an auger. Next to it hung an axe and a handsaw dangling from hooks on the opposite wall. Climbing on a pile of tires, he touched the wall for balance. Reaching up, he stretched and touched the auger. He was too short. Climbing back down, he picked up a long-stemmed wrench. Reaching again, he knocked the auger down. He touched the other two, watching to see where they fell.

Carefully he stepped down and clutched the tools. On the way out, he bent to grab the end of a coil of rope and dragged it back to the apartment. He left the tools inside the stairwell and bounded up the stairs like it was nothing.

Everyone looked up as he busted in. He rushed to the kitchen shelf.

"Out of my way." He pushed Katerina aside. She lost her balance and steadied against the stove.

"What are you doing?" Katerina, now an elderly woman, shoved back. No one touched food. She was the "controller of meals."

He rummaged through the sparse shelves and grabbed the last two tins of sardines that Yevgheni had found in an abandoned apartment.

"Put them back," she ordered. "It's all we have." She grabbed his forearm. He shook her off like a storm of tundra gnats. "He's mad." She tried to pry off his fingers and wrestle the tins out of his hand.

Tariem lifted them high out of her reach and then swiped the black hairnet right off her head.

She shrieked and grabbed her hair. "He's trying to kill us," she hollered in Chukchi.

No one moved to stop him. Twelve heads were riveted, their bodies still facing the television.

"All of you—" He turned to them and ordered, "Get up. Come with me."

Tariem rushed down the stairs, grabbing the pile of tools he left at the bottom. He strode towards the city square and back down to the dock. Those sober enough fell in behind. A few others wobbled, curious to see what the crazy old man was up to now.

Katerina ran after in only her housedress and slippers, screaming in Chukchi about stealing food out of the mouths of starving children.

He climbed over frozen heaves out onto the ice. Walking past the towering steel hull, he looked beyond the growing pressure ridges to where the ice was flat. The fast ice near the shore was too thick. Aquarvanguit had always forbidden hunting sea mammals so close to the shore; Tariem walked a bit farther and asked forgiveness.

As he scanned the surface for irregularities that might be seal breathing holes, the bright sun made it hard to distinguish natural ice formations from deliberate ones. Seals keep their breathing holes open by regularly popping their noses up and using their claws to scrape off accumulating ice. You'd see little piles of ice shavings on the surface. They had a distinct look. This was how they used to catch the seals. They'd be out for the better part of a day with dog teams searching. Often stalked by polar bears looking for the same meal. Spying on them from the tops of pressure ridges, thinking they could outwait the hunters.

Tariem spotted a breathing hole. The group huddled along, tagging after the old man. Katerina was gaining on him. Someone had thrown their coat over her shoulders. He reached the seal hole, but it looked abandoned. Probably too small for a seal, but at least they could set a line for fish. He stood thinking, scanning the horizon. None of them had enough stamina to go in search of seal.

Tariem handed the axe over to one of the young men.

"Here. Break it." He pointed to the round space of ice inside the abandoned breathing hole. He kicked the frozen ocean with his rubber boot. "What are you waiting for?"

The young man looked to the shore, scanning for patrol vehicles. They had no permit.

They all glanced sheepishly towards the shore.

"What the hell are you looking at?" Tariem yelled. "Look here." He kicked the sea ice with his heel again. "This is life now."

Tariem's black eyes smoldered. He grabbed the axe and began bashing the surface of the sea ice himself. Ice shattered and sparkled; it flew in all directions. They shielded their faces. The old man's muscles worked together in groups he hadn't felt in years. Then he stopped, handing the axe back over to the young man.

"Here," Tariem ordered. "Now you do it."

The young man worked until Tariem touched his shoulder.

"That's enough." The old man then squatted down to study the surface. "See the changes in ice color?" Tariem instructed.

They peered over his shoulder, studying the color of the surface.

"Now you." Tariem pointed at another man. "Come here." He handed over the auger. "Drill until you hit water."

"How will I know I hit water?"

"You'll know."

The young man began drilling, working it until the handle of the auger went slack. He looked at Tariem the instant it did.

"Now pull it out," Tariem instructed. "You come here." He pointed to another and handed over the handsaw. "Cut a hole this big." Tariem cupped his arms to show the circumference.

"Go," Tariem ordered.

Everybody watched as the hole was sawed to Tariem's specifications, the young man shaving ice from the sides. Then the old man reached down with the auger to move the free-floating circle underneath the surface.

He then opened each sardine tin.

"Stop him," Katerina shouted.

They all ignored her.

Tariem plopped the tangle of fish bodies into Katerina's hairnet. He tied off the ends. Grabbing the end of the frozen rope, he secured the bait. The smell was painful. One of the children dove onto the discarded sardine tin, licking out the oil in spastic motions.

Tariem handed the rope to Yevgheni. "Here," he instructed his grandson. "Lower it down, way down. Let's see what's down there." His voice was almost playful.

The teenager carefully dipped the bait deep into the frigid slushy mix of salt water. Tariem plucked at the rope as if it were a violin string to test its tautness; he then tapped his grandson's arm.

"That's good," Tariem directed. "Now we wait."

Katerina began slapping Tariem's back and cursing him. She ordered him to pull out the bait as she was so hungry she would eat it right there herself. No sooner had she fallen back onto the ice, sobbing in a heap, when the rope moved.

"Pull." Tariem laughed. The men grabbed to help the boy. The nose of a ringed seal popped through. Everyone looked at each other stunned.

Tariem shouted instructions. "Grab it, quick; pull it up."

The men struggled to pull out the slick body. It slid wet onto the surface of the ice. They stared in amazement at the fat mammal; the seal blinked several times and looked back.

No one knew what to do next, except Tariem. He drew his knife and bowed his head. Praying the old Chukchi prayers, he asked the seal to forgive him, giving thanks to Aquarvanguit—the Keeper of the Sea Animals—for saving the lives of the Chukchi. He prayed loud enough so that they would all hear and come to know. He killed the animal in an instant.

Within days, they began using the seal entrails as bait, each maintaining their own fishing holes cut into the ice. Tariem, Yevgheni and a few of the others began traveling farther out to scout breathing holes on the pack ice. They sat in silence for hours, waiting for signs.

That winter they stored up enough meat and, scavenging wood from doors and window frames, built fires in the middle of the streets to keep warm. This is what kept them alive until they stocked up enough food to make the return to Uelen.

CHAPTER 31

It was early. The sky grew progressively darker in that moment before light broke from behind the hills.

Rosalie hurried to ready Team A. Team B would get their turn at the end of the day. She was due at the Dreamcatcher clinic by seven to assist with Wednesday's "surgery day" for shelter animals. Jan had agreed to change Wednesday's hours so Rosalie could gain valuable surgical experience.

She sorted through dog harnesses in the dark, using only her headlamp. It kept dimming out. After she tapped the battery pack, it would brighten for seconds and then fade. Annoying as hell, though not annoying enough to stop and get fresh batteries. She could flip on the outside lights but hadn't wanted to wake Arlan. One shone directly in his bedroom window like a "German spotlight," he'd contend. Yet once the dogs started shrieking with excitement he'd be up anyway, complaining.

A car was in the road. She stopped. Gradually straightening, she tilted her head to listen. It was the Bronco; she was sure of it. A little over a week had passed since the fight, four days since the plant closed. He knew her schedule. She took Dan's earlier promise to help as being null and void. Just then headlights flashed and the Bronco pulled in.

Dan hopped down from his truck. "I said I'd help."

Okay, she thought. Despite the disclaimer, it was hope—even affection—that he remembered her Wednesday schedule. The outline of his back was barely visible as he stepped quickly to fetch the rig from the shed.

The chill of winter had set in. Dogs ricocheted off the fence like stray bullets once Dan wheeled the rig into position by the white pine. Squeals broke into a deafening roar. The kitchen light flipped on, then the outside lights. Arlan was up and probably bitching. She switched off the headlamp to save the batteries for the trail. Though dogs ran more efficiently in darkness, the headlamp would clear off raccoons, possums and other night creatures.

Frozen mud footprints dotted the driveway. Slushy ice floated down in Sand Bay. It looked like an oil slick as it undulated with the current—frazil ice, the first stage of freezing. Too unstable for even the weight of a seagull. Superior was finally considering winter.

The ground was still bare, except for isolated patches of snow in the woods and measly bits along the trail. A snow drought—nothing compared to last year's bounty. Nowhere near enough for Jan and Dave's old wooden sled they'd "bequeathed." "Knew there was a reason I've been hanging on to this old thing," Jan said. Last week Rosalie found it in the bed of her truck with a big blue bow tied around the handle. "Now you can enter that race, no more excuses."

Under pressure, Rosalie turned in an entry form for the Apostle Island Sled Dog Race in February. A nine-dog, ninety-mile race meant two dogs stayed home. That bothered her. Whichever two it was would be crushed; huskies were like that. She foot-dragged until Jan wheedled about the application deadline. Finally Rosalie turned it in, practically yessing Jan to death, knowing full well she'd withdraw at the last moment.

Pressure even from Arlan: "Don't you wanna test your mettle?"

She already knew their mettle. Nothing was better than running dogs through snowy woods as the sun was rising or setting. To see their unbridled joy as they ran and grew strong. After a good hard run, how proud and satisfied they were. They were already winners who needed no other proving grounds.

. . .

Rosalie rushed to harness the remaining dogs, afraid that if it took too long Dan might change his mind. Her fingers were stiff. She fumbled and dropped Clowny's harness twice. "Shit." She bent over, groping to make sure it was Clowny's. She'd already harnessed her once in Panda's.

The first light of dawn traced the outline of a great horned owl perched on top of a gray splintery utility pole. Its head swiveled contemplatively as if thinking about breakfast.

As Dan wheeled the rig past to secure the snub line, she smelled liquor. She escorted Clowny and King to the gangline, hooking them in lead. Dan huddled on the platform of the rig. He flipped up the collar of his jean jacket.

"Where's your coat?" she asked.

No answer.

"Your gloves?"

She hooked Panda and Junior in wheel position. The dogs broke into a fresh frenzy of howling, dragging the rig to the end of the snub line.

"I'll grab Arlan's parka," she shouted, and motioned to the house.

"No." He sounded irritated. "Let's just go," as if there was somewhere else he had to be.

"It'll take a sec."

"Let's go." He wouldn't look at her.

She frowned and hopped onto the platform beside him. "Freeze your ass off, see if I care," she muttered, and then pulled the quick release. The dogs surged.

Speed generated windchill. It was a long ten miles to be cold. Standing on the rig you were just ballast for the wind. Cold air infiltrated zippers and seams, greedily stealing body warmth. It wasn't like the sled, where you'd jog or run, quickly breaking a sweat even on the coldest days.

She'd treat him like the 180-pound meatball he was. But right now she needed Mr. Meatball's weight. Once the snows came she'd safely run the whole team alone. They turned onto a newly constructed section of the Quarry Recreational Trail just opened that week by the Forest Service. She was curious, as this part of the Peninsula had not been navigable.

"How was your weekend?" she asked, the hint of sarcasm not lost.

"I said I'd help." He was beginning to shiver.

"We can head back." She softened.

His nose was already a deep pink. He held the cold metal bar with one bare hand, his other tucked into the flimsy pocket of his jean jacket.

It was going to be a long run. The rising sun seemed to ease things. The stark barrenness of late fall was a beauty that few understood. Most complained about the depressing wasteland of November, but it revealed a beauty if you only knew how to see. Dried brown grasses and scarlet-stemmed bushes were frosted, spilling out into open meadows and fields along the trail. The orange sun illuminated with a sublime glow. Above their heads burnished oak leaves shuddered in the breeze on contorted wooden arms, rattling like the bones of paper skeletons leftover from Halloween.

The dogs ran with extra zest as they turned onto Quarry Trail. Their thick breath crystallized and zigzagged above their heads. Clowny ran in double lead with King, her copper hue the same spectral color as the fall grasses. Clowny was the apple of King's eye, not to mention his carbon copy. Arlan pointed it out one evening as the dogs were lying parallel in front of the TV. Even their front paws leisurely crossed in the same way.

Two miles into the new trail, the dogs stopped. They never halted in the middle of a run. "Well, that's weird." Rosalie locked the brake.

A wooden plank bridge spanned out before them. They regularly crossed bridges over ravines and creeks on just about every trail. She hopped off and ran in heavy boots up to Clowny and King. As she touched the tops of their heads, Rosalie peered over the edge into a deep purple granite gorge.

"Holy smokes," she said. No wonder they stopped. An old railroad trestle spanned what looked to be the rock quarry. Its braid of iron girders filled the gorge, new use for the old iron ore route built to last forever. The Raspberry River raged below, gushing through boulders with fall's heavy rains, echoing off the granite walls. The trail surface was retrofitted with treated wooden planks where train tracks had been.

Thick velvety moss grew in clumps on broken boulders, some as big as houses. It looked as though giants had lobbed them over the edge. Fir and birch trees grew out of brown and red granite, some several stories tall. Brown granite was cut from the very same quarries in the nineteenth century to face buildings in Manhattan and Chicago. Buildings that had come to be known as "Brownstones."

Her stomach squeezed. Between each wooden plank was a two-inch gap. No big deal for a snowmobile, but for a dog's foot it could be dangerous. There were no side rails either. And if that wasn't intimidating enough, the surface gleamed with icy morning dew. Though the trail was plenty wide, leaving at least two to three feet on either wheel, if one dog slipped or panicked it would be scary.

Rosalie ran back to Dan. She gestured skeptically with her hands. "I don't know about this." She hopped up beside him. Charlie's mushing axiom was: "Don't ever ask them to do something you know they can't."

"Want me to look?"

She watched Dan's shoulders as he jogged down five sets of huskies to King and Clowny. Dan's rumpled black head looked down. He stepped in front of the two onto the trestle; he jumped and tried to get it to wobble. Then he bent over, talking to Clowny and King.

"What do you think?" she called to him as he ran back.

"Seems solid enough." He stepped onto the platform. Dan's arm leaned against hers for only a moment and the pressure felt good.

"Let's see," she considered. Jan always said, "Trust them; they're smarter than us."

"Fifty bucks she won't cross," Dan blurted out.

Rosalie held out her hand to shake. He didn't look at it. *Asshole.*

Clowny's head swiveled as she calculated the risks. The dog stepped up to the first wooden plank. King reared back, but Clowny stood firm. The red dog was all fun and games until she slipped her head into a harness, giving the icicle stare to any who dared horse around. Her chest pressed into her harness with absolute certainty.

"You owe me fifty."

The dog proceeded as if not having a care in the world. The team mimicked her body language, falling in line as they followed.

Dan shook his head in amazement. Even the wobbly ones, who acted like they were being marched off to the slaughter, fell in line.

Once back at the house, Dan helped unhook and situate the dogs. He and Rosalie worked without speaking. After the dogs had been watered, she took baby steps towards him. Following as he pushed the rig into the shed, shut the door and latched it. She stopped and waited, hoping he'd turn and come back to her. He paused for a few moments as if deciding. Like Clowny standing on the edge of the trestle—which way, Dan?

He turned towards the Bronco. Marching across the driveway, he opened the door and climbed in without as much as a glance or wave good-bye—like a hired hand who never kissed or made love with her—she was now the furthest thing from his mind.

She sighed loudly as the Bronco backed out. If only we could all be brave like Clowny, or have the openheartedness of the Noodle.

. . .

All morning at the clinic, Dan was the topic of discussion while Rosalie was snipping out ovaries, uteri and scrotums.

"I'll bet you he's dyslexic and he's ashamed," Helen called from her desk. She sat closing out the monthly statements. "Probably feels he's got nothing to offer like his dad."

Rosalie perked up as if suddenly growing three inches taller. It was the first mention of Dan's father from someone who knew the man. She struggled to keep focused on the surgery table. Charlie was teaching her to suture. He watched closely over her shoulder, checking as she closed the last dog.

"Tie off both ends," he quietly instructed. "Don't give little Fluffy cause to chew them out."

"Little Fluffy" was any dog, excluding puppies, not tall enough to drink out of a toilet.

"Yikes, it's cold," Helen remarked. She stood and began rustling about in the waiting room. "That northwest wind—feels like someone kicked a hole in the wall." Helen tossed logs into the newly installed green enamel wood-burning stove, the compromise. Charlie would razz her about sitting in her down coat all day, too miserly to turn up the furnace.

"Men are like that," Helen called, and resumed stuffing bills into preaddressed envelopes. "All that 'pride' crap."

Charlie vanished for seconds from Rosalie's side. He sneaked off to confiscate billing envelopes before Helen could smack away his hand. He folded and tucked them into his pocket, ignoring her. It was a twenty-five-year battle. Her sigh accused him of "giving away everything." His swift hand countered her as being a "tightwad" like her mother. Grumpiness volleyed during every monthly billing. From jokes, to annoyance, back to jokes—the tip-tapping sound of Helen's nails on the adding machine telegraphed precise figures of "just how much you've put us into the hole this month." As always, Charlie pretended not to hear.

"Dan has to find his niche," Helen explained.

If only it were that simple.

"I never thought Shannon would."

Rosalie remembered their daughter.

"She finished college with my foot kicking her butt all the way down the aisle to graduation," Helen said. "Then I was a bitch—now she thanks me." She tucked the remaining envelopes into her purse before Charlie could do any more damage. "She's a graphic artist in the Cities."

"Art Director," Charlie called out to correct.

Helen stepped into the surgery room and rolled her eyes. "Yes, Charlie, Art Director." Helen made eye contact with Rosalie as if to underscore how he was the biggest pain in the ass to have ever been spawned. "Shannon's artistic like Charlie."

His eyebrows arched comically in sudden embarrassment.

"You?" Rosalie held the roll of gauze and surgery clamps in her hand.

He was speechless. Rosalie enjoyed his flushed face.

"All those woodcarvings of animals out front?" Helen pointed with her pen to Charlie as if identifying a perp from the witness stand.

"Sh-h-h," he said. "Everyone thinks I'm a perfect asshole."

"You *are* a perfect asshole," Helen interjected without looking up.

"Don't want to spoil it by letting them see my softer side."

"Don't worry; you won't." Helen crumpled up the long tape from the adding machine and threw it at him.

Rosalie prepared surgery packs for the morning's large animal calls using Charlie's checklist—Buster, a lame horse; a cow with mastitis; and more urgently a call had come in about a goat having trouble giving birth. The goat came first. It would be the first goat she'd get to assist.

"You knew Dan's dad?" Rosalie steered the talk back to Dan's father.

"Ah, yes, Edwin." Helen shook her head, smiling. "Handsome

bugger—Dan's the spitting image; third cousin on my father's side. Don't think Edwin even finished eighth grade. Something was up with him too," Helen said. "He left to go out on the tankers. Did all right for himself, though, becoming a captain and all."

"Dan'll figure it out," Charlie said.

Rosalie recognized the tone; he didn't believe it.

"Who knows?" He looked up at her. "Sometimes you *can* teach an old dog new tricks—"

"Hey—I heard that," Helen called from the desk. "So, old dog, there's hope for you?"

He looked at his wife. They both grinned.

"They probably have classes for people with learning disabilities. Would Dan go get screened?" Helen looked to Rosalie.

"No," Charlie answered for her.

"Why?" both women demanded as if Dan were there to answer for himself.

"Hell, I wouldn't."

"But he's so young, Charlie," Helen insisted. "He's got a whole life ahead of him."

But Rosalie knew Charlie was right. No way could she picture Dan pocketing his pride to get help. It would be an uphill bloody battle that would yield nothing; she knew at least that much about Dan.

"Might as well neuter the man."

"Oh don't talk stupid." Helen turned away from him.

"What's he to do?" Rosalie looked to Charlie.

Charlie looked at his watch and then leaned against the surgery table. He pushed up his glasses from where they'd slipped down to the end of his nose.

"I couldn't say." His voice was hushed. "Let's go." He gestured with his head for them to leave. "Goats wait for no one."

CHAPTER 32

Things looked quiet at Dan's house the next day. She started driving towards Aunt Edie's to pick up the next project but instead found herself heading towards Dan's.

Rosalie sat in her idling truck, trying to decide what to do. Snow collected like dust around the stone foundation. She glanced in the mirrors; no traffic to pressure her either way. No sign of his truck either. Lord knows there's nothing like an empty driveway to extend an invitation to snoop. Taking one last look around, she pulled into his driveway and shut off the engine.

The coast looked clear. She slid out of the seat, knowing any moment Dan could come barreling down the road. Ordinarily just the thought would be a deterrent. But so what—what would he do? Stop talking to her? Arlan would kill her if he knew. She should have called Lorraine; she might have talked her out of it or at least come along.

She circled the front of the house. The old stone foundation set high enough to make it impossible to peek in the windows. Inside shutters blocked a clear view. She'd have to find something to stand on. She glanced around for a bucket, a salt block, anything. Around the back a huge bay window didn't have shutters. Grabbing on to the window ledge, she stood on her toes, cupping her eyes in her hands to see inside.

The curved wooden legs of a dining room table and matching ladder-back chairs, nothing remarkable. Yet what would be remarkable? Dan sprawled out naked on the dining room table, spooning a bowl of fruit? She laughed nervously.

Branches of a low-growing fruit tree scratched against the side of the house. She grabbed the lower branches and climbed to a height well above the inside shutters. Leaning over, she balanced a hand against the shingles, squinting to see into the main room.

She leaned her forehead against the glass. Just as she cupped her hands to see, loud piano music startled her. Her forehead bashed the windowpane.

The music halted. Seconds later Dan peered back at her.

"Ah-h—" She lost her balance and toppled back. Her hips wedged into the crotch of the tree. Shifting herself around, she wriggled frantically. Panic set in. She was wedged tight. *Shit*. No way to run for the truck.

Dan walked around the side of the house and towards her in his socks. Hands on hips, he stood on the mix of snow and gravel.

"Help! I'm stuck." An embarrassing laugh escaped. She wiggled her hands and feet, trying to be comical.

But his was a strange and bitter look, as if he'd just as soon leave her.

"Help me, Dan."

He seemed reluctant but walked over and lifted her in one motion. She reached to grasp his warmth, hold him close, but instead he set her down.

"I tried to call."

"What are you doing here?"

She smelled beer. "I want to talk."

"I said I'd help tomorrow." Dan turned to walk back to the house.

She hurried after him. At the front door she ducked under his arm before he had the chance to shut her out. The house smelled like Dan's coat; she wanted to wrap herself in it. Button up and settle in. A large black piano filled the front bay window inside the shutters.

"I didn't know you could play."

"What do you want, Rosalie?"

Before she could answer, she saw Smokey's face tacked on the wall just above his shoulder. She covered her mouth with her hand without even realizing it. A drawing of Clowny from the other day on the trestle. Another of the Noodle earlier that year, cuddled with her puppies in the plastic kiddie pool.

"Did you draw these?"

He said nothing.

"They're incredible," she whispered. She stepped up to the Noodle's face. Some drawings were in black ink, others softer charcoals, each neatly thumbtacked to the wood frame of floor-to-ceiling bookshelves. The only color was the pale shimmer of Superior painted into each dog's eyes. Her eyes couldn't dart around fast enough, hurrying to take it all in. The clack of her boots echoed off the dark, dustless wooden floors.

"My God, you're an artist."

Fingers tucked into both front pockets of his jeans, Dan rocked back onto his heels. He glanced at the drawings as if noticing them for the first time.

It was humbling to learn she hadn't known him at all. Drawings of seagulls in flight, an eagle perched on the top branches of a dead tree, the view of the Lake from their cabin hung along shelves that flanked the fireplace. She turned. More shelves covered the opposite wall almost to the crown molding. The bookshelves packed with volumes lettered in gold along their spines, all neatly arranged. Three music stands of varying heights stood off to the corner; each held pen and ink drawings of the same tree from different angles.

"What do you want?" He stood corralled on all sides by towers of books.

"You," she wanted to say.

He took her arm and escorted her towards the door. "I'm busy."

"With what?" She looked over her shoulder like a student being removed from the classroom. All his shoes were lined and evenly spaced by the front door. No smell of rotting garbage or dirty socks strewn, the usual hallmarks of men living alone. She spotted a TV in a back room. The same Packer game Arlan was at home watching. A bottle of Budweiser stood like a hot date demanding Dan's attention.

"You're drunk," she said.

"Not yet." He opened the door, ushered her out and closed it.

"Dan?" she called, knocking with open hands.

"I'll see you tomorrow." His voice grew fainter behind the door.

A raw gust blew her hair. She clutched the sides of her parka against her ribs, crushing it to shut out November's bony fingers. "Dan." She rested her cheek against the peeling varnish of the raised-paneled door as if it were the side of his neck. Rosalie knocked, knowing he wouldn't come. She wanted to sit with him and make the dark tangle of emotion go away.

"I love you," she said into the wood.

"Now gosh darn it—why'd you go and do somethin' like that," Arlan scolded without conviction as he watched the game— more concerned about whether or not the Packers would make the first down. Her coat was still on. Arlan's battiness was comforting.

"I told you to leave him alone." Arlan watched the TV, waiting to learn why the refs had thrown down a penalty flag. He motioned for her to sit and eat. "He can draw, all right."

She sat. "You've seen him?"

"I've told you."

She looked away. He probably had. Arlan moved with the players, as if running the ball down the field himself. The time-out buzzer briefly released him back to his dinner. He began shaking the can of Parmesan cheese until his plate resembled a snowy hill.

"He'd draw the garbage can, Duffy the safety manager," Arlan said between swallows. "Drew King's face in the corner of a memo pad when we first got him—looked just like him." Arlan gestured with his fork as if to re-create King's face in the air.

King stepped up after hearing his name, following Arlan's fork with his one eye. His ears were alert, black lips moist with anticipation. Six sets of blue eyes sat hoping a meatball might roll off the plate. Bella's chin in begging position on Rosalie's thigh, pressing down with such force she swore it would leave a bruise.

"He can fix anything too. One time the front loader at the pulp boiler busted. Whole operation shut down; they were threatening to send us home. Then Dan takes the whole thing apart and fixes it before the engineers show up. Got written up for it, though; only certified technicians were supposed to touch machinery." Arlan leaned back, glancing over at the halftime show. "Figured drawing was just his way of killing time."

They searched each other for an instant, as if recalibrating Dan.

"Did one of you last month, just before the lockout. A 'Hazard Materials' update. Makes you wonder why they even bothered." A bitter laugh escaped. "Looked just like you. I tell him, 'You ought to keep them things.' But he just laughs, crumples 'em up, takes a foul shot into the trash can on the way out."

"Did he keep the one of me?"

He shrugged.

"Arlan, he's an artist; I'm serious—"

"Dan could be a lot of things."

"He could get a job like Shannon," she said.

"I've told him. 'Art's not a job,' he always says."

She twisted a strand of hair, thinking. Charlie's daughter was coming next weekend. Maybe Shannon could look at Dan's drawings.

The game came back on.

"Don't do that again," Arlan said, watching the kickoff. "You hurt the man's pride."

She made a face. "Bullshit. He's drinking—what pride is there in disappearing into a beer bottle?"

"Dan's a proud man."

"So what?" she said.

Arlan shook his head slowly. "My God, you're your mother all over again."

Arlan noticed a light scatter of freckles forming across her broad cheekbones, disappearing into the roots of her hair on either side. For some reason they awakened memories of new love and the terrible desperation that often rides on its heels. He sighed. She was so young and knew so little about men and love.

"I'm afraid for him, Dad." She lowered her head and began to cry over her plate of spaghetti and meatballs. "I don't want to lose him."

"I know, missy." She reminded him of when she was little. Right after Anna Marie died. "I know." Arlan reached over the blue-checked tablecloth, awkwardly touching her hand.

CHAPTER 33

She caught up with Charlie that next afternoon for rounds.

The Dreamcatcher truck was parked alongside the highway near a stable they'd visited the previous week. Parking behind him, she shut the door and crossed the highway to the fence.

"Charlie." She waved as soon as he looked up.

Opening the gate, she let herself in. Charlie was bent over, examining a horse named Buster's front leg in a field of broken snow. Buster's two sheep friends stood nearby. They followed him around the field, never far from his side.

It was hard to miss Charlie's blaze orange vest. She'd tease him, calling it his crossing guard outfit. "Well—say what you want," he'd grumble. "Better a crossing guard than shot dead by some trigger-happy man-for-a-day Chicago deer hunter." His work boots were left chronically untied because of rushing 'against the schedule.' His long, ratty ponytail trapped somewhere beneath all those layers of clothing.

"You're early," he called back. His dark eyes—framed by wiry eyebrows infiltrated with gray—looked huge, magnified by his lenses.

It was another recheck of Buster's knee after an equine orthopedic surgery three weeks earlier in Minneapolis. The horse's slow recovery was puzzling.

"We finished early, so Jan said to go," she said. "Helen told me where to find you." Rosalie was breathless and red cheeked from scurrying across the field of winter wheat. She leaned onto her knees to catch her breath once close enough to not have to shout. "Dan can draw—I saw it."

"Great," Charlie said with so little enthusiasm it made her laugh. "So could my kid when she was three." He was absorbed with the horse's knee, wondering what was causing instability in the joint. He flexed Buster's leg again, having compared its range of motion with the healthy one

"I'm serious, Charlie—I swear."

He looked cold and grumpy. Peering over the rims of glasses that rested on the furthermost tip of his nose, he seemed to say, "What makes you think I'm not?"

She laughed.

Nudging up his glasses with a shoulder, he stooped over the horse's brandy-colored leg. No sooner had he pushed them up than they slid back down, adding to his irritableness.

Placing Buster's leg down, Charlie stood and stretched out his back. He was about to ask her to draw a syringe of Adequan, a standard anti-inflammatory for horses, but instead motioned for them to change places so she could examine the horse. He touched Buster's halter to steady him. Quietly smiling, Charlie murmured to the horse, stroking his white velvet nose. Buster then nosed Charlie's pocket. He chuckled. The horse was used to the routine; he knew in which pocket Charlie kept the treats. Charlie opened his fist and Buster snorted as he gobbled them up with delight.

"God, I love horses." Charlie said it with the tenderness of a young boy's confession. He was such a funny man—knowing people inside out, yet being so much more comfortable with animals.

She bent over Buster's healthy leg and lifted his hoof, flexing the knee as Charlie had shown. "I saw Dan's drawings," she said, testing Buster's range of motion. She described the drawings of Smokey, the Noodle and her pups.

Despite Charlie's foul mood, Rosalie's conviction made him smile.

"Sounds like a bad case of love."

She laughed. "No, I swear to God, really, Charlie. Even if Dan was a stranger, he's really good."

She set the healthy leg down and lifted Buster's injured one to compare its range of motion. After she let the other leg go she stood. Stepping back, she noted how Buster shifted his weight onto the healthy leg. She looked quickly to Charlie and then back at the horse.

"I think his ligament's torn," she said while watching Buster. "Maybe it tore when he injured the knee, only it didn't show in the MRI or X-rays because of the swelling." She turned to see what Charlie thought. She'd grown used to him ignoring her. Only he had the strangest look, an expression that she couldn't read. There was a very long pause. The silence made her uncomfortable.

He let go of Buster's halter.

"Who the hell are you?" He placed both hands on his hips and stared.

Their eyes met for an instant. She quickly looked at the ground, embarrassed. She shrank. What had she done? What boundary had she overstepped?

She looked down. "I-I-I don't know what you mean." Laughing nervously, she toed a clump of frozen wheat and snow with her boot.

"Explain why you think it's a torn ligament?" he asked without moving. His stare had the force of law.

She couldn't meet his eyes. "Uh-h, I just guessed."

"Well, that's a pretty good goddamned guess."

His silence demanded an answer.

"The other day on Helen's desk was a vet journal. It had an article about a horse with Buster's problem."

Charlie was silent, his gaze unbroken.

"I wasn't snooping around or nothing—if that's what you think."

"No, no, I know you weren't." He crossed his arms, resting his chin on the knuckles of one hand as he listened.

"I was bored. Helen was at the post office," she explained. "So I read the article while waiting for you."

He was quiet for a few moments. "Explain your process, how you've arrived at a torn ligament."

"Well, last week the injured knee felt loose—different from the healthy one. Remember how you said he should have been making better progress?"

He nodded.

"In my mind I pictured his leg muscles, tendons, ligaments and the skeletal structure and compared them with the ones in your equine anatomy book."

He motioned with his hand for her to continue.

"You always say 'process of elimination,' right?" She looked at him. "I figured since you said the bone is healing okay it only makes sense that a torn ligament would cause the instability."

"So you pieced together the equine anatomy book, the journal article and Buster's presenting symptoms and came to this conclusion," he confirmed.

"Was that the wrong thing to do?" She was ready to cry.

He nodded slowly with no expression. "That's exactly what you're supposed to do." His voice was quiet.

"It's just plain common sense, isn't it? Most people would think that."

"Uh-h, no, Rosalie." He shook his head as he said it. "Most people wouldn't think that. They wouldn't pull it all together, at least not so quickly."

She watched as Buster nosed around in the wheat, sniffing puffs of steam through clumps of windswept snow.

"Tell you what." He shifted his weight as if needing to hear nothing more. "Finish the vet tech degree at Indianhead, and then Helen and I'll help you with vet school."

"Vet school?" Her nose wrinkled as she laughed. "Oh right, Charlie, like they're gonna let someone like me into vet school."

He smiled sadly and knowingly, vowing not to let her out of his sight for the next six years.

"You think Shannon'll look at Dan's pictures?" Her voice was meek as she directed him back to the subject of Dan.

He blinked and sighed, shaking his head slowly. "You really have no idea what you've got, do you." Charlie placed his hand over his forehead as if it had begun to ache. "You're about as far away from yourself as a person can be." His voice had the same tone as if talking to Buster.

It was embarrassing not to understand him and to know that something important had just happened. Something had changed. How was it possible to amaze and disappoint Charlie in only a few short breaths?

"Yeah, yeah." He waved his hand, motioning for them to head back to the road. "Of course she would." He shoved up his glasses as if they'd Velcro to his eyebrows, leaning over to brush off frozen bits of hay from the front of his pant legs. "Your timing couldn't be better. Baby's due next month; after that they won't be coming up for a while." He motioned for them to keep walking.

"That's right, Grandpa," she said, knowing it bothered him.

He frowned.

"How come being Grandma doesn't bother Helen?"

"Because Helen is better than me," he said in such a matter-of-a-fact tone, as if asking Rosalie to spin a blood sample. "Tell Dan this Saturday. Dinnertime. Tell him to bring some drawings," he said on the exhale.

They stopped at the truck. She nodded and cast down her eyes. No one told Dan anything.

Charlie studied her face. "But then you know he won't come, don't you."

Rosalie studied the cracks in her gloves. She looked to the surrounding hills just above where Buster stood in the field. The horse watched them as if wishing they wouldn't leave. She couldn't say what Dan would do.

Charlie opened the driver's side door.

"Well anyway," he said in a way that indicated he knew it was a lost cause. "Hop in. Another horse, a beagle and a cat await us in Hayward."

There still wasn't enough of a snow base to safely run the sled. Though the weather report promised overnight totals of four to six inches, by morning there was only a dusting. Because the snows were so late in coming, mushers everywhere still trained with their rigs and ATVs. No one had gotten an edge by running on snow. Jan and Dave, along with other competitive teams, obsessed about the conditions. Mushers called around, trying to get the scuttlebutt on who had snow and might be getting the better of them.

The snow drought was no respecter of persons. From Alaska down throughout the lower forty-eight, even the most competitive teams were waiting. People scoured radar searching for precipitation. Many talked a good game, especially the hopefuls and front-runners, trying to psych each other out: "Well jeepers, I think maybe we got just a tad bit more than you guys down there." It was code for the ground being completely bare under the bullshitter's feet.

In general, "snow stories" were far more corrosive than fish tales. They implicated the future race-readiness of a team, and would send mushers into tizzies in the endless pursuit of snow.

There was already talk of shortening the Beargrease if the heavy snows didn't come soon. Even more talk about how years of warm winters were affecting training. Though the *Farmer's Almanac* had predicted a snow drought, everyone hoped for once its mysterious wisdom was wrong. While sportsmen cursed the mild winter, locals were far too superstitious to rejoice. They knew Mother Nature might retaliate by hammering them on the other side of winter, come April, when everyone was desperately seeking signs of spring.

· · ·

Jan and Dave both entered the Iditarod for that March. All of them would make the five-day drive to Alaska in early February. It would give them a whole month of training and acclimating to high-altitude and mountain conditions. Much of the Iditarod traveled through mountain passes and high country. Dogs adjusted in three to four days, humans in two to three weeks. Rosalie would then join the army of vet assistants to work with Charlie and the other race staff. She would be flown by the "Iditarod Air Force" and dropped off to work remote checkpoints like Unalakleet. There she'd assist with health checks on dog teams and medical care for dropped dogs, caring for them as they waited to be flown back to Anchorage.

At the Iditarod, handlers were forbidden to assist in any way. A team could only get assistance from another dog driver on the trail or risk disqualification. Only officials were allowed to intervene, especially in the event that a team was way overdue arriving at a checkpoint.

The rig was all set up and ready to go by the time the Bronco pulled in. All the nervous energy had prompted her to set up the rig and gear before he arrived.

Dan looked out the truck window, puzzled. Setting up the rig together had become part of their ritual. Maybe one of the last understandings they shared. He would wheel the rig into place and secure it to the pine as she ran over with pairs of dogs. This was the first time she hadn't waited.

"Wow—am I late?" he asked.

"No. Just had a little extra time, thought I'd get all set up."

Rosalie felt him watch as she fumbled with the brass snaps on the neck- and tuglines. She walked past him with King and Clowny. Then she tripped over the water jug and accidentally kicked the metal bowls as they went rolling. Dan stepped to scoop them up, tucking them into the gear bag as he studied her face.

"Funny how it's getting so dark now," she remarked, trying to make small talk.

"It's almost December, Rosalie."

Dan walked Panda and Junior over. She quickly clipped the back loops of their harnesses onto their tuglines. Dan stepped onto the platform. One last check of the gangline and she stepped up behind the steering bar. The dogs were yelping and slamming into their harnesses. The rig lurched.

She pulled the quick release and the dogs took off in silence. Neither of them mentioned Rosalie's attempted breaking and entering of the day before. With such icy conditions, her neck and shoulders tensed as she gripped the steering bar. The feel of the rig floating on the icy trail was not good. The dogs could easily get injured, but there was no way to stop now.

The dogs made the sharp right. Clowny slipped and fell down, Bella too. Running on ice was tricky business, especially once it had melted and refrozen into uneven tire tracks and rock-hard footprints. The slushy snow of the last few warm days was now camouflaged ice beneath last night's dusting. She should have used better judgment and not gone out. Sometimes injuries received in such conditions never healed, or so Charlie would fume under his breath.

"We're not going out again until it snows," she said.

Dan nodded.

"They're saying three to six again tonight," she said. "Sorry about yesterday, just showing up like that," she apologized.

Dan looked off into the woods. There's nothing quite like being trapped for twelve miles with someone who won't talk.

"Charlie's daughter is a graphic artist." She forced out the words despite her better judgment.

"I know Shannon."

"I told him about your drawings. She's visiting this Saturday. Charlie's invited us over for dinner."

He bristled like the guard hairs of an aroused dog. She studied the side of his face, looking for a response. The black stubble made his skin look blue.

"Maybe Shannon knows people, has connections."

He was silent.

"Maybe she can help you be an illustrator or something." She anticipated his protest. "Hey—beading's sort of like art. Nothing wrong with making money from art—it earns me more money than Charlie and Stormwatch combined."

"This is none of your business." Dan turned and looked at her. The rims of his eyes were red and inflamed.

Panda and Junior, the two wheel dogs, glanced back at his voice.

"You just don't listen. You never do."

With that he stepped off the rig and started running back towards the house. The team darted a quick glance at the sudden weight change before bursting forward with fresh excitement.

"Dan," she called, "Dan!" and stomped the platform with her foot. She braked, but the rig just slid on the ice. It would be impossible to turn the team around at this point. She turned and watched him run.

"Dan!" she called once more, but the laws of physics were working against her. He was heading back past long fingers of frozen bogs. In spring they were like black mirrors, silently reflecting a more darkened and complex world beneath. An occasional cheery marsh marigold would grow, its reflection obscured, deeply rooted in the uncertain bottom. In some places the skin of the bog's surface was dank and cloudy as a dead animal's eye.

"Shit, shit, shit," she hollered in frustration, and pulled up her hood.

CHAPTER 34

Rosalie guessed that Dan wouldn't show. He was never late. She stalled and frittered away an hour in hopes he'd prove her wrong. The late afternoon sky was darkening; any longer and she'd risk being tardy to her first GED evening class. Not the best way to break out for a fresh start.

Three inches of heavy snow had fallen. Though not enough to safely run a sled, it was welcome traction for the rig. She surveyed Ridge Road and looked towards Scheffel. When she kicked the surface with her toe, the trail seemed better. All eleven sets of eyes watched along the fence as she walked back to get out the rig.

Just opening the shed door triggered the dogs. She pushed out the rig and slowly wheeled it into place; the dogs shrieked with excitement. She purposely stalled, unwinding the gangline in slow motion, still hoping Dan would show before they were ready to take off. She opened the gate and entered the yard, holding only six harnesses for Team A.

"Sorry, guys, the rest of you have to wait," she said. The ones left behind would look so forlorn she could hardly stand the thought. And to make matters worse, they'd have to wait until she returned after class.

Smokey and King watched as she entered the yard. "Look at you two." She chuckled and knelt, thinking of what Jan always said: "If you guys had thumbs and car keys you'd be dangerous."

She crouched down, eye-level with King, holding on to his harness. "Whatcha think, Kingster?" His long plume of a tail swished slowly, amused by her posture. "Wanna be my new boyfriend?"

She held out the harness and he shoved his head through the opening. "I take that as a 'yes.'" She chuckled and stood, walking him out of the yard first.

The GED teacher commenced with introductions, explained what was required to complete the program, and then mercifully let them out early. Rosalie was relieved to get back and run the rest earlier. She pulled into the driveway, shocked by the Bronco. Her heart jumped. She turned off the engine, left her purse on the seat, and couldn't race up the stairs and in the front door fast enough.

It was Thursday evening, weekly Pork Chop and Bingo Night at Isle Vista Casino. Arlan would be there with Noreen.

"Dan?" she called from the doorway, her hand on the knob. The doggie door was closed. "Dan, you here?" She stormed the house, peeking into each bedroom, the kitchen, and then headed outside to the dog yard. The floodlights were on. She rushed around back. Maybe he'd reconsidered and was readying the dogs and rig to surprise her. But the shed door was open and the rig was gone. He'd never taken out dogs by himself.

She opened the gate and slipped into the yard. Team B was missing.

"Hi, guys." She squatted near the dogs. They were oddly still. Their body posture was strange and droopy. No one rushed over as they usually did for the pack greeting. But then again she'd never been with half of them while the others were out running. When it came to running, reciprocity was a tough concept for dogs to grasp. Clowny, Smokey, the Noodle, Panda and Rascal were on the trail.

"Why so glum, chums?" She stepped to quickly pet King. It was something Dave would say. The dog seemed not to notice. "Come on now—you guys went earlier; now it's their turn." She snorted a laugh. Squatting down, she invited a puppy pile, but no one moved except for Bella. Even then Bella stepped restlessly, sniffing in corners, as if looking for something she'd lost.

Their faces were somber, eyes round and worried. They sat tall, flush against the fence, lined up as if before a firing squad. Sniffing the air, they exchanged somber looks with wide-eyed expressions she'd never seen.

Quickly she turned to listen. Something caught her attention. Unusual noises echoed in the distance somewhere down by the cliff's edge. Ice fishermen weren't out; the lake ice wasn't yet solid. Sometimes you could hear weird echoes from their radios or from arguments with their wives. It was hard to pinpoint its origin. There was no moon; no wonder Dan had flipped on the floodlights. King caught her eye and howled, looking with a significance that struck her as odd.

"Jesus." She turned and hurried out the gate. Latching it, she raced down the driveway and stepped down sideways, negotiating the icy hill towards the cliff. Sounds amplified as she neared. She was instantly sick.

"Oh my God. Dan?" High-pitched distress cries intensified at the sound of her voice. Her chest seized. She reached the guardrail in the dark; only two side sections remained. She hadn't thought to grab a flashlight from the kitchen drawer.

"Dan, oh my God." Rosalie gasped. She dropped to her knees and felt along the icy cliff's edge.

"Dan," she screamed. The dogs whimpered just below. They sounded closer than the shore—maybe on the sandstone shelf fifteen feet below. It broke her heart. She didn't know what to do first.

She reached over the cliff, feeling for exposed roots, rocks, anything solid enough to grab hold of to lower herself down. The crumbling sandstone shelf was undercut and dangerous. It was anchored by two rather twisted, tortured-looking juniper trees that grew from the cliff. From there it dropped thirty feet to the rocky shoreline and sea caves. As children they were forbidden to play on it.

An eerie bluish glow shone from the shoreline near the entrance to the sea caves below. He must have been wearing her headlamp. Her eyes adjusted. On the sandstone shelf the outline of the back wheel was visible on its side, wedged against a juniper trunk. The dogs were there.

"Dan?" she called. Maybe the headlamp had fallen off. Maybe he was knocked out near the rig or the dogs. She shuddered at the thought of him fifty feet below on the shore. He had to be on the shelf.

"Dan," she called. "Do something if you can hear me." No sound. Not one movement. Grabbing exposed loops of tree roots poking from the side of the cliff, she lay down on her stomach and maneuvered towards the edge. Positioning to climb down, she transferred her weight and rolled over, one foot touching the face of the cliff, then the other. Stepping into air, she went rigid. The sensation was terrifying. Her frightened cry mixed with the dogs. The feel of nothing below, she'd fall to her death. Cries from the dogs compelled her. She gained a foothold on a rock, but it dislodged the instant she rested her weight. The rock careened down, missing the shelf, tumbling into dark silence towards the shoreline. She didn't hear it hit bottom. She hung; frantically kicking into the side of the cliff, her foot found another protrusion. It held. A boom of lake thunder startled her. Plummeting temperature triggered changes. It crackled like static electricity, ripping at light speed across the bay.

She climbed down, reaching with her foot to touch the shelf—only empty space. She hadn't a sense how much farther. She groped, feeling for more roots, and then carefully lowered herself, reaching to gain another foothold. The dogs' urgent cries made her want to hop midway down to the shelf. She fought the compulsion. Feeling with her toe again, she finally touched down. She let go and gingerly stepped away from the overhang. The ledge felt oddly hollow. She wasn't sure it would hold. Reaching to touch the dogs, she counted all five, but no Dan. She crawled, feeling along the icy surface, searching until her fingers cupped edges on all sides. He wasn't there.

"Oh no, oh no." She cupped her face in her hands, hugging her knees and rocking. It couldn't be true. Lake access began a good three-quarters of a mile away on either side of the red rock cliffs. If he crashed through the fast ice he'd be hypothermic. The enormity settled into her.

She crept to the rig on her knees, feeling safer the lower she was to the surface. Touching the juniper trunk, she stood slowly and leaned over, getting a better look at the shoreline. The blue light was stationary. It emanated from below. She sized up the cliff wall. It was a sheer drop—there was no way to climb down. She had to go get help. Rosalie knelt and crawled back to the base of the cliff. She stood, touching the face of it to steady. Where had she come down? The climb back up hadn't occurred to her.

"I'm going for help, Dan. Hang on, okay?" she called out.

She touched the rig. The whimpering and shivering dogs were going into shock. She started to panic. Feeling her way to the front basket, she found the carbineer and connecting gangline. She'd carry one up and go call for help. But could she? Would the roots hold more weight? She might lose her balance. She touched the first dog; it was the Noodle.

The dog's frame was draped around Panda, her puppy, as she tried to be the shock absorber to protect him. Rosalie unhooked the dog's neckline and tugline. She gently rolled Panda off and lifted the Noodle's petite frame.

"It'll be okay, my little sweetheart," she murmured to the dog. Struggling to gain composure, Rosalie squinted in the bluish light, feeling for the roots. Grabbing the first handhold, she clasped the Noodle to her with the other arm. Her muscles burned from strain. She stepped and hoisted up. It felt as though the Noodle was pouring out of her arms like beach sand.

"Come on, Noody," she whispered. "Help me." She balanced the dog on her hip bone and felt for the second set of tree roots. The Noodle shuddered. Lifting her was risky.

"Help me, please," she whispered, calling out to whoever

would listen. Kicking her toe into the cliff at different angles, she inched up, feeling for roots, trying to get a better foothold. Midway up, she almost fell backwards. Gravity teased at her back, luring her to surrender. Her arm trembled as if it would give out. The Noodle was sinking, becoming more difficult to hold.

Near the top Rosalie hooked her arm through exposed roots of a juniper. Balancing herself, she rolled the Noodle up onto the top near the fence post. Rosalie was then able to sling her leg over, leverage her weight and roll onto her back. Exhausted, she caught her breath, rolled over and got up.

Lifting the Noodle, she steadied herself, shaking fiercely as she plodded up the icy road towards the house. Headlights started down Ridge Road towards their driveway, illuminating the top of her head.

"Dad," she screamed. It was too far to hear. If Arlan was sober enough he might have noticed. The truck turned partway and then stopped. It backed out. Slowly, Arlan rolled down the road towards her.

"Dad," she screamed again.

The door opened. Arlan came running.

"They went over," she choked out the words. "Dan . . . he's down somewhere on the shore."

"Oh my God." Arlan loaded her and the Noodle into the truck. They backed up the hill, into the driveway.

"He doesn't answer. I think he fell by the sea caves." She started sobbing.

"Call Red Cliff and Bayfield Rescue. Call Franklin, Buck, Charlie, everyone."

She nodded.

He helped her out of the truck with the Noodle. Arlan rushed back; she heard him backing out.

She laid the Noodle down onto the couch, wrapping her up in the throw blanket, kissing her face. "I'll be right back." The dog's eyes opened in slits, looking lazily at her.

Rosalie's arms were rubber. It was hard to get them to keep pace with her thoughts. Her frozen fingers stiffly dialed numbers she knew by heart, reaching everyone but Charlie. Helen had mentioned they'd be out for the evening, having dinner at old Doc Hanson's. Rosalie paged Charlie.

She flung open the kitchen drawers, grabbed the flashlight and ran back down the road so fast she almost tripped and fell in the darkness. The flashlight glowed dimly and then went out. "Goddamn it." She smacked it with her hand as if trying to wake it. It glowed anemically before dimming out again. "Shit." She threw it down.

The top of Arlan's head was visible just over the edge of the cliff, illuminated by the headlights of his idling truck. *Don't let them fall. How had he made such a climb?* As she neared the edge he was struggling to roll Panda over onto the top. Arlan grunted from effort. Panda, the heaviest dog, started to panic. She knelt down and grabbed the back of Arlan's jacket, hauling him over.

"Grab here." She tapped the twisted pine root.

Arlan hooked his arm through. She reached for Panda. The dog began to fight her, thrashing in midair. The fall could kill him. Sixty-five pounds of sheer panic could pull Arlan right over with him. She rolled Panda up and lay on top of him, talking to settle him. Arlan rolled onto his back, his chest heaving as he scrambled.

"Didn't see him anywhere," Arlan said. "He's gotta be down there. Don't know how much more that ledge'll hold," he warned.

"Can you put him in the truck? I'll climb down for the others." She began the climb back down, less fearful. "Dan," she called again, feeling along the rig for the next dog. It was Smokey. She unhooked and lifted him. "It's okay, good boy," she assured him.

Smokey trembled, his head outlined in the bluish glow.

Arlan appeared on the ridge with a flashlight from his truck, shining it down onto the area. "Want me to come down?"

"No. Help me up." She climbed.

Arlan grabbed on to the collar of her jacket and hoisted her up. "You call Charlie?"

"I paged him." She rolled over onto the top after Arlan took Smokey. There were two more dogs. "They're at Doc Hanson's, Helen said this morning."

They laid Smokey down on the seat. In the dome light of the cab, shards of bone pierced through the skin on his blood- and sand-encrusted leg. She climbed down two more times, handing the last two off to Arlan at the top. They were alive, though in shock.

As Arlan backed up to the house, a brigade of trucks slowly inched down Ridge Road. Floodlights blared from the roofs, carefully negotiating the icy road to the cliff's edge. In the distance ambulances and rescue vehicles screamed.

Rosalie laid Smokey on the couch. Both he and the Noodle were still. Rosalie had never seen an animal going into shock and guessed there were more injuries than she could see. She ran into the bedrooms, tearing off blankets and sheets in one swift motion. Ripping heating pads from Arlan's bed, she bundled up Smokey and the Noodle. They seemed to be the worst off. She called Charlie again. *Damn.* They needed immediate attention.

Maybe he hadn't brought his pager or had turned it off. She had to find him. Knocking clutter off the kitchen counter, she found the phone book. Fumbling with the pages, her fingers and arms were almost useless from strain and the cold. *Fuck, fuck, fuck.* She'd forgotten. Kicky had chewed up the pages just last week. A huge gouge out of the midsection, pages either missing or too chewed to read. *Shit.* She threw it down.

The Noodle was becoming listless as Smokey began shivering. Rosalie phoned and paged again. *Goddamn it, why wouldn't he call?* Shouts from the road got her attention; men were calling to each other. She ran out and down the driveway.

Arlan caught her arm. "They got him."

"They're raising him now," Buck reported, relaying information from his radio. The EMT ambulance carefully drove down

Ridge, getting as close as was safe to the edge. "They lowered Walt in the basket. They're bringing him up right now."

She closed her eyes in relief. "Is he okay?" She didn't wait for an answer and rushed towards the road to go watch. Arlan caught her arm and stopped her.

"You get hold of Charlie?" he asked.

She shook her head.

"Still not answering his page?"

She looked down. Every moment was critical.

"Dan's in good hands. Your dogs got no one." He motioned with his chin to her truck. "Go get Charlie."

"You know where Doc Hanson lives?"

Arlan let go of her arm. "In Bayfield. North, kitty-corner to the County Seat building."

Rosalie flew towards her truck. She'd drive the streets, find Charlie's truck.

Buck stood in the driveway with his radio. As she backed out he motioned for her to roll down the window.

"I'm going to get Charlie."

"You okay to drive?" Buck asked.

She'd make herself be okay.

She fishtailed down the frozen driveway, out to Highway 13, gunning the engine. "Damn you, Dan," she yelled, crying. She hit the steering wheel with her palm, choked with emotion. "Damn you, what were you thinking?"

In Bayfield she turned at the County Seat. Arlan had said it was near. Driving the streets, she had no idea how to find them. Then she spotted the Dreamcatcher truck. Rosalie stopped in the middle of the street, driver's door wide open. She ran up to the house. The top of Helen's head was visible through the window in the living room.

Opening the storm door, Rosalie began furiously knocking.

"Open, please."

A kindly-looking elderly woman peered out inquisitively.

Rosalie started shuddering. "Charlie, Helen—" She couldn't catch her breath to speak, her chest heaving.

Doc Hanson's wife stared. Smokey's blood covered Rosalie's vest, face, hands. Mixed in with her own from gouges and cuts, her hair crusted with red sand and ice. Helen appeared next to the older woman.

"My God, Rosalie?" Helen stepped outside, touching her arm.

"There's been an accident. It's terrible, Dan, the Noodle—" She broke down.

"Charlie," Helen called into the house. "Charlie," she raised her voice to get his attention. "There's been an accident."

Charlie appeared in the doorway.

"Get my coat," Helen ordered. "My purse is by the couch."

"I'll drive your truck," Helen said. She bundled Rosalie up and tucked her into the passenger side.

Rosalie wanted to explain but was too exhausted to get out the words.

"The Noodle. Smokey's leg," was all she could say.

"Doc?" Charlie called into the house.

"We're on our way," the older man said. His wife began scrambling to gather coats and turn off lights. They followed Charlie all the way back to the house, passing the ambulance screaming in the opposite direction towards Ashland Hospital.

At the clinic Charlie looked into her eyes.

"I know this is tough," he said. "But I need your help."

She was sobbing, looking at their bodies.

"Look at me." He grabbed her shoulders. "*They* need your help. Love them more than yourself. They're going into shock."

She nodded and wiped her nose on her sleeve.

"Get me seven IV fluid bags, the ones with the red stripe."

She started to tremble.

"Get your shit together," he said sternly. "We have five dogs and two vets. Do what I tell you now," he ordered.

Rosalie snapped into action. Charlie barked order after order, almost bullying her, but it felt good to have a purpose. The clinic door opened. Cold air entered along with Dave and Jan. As they stomped off their boots, the swishing sound of their down jackets was all she could hear. The static-cling sound of knit hats being pulled off in dry air as Jan rushed over to hug her.

"Tell me what to do," Dave said to Charlie, standing with open hands.

Charlie instructed him how to check for internal injuries and bleeding as they sorted the dogs from most to least critical. Rosalie scurried about, assisting with clamps, typing blood, filling syringes and anesthesia.

Helen, Jan and Rosalie gathered all the clinic heating pads. They spread dog beds and blankets, transforming the waiting room floor into an ICU. The X-ray machine seemed to run all night, the surgery table continuously occupied. Jan sat next to the Noodle, holding the bag of blood as the dog was being transfused.

"Panda's ready," Doc Hanson said. After each was finished on the surgery table, the women would lift the anesthetized dog onto the warm pads. Dave and Rosalie continued to monitor vitals.

The phone rang at about 2 a.m., it was Arlan. Dave talked with him for a good long while, and then with the attending physician before hanging up. He looked at Helen.

"Will he be okay?" Rosalie asked.

Dave didn't answer.

She looked at Helen, who was looking down at the floor.

"Will he be okay?" Rosalie demanded.

Dave said nothing.

"I'm going." Rosalie peeled off the surgical gloves and tossed them.

"Don't. You're of more use here," Dave said curtly.

"But I can be there for him." She was getting angry. Why weren't they looking at her? She grabbed her coat, glowering at them, and stormed out the door.

"Rosalie, wait," Helen called.

Rosalie ran across the clinic parking lot. "Leave me alone," she yelled. Fumbling, she flung open the rusted door, jumped in and slammed it. She reached to turn the key. They weren't dangling from the ignition. *Shit.* She dug into her pockets. *Where the fuck are they?* Then she remembered. Helen had driven her truck. *Oh shit.* She started crying, lowering her head onto the steering wheel. Dave slowly opened the door.

"No, no, no," she cried, crumpling over as he leaned on her back.

"I'm sorry, Rosalie," he said. "I'm so sorry."

Helen and Jan stood next to him. Dave helped to lift her down. She crumbled in his arms. They all stood holding her. It couldn't be; it just couldn't. Yet she knew it was true. She'd known it back at the house, when Arlan insisted she go find Charlie.

The world was silent. Only the sound of wind as it sifted through bare branches of oak. Helen began to sing a prayer. It was familiar. From back when Rosalie had stood at her mother's graveside. Only now Helen was singing it for Dan's spirit.

It wasn't clear if Smokey and the Noodle would make it through the night. Smokey was still in shock. Half the Noodle's liver had been removed. Doc Hanson assured Rosalie that if the Noodle made it through the night, she'd be fine and her liver would regenerate. Rosalie lay on the mat next to the Noodle, stroking her cheek.

Helen quietly walked over to the stove and scooped out ashes. She smudged them across Rosalie's forehead as well as the foreheads of both Smokey and the Noodle.

Rosalie looked up at her.

"This is to protect them and you. Spirits are afraid of black. Sometimes when a spirit is confused or lonely, they will try to take someone with them for company. These two are especially vulnerable right now. The smudge will keep anyone from stealing their spirits before it's their time."

"Don't go," Rosalie whispered to the Noodle, and spread ashes with her index finger across the dog's forehead. Dan had always called the Noodle "their" dog. The Noodle's eyes focused on her, fluttering and then sinking back. She drifted in and out, the contours of her skull visible beneath the fur around her eyes. The way she must have looked as a puppy, what she might look like as an old lady. The Noodle's expression seemed to say "sorry" each time she began to drift.

"Stay, Noody. We need you here," Rosalie whispered, wanting to follow wherever it was the Noodle might need to go.

CHAPTER 35

Bakki hadn't been to the Cove in a decade and Jeaantaa wondered if he remembered the way. Heavy snowfall was obscuring the familiar landmarks.

The team slowed after the initial burst. Loping for half a mile or so, then walking. As snow blew into sculpted drifts, she let them set the pace. It was a light load. They followed the trail that the Brother Spirit had broken on his way to Rochlit. For the first miles, Jeaantaa kept glancing back, looking for Tariem. Afraid he'd follow. Relieved he hadn't.

The lazy sun lingered, hovering on the horizon. It illuminated the clouds in a round disc, refracting pink rays, and made the snow fluoresce with a deceptively warm yet sinister glow.

It was six miles to the Cove. A trip she made daily the year after Uptek's death. Back then they could run it in no time; now it would take the better part of the morning, if they made it at all. The snow was piling up fast, in some places it was almost up to their chests.

"Good dogs," she said, encouraging them, their ears perked at her voice. She walked on the side of the trail beside the sled to keep warm, the snow reaching the tops of her thighs. The dogs leaned into their harnesses, heads down, battling the fierce wind.

She choked up as she thought of Tangek's scream when Tariem struck her. Ankjem's cries as Cheyuga shielded him. But there was no road back.

"Sweet ones," she encouraged. The dogs grinned with broad toothy wolf smiles. "You're so brave." Some of them wagged their tails. They were so proud to be working again. None had lost

their lust for the trail. Though advanced old age robbed them of
strength, it hadn't touched their will. Ears set high, they walked,
wide-eyed.

Another couple of miles. It was getting harder to walk and
even harder to watch as drops of blood darkened the snow. The
skin of their footpads were thin from age. It was the worst kind
of snow. Icing up between their toes made walking painful. If
left to accumulate, it could crush the bones in their feet. A few
paused to shake heavy blankets of snow from their backs.

"Whoa." It seemed cruel to go any farther. A few dropped to
chew on their feet. Their faces were almost completely crusted
over with snow. Even Bakki slowed, though still leaning into his
harnesses. They lay down in the pillow snow to rest, circling to
tramp it down. She leaned over the dogs who were chewing
their feet and pulled up a paw. Jeaantaa crushed an ice ball between her teeth. Instant relief.

She sat on the edge of the sled and leaned back. Too tired to
cry, think or remember.

Bakki glanced back at her. His face bearded over with ice. At
his prompt the others stood and doubled back, leading the gangline back to circle her. Bakki's crystalline eyes sparkled for her.
"My good boy, Bakki." She held out her arms and cradled him
under her torso like mother dogs do. He pressed his flank
against her thigh. "Bakki." She whispered his name into the fur
of his neck.

Her hat burst off with a wind gust, startling them both. She
watched it tumble as it entered a tunnel of dimly lit snow and
disappeared.

The Cove was close.

She held out her mitten, inviting the others. They lumbered
over like snow bears, falling together as one. She gathered them
up like a bouquet of tundra flowers, leaning on them all. She
cooed to them in her comforting way. They pushed their bodies
against her, heads drooping down. Too tired to lick her face.

"We can stop here."

. . .

Bakki woke. He shook off and stared intently at Jeaantaa's face; she didn't move. He bumped her sharply on the forehead with his nose. He bumped harder.

"B-Bakki—" She tried to raised her hand. She looked for Uptek. He was somewhere close by, maybe hiding, playing a joke.

One sharp bark startled her. The others stirred. On his cue, they stood and shook off. Bakki unwound the gangline. He pulled it taut; they were ready. Leaning forward, they slammed in unison. The sled budged.

"Uptek." The pain in her feet was unbearable as Jeaantaa stepped onto the runners. The dogs bolted but slowed just as quickly in the deep snow. She stepped off, walking through the pain; it was too late for warmth to return. Her mittens were gone.

The dogs' breath billowed into heavy streams of frozen air. "Sweet ones," she encouraged. A few began limping exaggeratedly. More ice between their toes.

She unhooked Gorkka. Using her teeth to pull off the collar, she placed him into the sled bag with the others. Jeaantaa hooked her arm in the dog's place and pulled as Bakki pressed on.

The wind blew from all directions. "Bakki," she shrieked. She lost sight of him in the blowing snow.

The dog stopped and sniffed with interest, and then looked at her.

"Is this it, Bakki?"

He surveyed the area. The bluff was off to the left. The dogs seemed reinvigorated, wagging their tails as they inched down the steep path to the Cove.

At the shoreline Bakki stepped over steep pressure ridges. Waves had frozen into razor-sharp heaves with layered edges like the rim of a clamshell. The snow had blown into a hard crust. The sled glided effortlessly. The dogs ran, slowing through drifts, and then taking off. The sled fishtailed on the glare ice.

The storm intensified. Bakki stopped to lie down. He'd never once lain down on a run.

Jeaantaa unloaded and spread the tarp quickly. No sooner had she laid down a pine bough than the dogs stepped onto tarp, circling and settling down to face east. She unfastened the gangline, pulling off each collar with her teeth. They'd all be free. She lay down on the pine boughs with them, cradling the three pouches containing her children's afterbirth and the remains of her daughter. Reaching with her foot, she felt for the sled. One last thing to do.

There was the sea, shimmering gold from the sun. Just as it had been the day of their betrothal. She swore there was sand between her toes. Jeaantaa felt the sled stanchions with her leg. "Forest Keeper." She asked for help. With one shove, she pivoted the sled to face east. The entry point into the sun.

She grasped the tarp and pulled it over them. Jeaantaa kissed Bakki's nose. She was so tired. Holding her children in her heart. The Guardians. Her parents. And there was Uptek. The flash of his white teeth as he smiled that day, modeling the anorak. The shivering stopped and curious warmth flooded her. The sun was bright and the whole world as warm as a cook fire.

Cuddling into the warmth of Bakki and the others, she went to sleep.

CHAPTER 36

The ceremonial gathering was held the next day by the edge of the cliff. Tobacco was tied in pouches to the branches of the pines, and a large fire pit had been prepared by the edge. Snow was dug out. The circumference lined with stones to mark where Dan's spirit was released from earth. Fallen trees were chainsawed and placed as benches for the elders to sit. The fire popped and crackled. Smoke from the birch logs, bark and twigs twirled up in fragrant plumes. The drummers began singing as snow fell like a heavy blanket, shrouding them as it bound them together. There was no wind to break its fall, only quiet puffs falling through the mist to cleanse the air.

The ceremony to help Dan make the journey started in their driveway at the white pine, where it was believed his spirit began its point of departure. The procession traced his path down to the cliff's edge.

Arlan stood alone. Noreen had just arrived. She walked over and slipped her arm through his.

The older men began singing, men who grew up with Dan's father. Some of them his relatives. Recalling how proud his father had been the day he brought Dan to Red Cliff to show everyone his son. How Dan's musical talent had been apparent early on. They told stories of Dan's father and his bravery as a sea captain and how he was now waiting for Dan, to help him make the journey, to stand beside him and help him navigate.

The ceremony lasted for hours. They talked to Dan's spirit, encouraging him, telling him how he was loved and honored. They began smoking the sacred pipe and passing it as they all witnessed the beginning of his crossing. The smoke intertwined with their prayers, soothing Dan from where they believed he was watching, and explaining to him in case his spirit was confused.

And strangely, Rosalie felt him in the trees as the old men conversed. She imagined his spirit twirling about with the sacred smoke, as light as a feather now, their words and stories offering assurance. Memories of how her mother's ceremony had comforted her, back when there was only darkness. She could feel the gentleness of the older men's words, as a father calms his frightened son.

After the final blessing, everyone turned and began trudging back up the snowy hill. The falling snow had already softened their earlier tracks. Even the old men walked, including Earl. People had brought food to the house as Pearl stayed at the cabin, readying it so they could return to a hot meal.

Charlie caught up to Rosalie as she walked arm in arm up the hill with Jan and Dave on either side.

"You and I are taking a trip."

Rosalie briefly looked at him. And then back down to watch her feet as they parted the fresh powder into two continuous tracks.

"In March after the Iditarod ends in Nome, we'll rest a week, then go west over the Bering to Siberia."

She was too exhausted to care.

A week later, Rosalie and Lorraine, mostly at Lorraine's prompting, broke into Dan's house. They heard that Dan's sister was on her way to claim her brother's body and meet with a Realtor about his property.

"Hey, what's a little breaking and entering between friends?" Lorraine muttered as Russell, her boyfriend, jimmied open Dan's back window.

Once inside they stood looking around. So quiet, empty and

lifeless, though Rosalie had only been inside that once. It was odd, as if standing on consecrated ground.

"Look at all of this," Lorraine whispered.

"I just want his pictures," Rosalie whispered back, looking at King's face. But she couldn't move to take them. She looked to Lorraine.

"Well, shit." Lorraine began to pull out thumbtacks, tucking each one under her arm in assembly-line fashion. "What's a little petty larceny too?"

Rosalie heard the rustling of plastic grocery bags from the kitchen.

Lorraine emerged with the drawings safely protected.

Dan's jean jacket lay on the back of the couch. Rosalie picked it up, touching it to her nose.

"I'm taking this too," Rosalie said. She peeled off her parka and slipped her arms through his jacket, buttoning it before she slipped her coat back on. Then she stepped into Dan's bedroom. His shirts all hung evenly spaced in his closet. Spare change was sorted in a ceramic coffee cup with *Beargrease* stenciled across.

She lay down on Dan's bed and breathed into his pillow. Waves of pain broke as she curled up, grasping the pillow to her, clutching it with her knees, sobbing without tears. As her feet came together, the soles of her boots felt hard. "Why, Dan?" she said his name. Why had he gone alone? No sound came out. "Why?"

But she knew why. Arlan knew him better than anyone. "He was probably trying to make up with you, missy, show you he cared and that he had second thoughts," he said after the funeral. "Probably took them out alone as a way of saying he was sorry."

Rosalie felt Lorraine and Russell standing in the doorway.

"We better go," Lorraine said quietly, the drawings tucked under her arm. Several cars had passed along the highway. Russell looked itchy to leave.

Looking around Dan's bedroom, Rosalie took his pillow.

Standing in the center of the living room, she spotted a photo of Dan on one of the bookshelves. She stepped closer. He looked about eight. Dressed in a suit, a violin posed upon his shoulder, and a haughty-looking woman, presumably his mother. Dan looked as bewildered as a lost little boy in a department store—someone, anyone, should have grabbed his hand.

They left through the front door.

Back at the cabin, Rosalie tacked Dan's drawings up on the walls. This would be all she had of him. Unzipping her parka, she pulled his gloves out of the jean jacket pockets and slipped them on.

That night Rosalie lay in bed, wearing Dan's jacket and holding on to his pillow. She turned over each action as if she could reverse events and alter what had happened. If only they'd waited to run the dogs; now there was plenty of snow. A matter of a day had meant life and death.

Arlan too had been up. They'd both stopped sleeping. She finally got up and walked into the living room in her sweatpants and T-shirt.

"I'm going to the clinic." She reached for her coat. "Gonna check on Smokey and the Noodle."

Arlan didn't say anything. The darkened form of his head perfectly outlined as it blocked the light from the TV.

The parking lot of the Dreamcatcher Clinic was freshly covered with snow. The truck tires squeaked as she parked. Only the lights inside by the surgery table were on. She glanced up the incline towards Charlie's house. The blue light of their TV illuminated the front room; they were still up. She unlocked the clinic door with her key. Smokey was up, greeting her at the door.

"Hey, guy." She knelt as he licked her face. "You shouldn't be up walking."

He was bouncing back, moving about happily like a pirate with a peg leg. Charlie had pinned the broken femur only the day before, immobilizing the leg from the armpit down with a cast. It made a Captain Kidd thump and drag noise on the floor. He was making a game of it, wielding it and dashing from side to side, excited to see her.

Rosalie knelt down where the Noodle was sleeping on a bed in one of the cages. She opened the door and crawled inside. The Noodle's tail thumped the bed as she lifted her nose to greet Rosalie.

"Hey, good girlie."

Not long after the front door opened, Charlie stomped in with his heavy boots.

"Saw your truck," he called to her.

"I can't sleep," she called back.

"I'm not surprised."

"Thought I'd come and check on them."

"You can take 'em both tomorrow." The three others had already come home that morning. "Probably do better at home anyway." He pulled up a stool, placing down a half gallon of ice cream as he slipped off his parka. "Helen insisted."

Charlie rummaged around in the lab area and returned with two stainless dog food bowls. "Sorry." He held up his hands. "Forgot to grab bowls from the house."

Rosalie shrugged.

He began raking out clumps of ice cream with a fork, handing off a chunk to Smokey. It disappeared in seconds. The Noodle whined from her cage.

"Oh-h—" Charlie chuckled. "Look who's feeling better."

The dog rolled back, lifting her leg, offering up her sutured belly. It looked like a sternum to hip bone zipper had been installed. Her tail thumped again as Charlie opened the door, letting the Noodle lick all the ice cream off the fork.

"Once they're begging," he said, "you know they're feeling better." He handed Rosalie a dog bowl after he scooped them each a respectable heap of ice cream. The bowl sat on her lap.

"Ramsay called a few nights ago. I didn't have the chance to talk to you about it."

She smiled, remembering Ramsay.

"He got this call from an old man over in Chukotka—literally across from his backyard. Remember him talking about the woman who gave him the dogs?" Charlie looked at her. "Well, apparently the woman's husband called and wants them back."

Rosalie looked up. "Her husband?"

"After the Iditarod ends in Nome, we'll take a week to recover, and then we're taking a little trip with Ramsay. We're borrowing Jan and Dave's teams."

"You mean run dogs to Siberia?"

"Yup, that's the plan."

"Won't we get in trouble?"

"The whole country's collapsed. Ramsay says we'll make it no sweat. He specifically asked for you."

A few days later she began dozing, thankful that sleep hadn't deserted her for good. The Noodle was home and lying beside her. Kicky sprang up onto Rosalie's bed to nestle and sleep alongside the Noodle; the dog wasn't used to sleeping without her mom. Rosalie welcomed the addition of another sweet canine scent. It slowed her mind down enough to drift off into the arms of sleep.

Soon she was dreaming. Once again Rosalie stood barefoot out on the ice road. The ice was clear as glass, though not cold. Underwater plants undulated in the wake of the waves. The wall of cliffs felt as if they were snuggling up closer, either to comfort or to absorb her. The woman with the long black hair was curled up on her side, holding the small shrunken body of an infant. Then Rosalie noticed other snowy mounds surrounding them. Huskies, all asleep. The smell of pine resin so pungent she could taste it in her mouth.

Wisps of Rosalie's hair blew as she watched, tangling in her eyelashes. She brushed it away.

She was aware of Arlan standing there.

"Missy?" He shook her as if life depended on it. "Wake up."

Tears wet her eyes.

"You okay?"

She nodded, not wanting to open her eyes.

Arlan studied her. "You were crying out, trying to say something. Look at me."

Rosalie looked at him but couldn't speak. She lifted her hands out from under the blankets, her fingers like white icicles.

"What the hell?" Arlan cried.

"So you see them too." She held them up.

His alarm turned to puzzlement.

"It's happened before. Whenever I dream of her."

"Who?"

She motioned for him to come closer and touched her icy fingers to his face.

He pulled away.

It was real.

"I'm going with Charlie, Arlan," she said. "I'm crossing the Bering with him in March."

CHAPTER 37

Uelen was virtually unrecognizable. Down on the cape were cement apartment buildings and messaging stations for the farthest eastern outpost. The town had been abandoned since 1986, after the Soviet Union collapsed. For a few years, only a skeleton crew of Government workers remained. After their paychecks stopped it didn't take long for them to evacuate with the rest of the non-Chukchi residents.

The narrow strip of land was crammed with buildings, most of them empty. Shore to shore filled with cement boxes. Tariem walked to the tip of the cape and looked out to where the seas roiled together. During the frequent and rough autumn storms, giant waves thudded against Government buildings, loud enough to startle a person out of a deep sleep. Seawater froze over windows. It all existed so precariously, as if one good autumn storm would roll over to swallow the whole village.

On that first approach, Tariem and Yevgheni drove up on the ridge towards Cape Dezhnev and the Cove. Tariem choked up with recognition at the crescent stand of trees. Had it not been for the pines, he would never believe his people once lived there. Tariem dismounted from the snowmobile and stood. The emotion was too great. The old man's legs buckled as his grandson caught him and lowered him to sit.

Since 1929 the area had been used as a storage and junkyard for State mining operations of tin and tungsten. All left abandoned. Piles of cinder blocks, rusted gasoline tanks, junked trucks and cars. Junkyards had formed wherever someone got tired of hauling scrap from one place to another across the vast tundra.

Like an ant programmed to reconstruct an ancestral hill, Tariem was inexhaustible. He'd not wanted to stay in the apartment buildings. Instead he and Yevgheni scavenged birch wooden poles along with skins he found in defunct fur collectives. He began instructing Yevgheni on how to make the *yaranga* airtight and waterproof.

Their other relatives, content to stay in their apartments, couldn't tease him enough: "Ha! A *yaranga*, how charming. We'll come to pry out your bodies this spring, when you thaw a bit." They chuckled. "Set you up on stanchions for the ravens to pick at."

But power in Uelen proved even more unreliable than in Anadyr. After three days of prolonged outage, several ate their words to hike up the mountain towards the Cove and Tariem's cozy *yaranga*. He and Yevgheni sat, stuffed with seal meat, as the boy listened with his radio to basketball games broadcast from Rochlit or Nome.

Soon the *yaranga* was packed with twenty-some distant and not-so-distant relatives. All piled in, practically on top of each other, dozing and eating seal meat and dried salmon in the warmth of the fire. Their babies and grandbabies toddled around in diapers as the outside temperature plummeted to fifty-five degrees below zero. They wouldn't shut up about building more *yarangas* once the storms quit, how they would get their hands on more reindeer skins and birch poles.

As soon as the weather broke that spring, even more relatives showed up with blowtorches and tools they confiscated from the mines and ports of Anadyr. Dismantling and hauling off junk, they made repeated cross-country trips—teetering in overloaded trucks across the tundra—since gasoline, like alcohol, seemed to be mysteriously abundant. The goal was to contain it all in the wasteland outskirts of the city. Together they worked into the "month of lengthening days," purging their village of reminders of the Soviet presence.

The crescent stand of trees had been used as a resting place for non-Chukchi workers from the Ukraine and Irkutsk who died in the work camps. While the bodies of soldiers and Party officials were promptly sent to Anadyr and shipped off to families, the remains of poorer workers—a total of about fifty in their village alone—were entombed in cement sarcophagi piled on top of one another. The corners of each had begun sinking, lopsided, down into the permafrost. For all Tariem knew, the bodies of his own family might be there. Since 1929 they'd been scattered. No longer could he feel the spirits of the ones who'd passed. There was no central place to leave food or offerings to the Old Ones. No place to ask for their wisdom and comfort.

He had one of the younger men phone and make a formal request to Anadyr to have the bodies removed. Tariem guessed it would take another hundred years, maybe longer, and he'd run out of that kind of patience. It was time to clear the space for the return of the Guardians.

That summer Yevgheni's much older brother, Gregori, appeared. Cigarette dangling from his roguish smile, brimmed by his spiky mustache. He touted a flatbed truck with an industrial hoist he bragged about having commandeered from a power plant. Each sarcophagus was carefully loaded to make the precarious trip down to Anadyr, four trips in all. The boxes were stored alongside the rest of what the Invaders left behind. Gregori returned with several rolls of welded wire fencing to prepare a kennel system.

For the start of the second winter they were happily immobilized. Huddled together in the *yaranga*'s warmth, listening to basketball games, assured by Tariem that next year's food caches would be even better. They'd be able to dry and preserve fish and mammal meat. The hunters would come from Rochlit. Spring would bring new gifts.

It had been a week since the meeting with the Alaskan contingent.

"I hear something." Tariem clapped Yevgheni's shoulder.

"Yuri's truck." Yevgheni scrambled up to his feet in seconds. Up from where he was fiddling with his portable radio to get better reception. He was catching just enough English now to make out the scores and some of the action of the game. The radio was powered with the last few precious batteries he'd picked out of an old commissary in Uelen.

Yevgheni hopped over the sleeping bodies of relatives already dozing on the *yaranga* floor. "Watch out," a few yelled. Yevgheni laughed as he stepped around them, scurrying towards the door flap.

"It's him," he called, and grabbed his boots.

"Who else would it be?" someone yelled.

It was beginning to storm. Katerina had stuffed them with a good stew of seal meat and fish roe. Yevgheni shut the inner and outer flap doors and dashed outside. Hopping towards the truck, he jammed his feet into rubber boots. He listened to the familiar straining whine of his friend's truck and ran to greet him. The truck slowed. The engine coughed and idled, sputtering alongside the *yaranga*.

Even with the short drive from Uelen, the truck was glazed with thick ice. With a metal shovel, Yevgheni pounded the outside of the frozen door as Yuri pushed back. Then the teenager began chipping away at the glacial sheet that coated the side of the truck. The blade broke through enough to wedge the edge of the metal shovel between the door and the frame. He leveraged the handle against the doorjamb, without even breaking the window this time, a delicate art form in Chukotka. Yuri lay down on the seat, pushing with his feet.

"They called," Yuri blurted as soon as the door gave way.

"I knew it," Yevgheni yelled. He held up the shovel and began laughing in victory. He danced around, slapped the door of the truck with his hand several times and then dropped on the ground to roll in the snow.

"Get up, you idiot," Yuri scolded him. "What are you suddenly two years old again? We have to go; they're waiting for you to call back. Go get your grandfather; it's getting bad," he advised, looking around to gauge the wind speed. "We'll wait out the storm there. My cousin's visiting from the university in Leningrad. She speaks English. Stupid bitch thinks she's leaving early tomorrow to go back to Anadyr." He gave a nasty little laugh.

"In this?" Yevgheni laughed, holding up his hands in the wind.

His friend shrugged. "Irina wants to get the hell out of here. She's sick of freezing. Go get your grandfather."

As Yevgheni turned, Tariem was already at his side. The old man was fully dressed with his grandson's overshirt and gear hanging on his fingers.

The three of them worked to open the passenger door; the ice was not quite as thick on the other side. Yevgheni helped Tariem up into the truck cab. They slowly began the trip along the hard snowpack of the coast, teetering along the cliff edge. They could barely see to the front of the hood. Yuri drove carefully over hills and swales, where the snow was piling up fast. Even though it wasn't far, people were known to freeze to death in storms like this, sometimes just strides away from their front doors.

Straight-line winds obscured the way. Ice froze the windshield faster than the defroster could fight. Yevgheni popped open the door and stood. Leaning over the windshield with the shovel, he tapped to break up the rapidly accumulating frost.

"Easy, easy, enough already," Tariem yelled, annoyed at his grandson's zealousness. He smacked Yevgheni on the top of his thigh, scolding him in Chukchi, afraid he'd bash through the windshield. Yevgheni laughed in his giddy way, which annoyed the old man even more.

At last they approached the steep descent to the cape and out to the village. Faint lights were barely visible, a sign the town generator was holding.

They parked in front of the apartment building, leaving the truck in the middle of the street. Yevgheni helped Tariem down. Yuri's mother greeted them just inside the building's foyer, a heavy blanket wrapped around her shoulders. She extended a round brass tray with three clear glasses of steaming tea. Yevgheni accepted, cupping his hands around the small cylinder of hot tea to thaw his hands, but Tariem politely declined.

Upstairs the university cousin sat cross-legged in a chair by the phone, bundled up in her coat, hat and blankets. Irina's pale face was a scowl of resentment and crankiness. In her lap was the telephone and a piece of paper with numbers scrawled. Irina rolled her eyes when she saw the old man. Picking up the receiver, she dialed as soon as they were situated. Soon she was speaking the language of Rochlit. Her breath steamed, fogging up the receiver with tiny drops of moisture. Her face softened. She smiled at the old man and nodded, and then smiled into the air; she talked as though the person were sitting right there in front of her.

"Robert Ramsay?" Tariem pointed to the receiver.

Irina nodded. Something about the old man's gesture made her smile. There was an innocence about him that disarmed her.

He furrowed his brows and shook his head, mystified how the voices of people could live in there.

"Ask him where my wife is," Tariem said.

They all looked at him.

"Your wife?" Irina asked.

"Ask him if he knows where she is."

Irina started talking, her eyes fixed on Tariem. "He says he remembers your wife and the day he came to get the dogs," she translated.

"Does he know where she is?"

Irina spoke for a few moments. "No. He hasn't seen her since that day sixty years ago. Says he's wondered what happened to her."

"It can't be—she's not in Rochlit?"

Irina spoke again, and then shook her head. "No."

"He doesn't know where she went?" Tariem asked, feeling like it was only yesterday that she'd taken off. He sat forward, looking down at the floor. "How can that be?" he said to himself, rubbing his brow, switching to Chukchi. "Where did you go, Jeaantaa? Where have you been?"

Tariem sat for some time, his forehead resting in his hand, saying nothing.

Irina looked at him, waiting.

"It's a long time not to see her," Tariem said in Russian. "Ask if he knows anyone else who knows where she went?"

"He says he wishes he knew," Irina said. "He's wondered too over the years."

"Does he have her dogs?" the old man asked.

"Yes, they have many, many generations of Guardians," Irina went on. "Great sled dogs. There's an old red one sitting on his foot right now. Reminds him of the red puppy your wife put into the cage."

Tariem closed his eyes and sighed loudly. He sat back, pressing his shoulders against the back of the chair. It was too much to imagine, too much to remember. The weight was suddenly enough to grind him into dust.

"He says they will come in March," Irina said. "They'll bring puppies and young dogs. Someone who speaks Russian will call here. Give you the date and instructions where to meet. He wants to know if you have a safe place to keep them."

"We are home now. We have our place back. We are all safe," Tariem confirmed.

"How many do you want?"

"How many?" Yevgheni repeated as if he didn't understand or couldn't believe it.

Irina looked to the two of them, waiting for a response. Tariem and Yevgheni glanced at each other, and then back at Yuri's cousin.

"Tell him to bring as many Guardians home as he can," Yevgheni said.

Tariem stood and walked over to where Irina sat, motioning for her to hand him the receiver. Everyone looked at the old man, waiting for him to speak. He awkwardly positioned the receiver along the side of his head.

"Robert Ramsay?" he shouted as clearly as he could enunciate.

"Yes?" the man answered.

Everyone watched.

"Brother Spirit," Tariem said in Chukchi. "Come back. Bring the Guardians home. They have been gone a long time." He then handed the receiver back to Yuri's cousin.

Tariem sat back in the chair as if he'd fallen asleep. Covering his face with his hands, he started to tremble. A lifetime descended upon him in an instant. He started to cry.

Everyone looked at him, then at each other, not knowing what to do.

"Tell him we will be there," Yevgheni piped up, eagerly scooting to the edge of the wooden stool where he was perched. His eyes sparkled, watching his grandfather. "And tell him we will be good to them and not to worry."

Irina laughed out loud as she translated the teenager's words.

"He's not worried," she said, smiling as she relayed the message.

"Michael Jordan great," Yevgheni blurted out in English, yelling at the black receiver.

Irina laughed.

"Yes. He wants to know what size is your foot?" she asked Yevgheni.

"My foot?" Yevgheni looked down at his foot, puzzled.

"Yes, how big is your foot, idiot?" Yuri smacked the back of his head. "What size?"

They all looked down at Yevgheni's feet.

Yevgheni shrugged.

"He doesn't know," Yuri reported.

Hardly believing how someone didn't know his shoe size, Yuri's cousin looked at Yevgheni's Soviet-issued rubber boots. They were stuffed with newspapers. Then it dawned on her that Yevgheni had probably never owned a proper pair of shoes.

Yuri's mother pulled off her son's boot, holding it up to Yevgheni's foot. "Mm-m . . . nine American, forty-three European," she reported to the cousin who translated. "Give it a size up, room to grow."

"He says good-bye for now, they will call here and leave instructions. He will see you in March."

Tariem sat up and motioned to Yuri's cousin to wait.

"Tell him does he know the Cove?"

"Yes, he knows the Cove. He says that's the way he came before. He will come the same way when he returns in March. He's bringing helpers with him."

The old man nodded. Tariem's mind and heart stirred once again with a love and disappointment that never seemed to finish.

CHAPTER 38

March weather patterns triggered storms of unpredictable fury. Warm Japanese currents began seeping northward into the Bering like dark, quiet fingers: the beginning of the melt. Evidence of their arrival could be seen in elongated black streaks deep within the sea ice. Within weeks these would spread like ink spots until the Bering would open once again.

But it was still early enough for the runners of a dogsled. Standing in Ramsay's backyard, on the shore of the Seward Peninsula, Rosalie and Charlie loaded wire dog cages into the sled bag of a freighting sled. Two litters of puppies from Ramsay's kennel would be delivered. Ramsay would also run a team of yearlings that he and Charlie had handpicked to be returned to the old man.

"I kept their genetics consistent," Ramsay explained. "Always felt it was important."

Rosalie listened as she gently lowered each pup onto a bed of straw. The scent from Dan's jean jacket wafted up under Jan's arctic parka. It made Rosalie stop. Waves of unbelief still crippled her.

Snowmobile engines revved as timing was checked for the trek across the Bering. The smell of gasoline was sharp.

Ramsay turned and looked back at his kennel. "That woman's dogs saved my life. Pulled me out of the Yukon River one winter," Ramsay said. "It's time to return the favor."

. . .

That next hour everyone stood on the shore of the Bering Sea, packed and ready to go. Charlie looked at Rosalie's loaded sled and spotted Smokey's head in the sled bag.

"So, you decided to take him." He grinned.

Smokey's leg was still not healed enough to run, so she left space for him to sit comfortably. Rosalie stepped onto the runners of Jan's sled. The Stormwatch teams had finished the Iditarod only a week earlier.

"You ready?" Charlie asked.

She nodded. Clowny and King were hooked to run lead in front of Jan's team for the fifty-mile trip.

Ramsay stood on the runners of his sled, piled high with warm clothing and supplies.

Charlie reached to touch Rosalie's shoulder. He then looked around at the contingent of fifteen Alaskan Inuit on snowmobiles. Each had drag sleds loaded with ice-fishing gear, blankets, fuel and generators, cartons of canned food, frozen fish and meat for their cousins in Uelen.

Clouds of blue iridescent fumes filled the air as they powered up their engines. The provisional Russian government had refused their official offer of humanitarian transport. The stated reason was fear of spreading vermin. Nome's Inuit community politely ignored the ruling.

"Ready, old man?" Ramsay asked Charlie.

Charlie grinned.

"Everyone ready?" Ramsay called back.

Snowmobiles revved in acknowledgment and then took off.

The dogs began squealing in deafening roars.

"Let's go," Rosalie called.

Clowny and King jumped as the sled jerked forward. Rosalie pulled the snow hook. The dogs took off running in truth and earnestness towards Chukotka, chasing the snowmobiles. Rosalie's hat flew off and her dark hair blew out behind her.

. . .

It was a clear day as Yevgheni and Tariem departed for the Cove. The engine on their elderly snowmobile whined. Tariem sat in the drag sled bundled in reindeer blankets and kept an eye out for polar bears, looking for glimpses around the rifle slung across the teenager's back. Yevgheni held up binoculars and scanned the horizon for dark specks, steering with his free hand.

Atop towering cliffs surrounding the Cove, their relatives lined up to keep watch. Their snowmobiles and battered vehicles were parked along the edge. They scanned the horizon for signs of anything that might identify their cousins from Rochlit. Once they spotted them, three shots would be fired, signaling to Yevgheni and Tariem.

Children romped and played on the ice in the Cove. A special festival celebration was organized to mark the return of the Guardians. Dancers dressed in furs and drummers welcomed the spirits of all who'd passed before them. Many had come as far as Anadyr and Bilibino to welcome the people from Rochlit.

"It's them." Yevgheni sat up even straighter.

Shots were fired from the Cove, but Tariem had already seen. Tears collected in the outside corners of the old man's eyes. He watched the dark forms on the horizon grow larger.

Rosalie waved. The visiting party had agreed that the dog teams would approach first.

Yevgheni stood up, waving his whole arm vigorously.

The two groups neared and slowed to a stop. Ramsay set a snow hook and young Thomas parked his snowmobile.

Rosalie kicked in her snow hook and stepped off the sled. Smokey sat up in the sled bag, his ears alert. She patted his head and hurried past. He cried forlornly, watching her walk swiftly towards Yegheni and Tariem. She felt their scrutiny as she approached and slowed to a stop. Aware of their caution, she kept her distance. Eyes burned from beneath the old man's sealskin hood. They were eyes from another century—as ancient and unworldly as one might see in the wild.

"Come closer," Tariem said in Chukchi.

She stepped towards him and took off her mitten. She reached her hand.

"They don't shake." Thomas caught up and bumped into her shoulder.

"Oh." She withdrew her hand.

"It's not rude," he explained. "That's how they are."

"Okay."

Ramsay caught up too and stood. "Robert Ramsay." He touched his chest.

Tariem slowly nodded. The two men stood in silence.

Tariem slowly gestured towards the Cove, keeping his eyes on Rosalie. He said something to her in Chukchi. Thomas stepped closer, tilting his ear, but the old man's voice had been too soft. Rosalie looked for a translation; instead Thomas shrugged.

Behind them dogs yipped excitedly, impatient with the delay. Yevgheni steered and turned the snowmobile around. Rosalie stood watching as they took off. Behind them engines powered back up and began to follow.

"Roz," Charlie called over the engine noise. "Rosalie," his voice kicked her out of a stupor.

She turned to see Charlie gesturing impatiently; she was keeping them waiting. Rosalie jogged back, stepped onto the runners and pulled out the snow hook. Clowny and King surged, rushing to catch the others to the Cove.

Rosalie and Ramsay unloaded puppies into the fenced area in the crescent stand of trees. Children ran inside to play with the them as Tariem looked on. Rosalie showed Yevgheni and some of the braver children how to kneel down and hand-feed the puppies. After, she and Ramsay fed and watered the dogs. They broke up and spread a few bales of hay they brought from the Iditarod finish line in Nome.

That evening everyone gathered outside the *yaranga* around a bonfire. Katerina ladled out bowls of a stew made of seal meat, fish roe and seaweed. Children walked about, distributing a bowl to each guest. Rosalie grasped her bowl, feeling its warmth down into the bones of her hands. She sniffed it. It smelled with an earthiness of the sea. She waited until everyone else had a bowl. She looked around for soupspoons but took her cue from Tariem as he tipped up his bowl and drank.

Platters of raw fresh whitefish and roe were passed around along with a knife. She watched Yevgheni slice off a piece, dip it into a cup of seal oil and then eat it off the knife. Tariem's grandson closed his eyes in bliss.

Then the bowls were collected. Katerina barked orders as another woman helped fill each bowl with something resembling pink Cool Whip. The children began to distribute bowls to the entire party.

Rosalie turned to Thomas. "It's a type of dessert," he explained. "We eat the same thing, only we call it 'Eskimo ice cream.'" Walrus tallow whipped with seal oil combined with frozen cloudberries and salmonberries. The others began to scoop the dessert up with their fingers. She did the same.

Everyone sat back, leaning against piles of gear as they warmed hands and feet. Tariem began to speak in Chukchi as they all sat listening. He told of the Red Army. Of Jeaantaa being the Keeper of the Guardians. Of the old ways of sacrifice. Of Jeaantaa's love for her dogs. He told of their fight the day she left. His voice faltered. The old man spoke in torrents as if trapped memories had finally dislodged.

Yevgheni translated into Russian, Thomas into English.

"She left. I don't know where she went," Tariem explained.

Rosalie looked at the old man. His face was wet from emotion as their eyes met.

"I think I know where your wife went."

They all looked at Rosalie. Only the fire popped to break the silence. Lights from apartment buildings were twinkling in Uelen. The spicy scent of pine resin from the crescent circle of trees. She thought of Jeaantaa on her sled with the old dogs. It was all clear. Rosalie gazed out to the sea ice where the Arctic and Chukchi seas joined. The tops of distant granite cliffs that had risen up—millions of years before—to form the shelter of the Cove.

She turned to the old man. It was crazy, but everything there was otherworldly, as if being at the end of one place and the beginning of another. The dreams, the woman with long hair, the cliffs, the white mounds of sleeping dogs covered with snow, the woman's underwater home.

"Sir," Rosalie said, looking to Thomas to translate. "I think your wife died out there"—she pointed out towards the Cove— "with her dogs."

Tariem looked into the fire. He closed his eyes and his chin tipped down slightly.

"I think she curled up with them right out there in the Cove and died in a storm."

Singing woke her the next morning. The light was dim in the *yaranga*. Rosalie opened her eyes, startled to see Yevgheni sleeping bare chested, his nose inches from her face, cuddled under the same reindeer blanket. She turned over. Yuri, Yevgheni's friend, was also stripped from the waist, even closer, his breath on her face as he snored loudly.

Rosalie sat up quickly. Both stirred on either side. She hadn't remembered falling so deeply asleep, much less being flanked on either side by two young men. Last she remembered, they were all sitting inside as one of the elderly women told a story in Chukchi. Rosalie remembered the weight of the reindeer blanket on her chest and looking up at the *yaranga*'s ceiling. The skin stretched over the poles made her feel like she was peering from inside the rib cage of a whale.

Smokey had been sleeping on her feet. He looked up at her; everyone else was asleep. The singing was coming from outside. The *yaranga* floor was carpeted with bodies interlaced with several of the pups. A few of the Nome contingent slept in down bags; others were sandwiched between the reindeer-fur floor and the top blankets. Carefully, she slid out and looked for her boots and parka.

"Come on, Smokey," she said.

The dog stood, limping after her with his cast. Together they stepped to the outside of the *yaranga*. She climbed over Charlie and Ramsay and crept past the cookstove, edging around as she felt for the door flap. She couldn't detect an opening but then spotted the tie that distinguished it from the other panel walls. They stepped through the flaps and sealed out the cold air by smoothing the panel shut. The outside air felt sharp, almost searing her lungs. She followed the singing.

Circling the *yaranga*, she spotted Tariem. He stood facing east over the rooftops out toward the Bering shoreline. His arms were outstretched towards the farthest point of land. He stood praying, as if encouraging the sun. The old man turned the moment he felt her and gestured with his hand, motioning for her to stand with him.

Rosalie stepped slowly.

His cloudy eyes regarded her with an ancient gaze.

As she stood there, she towered almost a whole head and shoulders above him. Smokey sat down beside her.

"We will welcome the sun," Tariem said in Chukchi. The sky was a strip of scarlet. He raised his arms again and began singing.

Rosalie didn't know what to do. She felt foolish. He stopped and motioned for her to lift her arms. Tariem pointed to his throat, as if he wanted her to sing.

She thought of an Ojibwa song that was sung at her mother's graveside funeral and at Dan's ceremony. The haunting words promised, "We will remember your name forever. Forever your memory will burn as a light inside us all." Emotion choked her words. Her chest tightened, thinking of Anna Marie, thinking of Dan. The moment of release she felt the night she'd taken

Smokey. As if that one act defined everything that was yet to come. She felt the cruelty and suffering of the earth—of animals, people, the pain of the mountains and rivers. Her voice faltered.

Tariem was smiling at her. He nodded. Then the old man closed his eyes and lifted his arms as he joined in with her song.

She hadn't known how long the two of them had stood there. When she finally opened her eyes and looked around, Charlie and Ramsay were standing next to her. The sun had fully risen. She was surprised to see Chukchi and the Inuit contingent all bunched up behind her. Some in their parkas, others wrapped in reindeer blankets, there was a peacefulness as they held the moment.

The smell of bacon and eggs came from the cook fire by the *yaranga*. She thought of Arlan.

"Jesus." Ramsay turned to her and patted his rib cage with both hands. "God, I could eat a moose!"

"You all hungry?" a woman from the Nome contingent called out. "Breakfast American-style. Be ready in twenty minutes."

"Those dogs need to eat," Ramsay said.

"You know," Charlie said, "the Ojibwa believe it's a sin to eat if your animals are hungry."

Thomas translated.

Tariem nodded. "We believe that too," the old man acknowledged, and then turned to Rosalie.

"My wife knew—," Tariem began. Quickly looking away, he touched his lip with realization.

"—that by saving the Guardians, she'd save us, the People of One Fire. That long after the flame was stomped, the Guardians would return to rekindle us." The old man's shoulders drooped. "She was the Keeper. She knew such things," he said. "But I didn't. I wanted to sacrifice—to kill them." His eyes narrowed, darting with memory.

Then he glanced at Rosalie and smiled in an unsure way. "Back then it was our way." He turned towards the Cove and raised his voice. "You knew better, Jeaantaa."

Then he turned to Rosalie.

"She brought you back, Daughter Spirit." He raised his weathered hands towards her, surrounding her face. "She led the Guardians home. This is her gift."

Rosalie absorbed his words. She studied Tariem's lined face, trying to imagine him as a much younger man. Rosalie wanted to hug or touch him. She glanced at Thomas, who seemed uncertain of what to do.

Instead she slipped her mittens back on and smiled.

Then Tariem gestured towards the smell of the food. He raised his eyebrows several times in quick succession.

She chuckled and nodded. Children laughed as they raced each other towards squealing puppies, excited at the anticipation of the coming meal.

After all the dogs were settled, Thomas and Yevgheni distributed bowls heaped with scrambled eggs and bacon. Many residents from the apartment buildings in Uelen hiked up, some riding double on snowmobiles, carrying trays of food.

Tariem lifted a wavy string of bacon and spoke in Chukchi. The old man turned it over, examining it before he took a bite. He continued studying it as he chewed, and then said something to Yevgheni.

"He likes it," Thomas relayed.

After breakfast the sleds were unpacked. Generators and supplies stacked and lined up next to the *yaranga*. Tariem took them on a tour of the five umiaks that he and Yevgheni had built. The old man lifted the blue tarp, discussing construction techniques of the old days. Several young Chukchi men eagerly voiced their desire to the Inuit men; they wanted to learn the hunt.

Ramsay unpacked several pairs of basketball high-tops, lining them up according to size. Bulls jerseys plastered with *Jordan* across the back and seven basketballs were donated by a sports store in Nome. Tariem picked up each item and inspected it, nodding in approval before commenting to Ramsay in Chukchi. The two old men seemed to have worked out a system whereby they understood each other perfectly.

Tariem sent Thomas to corral Yevgheni from the crescent stand of trees and bring him over. Yevgheni ran back, followed by Thomas and Rosalie, Smokey, Clowny and King. They stood next to Tariem, watching.

"Try this size." Ramsey handed Yevgheni a pair of high-tops.

The teenager pulled off his boots. A wad of ratty newspaper tumbled out. His foot was wrapped in an indistinguishable cloth vaguely resembling a sock. Clowny started sniffing his foot with interest.

"Put them on," Rosalie motioned.

Yevgheni slipped on the high-tops.

"Now stand." Ramsay gestured.

He stood and Ramsay checked for size. Rosalie began to lace up one foot, Ramsay the other.

"How do they feel?" Ramsay asked.

Yevgheni nodded and gave a thumbs-up.

"Walk around." Rosalie motioned with her hands.

He walked around and smiled. "Michael Jordan," Yevgheni pointed to himself. He then began to ham it up, running in circles as if he were dribbling a basketball.

They all laughed. King began to howl.

Ramsay took out one of the Bulls basketball jerseys and turned it so Yevgheni could see the name on the back.

"Ah—'Jordan,'" Yevgheni read.

"Put it on." Ramsay tossed it to him.

Yevgheni quickly slipped the oversized shirt over his sealskin anorak.

Rosalie reached over his head and helped pull his hood through the neck opening. "There," she said as the hood slipped through. "It's perfect."

"Perfect," Yevgheni repeated in English. Then he raised his hands and twirled, looking for their approval. Clowny followed after him.

"You'll need one of these." Ramsay pulled out one of the basketballs.

Yevgheni's eyes grew large. Ramsay threw and Yevgheni caught it. He started chattering in Russian. "The ball at the community center bounces like a flat tire."

Ramsay produced several pumps and other balls. "This'll help you get your own team."

Yevgheni started dribbling the ball on the icy surface and pretended to shoot a basket. Clowny barked, wanting to play.

"Yuri," he called his friend. He held up the basketball. "Let's go." He looked at Thomas. "There's a hoop in Uelen, in the schoolyard by the shore."

"It's easy to hike down," Yuri said.

Thomas began mimicking layups. Blocking Yevgheni, he pushed him with his back, and the two began laughing as Yuri joined in.

Then Yevgheni stopped and looked at Rosalie.

"Rosie?" Yevgheni asked shyly, still not able to say her name correctly. "You too?" he asked in English. "Smokey too?"

She smiled. "Wouldn't miss it for the world."

She turned to Ramsay. "You game?"

"Nope. Thanks, but—" Ramsay turned. He glanced at Tariem, who stood by watching. "I'm staying up here with the old farts. You kids go on and have fun."

"Thank you," Tariem said to Ramsay in English, and grasped his arm. Then the old man smiled and leaned towards Rosalie, saying in Russian so Thomas could translate, "He's a good boy." Tariem was moved by emotion, and then chuckled awkwardly. "Look how crazy he is for this basketball." Tariem's voice broke as if his grandson was the only thing in life he was reluctant to leave.

Ramsay and Tariem watched them hike down the steep hill-side towards the village. Shoving and chasing each other like a bunch of playful yearlings, Yuri kept grabbing Yevgheni's spot-ted sealskin hood, chuckling at the spectacle of him in the jer-sey. Yevgheni took two leashes from Rosalie and raced with Clowny and King towards the shoreline.

Rosalie's dark hair streamed out behind her as she lagged behind, walking with Smokey.

"Come on, let's go," she said to Smokey. "We're missing all the fun."

They walked carefully down the hill onto the sea ice and be-gan passing the ball. The dogs were running and jumping as they chased after the boys.

ACKNOWLEDGMENTS

Thank you to Marlene Stringer of the Stringer Literary Agency, who took a chance on me and loved this story from the very beginning and persevered until the book came into realization. Thanks to Stephanie Flanders at Forge Books for her sharp mind, skills, and patient direction in helping me through the editorial process. To Ron Kuka, University of Wisconsin, Creative Writing Program—my good friend and mentor—for his guidance and feedback on some of the earlier, more torturous versions of the manuscript. To Bryan and Cherry Alexander and their amazing company, Arctic Photo (arcticphoto.co.uk), for their wondrous archive of cold-weather photography that served as the primary inspiration for much of the novel. To Beargrease .com for their clear, concise page of race rules and regulations and to Nell Thalasinos, my stepmother, for the amazing Web site design and for being a faithful and tireless Beta Reader along with Karen McGovern. Their honesty and encouragement cannot be overstated. To Emily Nelson, my longtime friend, for giving me the first live feedback, as scary as it was, and to my mother, Mary Moustakaikis Thalasinos Zucconi, and to both my sons, Michael and Adrian, for never wavering in their love, patience, and belief that I could see this story through to the end or, more important, to the beginning. And lastly to John Tomczak, who helped me to fall in love with the land and the people of Wisconsin.

READING GROUP GUIDE:
AN ECHO THROUGH THE SNOW

1. Throughout the book we learn about the struggles of the Chukchi people, beginning with their forced eviction in 1929. What parallels do you see between the Soviets and the Peoples of the Native American nations and how is this theme explored in the story?

2. Both Rosalie and Jeaantaa risk their lives for their dogs. Discuss Jeaantaa's role of being a "Keeper" of the Guardians. What might be some of the duties and responsibilities of being "called" into being a Keeper? Is Rosalie an "unspoken keeper" of her dogs as well?

3. Tariem spends much of his life wondering about Jeaantaa. Did your feelings about Tariem's character change throughout the story? How does Tariem deal with his emotions and how does Rosalie help him find resolution in the final chapter? Have you ever been in a situation with negative feelings that "ate" at you for a very long time?

4. The relationship between Rosalie and Dan starts out as a precarious one. What might be some of the reasons why Dan keeps his distance? Explain Dan's reaction after Rosalie reveals her plan to get a GED and encourages him to do likewise. What does Arlan's revelation about Dan tell Rosalie?

5. Rosalie and Arlan have a falling out after the revelation that he and Jerry's mother became romantically involved immediately following the death of Rosalie's mother. Do you think Rosalie is justified in being so angry?

6. What do you think might be the motivation behind Jan telling Rosalie about her past mistakes? How does Rosalie react? Do you think seeing Jan in a more "human" light gives Rosalie the strength she needs to face her own struggles?

7. Had Dan not taken out the dogs that evening, how do you think Rosalie's life might have been different? Do you think their relationship could have survived given Dan's background and challenges?

8. In Chapter 24, Tariem makes the trip by reindeer to "kidnap" his sons from the Soviet State Boarding School. Explain the reasons behind the Soviet government setting up such schools for "Primitives." What were the effects of this separation and forced assimilation on children, their families, and Chukchi culture?

9. How were the Inuit communities of Nome, Alaska, instrumental in helping the coastal Chukchi survive after the breakup of the Soviet Union? What had happened to Tariem and the coastal Chukchi that made returning to their traditional way of life so difficult?

10. Rosalie has a habit of always expecting bad things to happen. Have you ever been in a situation where you expected the worst and were surprised by something good? Explain why Rosalie has developed a practice of not hoping for anything so she will never be disappointed. What were the events in Rosalie's life that might have brought her to this conclusion? Do you think after meeting Smokey, Jan, Dave, and Charlie that things might be turning around to show her otherwise?